I0693103

DOORWAY INTO FAERIE

A PROCESSION OF FAERIES ~ 3

ALEXANDRA BRANDT   BRIGID COLLINS

DIANA BENEDICT   ANNIE REED

DEANNA KNIPPLING   DAYLE A. DERMATIS

KAREN L. ABRAHAMSON   LOUISA SWANN

LISA SILVERTHORNE   DEB LOGAN   BRENDA CARRE

REI ROSENQUIST   LINDA JORDAN   ANTHEA SHARP

JAMIE FERGUSON   SHARON KAE REAMER

Edited by
JAMIE FERGUSON

COPYRIGHT

Copyright © 2018 Blackbird Publishing
Cover design: Blackbird Publishing
Cover art copyright © Kharchenko_irina7 | iStockPhoto

ISBN-13: 978-1-939949-14-1

Doorway into Faerie is a work of fiction. Any resemblance to actual events, places, incidents, or persons, living or dead, is entirely coincidental.
All rights reserved.

"Sidewynd" © 2018 by Alexandra Brandt
First published by Tangled Sky Press, November 2016

"Midnight Thread" © 2018 by Brigid Collins

"Dancing in the Moonlight" © 2018 by Diana Benedict

"How We Danced" © 2018 by Annie Reed
First published by Thunder Valley Press, November 2013

"The Good Neighbors" © 2018 by DeAnna Knippling

"At the Mirk and Midnight Hour" © 2017 by Dayle A. Dermatis
First published by Soul's Road Press, August 2015

"With One Shoe" © 2018 by Karen L. Abrahamson
First published in *Playground of Lost Toys*, December 2015

"One Good Sneeze" © 2018 by Louisa Swann

"Dust" © 2018 by Lisa Silverthorne

"To Have...and to Hold" © 2018 by Deb Logan
First published by WDM Publishing, August 2018

"Venom" © 2018 by Brenda Carre

"Along These Lines" © 2018 by Rei Rosenquist

"At the Crossroads" © 2018 by Linda Jordan

"Waterborne" © 2018 by Anthea Sharp
First published in *The Shapeshifter Chronicles*, July 2016

"And Then There Are Cats" © 2018 by Jamie Ferguson

"Night Shepherd" © 2018 by Sharon Kae Reamer
First published by Terrae Motus Books, November 2018

If you catch a glimpse of the Faery Queen
Consider whether you should remain unseen

If you come across a faery ring
Listen to the wind laugh, and murmur and sing

But beware, for if you enter the world of the Fae
You may have no choice but to stay...

CONTENTS

INTRODUCTION

Doorway into Faerie, the third volume in the series *A Procession of Faeries*, is a collection of stories about faery paths, portals, and passageways.

What if you followed a path through a city park, and found yourself in another land? What if the archway you just passed is really a portal to Faerie? What if the guardian of an opening into our world has perished, and left the doorway unattended?

Walk through the doorway and into sixteen different worlds of magic and enchantment.

—Jamie Ferguson
Editor

SIDEWYND

ALEXANDRA BRANDT

S ky Patel stood with her oldest friend under the arch of Borthwick's Close and knew things were drawing to an end at last.

She leaned against the wall, hands in the pockets of her faded summer-weight anorak. The old alley's cold musty smell of damp stone, the uneven paving under her feet, the rough surface of the crumbling old walls all seemed sharper, clearer, more significant today. The sounds of the crowds of Edinburgh tourists and motor vehicles on the Royal Mile seemed so distant, for all they were just outside the entryway.

His hand on her shoulder, Ramsay gestured in the other direction, down the short, narrow alley. "Shall you do the honors, my dear?"

Sky shook her head mutely. She was as adept at opening a Sideway as any Wyndling, but this was too much to ask today. The familiar hum of ancient power that lay in the roots of the city, in the stones of these close walls, didn't seem particularly comforting this time.

Ram seemed to understand. "Ah well, once more for old time's sake, then. My last Sideway."

Sky's eyes stung. She blinked rapidly to clear them as she began to follow him further in. A grown woman—especially one of her age —had no business crying over her best friend's retirement. And yet...

"Wait," she found herself saying. "Just let me...look at you a minute." He smiled and paused mid-stride, turning. He patiently allowed her to finish drinking in the details of his worn old form, with its well-used crown of white curls, the wire-rimmed glasses hiding sharp earth-brown eyes, the stooped posture and gnarled hands. He still insisted on wearing a kilt every day, a bit unusual for this day and age, but on him it seemed charmingly eccentric. Oh, she would miss this version of Ramsay Whitebridge.

But she couldn't stall any longer. Her resigned expression must have said it all, for Ram nodded once, his eyes kind, and began the gesture to draw on the deep, slow power within the medieval bones of Borthwick's Close's walls, to pull and shape it into the opening that would bring them to the Sidewynd. No one on the street noticed, of course. They never did.

Then the two of them stepped through, and transformed.

The close itself remained a winding little tunnel-like alley of crumbling stone, but everything else changed in an instant. The sounds of motorists and babbling tourists and street performers were gone, replaced by the chatter of voices that weren't human, the sound of faint music coming from somewhere, the tinkle and rustle and patter of beings of all shapes and sizes moving just beyond the archway.

Ram stood six inches taller than Sky now, his shock of white curls longer, wilder. Great, curling horns now framed his face, which had elongated and changed shape to resemble a goat or a sheep more than a man. His legs had changed shape too, now covered in white woolly curls beneath his kilt, although his feet more resembled a gargoyle's than hooves of a goat.

It never ceased to amaze her, that her friend could conceal all of that beneath the form of an eccentric old man. But Ram had always been very good at illusions, what folks on the other side would call "fairy glamour." Not that he would need to use it again.

Sky was lucky that she required so little glamour of her own to blend in with the humans, and still it was always with some relief that she dropped all illusions in the Wynd. Sky's warm brown skin and features of a pretty fortyish East Indian woman remained the same, but her ears were now oddly-shaped and tipped with golden-brown fur. A slender tail swished below the hem of her anorak, like-wise shading to deep, soft gold and ending with a plume-like tuft of fur. Her eyes had changed from light brown to bright blue—not an abnormal human color, but so vivid in her brown face as to be a bit too noticeable on the streets. Summer Sky Blue, her own true self.

She faced Ram—Old White, as he was known on the Wyndside—and looked him up and down again. "Are you sure you want to do this? Leave Edinburgh, leave humanity's side of the city for good?"

He rumbled a laugh, and gestured for her to follow him onto the

Spine, the Wyndside version of the Royal Mile. They had a purpose here, and he was becoming wise to her stalling tactics.

"My retirement is long overdue, dear Sky Blue," he reminded her as they dodged a swarm of whirring creatures in the balmy air and turned right to go down the steep hill.

The Spine echoed the shape and length of its human equivalent, although the buildings along either side didn't seem to follow the laws of physics in any way. Nor, for that matter, did the Spine itself. Time to get from one place to another always seemed to vary wildly. Everywhere here the colors were unnaturally bright, and the sounds and smells seemed to have their own shape and texture. Sky remembered well the feeling of wild disorientation and delighted wonder that had accompanied her first sojourn into the Sidewynd. These days, she preferred the experience in small doses, and it was always better with Old White at her side. How would she manage in the future?

She linked her slender arm with her friend's woolly one, muttering something about it all being far too soon. Surely he had years yet.

Ram put his hand on her arm and squeezed, but continued to gently propel them down the street. "Now, now. I've put in my three hundred years and seen the face of that city change beyond anything we could have imagined. I'm looking forward to finding a corner of the Wynd to settle in. Maybe I'll raise a family at last. Surely you can't deny me that?" His eyes twinkled.

There wasn't a good argument in response to that. Of course he was allowed his happiness. And the city wouldn't go unprotected— some other powerful Wyndling, equally qualified, would take his place as Protector soon enough.

They were at their destination now, a white building, deceptively small and plain. Wynd Law, read a severe black sign by the door. Three symbols accompanied the text: Wyndling name-stamps of the lawyers within.

"Come on, then," Ram said, and ushered her in the door.

～

W hen they emerged some hours later, the finality of Old White's retirement had finally sunk in. Ram had bequeathed to Sky all the tools of his position, despite her protests. Whatever new Protector came to Edinburgh would have his or her (or its) own tools, he'd explained. Who else deserved the Far-Seeing Eye, the Universal Map, and the assorted amulets of protection, but the woman who loved the city even more than he?

More importantly for Sky, they were pieces of Ram, and therefore she accepted them without too much argument. Well, no more than an hour's worth, anyway.

Now they stood again in Borthwick's Close, Wyndside. She now had a large gunnysack (illogically roomy on the inside, of course) that contained the tools and a heavy stack of papers bound by Wynd magic. With those, no Wyndlings could contest her claim to Ram's items of power.

It was small comfort, really.

They gazed at each other silently, leaning on opposite walls. Ram had put on a good face before, keeping up spirits with his trademark good humor. That was gone now, replaced by sad eyes and a serious set to his mouth. For him, this was not just a good-bye to Sky, but to the human city he'd guarded for so long.

Traveling between the two worlds via the closes and alleys required special dispensation by Wynd law. It required the traveler to have a bloody good reason, like Old White's Protector status, soon to be gone. Sky understood the law, because it wasn't so terribly long ago that the Wynd was a place of feudal savagery and blatant enslavement of humans. Every Wyndside Lord and Lady had captured human children at one point or another for his or her own amusement. The current powers in the Wynd had seen the damage and put an end to such behavior, but because of this, Wynd Law meant Ram leaving forever.

And yet—"Are you telling me that a *retired Protector* doesn't still have special dispensation?" She was fairly sure that was exactly the case, and the way Ram ducked his head confirmed her suspicions.

"It's the principle of the thing, Sky Blue. I upheld Wynd Law for three hundred years. I'd do best to follow it. But speaking of special dispensation," he said quickly, "I was able to get you official Observer status. You will be free to move in the Sideways at will, provided you don't abuse the privilege. Since I won't be here to give you express permission anymore."

"How did you manage that?" She was delighted, but shocked.

"I argued that you had the right to choose the world of humans as your side rather than the Wynd, being a half-human, but should still be able to enjoy your Wyndling heritage. I vouched for your lack of interest in human domination, too. That, and frankly you aren't powerful enough to concern them."

That last bit made the most sense. More importantly, it meant that she could still visit Ram...albeit maybe once a year, at most. She couldn't be seen to be abusing her privileges.

Ram touched her shoulder, making sure she looked at his face. "I also sincerely want you to keep watch, Summer Sky Blue. That's why I gave you my tools. I don't know who my successor will be, but I trust you to care for Edinburgh as I would. Keep watch for us both, and report to the Protector if you see anything wrong."

She found herself nodding solemnly, although part of her still didn't understand why he was asking this. Perhaps it was just that she was a known quantity, for all her own powers were limited.

But of course she would do what she could. For Ram. For Old White. For the closest thing to a father she'd ever had.

She let out a long breath. "I guess this is where I leave you, then." It wasn't as though he was dying. He just wasn't going to be *here*. He was the only person in her life around whom she could be her true self, and she would only see him rarely, now. Very rarely.

Ram enfolded her in his arms, and she found she had nothing more to say. "Take care, my Sky Blue," he said quietly. "Keep your eyes and heart open. I would have stayed..." he trailed off and she blinked, startled. But then he released her abruptly and swiped at his eyes. "Off you go then."

She nodded as he stepped back. Placing her hand on the wall of the Close, Sky let the power that lay in the bones of its stonework, the power fueled by the spirit of the city, by the vibrant lives of millions who had worked and loved and lived inside its walls, pull her back to the world and to Edinburgh.

∼

His words still bothered her, days later. Why had he seemed reluctant to leave after all? Why was he so insistent that she should keep watch?

Certainly, she had been a casual informant through the years they had known each other, but she had never thought of it as a job description. She had a perfectly adequate human job at the Bank of Scotland. It wasn't as though Ram or any other Wyndling had paid her to watch the streets of Edinburgh.

But to be fair, she always had done that to a certain degree. Edinburgh was the kind of city that required your attention. Once her hooks were in you, your heart would be completely hers forever.

Sky had spoken to countless people at the bank, people who had once been tourists and had fallen in love with the city.

Some fell for the classical, ordered beauty of the New Town, where graceful Georgian townhouses held court in clean lines, their walls the color of honey and smoke.

Some, like Sky, had given their heart to the Old town, with its jumbled mix of buildings ranging from the medieval to the postmodern, its throngs of tourists—all noise and color—heading for the castle. And of course its myriad alleyways in the forms of old closes, courts, and wynds, all trailing off of the main spine of the Royal Mile, each quaintly still bearing its name from the past, even when a modern building engulfed it. Each bearing the weight of history and memory in its bones, a power that uniquely tied it to the Sidewynd.

Being who she was, how could Sky ever have resisted this place?

So she watched now, from the closes and the courts. Ram's replacement still hadn't arrived yet—or if he/she/it had, they hadn't seen fit to seek Sky out. So she wandered to the Old Town every moment she wasn't working at the bank. Even on her breaks she found herself looking through the Eye that Ram had left her, a small disc of milky glass that would, if she concentrated on it long enough, reveal parts of the city to her—especially parts like the Royal Mile, where the power was strong and the connection to the Wynd was at its closest.

She wore Ram's amulets now, although she still hadn't found the papers that described what each was supposed to do. It was a way of keeping him close, and that was what mattered right now. She had the Universal Map tucked in her purse, but knew the city well enough that she hadn't opened it yet. Whenever she finished work, she would check the Eye and make her way to whatever place showed on its surface. Nothing seemed to happen under her observation, but she didn't mind watching the city every day. She never minded.

Then, a week after she and Ram had parted ways, something happened.

It was early evening. Sky had leaned against the gate of a private close, in the section of the Royal Mile known as High Street, to eat her take-away curry and watch a young couple in their late teens—definitely tourists—take a meandering tour down the length of the Royal Mile, from Castlehill to Canongate.

At least, she assumed that was their goal, as they seemed to be stopping in every close, court, and wynd that was open enough for them to duck inside, or at least peer past the gates.

Oblivious to the intermittent summer rain, they had already come up the South side of High Street, crossed over, and headed down the North side. Sky very much enjoyed their delight in reading aloud the names—Toddrick's Wynd, World's End Close, Fleshmarket Close—and trying to figure out where the alleys led.

The Eye had indicated this place, and something about that young couple pulled Sky's attention. She could focus her observation skills very well, if she so chose—including hearing words spoken across the busy street, in the rain, with many conversations swirling between. The couple was American, she thought. Or possibly Canadian. The boy—lanky, blond, with a crooked nose and a rock band T-shirt, was explaining to the girl—petite with Asian features, similarly dressed—that they could totally move to Scotland if one of them went to college here. Or got a job at the museum. Or something.

Ah, youthful optimism.

Then, she felt a tug at her insides, one that indicated Sideway activity of some kind. It came from across the street. Bailie Fyfe's Close. Right as the young duo had ducked in by the gate to escape a particularly vigorous downpour from the capricious Scottish weather.

Coincidence? Not bloody likely.

Cursing under her breath, Sky dodged across the road, trusting her not-quite-human speed and luck to get her there in one piece. The magic flared as her feet landed on the curb of the North side, and faded as she ducked around an elderly couple heading into a kilt shop.

When she got to Bailie Fyfe's Close, the youngsters were nowhere to be seen.

Of course they weren't.

Due to the sudden downpour, the sidewalk had fewer people than usual and most of them had had their heads down. None looked shocked to see a pair of kids suddenly vanish, although a skilled user of the Sideways would be able to hide signs of passing at any rate. One oncoming young man looked mildly bemused at Sky's hasty arrival and frantic search around the close and the restaurant next door, but he moved on.

Something in her gut told her the couple had been pulled through a Sideway. She doubted it was by choice.

It seemed she was the only one who could do anything about it, so she ducked around the corner and pulled a "forget me" glamour over herself—a particularly difficult trick, but she had practiced it under Ram's tutelage until she could do it at a moment's notice, provided she had the power for it. Then she put her hand on the stones and pulled herself into the Wynd.

It was only after she stepped out into the Spine that it occurred to her that this wasn't her job. She was supposed to be observing, not Protecting.

Well, she was all those two had, and she was here now.

No sign of them on the street in front of her. Something tugged between her shoulderblades and made her turn around and look through the close she had just exited. Intuition, maybe, or perhaps one of Ram's little tools...

Or just common sense, because where the closes of *Edinburgh* led to other parts of the city, their equivalents *Wyndside* led to other parts of the Wynd itself.

In this case, Bailie Fyfe's Close led from the Spine to what appeared to be a copse of trees, with hills beyond. And there, three tall Wyndlings escorted two smaller, familiar figures through the trees.

This was not good.

Sky's sharpened sight marked out a tall, willowy sort in the front, with long, pale-gold hair. The other two were clearly some sort of muscle, chosen to intimidate. One seemed to be made of rocks. The other was of a similar type to Old White, although distinctly more goatlike, with short horns and brown-and-black coloring.

The two youngsters clung to each other. She couldn't see their faces, but she could imagine the dazed confusion of emotions they must be feeling right now. And *she* was going to be the one to get them back?

Surely this wasn't even within her meager capabilities, let alone her job description.

But Old White was off making a home in some peaceful corner of the Wynd. The new Protector had never arrived. Clearly these Wyndlings had thought they could get away with the older, darker ways—snatching human children away for their own amusement— because no one currently guarded the Sideways, upholding the reformed Wynd laws.

Well, Sky knew enough Wynd law to keep herself from inadvertently breaking any rules; Ram had made sure of that. And she also knew that what those three Wyndlings were doing was quite illegal.

And it appeared that she was the only one in any position to stop it.

So she followed after the group, frantically going over her available actions. She couldn't take any of them on in a fight of physical skill or magic, but they didn't necessarily know that. They might recognize that she was only a half-Wyndling, but she also had Old White's tools of authority.

Now there was a thought. Sky untucked Ram's amulets from inside her shirt as she approached, hoping they might help.

Her only choice was to brazen this out.

They had noticed her now. The two Wyndling muscle turned to confront her, and she schooled the trepidation from her face. She drew on a bit of her limited power to amplify and project her voice, to give it badly needed authority.

"You are breaking Wynd law. Release the humans immediately."

The leader—the one with the long hair—had turned as well. He was one of those 'unearthly beauty' types, with cheekbones sharp enough to cut, and eyes the same pale gold as his hair. He wore traditional robe-like garments, also pale yellow, rather than the modern human dress that many Wyndlings had adopted these days.

He looked her up and down, his gaze sharpening on the amulets she wore. "Impossible. There is no Protector in Old Town."

The goat-man turned to his leader, his voice a low rumble. "Alabaster, you said our Lord had arranged—"

Alabaster silenced him with a hiss. Sky swiftly buried her shock.

Instead, she barked a laugh. "Your Lord was mistaken, clearly." Inwardly she thought furiously. Was one of the Lords pulling strings with the powers that be? Had Ram's retirement not been entirely voluntary? Was there truly no other protector coming?

The eyes of the two teenagers were fastened on her face, huge and desperate. She had to keep talking. She had to be convincing. Especially with the rock creature and the goat-man beginning to look uncertain, glancing between her and Alabaster.

She planted her feet and faced Alabaster squarely, resisting the urge to clutch at Ram's amulets or take any action that appeared uncertain about her authority. "Release the human children to me, and your actions will have only been an infraction. If you attempt to take them further, I will stop you, and the law will come down upon you." It had better.

Alabaster pursed his lips and looked her over more carefully. "No, I don't think so, halfblood girl. They would never appoint someone like you to protect the Sideways. Be gone." He flicked a hand at her, and she felt a force attempting to pick her up and fling her back toward the close from which they'd come.

One of the amulets on her chest flared with warmth. Somehow, her feet stayed where they were.

Bless Ram.

Still, even with protection she could be no match for the three Wyndlings.

But the close, now—if she could bring them back there somehow, she would be on home ground. She could catch the attention of some denizens of the Spine, perhaps. Get enough people involved, and Alabaster would have to give up. Wouldn't he?

The pale man was quickly recovering from the surprise of his failed spell. Although Sky's heart quailed, she strode forward, glaring at the goat-man and the rock creature, daring them to make a move. They didn't. Yet.

She grabbed the boy and the girl by their arms. "Run for the doorway. Now," she hissed, and shoved them behind her. She clutched at the pendants around her neck and thought of that feeling of resistance. Could she amplify it long enough to keep Alabaster and his lackeys from moving forward? Long enough to get the children back to Bailie Fyfe's Close?

The three Wyndlings leaped forward, and she pushed back with everything she had.

It worked.

The Wyndlings strained against the invisible force, enraged. She gritted her teeth and felt herself slipping. She had little magic of her own—this was all the amulet, and it wouldn't hold for long.

She glanced behind her and saw that the two humans had reached the mouth of the close. They halted inside, unsure of how to proceed.

She slipped another inch. Could she get to them in time, if she let the spell go? Now would be an excellent time to have some force flinging her toward the door again. Could she...? She tried to remember how that had felt. Clutching the pendant, she envisioned its force of resistance as a quick blast outward instead.

The spell ended with a bang and she flew backwards, landing winded in front of the stone opening. Perfect, although painful.

No time to congratulate herself. The force had been much less effective against the strength of Alabaster and his muscle, and they leaped toward her now.

She scrambled into the narrow alleyway, urging the humans toward the other door. The power of the stones, of Edinburgh and humans and memory, remained the same—Wyndside or not.

This was home. This was hers.

"ENOUGH!" she bellowed as Alabaster reached the doorway. "I will not let you break Wynd law. Have you no respect for the powers that be?" Appealing loudly to the law should draw other Wyndling attention, she hoped.

"You are not the law, halfblood girl. Give me what is mine." His voice was cold, but she noticed he spoke quietly.

So of course she spoke louder. "Nothing of the human world is yours, Alabaster. Who do you think you are, flouting the law and taking human children?" Oh, that had gotten some attention. A small crowd began to gather on the Spine side, peering through the close doorway to see who the lawbreaker might be.

She stared him down, daring him to argue further. Yes, I will shout your name some more. Yes, I will cause as big a stink as I can. Your Lord might be pulling strings somewhere, but I doubt even he can openly flout Wynd law.

Alabaster's gaze was a cold knife. "This isn't over, false Protector," he said softly, and she shivered involuntarily. But he motioned his lackeys away and faded out of sight.

She couldn't waste time thinking about what she had just done. "Stay close," she said to her charges, and put her hand on the stone of Bailie Fyfe's Close.

A pulling sensation, and they were through. "Quickly now," she hissed, pushing at the bewildered humans to get them through to the sidewalk, hastily remembering to pull her glamour back on. She had a feeling this wasn't quite over yet.

The children stood outside the kilt shop now, blinking at Sky through a light drizzle of rain. They hadn't said a word Wyndside, which made her wonder if Alabaster had bespelled them somehow. Now, the boy burst out, "You had a tail!"

She gaped at him. Really? "And you were just kidnapped by fairies," she said flatly. "You might say thank you," she prompted as they stared.

The girl spoke for the first time. "Thank you," she said. She shivered. "Why did this happen to us?"

Not the worst question she could ask. But Sky wasn't sure how to answer. "I don't know why you, specifically. But I think something is changing here. Someone from the other side wants humans, and I'm going to find out why." More than ever, she wanted Ram back. Especially since his absence was clearly the impetus for this blatant break in Wynd law.

The boy and girl continued to stare at her, and she sighed. She had been taught a spell of forgetting when Ram decided she might need to protect her identity, but she didn't want to use it. She wanted these two to stay alert. "Don't go into any more closes," she said. "Or courts, or wynds. Are you going home soon?"

"Tomorrow," the girl managed.

"Good. I wish-"

Power built up nearby. Paisley Close. It had to be Alabaster. Who knew what he would try to do?

Sky couldn't get there in time...but maybe she didn't need to. The power of Edinburgh hummed in the concrete under her feet, in the old stones and the new plexiglass and everything in between. It was more faint than what lay in the closes, but it was hers.

She might be half Wyndling and half East Indian, but she was all Scottish, thank you very much.

She focused on Paisley Close and pushed.

The force on the other side sharpened. She could picture Alabaster growing angrier with every passing second. But she held on, because this was her city.

Edinburgh had always had Sky's heart. Now Edinburgh had her protection, too. And in return, the city was Sky's power.

The pushing stopped and the power drained away.

Sky stayed alert, knowing she must appear rather odd, standing on the sidewalk facing toward Paisley Close, her eyes closed and fists clenched. The kids still stood behind her, questions in their eyes.

"He's trying to come back. You should go back to your hotel," she said. "I think you will be safest there." They nodded mutely and all but ran down the street.

She kept them in her sights until they reached the road that would take them to New Town, then she stayed on the Royal Mile as the sky darkened. If Alabaster—or anyone else—tried to use another Sideway before night fell, Sky would stop him.

She'd have to get a new apartment in Old Town, she realized. She might have to quit her job, although she had no idea how she would manage.

No other protector was coming. Maybe Ram had known this all along. Maybe he had left her his tools because he knew she would take on his mantle. He knew her better than anyone, after all.

Sly old goat.

Against all common sense, Sky found herself smiling. She had a feeling she would need to dig up those papers when she got home. And then she'd get about the business of protecting her city.

ABOUT THE AUTHOR

Alexandra Brandt spent most of her childhood dressing up in fairy wings and parading in front of the mirror telling stories to herself. Not much has changed: she still loves a good costume, and tells herself stories every day.

Her short fiction appears in *Fiction River* and other anthologies, and has made it onto *Tangent Magazine's* 2017 and 2018 Recommended Reading lists. "We, the Ocean," her story in Fiction River #22: *No Humans Allowed*, was described as "inventive, heartbreaking, and wholly original" by Hugo award-winning writer and editor Kristine Kathryn Rusch.

When not writing, reading, or debating worldbuilding details with her writer husband, Alex writes marketing copy for a medical practice and does graphic design work, including freelance book cover design. She occasionally sings in a choir, and always welcomes any excuse to sit down and play tabletop games—from D&D to board games to cards.

Find out more about Alex at:
alexandrajbrandt.com

f facebook.com/AlexandraBrandtWriter

g goodreads.com/AlexandraBrandt

BB bookbub.com/authors/alexandra-brandt

MIDNIGHT THREAD

BRIGID COLLINS

Deep night had fallen over Mack Avenue. The crickets sang their love songs with little regard for any others who might be listening. Leaves rustled in a strong wind still warm from the heat of the day. Moths beat their juicy bodies against the human-made moons that lined the avenue, some falling prey to the traps clever spiders had laid for them there. Though the human world slept, the occasional car swept down that black line, the hiss of its tires swelling and exhaling like the gasp of a dreamer almost wakened. And faintly, faintly, if a listener strained for it, the crash of waves could be heard from Lake St. Claire a few blocks to the east.

Under the road the humans had laid over it, the ley line thrummed as the heartbeat of the world.

Cassandra moved along her thread, adding no sound of her own to the deep night. She kept the spiders' way, unheard and unseen as she closed towards her trap. Below her belly, within easy reach of her back legs, hung her spool of midnight thread, ready for making repairs to a web damaged by prey.

She hoped she'd need it tonight. If she hadn't caught anything for a third night in a row...

No, she wouldn't allow herself such defeatist thoughts. She also wouldn't allow herself to drift into annoyance at her sister's inability to help. Breida didn't have the magic, couldn't tap into the ley line to create the midnight thread the way Cassandra could. And while Breida had no problems making the unmagicked threads spiders who didn't have access to a ley line used, she simply didn't have the mindset of a hunter. She was too interested in letting everyone see her work. As the Mother Weaver said, "a trap seen is a trap unsprung."

So it fell to Cassandra to be the hunter for the ragged remains of their family, and she took to the task with pride. She was happy to let Breida do her flashy thing, the thing she called "art" with embroidered leaves and pictures in webs, or her latest obsession, individual dewdrops somehow strung out to catch the first rays of sunrise but fade to invisibility at high noon. Seeing her sister happy made Cassandra happy.

But their preserved stores were running low, and if Cassandra couldn't bring anything home for another night...

Like many of the Mack Avenue spiders did, Cassandra had placed her midnight web parallel to the road in order to use the lure of the ley line as bait. Her web hung between two brick pillars of a building on the east side, high enough that the humans who walked here during the day to collect their own accumulated food wouldn't tear through it. The midnight thread could catch any insect and withstand more thrashing than unmagicked thread, but it wasn't indestructible, and Cassandra could only make so much at a time.

But still, she hoped, hoped, *hoped* she'd caught something that would require her to make repairs.

They just had to make it 'til the lake pixies swarmed. It was getting closer as the air grew heated and heavy with moisture. Closer, but not quite here. True, a few lake pixies had already risen from their year spent dormant underwater, but they were nowhere near enough to be the swarm that would feed the spiders of Mack Avenue for months. A single pixie was good eating for two spiders for multiple days.

So if Cassandra could only catch something big that would last them until the swarm started, a lot of her worries would drop away. She was hoping for a moth, for moths were nearly as mindlessly attracted to the ley line as they were to lights, or maybe a butterfly from earlier in the day. She had no reason to hope for a cricket, with how high she'd placed her web, but—

Something thrashed in the middle of her midnight web.

She stopped, and the thread she walked on dipped and bobbed with the suddenness of her halt. Her hunter's instinct hummed to life, and her focus narrowed to her still-living prey.

A glint of light from the man-made moons caught on a pair of gossamer wings, danced off a pale, four-limbed body like starlight on the surface of still water. It reflected off a grimacing visage like that of a tiny human, but with a set of jeweled compound eyes to rival any dragonfly.

A lake pixie! Caught by the left arm and wing in the sticky

threads of Cassandra's midnight web, and nearly set to break free if Cassandra didn't act now.

Unheard, she moved swiftly along her thread.

Unseen, she filled her sting with the venom that would still her prey's movements.

Remain undetected even when your prey is trapped, said the spiders' way, *and it will never have the chance to escape you.*

The lake pixie didn't glance over its shoulder as Cassandra drew up behind it. It didn't prepare to fight back as she brought her sting a hair's breadth from its neck.

"Cassandra, wait!"

Cassandra jumped at her sister's voice, and the pixie turned its head. Its compound eyes glittered with hatred and building power from the ley line.

"Stop, don't hurt each other!"

Breida scuttled up Cassandra's thread, setting it trembling enough to alert the entire neighborhood to their presence.

Cassandra clicked her fangs. There was no point in suppressing her frustration now. "What are you doing here?"

Before her sister could answer, pain bloomed under Cassandra's right eyes. The lake pixie had punched her. Growling, Cassandra brought her sting back up.

"No!"

Breida stumbled to the web, unused to dealing with the midnight thread, and thrust her front legs between Cassandra and her prey.

"Breida," Cassandra said. "We need this. I know you've been paying attention to our stores."

"You'll catch something else."

Cassandra almost laughed at the certainty in Breida's voice. "This is the first thing I've caught in three days! Not to mention you're asking me to let about three days' worth of food fly away."

"This one's not food."

"Looks like food to me," Cassandra said, dodging another blow from the pixie. "It thrashes like food."

"It's an artist, Cassie."

Breida reached one of her back legs under her belly and produced a pink petal browned around the edges, one of the ones she'd saved from spring. It shone like silver now, crisscrossed with Breida's threads and studded with tiny crystalline dewdrops. It threw the light of the man-made moon into a thousand rainbow speckles as she shoved it under Cassandra's eyes.

Cassandra blinked, then blinked again. Her face ached where the pixie had hit her. She sighed. "You've been collaborating with a pixie?"

Breida pulled her fangs apart in a smile. "Isn't it beautiful? The dew adds such a different feel than what I would have made on my own, but I still love it. Don't you love it?"

The pixie stopped thrashing and turned its compound eyes to the enhanced petal. Its grimace twisted into a look of pride.

Cassandra wouldn't say she loved the piece, but it did have a certain allure. It made her feel...something when she looked at it. Something different from when she looked at the things Breida had made by herself. She didn't know what.

The words of the spiders' way burned in her throat, as they always did when she was confronted with Breida's blatant flaunting of them.

But Breida's face shone with a recognizable desire to create more pieces like this one, and Cassandra knew there would be no winning this argument. She swallowed the words back down.

Ignoring the threatening emptiness in her belly, Cassandra reached out with the sharp edge of one leg and slashed at the midnight threads that held the lake pixie captive.

The pixie tumbled to the bottom of the web before it caught itself on its gossamer wings and brought itself even with Cassandra and Breida where they stood on the thread. Though it wore nothing resembling a human dress, it sketched a midair curtsey to Breida, threw a smirk at Cassandra, and darted off into the darkness of deep night.

Cassandra felt her insides writhe with the hunger pangs she'd ignored earlier.

Breida shifted beside her, and the thread shivered. "Thank you for understanding."

Cassandra didn't understand, but she only said "what are sisters for?" before unspooling her midnight thread to make repairs.

∼

Summer burned onward. Cassandra's midnight web caught a meager share of mosquitoes and gnats, and even one pathetically tiny moth. The crickets sang their songs every night, taunting, making Cassandra debate moving her web lower. But she couldn't risk wasting the midnight thread like that. If she pulled too much power from the ley line all at once, the line would lose its allure as bait.

So she kept her web at its customary height and made do with the single meals she snared. At least Breida was happy, setting up her "art" all around the brick pillars the two of them lived in. Cassandra tried to turn her eyes away when she caught glimpses of it, but inevitably another piece would lie precisely where she next turned her gaze. Her sister was becoming more prolific as she collaborated with the pixie. Cassandra still didn't know what to call the thing these pieces made her feel, but it didn't sit well with her growing sense of failure each night.

It wasn't until the Mother Weaver came to call that she realized the failure spread farther than home.

The Mother Weaver tapped her front foot on the threshold of the cozy hole in the brick pillar Cassandra and Breida had made into their home. The rest of her body remained motionless, but anger radiated from the posture. She looked at Cassandra like one would look at an entangled fly.

The dew-speckled fragment of lavender she'd thrown to the floor lay between them, an accusation.

"This has gone beyond far enough," the Mother Weaver finally said. Her voice did not rise above a whisper, even now keeping as close as she could to the spiders' way. "You may allow your sister to

25

sabotage your family's take if you want the extra challenge to your hunting. But when her brazenness affects every spider on the ley line, I must step in. No spider in the whole block has managed to catch more than a mayfly for the past week, Cassandra. We are too visible!"

"I apologize. I'll speak with her tonight," Cassandra said. She somehow managed not to cower or tremble. She had no idea how she was going to convince her sister to abide by the spiders' way now that a creative fever had caught her.

"It is too late to simply speak with her. Too much midnight thread has already been wasted making new webs in new places, and still your sister insists upon putting her flashy projects nearby. Lake pixie season is nearly upon us. These *things* will be taken down, one way or another."

The Mother Weaver ground her foot into the piece of lavender. Bits of dew and scented oil splashed over Cassandra's front feet, and she flinched. Without another word, the Mother Weaver climbed outside and disappeared into the shadows of evening.

Cassandra sagged. Dread mixed with hunger to make her movements lethargic. The spool under her belly scraped against the mortar, reminding her that it was nearly depleted. She'd have to draw more from her dwindling stock in the chamber below after this evening's hunt.

She didn't want to break Breida's heart, but how could she let her sister's happiness reign over the wellbeing of the whole of the Mack Avenue spider community?

She couldn't let everyone starve for Breida's strange, unnerving "art."

The crushed lavender lay on the floor before her, an order unspoken.

Silent and invisible, Cassandra slipped out into the night to follow the spiders' way.

S he returned home as the first rays of the sunrise streaked from the east, burdened with the guilt of her deed as well as the carcass of the largest moth she'd ever trapped. She carefully avoided looking at the place outside their door where Breida's first dewdrop collaboration used to hang.

The moment she let the carcass flump to the floor she knew Breida was not at home, though she had been. The emptiness echoed all around, humid with anguish.

Cassandra tried not to feel it. She'd already indulged her sister too much.

Instead, she hooked a front leg into the moth and dragged it to the chamber they used to store their food. They'd eat off it for the next few days, enough time to get them into the start of the lake pixie swarm.

This was good. This was how things were supposed to be, her providing food for her unmagicked family. This was the spiders' way. Breida would just have to live with it and find some other way to release her passion for creativity. Some less visible way. Some way that didn't cut into their food supply.

Cassandra paused. The moth was heavy enough it made her legs ache as she carried it. The ache made her spread her fangs in something like contentment.

But in that pause, something about the empty silence of her home struck her. Something that felt like the...something those collaborative pieces had made her feel. Something not right.

Leaving the moth where it lay, Cassandra moved, soundless, into the storage chamber and finally found the name for the feeling.

Betrayal and treachery.

Her midnight thread was gone.

O utside, in the growing light of morning, the lake pixies swarmed. It was too early, too soon in the season for the swarm, but here they were. The spiders of Mack Avenue were not prepared, their wider nets not cast to deal with the swarm.

As she stalked up the side of the brick building towards the roof, Cassandra felt the rustlings of the other spiders, heard their unspoken panic at the loss of the food they'd relied on, their silent wonderings about how this had happened.

Cassandra knew how it had happened.

Up on the roof, in full view of the sunlight, Breida built a web with her own unmagicked thread and watched the pixies swarm.

"They'll suck the ley line dry, you know," Cassandra said, climbing the support thread to join her sister at the top of her structure.

"Yes."

"There aren't enough midnight webs to stop them."

"I know."

"Did you give your friend all of my midnight thread so the pixies would wake up early?"

"And everyone else's. They just haven't noticed yet. One spool of midnight thread doesn't hold enough of the ley line's power to awaken the whole swarm on its own, after all."

Cassandra reeled like a lake pixie had punched her. "There won't be any more midnight thread! Every spider on the avenue will starve for this...this...what are you *making*?"

The sun had risen enough to reveal the full extent of Breida's web across the entirety of the roof, along with the beads of dew she had meticulously woven into it. The thing was monstrous, alluring, beautiful. Cassandra couldn't look away from it. Pixies flitted through it, guided by the sparkling dewdrops to pass unhindered from the lake side to the avenue and the exposed ley line.

Breida clicked her fangs. "If you'd bothered to try to understand my art instead of destroying it, you might gather what I'm doing here."

She affixed another drop of moisture in place, then climbed along the top thread to stand beside Cassandra.

Silent, unheeded by the single-minded swarming pixies, the two sisters watched as the power of the ley line faded. As the sun climbed higher, the pixies grew fatter, and the ley line dwindled to a trickle, then a sputter, then a mere whisper of power.

With no midnight thread, Cassandra was similarly powerless. Nevertheless, the need to do something remained untempered. Was this how Breida felt all the time?

But Breida was laughing now, the sound harsh and breathy, quickly turning to the sawing hack of pain and anger.

"You couldn't have stood up for me, sister? Against the Mother Weaver? You couldn't see any way forward that didn't involve destroying my life's work?"

"She doesn't understand you," Cassandra said.

"No one understands me. No one even tries. All you ever talk about is the spiders' way. Listen to yourself! You're even whispering now, when I can feel you shaking with anger. Why don't you yell at me?"

A growl built in Cassandra's throat, the words of the spiders' way burning to come out. "Fine! You're one to talk, with your brazen disregard for the way. You never even tried to follow it, not once. And now you've destroyed everything that makes up our way of life. We'll all starve because of you!"

Breida laughed again, her fangs spread wide. "We won't starve."

"*There's no midnight thread!*"

"You hunt in your way, sister, and I'll hunt in mine."

Breida pointed one leg at the ley line, and Cassandra looked.

The lake pixies, sated so their bellies distended grotesquely, lifted off from the diminished vein of power and drifted back towards the two sisters, towards the lake. The light of the noon sun beat down on them, turning their straining wings to blinding mirrors.

Cassandra watched first one, then two, then a whole mass of bloated pixies run straight into the unmagicked threads of Breida's web. In the high sun, the dewdrops Breida had placed to guide the pixies through safely in the morning had turned invisible, just the way Cassandra had seen them do in the other pieces that used to be displayed outside their home.

Speechless, Cassandra turned to her sister.

Breida spread her fangs, brandished her sting dripping with venom. "Well? Will you give hunting my way a try, sister? Even gorged as they are, the pixies can still break out of this net, and I can't get to all of them myself."

Silently, covered by the blinding light of the noon sun above them, the sisters descended upon their prey together.

And as she sucked the power of the ley line from the body of the lake pixie she'd released days ago, Cassandra decided she loved her sister's artistic interpretation of the spiders' way, even if the Mother Weaver didn't understand it.

Her sister was a true visionary.

ABOUT THE AUTHOR

Brigid Collins is a fantasy and science fiction writer living in Michigan. Her short stories have appeared in Fiction River, The Uncollected Anthology Volume 13: *Mystical Melodies*, and the *Chronicle Worlds: Feyland* anthology. Books 1 through 3 of her fantasy series, Songbird River Chronicles, are available in print and electronic versions on Amazon.

Find out more about Brigid at:
backwrites.wordpress.com

 twitter.com/purellian

bookbub.com/authors/brigid-collins

DANCING IN THE MOONLIGHT

DIANA BENEDICT

L odie stopped the truck in the parking lot of Hayden Mountain Park and turned off the engine. It ticked in the late afternoon heat. Flowers dotted the green grass of the open meadow ahead of her.

The air seemed brighter somehow, sparkly even. Maybe it was the meds. Maybe just the time of day. It was pretty, so she would take it either way.

She and Shawhene had spent many hours here riding, practicing, just spending time together. She was tired now, so tired, and that made her angry. Everything made her angry lately. And that made her angrier yet.

Lodie opened the door. The ground looked like it was a mile away from the truck's seat. Sighing, she thought of the days when she used to just bounce out of the truck and be on her way.

She took hold of the handle along the door frame and slid off the seat and onto the ground with a jounce that hurt her entire body.

How was she going to go for a ride if just getting out of the truck was so much work? She shook her head sharply. That was not a question. She was going for a ride on Shawhene. Even if it was the last one. Especially if it was the last one.

She slammed the door on the red one-ton Dodge truck and walked to the back of the horse trailer. She opened the manger door and smiled as Shawhene whickered at her. Lodie's heart swelled with love at the sight of the Arabian's black head and the long, narrow blaze on his forehead. He was not the easiest horse, but she had not been the easiest girl when they met fifteen years ago.

Shawhene had been a young colt when she first saw him. He was super intelligent, fearless, defiant, and immensely talented. It didn't take an expert to see he had all the right moves, the grace, the strength, and the smarts to do whatever a skilled rider could want. But the emphasis was on skilled. She had not been skilled in the beginning. She'd been a hard-ass teenager and he'd been a bastard of a colt. They fought for the first months after she'd bought him. Her trainer suggested that she stop fighting him and figure out what made him tick.

They spent days working on the lunge line in the corral at her house as she watched him, paying attention to his body language, his likes, his preferences. The first time she used that knowledge to work him was a Helen Keller moment for both of them. She could actually see him make the connection between what she was asking and what he was supposed to do. And she realized how she needed to work with him.

In that moment they both understood they had a relationship, and what their roles were. After that, they were unstoppable. He progressed by leaps and bounds, and soon they were competing. Then came the winning. Shawhene and Lodie, the darlings of the dressage circuit. The stable wall filled with ribbons and trophies. A feed company approached her about a sponsorship and they went on the national, then the international competition circuit.

She untied his lead rope and returned to the back of the trailer to open the door for him. The smell of a warm horse, hay, and fresh manure greeted her as she dropped the ramp. She stroked his haunch and said, "Back". He obediently backed out of the trailer and looked around. He snuffled the air, tossing his head and snorting.

He smelled something. Or sensed something that she was too dull to notice. If she listened carefully, she thought she heard bells far off in the distance. Shawhene's body language wasn't afraid or wary, just interested, eager.

Something whirred in the air above her head. It looked like a little Tinker Bell, and its gauzy wings buzzed like crazy. Was it some kind of new drone? How could those wings support the tiny body? The detail was amazing and moved incredibly lifelike, bowing its head as it looked at them, twittering something before flitting away with a twist of its tiny body. She'd never seen anything like it, but she didn't follow tech. She didn't follow much of anything these days.

Shawhene watched, unafraid but curious, as he craned his head to keep it in view when it circled above them and zipped away to the west. Lodie shrugged. Once she put his lead through the loop on the side of the trailer she retrieved his curry and mane brushes.

She was able to lean against him while she curried his body, resting her head, arm, and shoulder against him. His black coat was hot from the sun and glowed in the bright afternoon light as if he was covered in static electricity. She smoothed his white socks, ankle high in front and climbing all the way to his hocks in back. They contrasted nicely with the black of his body, and his blacker hooves.

Proud, handsome, and approaching the prime of his life, she was always amazed and delighted that Shawhene was hers. She glanced over in the parking lot and the open space beyond, looking for what he might be sensing.

Lodie traded the curry for the hair brush and worked over his mane and tail. She wished she had the energy to braid them, but had to settle for smoothing non-existent knots from the wavy mane, and pulling a couple of stray burrs from his tail.

He whickered at her when she ran her hand along his back and moved to his withers. She was glad she barely had to touch the back of his legs for him to lift his feet for her to clean his dainty hooves.

When she flipped the saddle blanket over his back and hoisted the saddle on it, she had to stop to breathe deeply after it was in place. Shawhene turned his head and nuzzled her, his breath whuffing warmly against her skin.

"I know, my boy. Give me a minute." He stood still so the saddle didn't slip and she stroked his shoulder, which quivered as her fingers slid over his silky coat.

She reached under his belly to pull the girth up and chuckled, remembering how he used to hold his breath to make the strap loose when he let it out. She fell for the trick early on and paid for it, falling off him as the saddle slipped around his barrel. He'd stood shaking his head and laughing his horsey laugh at her as she lay on the ground, groaning.

Never again. She hadn't kneed him as so many others would have, but instead puttered around, petting him, feeding him horsey treats until he released the air, then moving around to tighten it before he could suck in again.

At one point she wondered if he wasn't doing it to get the extra attention. Ever since, she cosseted him, petting, stroking, whispering sweet nothings to him. He doted on the attention and she loved giving it, so it worked out for both of them.

She tightened the cinch and petted him. "Shawhene, you are my King of the Sky. I love to dance with you." Pain struck her heart as she wondered again what would happen to him when... when she died.

Because she would die. Sooner rather than later. She was on the downside of this cancer. Fighting as hard as she could had brought her to this point, but she knew there was nothing that would carry her to any victory.

Her parents were gone, and any relatives were strangers. She'd wound down her training business when it became apparent that the chemo wasn't going to be the miracle her doctors thought it would be.

A reverse mortgage paid the bills when the savings ran out. Anything of any value, she'd sold and made arrangements with her neighbor to take care of the rest when the time came.

Nothing mattered in the end but Shawhene. And she had no answer for him. He was special. He was hers. Her partner. They had been competing for almost fifteen years. No one knew him like she did. No one loved him like she did.

He won everything she'd taken him to. She was always impressed when she watched the videos of their performances, how beautiful he was when he moved. Shawhene, king of the air, indeed.

As always, she put these thoughts to the side to concentrate on being with him here, now. Tightening the cinch again, she tucked the end through its keeper and went to get his bridle.

It was beautiful, rolled leather with silver hardware. The bit was delicate and light. Its loose rings tinkled as she shook it out for him. He accepted it and lowered his head so she could pull it over the top of his head and lift his ears through. He steadied her with his shoulder as she buckled the strap and flipped the reins over his head to rest on the saddle pommel.

The truck was locked, the trailer doors shut and secured. The last few times they rode, she hadn't had the strength to mount. He wasn't a big boy, just a shade over fifteen hands, but she couldn't haul herself up anymore. Anger rose up when she thought of how easily she mounted a year ago.

Lodie faced the saddle and tapped his left shoulder twice. He picked up his left foreleg and drew it back under his body. Stretching back on his haunches, he stretched out his right leg, sinking down until his left knee touched the ground.

Now he was low enough that she could reach the stirrup and swing into the saddle without struggling. He waited obediently until she leaned back in the saddle and asked him to rise with a squeeze of her legs. He rose gracefully and gently in one slow smooth movement.

Seated comfortably, she patted his neck and gave him a nudge and a cluck. He headed for the trail head. His hooves crunched on gravel, then thudded hollowly on the earth as they left the parking lot.

A breeze brought tweets and songs from the birds that flitted through the stands of trees and grassy expanse. The smell of grass and pine sap filled her nose, and she breathed in deeply. This was life; she was glad to be alive, feeling Shawhene's powerful body moving under hers, responsive to her slightest movement.

Anger vied with sorrow at losing these moments. The melanoma had found her despite everyday precautions like sunscreen and hats. Either that or the cancer was just that insidious.

Shawhene moved surefootedly, paying attention to her seat in the saddle as he went down the trail toward the open space. She appreciated his efforts to ensure her safety as much as she hated the necessity.

Fuck cancer. She was going to be present in this moment and not worry about anything else. Just be here with Shawhene. She let herself relax into his movements, trusting how careful he was with her. He had known how fragile she was, almost before she had.

When she gave him his head as they reached the open space, he ambled along the verge. She saw a doe and fawn in the shadows of the trees and smiled. Beautiful. Shawhene tossed his head and snorted at the scent of them.

She wished she could stop time and live this moment. The sun, now falling to the horizon, felt warm on her shoulders and Shawhene's black coat gleamed, his hooves sounded rhythmic and melodic against the grassy turf.

Lodie watched a bird fly over their heads, chasing insects that Shawhene disturbed in the grass. This whole situation was a shame. He was approaching his prime and he was a champion. People had begun asking her for stud rights last year. She accepted offers selectively, breeding him for a hefty fee.

Maybe she could talk to one of the other riders in the circuit. But her heart curdled at the idea of someone else riding him, competing with him.

They were nearly all the way around the meadow, approaching the pine trees when Shawhene's head jerked to the right. He stopped, his ears pricked forward, focused on the wooded area.

She patted him and looked where he was facing. The sun was nearly to the horizon, and she saw lights bobbing in trees. She heard the same bells she'd heard back in the parking lot, along with a thin piping and a drum beating.

Was someone practicing for parade? Several rodeos were coming up. No, it wasn't that kind of music. She could feel it in her bones even though her ears barely registered it. It pulled at her heart and set her fingers to tapping on the saddle pommel.

Shawhene felt it too. He started moving *a piaffe*, picking up his hooves, front right and back left, front left and back right, in a sharp, poised trot that moved up and down with no forward movement.

Lodie smiled. Shawhene loved to dance more than he loved to jump. She watched the lights approach. Several people wearing milky, shimmery robes rode pale horses—beautiful, lithe animals that seemed to flow from a fog, or perhaps they were the color of fog silvered by moonlight.

Wait. The sun had just been heading toward the horizon. How had it grown so dark? And where had the fog come from? Did they have some kind of machine back there in the trees? The idea was crazy. They'd need a generator, and she didn't hear anything.

Behind the riders she saw a huge stag with an immense rack of antlers step out from the trees followed by what looked like a unicorn. That couldn't be. It had to be a white horse wearing a horn headband like they did for the unicorn rides at the fair. People on foot danced out of the trees behind the animals, twirling in time to the pipes and drums they played. She could hear them singing now, with voices like silver bells at Christmas. But who had voices like bells? Maybe it was a recording.

One of the people moved oddly, like his legs were backwards. Then he moved into a beam of the moonlight and she gasped. He had horns sprouting from curly hair and furry goat legs. It had to be a costume, a very elaborate and clever costume. Maybe this was a rehearsal for a Renaissance Fair procession. Birds of every color flew overhead, wheeling over the line. Why were birds flying at night? And if it was night, how did she see all their colors?

She should be afraid, but the scene was beautiful, and all she felt was awe and excitement. Everything glowed, bathed in the argent light of the full moon that rode high above the clouds that scudded quickly across the sky. What time was it? Had she been standing here for that long? She looked at her watch, but it had stopped, the second hand frozen. What a time for the battery to die.

Lodie rubbed her eyes and shook herself, trying to shake herself out of what suddenly seemed like a waking dream. She had seen a *Cirque de Soleil* show once, and it had had this fantastical flavor.

Shawhene whickered, and she felt his excitement mirror her own. Whatever this was, he felt no fear, and waited to see what she wanted to do. She stroked down his neck, feeling his precise movements as he stepped in place in time to the music, feeling the rhythm move him the way it pulled at her. What kind of music was this compelling?

Lodie trusted his instincts. Her heart filled with joy the same as it did every time they danced. He was marking time to the music, waiting to see if she wanted to join him.

Her body connected to him through her legs and, to a lesser extent, her hands on the reins, and she noted the twitches of muscles as he moved. She squeezed her legs slightly, asking him to change the *piaffe's* up and down movement into a forward impulsion. She let him continue into the center of the open space for a couple of measures, synching her rhythm to his.

As he moved she sculpted his body with the pressure of her hipbone, a light press with one leg, a twist, and an easy backward movement of her left leg. There was no active thought as she pulsed with him in a beautiful trot. Simple pressures and movements of her legs told him to go higher or move forward

The music floated on the air and she guided him into a big, twenty meter counterclockwise circle, pressing to sculpt his body around her right leg. She struggled to hold herself in position and he lifted his back and rounded his body and neck, putting his head down to settle himself under her, giving her a more cushioned seat as he carried her forward.

Her heart rose up in her throat at his love, the tenderness in his knowledge of her illness, her weakness, and his care for her. She stroked his neck gently. Partners they were, compensating for each other over the years. Now, she was not well, and he took extra effort to be careful with her.

Rounding up as he carried her forward, she reversed her seat and changed his bend to the right. He flowed smoothly through the direction change like a yin yang symbol. They headed clockwise, making smaller circles and starting to create patterns. Moving in a shape like an ice cream cone, Shawhene changed leads, following the movements of her legs, the way she straightened her right leg, pressing her right hip down into his back lightly, pushing her left leg toward his rear legs. His body was a continuous curve from his poll between his ears to the dock at the top of his tail.

Lodie signaled him to move right in the same large circle, guiding him into smaller and smaller figure eight patterns, which meant he must change body positions twice as fast. Her legs and hips danced in time to the music and he danced with her, switching body position and length of stride all the time in response to her slightest movement. They were perfectly in balance. Two long time lovers that knew each other intimately.

As the music changed from four beats, to a three beat waltz, Lodie was vaguely aware that the procession had stopped to watch. She wanted to stop and look at the unusual spectacle, but couldn't bring herself to tell Shawhene to stop, didn't want to end this wonderful dance.

Instead, Lodie let the reins fall crossed over his neck, confident that he didn't need them as she gave revelers a show. She began to move her arms in graceful arcs, letting her body fly as he flew beneath her. She pressed him into a canter pirouette and suddenly he felt light under her like he really might leave the Earth, the sound of his hooves drumming into her heart. He was breathing hard, snorting as he danced, and she smiled in the pleasure of what felt like a never ending moment.

The music built to a climax and she gave him the signal to levade. He rose on his hind legs, front legs pawing as if they would strike the moon.

She felt joined to Shawhene as one single flame of love, partners in heart, body, and mind, so bright she thought she would burst from the abundance of joy. The notes faded away on the night air and a cloud streamed across the face of the moon.

Then she couldn't hold her position and started to slide backward. Shawhene felt her slipping and let himself down, curving his head to see to her safety.

He lowered his front leg and haunches so she could slide off. She leaned, legs quivering, against him, arms around his neck, stroking his silky coat in both love and gratitude, but also holding on from fear that her rubbery legs would not support her. "Oh, Shawhene, that was beautiful, no, beyond beautiful, that was heaven."

His sides heaved as he caught his breath, and he nuzzled her side, whickering softly. She smelled his sweat and her own on the gentle breeze that caressed them.

They stood that way until he lifted his head. She heard footsteps swishing through the grass and pushed herself upright, leaving one hand on Shawhene's shoulder to balance herself.

A man wearing old fashioned breeches and a linen tunic with tattered lace around the cuffs stopped a few feet from them and bowed. A harp hung over his shoulder by an ornate strap.

Lodie wondered if he actually played it and smiled at the intricate details these people indulged in for their play—the special effects, outrageous costumes, medieval characters.

"My lady, my lord," he said with a rich Irish accent as he nodded to them both, which pleased her.

She nodded back, and Shawhene tossed his head and whickered.

"I am Martin the harper. My queen was most pleased by your dance and wishes to thank you for your performance."

Lodie smiled, holding back a chuckle. It had to be a Renaissance group. Well, she could play at this, too. She inclined her head gracefully. "My thanks. We would be pleased to meet your queen."

"And how shall I introduce you?" he asked.

"Lodie and Shawhene."

Martin gestured to the head of the procession, and she and Shawhene walked toward the head of the line. The horse drew himself up and strutted like the proud stallion he was, every step like a coiled spring. Taking strength from his energy, she stood straighter, brushing imaginary lint off her trousers and smoothing her shirt. She pulled off her helmet, hooked it onto the saddle, and fussed with her long black hair.

Curls of fog chased moonlight through the line of revelers, even as she realized there was no fog anywhere else in the open space. Perhaps the machine couldn't push it that far. The moon glazed the grass around them, but it was brightest where they walked. Their costumes gleamed, but then she realized it was the people who were gleaming, no, glittering in the argent light, as if they had bought out the local craft store.

That was all strange enough, but still, there was that elk. Elk didn't live so far down into the foothills. And this one was immense, reminding her of a mockup of an extinct Irish elk she had seen once at a museum as it gazed down at her regally.

And the unicorn. From where she was, she could see no evidence it wore a headband. The creature stared at her with large, dark eyes, sporting a wispy beard on its chin. The twisted pearly horn was long, too, easily over a foot. His legs were narrow with curly tufts on his fetlocks, just above his hooves and, when he stamped one hoof, she saw it looked cloven, although that had to be the shadows.

As Lodie and Shawhene drew closer, she saw they trod a beaten path she had never seen before. And it glowed faintly. How had she never noticed such a path in all the times they had ridden there? She looked beyond the procession and saw that the trail glowed as it marched straight across the field and into the distance. She wondered where it went.

"Come this way," Martin said, leading them a regal woman riding a milk white mare. She wore a pale blue gown encrusted with thin silver braid and moonstones that glowed in the light. Her silver tiara was crowned with a large, faceted moonstone. It held her silver hair back from her face and two pointed ears poked out from the strands. The man next to her wore a dark blue jacket that gleamed in a moonbeam. He also had a circlet on his brow, holding back a complex silver braid that swung over his shoulder as he nudged a matching white stallion forward so he could whisper in the woman's ear. She smiled and stroked his arm.

Lodie was impressed with the horses. Their conformation was perfect: clean lines, beautiful necks, and deep chests. She felt Shawhene tense up in the presence of another stallion, and she shook the reins and whispered, "Down, my fine boy. There is no contest here. Just a greeting, then we shall go."

Go home and hold this ride in her heart to the end. The knowledge that it was the last and her end was likely close was a knife twisting in her heart.

"Your majesty," Martin said. The woman acknowledged him with nod of her head. "Queen Titania, may I present Shawhene, king of the air, and his lady, Lodie.

Impressed that Martin knew the meaning of Shawhene's name, she signaled the horse to bow, and she curtsied as well as she could. When she rose, she saw the woman smiling in delight.

Then she realized the name Martin had spoken. Titania was the queen of the faeries, which had nothing to do with the Renaissance. Lodie looked down the line. The revelers all stared back at her. She saw pointed ears, slanted eyes, and several small folks hovering on iridescent wings like the one she had seen in the parking lot. Suddenly, she wasn't sure this was simply a Renaissance group with a fog machine, clever costumes, and cunning drones. There were just too many odd things. Her belly went hollow and her heart pounded.

"Well met, King of the Air," the queen said, nodding to Shawhene, who tossed his head and bugled in response. "You and your lady do honor to the evening. Never have we seen such a beautiful dance. Lady, you are blessed to be the consort of such a regal and talented stallion."

Shawhene lifted his head and struck the ground with one hoof. Lodie looked back to the queen.

"Thank you, your majesty. May I ask what brings you to the park this fine evening?" There that would work. Polite, and a reasonable question couched elegantly.

The queen lifted her chin at Martin, who spoke. "We dance upon an ancient ley line on our way from my lady's winter court to her summer court."

A ley line. Those were magical lines that ran all over the world. And they were faerie highways, too, she remembered. Imagine that. It explained a lot of things—the glowing road she'd never noticed before, the flying fairies, the elk, the unicorn. Her heart fluttered at the idea she and Shawhene were standing in front of the queen of the fairies.

And winter court to summer court? Ah, it was the summer solstice today, a magical time itself. A summer she would be doing well to see to the end.

"And you, fair Lodie? What brings you out on this solstice?" The queen's voice was light like chimes or the pure tones of a silver bell.

She spoke with an accent more exotic than French or Italian, or that Jordanian prince Lodie had met in Germany at the International Cup. Combined, her voice and accent set Lodie's soul quivering in joy.

She was not one to share her trials, so she was shocked when her mouth opened and she said, "I'm dying and I wanted one last ride with my dearest friend."

The queen nodded soberly. "It is your fortune then that our paths have crossed. We are impressed with your dance and will grant a boon." She gestured to an old man with flowing locks and a long, wispy beard who stood behind her and her consort. Sort of like Gandalf, Lodie thought, and smiled as he walked toward her, using a tall staff tipped with a large purple crystal to support him.

Martin said, "This is Ilandor, the Queen's wizard."

She nodded at the old man, feeling a bit silly, and awed, still not sure what exactly was going on.

Ilandor nodded to Shawhene and the horse whickered, extending his nose to the hand the wizard offered.

"Yes, King, the wind loves you and the sun races across the sky, only wishing he was so handsome."

Shawhene tossed his head and pawed the ground with one hoof.

Lodie smiled, then wondered if the horse had understood the wizard. She knew he often understood her. Whether it was the words or the cadence, or just the sound combined with her body language, she didn't know. She just knew they communicated.

"With your leave, my lady." The wizard lifted his staff and the end glowed brightly. He pointed it at her and aimed it over the length of her body. She felt a tingle as the light touched her. He bowed then and returned to Titania, who leaned over her horse to hear what the wizard whispered. The queen straightened.

"I cannot cure you," she said sadly. "A bright and joyous light will go out of the world, and grief will be the end of your king."

The words hit Lodie in the gut. She knew she was dying. She knew Shawhene would grieve; their relationship was so close, she knew he would suffer. However, this woman knew it would be his end, Lodie believed it, too, felt it in her soul. She would die if it was him who was failing. Life would not be worth living without him.

She leaned against Shawhene. Her throat tightened and she took deep gulping breaths as her legs went rubbery. He was warm and solid, a comfort in this moment, but a tragedy coming. She was going to fail him. There was nothing she could do. She hated the cancer with a futile passion so powerful she felt it would break out of her, tearing her into pieces.

"I feel your pain and anger, Lodie," the queen said. "Such a love should not go down so unjustly. While I cannot cure you, I can give you your heart's desire."

Lodie looked at Titania, sitting so easily on her horse, so completely in control. She didn't doubt the queen's words, but she hated the hope it instilled in her breast. Because she didn't know her greatest desire if it was to not die of cancer and leave Shawhene bereft. The ignorance made her irritated.

"What would I desire then?"

Titania frowned. "Do not play with me, Lodie. You stand next to your king, your great love, and pretend to not know your own desire. Name it. Your obstinacy wearies me. Speak now or lose the boon."

What did she want? Lodie buried her head in Shawhene's neck, smelled his scent, his breath as he turned to nuzzle her. She was going to die and leave him alone. She couldn't bear that. She could lose anything, everything, but him.

"I want to be with him," she blurted. "Forever. Or at least to go together."

Titania nodded regally. "Such love deserves no less. But for that to happen, you must come with us to Faerie. I swear you will be together in a fashion befitting the King and Queen of Horses in my realm. And when the time comes, you shall cross the shining sea together."

Go with them? She looked at the procession strung out on the glowing road. She looked to Martin who said nothing, moved not a muscle. If she believed the queen, she had to believe the stories she'd heard: mortals tricked away into a land with no escape, or a return decades later to a world completely changed; either eating banquets of delicacies or dirt and spider webs; wearing fabulous gowns or torn tatters. Living forever in a fantastical realm or dying in a dream.

She had nothing here except Shawhene. Nothing to lose except him. But he trusted her. How could she take him into the unknown? How could she protect him?

How could she not? Any end they faced together was better than her dying and him alone, bereft.

She stroked Shawhene's neck and whispered, "Would you go with me? We would be together at least, no matter what."

He nudged her with his soft nose and whuffed against her cheek.

She stood as straight as her weariness would allow. "We gratefully accept your gift, your majesty. We will go with you."

The faerie queen nodded regally and raised her scepter. She gestured with it and spoke words in a strange language that shimmered the evening air, whooshing like a wave on a beach. When the wave reached them, it struck her like a blow, knocking Lodie down. Shawhene whinnied and stamped his front hooves.

Lodie felt a pulling, a pushing, a rush of pain, then a freedom she hadn't felt since she first felt the sickness creep up on her. She took a great breath and it seemed that the world streamed in: the smell of grass, the rustle of mice, the wind slipping among the pine trees, the cool dirt against her skin, the moonlight shining down upon Shawhene, who looked at her, amazement in his eyes.

She tried to stand and stumbled, her legs tangling with each other as if she had no control over them. She put out her hands and stared, confused, at the horse's legs in front of her, golden down to the ankles, then black all the way to hooves reflecting the sheen of moonlight. Whose hooves were they? Shawhene was black, not gold.

"What?" she said but heard only a frantic neigh. "What the fuck," she tried again, only to feel a whinny come from her throat.

Shawhene walked over and nuzzled at her. She tried to lift a hand to stroke him, but the horse's leg got in the way again.

Pulling herself together she scrambled to her feet but realized that she was still on all fours. When she craned her head to see what was going on, she saw her legs were a shining golden color with the black socks and black hooves. She turned her head to look down the length of herself and saw a horse's body, the same golden color. She shook her head and a long black mane flew around her face, then wiggled her butt only to feel a matching tail flick her haunches.

She was a horse. A buckskin. What had the queen done to her? She lifted her front hoof, stamped it. She felt strong, well, alive, except for a small black kernel in the center of her being. The cancer then, still with her, but tiny compared to the encompassing tendrils it had spread throughout her body. Joy filled her heart at the reprieve.

"Lodie, my love, you are beautiful."

She looked around wildly to see who was speaking, but saw only Shawhene, smiling his horsey smile. He leaned forward to nuzzle her ears.

"What is going on?" she neighed.

Martin the harper stepped forward. "Queen Titania has granted your heart's desire, Lodie. You and your king will always be together. And, when the time comes, she has promised you shall go together."

The king and queen of horses? Lodie was awestruck at the idea of herself as a queen. Her mane brushed her neck in the breeze and she liked the feeling so well she tossed her head so the lustrous black hair swished again.

He turned to Shawhene. "If you would allow me, your majesty?" He pointed to the saddle and Shawhene allowed him to remove it and the blanket, laying them on the grass. He put Lodie's clothes, her helmet, and the bridle on top of the saddle.

Shawhene shook himself, then laid down in the grass to roll enthusiastically.

When he stood again, Martin said, "Now we must continue the procession. Her majesty requests you take your place with her as befits the king and queen of horses." He gestured for them to precede him.

"Shall we go, my lady?" Shawhene moved in beside her and took a tentative step forward, waiting as always for her to make the decision. This time, though, he waited for her to join him as his queen.

"You talk?" Her heart exulted. Queen Titania had given her—and Shawhene—a gift beyond measure. She rubbed his cheek affectionately with her chin.

"I have always spoken. You have always understood me. Only now we speak the same language."

It was true. He had spoken to her in myriad ways—the way he looked at her, the way he arched his neck, perked his ears, curved his body, the way he whickered to her when he first saw her approach.

"I have, my king," she said, her heart swelling. "I have. And now I am with you completely."

"Then, shall we join the procession, my queen? I am eager to walk beside you."

Lodie tossed her head and laughed, a high pitched whinny. "We shall." She stepped out, neck arched, hooves lifted high, precisely striking the turf with a dull thud that rang in her heart. She shook her head so that her mane waved about, and she swished her tail for sheer happiness.

Shawhene matched her step for step. She was a bit smaller than him, and she noticed again how handsome he was, how powerful, how strong and agile he was. They complimented each other nicely.

"You are beautiful, as well, my lady. We are an exquisite pair, even more now than before. And I always thought you fine-looking, with lovely hands."

"You read my mind?" He thought her fine-looking?

"No, my queen. I see your appreciation, I smell your desire." He preened for her, tossing his head so that his own wavy mane moved gracefully.

She smiled her own horsey smile, her knees lifting a tad higher, and she moved into a canter around the open space. He matched her strides as they skipped their way back to the procession.

The queen smiled and nodded regally, gesturing them to join the line behind her and her husband.

Lodie bowed low, nose touching her leg, in profound thanks.

Shawhene followed suit, then raised up, neck arched as he

bugled, his ears pricked, his tail lifted proudly as he stood at attention.

"Well, met, your highnesses. Play on," the queen cried to the musicians, waving her scepter, and her mare walked on as the festive tune started up again. She stepped into a moonbeam, which dusted her and her horse with silver.

Lodie leaned against Shawhene, letting her head down to exchange breath with him before rubbing her chin against his cheek. Then, heart singing, she trotted after the queen in a joyous dance, together with Shawhene, her king, the love of her heart, along the shimmering ley line, into the future.

ABOUT THE AUTHOR

Diana lives in a small suburban Colorado city a mile away from where she grew up. She loves studying magic and history and will take any opportunity to combine them into a good story. She once tried to work a spell inspired by a tale her great aunt told her and has always felt lucky that it only turned her fingers green for a week.

Find out more about Diana at:
dianabenedict.com

BB bookbub.com/authors/diana-benedict

HOW WE DANCED

ANNIE REED

Tonight the test hurt.

Claudia let out an involuntary cry as the lancet pierced the pad of her index finger. Blood welled out, a fat red droplet, and she looked away.

"I'm sorry, Mom," Gary said. "I had to dial the thing up. Last time, I hardly got enough on the strip."

Claudia kept staring at the blank ivory wall of her room.

She didn't need to see the numbers on the tester's readout to know her blood sugar was too high. She'd had a fuzzy-headed feeling all day, the muzzy, sleepy grogginess that went hand in hand with her disease. No amount of wishing made the feeling go away, and now the high number would be charted, and tomorrow the staff would take away her pudding. They thought she wouldn't notice. They didn't realize she noticed everything.

Like the sickly-strong scent of the floral room freshener plugged into an outlet on the other side of her room, the aroma meant to mask the odor of bedpans and ammonia.

Like the steady moaning of the woman in the next room when she fell into a fitful, nightmare-filled doze.

Like the gradual loss of compassion in her son's eyes as he made his twice-weekly evening visits, always accompanied by the twice-weekly testing of her blood.

Her family couldn't afford to keep her in a nursing home, and no one in the family could care for her in their own homes. Gary was single, but his job barely kept him afloat. Claudia's daughter lived halfway across the country with a husband who had his own health issues. Gary had explained the situation to Claudia when he'd moved her into this group home after her stroke. He'd talked to her like everyone did, like she was a little child who couldn't understand anything.

Claudia understood everything. The stroke had left her unable to talk, unable to walk, unable to do almost anything for herself, but it hadn't left her unable to think.

The staff in the group home weren't nurses, they were caregivers. While they could parcel out Claudia's medication in neat little piles, some to be taken with food, some without, they couldn't test her blood, so that task fell to Gary. At first he had been squeamish about it. But as the weeks grew into months, and the months grew into a new year, Gary had grown callous.

Claudia supposed it was only natural. To him, she was only a hollow shell of the mother he had always known.

She wished she wasn't a burden. It was the thing that had angered her the most after her stroke. She'd never wanted to become a burden to her children in her old age. She never wanted them to resent her.

At times like this, Claudia wished the stroke hadn't taken her ability to speak. She wanted to tell Gary he was still a good boy and she loved him.

Most of all, she wished she could tell him about the Other Place.

"Your circulation's getting bad," Gary said. Claudia felt him dab at her finger with a wet cotton ball. The scent of rubbing alcohol almost over-powered the floral air freshener. "Are you doing your exercises?"

Claudia kept her eyes focused on the blank ivory wall, waiting. He wouldn't expect an answer.

This one-sided conversation was his attempt at normalcy. He used to do it more often, just like he used to talk to her about his life instead of just ask her questions about hers that she couldn't answer.

Gary moved her slack arm in a gentle curl, hand to shoulder, then stretched her arm out against the afghan his sister had knitted, a practical Christmas present Claudia could never thank her daughter for.

The left side of Claudia's body didn't work anymore. She hadn't responded to physical therapy in the hospital. It was almost like her brain forgot that half of her body was still there. She could move her right hand enough to feed herself, but her ability to write was gone. Perhaps she should have learned to be ambidextrous like her father wanted instead of reveling in the differentness of being a left-hander. Water long under the bridge, as her mother would have said.

She hadn't seen either of them yet in the Other Place, although she expected to. She hadn't seen anyone she expected. Anyone she yearned for, like George.

The ivory wall shimmered in the low light of the room.

Gary kept curling her arm. Hand to shoulder, hand to afghan, back and forth again and again, the slow, repetitive exercise for her unresponsive arm.

He hadn't noticed the wall.

She was supposed to grip her left wrist with her right hand and do the exercise herself, but she rarely did anymore, and never when anyone watched. When no one expected intelligence or interaction, it became remarkably easy to meet their expectations.

The shimmering grew more intense. Now not only did the blank ivory wall shimmer, so did the blinds covering the lone window in Claudia's room.

Was it all in her mind? A by-product of the stroke? She used to wonder, back when she resisted going to the Other Place. Back when she feared it, just like a child fearing the shadowy corner of their nighttime bedroom.

Only the Other Place wasn't nighttime and shadows. It was a happy place. An entire world full of light and music and the natural fragrance of flowers and green grass and fresh, ammonia-free air.

It was the only place where Claudia could still dance.

The muzzy headedness swept over her like a wave, filling her head with cotton and making it far too heavy to hold up on her neck. Claudia let her head drift back against her pillows even as the shimmering wall took on a definite glow. Her eyes closed, and now the shimmering was behind her eyelids, swirling silver motes that spread warmth throughout her down to her cold, cold fingers.

Gary still didn't see it. She knew by the soft disappointment in his sigh. In the way he said, "I've tired you out again." In the way he arranged her hand on the afghan covering her lap so that her fingers lay relaxed on the soft yarn.

The chair creaked as he stood up. The brush of his lips against her forehead was perfunctory, yet the smell of his gum—the one childhood habit he'd never been able to break—was a wash of mint that reminded her of Girl Scout cookies and the joy of eating an entire box with her children and giggling over everyone's messy fingers.

Kisses hadn't been perfunctory back then. Without the sanctuary Claudia had found in the Other Place, her heart might have broken a bit more every time Gary kissed her like she was a duty instead of the mother who had given him the last cookie in the box just to see him smile.

"I'll see you Thursday, Mom," he said, his voice more distant. He'd be standing in her doorway now, so sure she was lost inside her mind that she didn't even know he was there.

For that one moment the raw need to tell him she still knew *everything* was so strong, she was sure if she just tried hard enough, she could open her eyes, roll out of bed, and walk over to him, whole and undamaged, and ask him to dance with her like she had danced with his father.

But this wasn't the Other Place. Here she was broken, never to be repaired. Here she was housed and taken care of. Over there—over there, she lived. Over there, she was cared *for*.

Gary's rubber-soled shoes squeaked on the hardwood floor as he walked down the hall away from her room. She heard the soft murmur of his voice as he talked to one of the caregivers, and the caregiver's melodic, accented reply.

Claudia sighed and opened her eyes. The Other Place was calling to her from the shimmering wall.

She stared hard at the center of the shimmer, not squinting at the growing brightness, as the wall seemed to peel away, revealing not the skeleton framework of the place that housed Claudia and four other elderly women, all too ravaged by time and disease to live on their own, but rather a place of light and life.

As always, a young man smiled at her from the hole in her wall.

"Time for tea?" he asked.

He was as light as his world—light skinned, light haired, light in weight and attitude. Whenever he came for Claudia, he seemed to float on the very air, although his bare feet did brush the ground. His touch on her hand—her barely-functioning right hand—always imbued Claudia with strength and purpose.

She didn't know if her body actually floated toward the Other Place or if she only imagined it did, but she'd long ago stopped caring. If this was a by-product of the insanity left behind by the stroke, Claudia counted herself lucky. She could just as easily be trapped in the land of nightmares.

She never looked behind herself as she passed the boundary between her bed-bound room and the place on the other side of the shimmer. Sometimes her feet touched down on a grass-covered hill, other times on a sandy beach. Once she found herself walking along the side of a road, her feet scuffing the gravel next to the blacktop, blackberry bushes growing wild where the gravel ended. Claudia always thought about stopping to pick the blackberries, but she reveled too much in the very act of walking to want to stop.

Her guide, the light-skinned, light-haired, light-at-heart young man, never stayed with her long.

Claudia came to realize that he wasn't her true companion in the Other Place, but rather her conduit to take her from the reality of a body that had become her prison to this place where she was free to move and laugh and talk. He never came to transport her back. That seemed to happen automatically after Claudia had tired herself out and stopped to rest. She always woke up back in her room with her daughter's afghan covering her lap and the sickly smell of artificial flowers clogging the air.

Tonight she passed not into a meadow or onto a beach, but rather into a vast ballroom. The floor beneath her feet was a light blonde hardwood, the once-shiny surface scuffed by untold numbers of dancers. Soft music played in the background, not canned but the kind of sound only a live band could create, complete with the occasional off-key note or slip of elderly fingers on accordion keys.

Claudia looked down at herself. No longer was she wearing the nightgown Gary had given her for her last birthday. Instead she was dressed in deep blue chiffon, the skirt dusting the top of the floor, the waist pulled in gently with a large bow. A corsage of white roses and baby's breath was wrapped around her right wrist, and her wedding ring was shiny new on her left hand. A hand no longer covered in age spots or misshapen by arthritis.

"What is this?" she asked her guide.

He took her hand and bowed deeply. "I hear that instead of tea, you'd like to dance."

When he straightened up, she half expected him to no longer look like her guide, but rather like a younger version of George. They had been married for forty-one years when George suffered a heart attack. He never woke up again.

But her guide still retained his youthful, light looks. Claudia smiled at him, trying not to show her disappointment.

"Yes, I would," she said, and she put her other hand on his shoulder.

Claudia had loved to dance, but she'd never been very good at it. George would grumble good-naturedly whenever she stepped on his feet or tried to lead one way when he led the other. But now, here, in the Other Place, Claudia danced the way she always dreamed she could.

Her steps felt natural and smooth, and she glided across the dance floor so in tune with the music that it seemed almost a part of her. The air brushed against her face, bringing not the cloying odor of artificial flowers but the gentle smell of perfume and aftershave and lemon-oiled hardwood.

She thought the magic would end when the song ended, but instead the band gamely struck up another waltz. With only the slightest hesitation, her guide led her into the new dance. His eyes were brilliant blue, and they looked down on her kindly.

"Who are you?" Claudia asked, remembering Dorothy who'd populated Oz with all the people she saw in her waking life. Claudia was sure she'd never seen her guide outside of this place.

"Who do you want me to be?" he responded.

She almost said George, but stopped herself. This place had never been part of the life she'd spent with George. Neither had any of the other places she'd visited on this side of the wall. If this was truly all in her head, she didn't want to break the illusion.

Claudia smiled up at him. He was only a little taller than she was, but they seemed to fit perfectly together in the dance. "I've decided I don't need to know."

This waltz truly seemed to go on forever.

Claudia lost track of the number of times the band repeated the stanzas of the song, lost track of the number of times her guide led her around the vast dance floor. Her feet never faltered, and her gait never tired. The chiffon of her dress swirled around her legs, caught in the breeze of her movements. In her mind, Claudia could see how the two of them must look, one lone couple on the dance floor, caught in the magic of the moment.

"I never want to stop," she said, only slightly breathless.

"It's always been your choice," her guide said.

Claudia stumbled, and the dance came to a ragged end. So did the music, almost as if the band took its cues from her instead of the other way around.

"What do you mean, my choice?"

He only smiled at her. Apparently this was one question he wasn't willing—or able—to answer.

"So this really is all in my mind?"

Another question with no answer.

Claudia sat down on the dance floor as her legs abruptly gave out on her. The chiffon of her gown lay in tatters around her swollen ankles, the white roses of her corsage wilted against her age-spotted skin.

Worst of all, her wedding ring slid off, and she couldn't make the arthritic fingers of her stroke-impaired left hand work to pick it up.

"*No!*"

The word came out as a heartbroken wail. The lights dimmed on the dance floor, and her guide seemed to fade to a mere shadow of himself. Still, he looked at her with the same kindly expression.

In her head, she heard George's voice. "Your choice, sweetheart. It's always been your choice."

Stay and dance? She knew what that meant.

An empty bed.

An afghan boxed up and packed away, or donated to someone else who needed it.

No more testing. No more burden to her children.

No time for goodbyes.

She wished she could have said goodbye. Gary was a good boy. He deserved a goodbye.

"George?" Her voice was querulous, an old lady's voice, not the voice of the woman who'd danced with her guide. "I don't know how."

"Take my hand," he said, and suddenly there he was, solid and real and right in front of her where her guide had been.

He was young, as he'd been when they first met. He still had a head full of brown hair, and sideburns that were long since out of style, but he wore a blue navy suit that he'd never had in life, and his eyes were even more brilliantly blue.

She tried to make her body work, but the magic that had given her youth in this Other Place had fled.

"I can't," she said.

"Nothing this wonderful is easy," George said, an echo of the words spoken by the doctor who'd delivered Gary, Claudia's firstborn, when she'd complained about the pain. "You have to really want it. Work for it."

One thing. She just needed to concentrate on one thing, and the rest would follow. That's what George always told Gary when Gary was learning a new sport.

Claudia stared at the corsage on her right wrist. The flowers were almost completely gone, a dried-up, shriveled memory of what they used to be. Just like Claudia.

She focused on what they'd looked like the first time she'd seen them here on this dance floor. Only had that been the first time? The memory was dim. Something about a high school dance.

She hadn't gone with George, but with another boy who'd asked her first. The boy had given her a corsage just like this one. When

George had seen her at the dance, he'd cut in, leaving both her date and his own fuming.

George had touched the flowers on her wrist and told her he'd never seen anything so beautiful, only he'd been looking at her.

The flowers on her wrist transformed as her memory became stronger, and the stronger her memory became, the stronger her body became, too.

Was it really all just that simple?

The chiffon of her dress repaired itself. Her ankles became slim and trim and strong, and when she bent over to reach for her wedding ring, the fingers of her left hand closed around it easily.

When Claudia reached up to take George's outstretched hand, it was with a strength she hadn't possessed in years.

"Can I have this dance?" he asked her, a smile on his lips and a twinkle in his brilliant blue eyes.

Claudia smiled back.

"All of them," she said. "You can have them all."

ABOUT THE AUTHOR

A frequent contributor to the *Fiction River* anthologies and *Pulphouse Fiction Magazine*, Annie Reed's recent work includes the urban fantasy mystery novels *Unbroken Familiar* and *Iris & Ivy*, and the near-future science fiction short novel *In Dreams*. Annie's also one of the founding members of the innovative Uncollected Anthology, a series of themed urban fantasy stories published three times a year written by some of the best writers working today.

Annie's full-length novels include the Abby Maxon private investigator novels *Pretty Little Horses* and *Paper Bullets*, the Jill Jordan mystery *A Death in Cumberland*, and the suspense novel *Shadow Life*, written under the name Kris Sparks, as well as numerous other projects she can't wait to get to.

Find out more about Annie at:
annie-reed.com

BB bookbub.com/authors/annie-reed

THE GOOD NEIGHBORS

DEANNA KNIPPLING

THE GOOD NEIGHBORS

Lee Warnick leaned her head on her arms and watched out the window. Her mom said, "Come away from the window, Lee, why don't you call your friend Jenny? Or watch some TV?" but Lee ignored her. Her dad was working late at Smithfield Parts Fabrication —the factory—that night, and she wanted to see him come home.

Her mom wasn't fooling anybody. They were both nervous.

That day had been one of those fall days that are too beautiful, too perfect. The sky was a clear and artificial blue-green, and the leaves rattled as they tumbled along the streets and through the parks, picking up strays. Everything had come easy at school. For example, almost everyone had gotten an A on the math test from last week, and nobody had gotten lower than a C. The worst thing that had happened was that a couple of senior boys were smoking behind the building and had made rude comments to her, but their hearts weren't in it. It was the kind of day where no elementary school kids were beaten up for their lunch money, no stray dogs were kicked, and no soufflés went flat.

Those days, those days. Those terrifying days.

About four o'clock the air turned damp and cool and wet. "It'll be foggy tonight." About a dozen people called her mom to tell her that, as if she didn't know. With her husband working late at the factory tonight. Driving home in that fog.

"You never knew when something might happen."

But that was it, wasn't it? Nobody knew. Nobody knew why some people, on foggy nights in the town of East Smithville, just flat-out disappeared.

Or rather, everyone knew *why*. The fairies took people.

They would take one or two or three or six people a year. The records went back to 1875, and there were no years where no people were taken; the most was six, although one of *them* had looked more like a crib death than a taking, at least to Lee.

But it could have started before 1875. That's just when the records started.

The question was: how did the fairies decide who to take?

People disappeared when they were out walking, when they were driving (their cars running off the road, or that one time ten years ago that everyone was still talking about, just rolling along the road at five miles an hour for another quarter-mile with nobody in the driver's seat), or even at home, sitting with their arms under their chins, watching through the front window.

Lee had taken up every case she could find and graphed it all out. It had originally been a project for the science fair, until Mrs. Treen on the school board had found out about it. That was that. Lee had had to make a last-minute volcano, for which she had been given a punitive B-.

But in secret (or not so secret, because the school librarian, Mrs. Akers, wasn't stupid), she had combed through newspapers, books, and microfilm records to gather her data.

Painstakingly, Lee had sorted out every detail she could think of. Where the disappearance had occurred, what the person had been doing at the time, what time, how old, married or not, what kind of job they had, whether they had a history of making trouble, whether they had been picked out for doing something well, or even whether they had showed up in the paper lately.

East Smithville was a town of about forty thousand people.

Losing one or two or six people a year to the fairies wasn't that bad. And of course they came back eventually, so you could almost talk yourself into thinking that it averaged out eventually.

Except that sometimes the people didn't come back for a year, or ten years, or twenty. Or more—Mrs. Akers had showed her a list of people who hadn't come back yet. *She* kept track, too. One person, Virginia Blackinton, hadn't come back yet, and she'd disappeared on September 19, 1899.

Lee had looked at her data every which way, and hadn't found anything that stood out yet. As far as she could tell, you could be doing anything, anywhere, at any time, and still get taken. You could be a newborn baby, or an old person at the nursing home. You could be a man or a woman. Mostly people in town were white, but black people had gone missing too, and a couple of Chinese people back in 1880, who had disappeared together but who had come back separately.

Some people only disappeared for a few days, and Lee was always tempted to count those out. Sometimes you just had to get away from the town and the constant questions. Everybody wanted to know where you were. You couldn't walk to a friend's house for five minutes, but everyone wanted you to call them and let them know that you made it there safe. She would bet that most of the people who only disappeared for a day or two were faking it.

"Yep, stolen by the fairies. That was it."

But with most of the others, the disappearances seemed to be genuine.

Outside, the Newcombs' swingset creaked. There was just enough of a breeze to make the light plastic seats sway. The fog dithered around the front yard. The streetlights just seemed to make it darker and harder to see. A pair of headlights swung around a street corner down the road, then pulled into a driveway. Across the street she could see the lights flickering in old Mr. Emmott's front room as he watched TV. His wife was one of the missing, for almost four years now. The leaves stirred in the driveway, then went limp.

Waiting. It felt like she had always been waiting.

Nobody could be sure what it was that made the fairies take you; that's what her data said. But that didn't stop there from being a thousand rules about what you could or could not do. God help you if you broke one. Everything from not stepping on cracks to staying inside on foggy nights. *Don't ask questions, or you'll catch the fairies' attentions.* She knew that some people thought she was too nosy, that she would be next.

She thought that people were just making up rules because they were afraid.

Another set of headlights swung onto the street. These were the right ones. Lee smiled. "Mom!"

Her mom appeared in the kitchen door, wearing an apron and with a towel in her hand. The towel was ragged from being twisted up so much. It had a crochet loop on the top so it could be buttoned onto the oven door handle, and she'd torn it almost completely off.

"Is it him?"

"The headlights are right."

Her mom licked her lips. "Tell me when you *see* it's him." She went back into the kitchen.

The kitchen window overlooked the driveway and the street, same as the front room. But Lee's mom didn't want to look. If it was bad news, she didn't want to know until the last possible second. And if it was good news, she didn't want to get her hopes up.

The more you hoped, the more the fairies were likely to take the ones you hoped for.

Someday, Lee was gonna go to college. She wanted to go to Harvard to study math. Who knew? Maybe she would make it out of East Smithville someday. But

~

Someone came back that night.

Lee's dad made it back okay, looking tired and relieved. You could tell from the way he put his coat down on the back of the chair instead of on the coat rack, which he wasn't supposed to do, then kissed Lee's mom, then hugged Lee tight, that he hadn't been worried about himself. You just had to know that the whole time, he had been gripping the wheel of the car and wondering if Lee or her mom—or even both of them—would be missing when he opened the door. When you were driving, he always said, that was the worst. Because you could just imagine the phone ringing at work, someone trying to reach you to tell you the bad news. And the phone would just ring and ring, until someone else would have to run and answer it. "Hello? No, he just left. And that's a real shame. A real shame."

Lee had already finished her homework. She had gone to bed, ignoring the low voices from the other room. Her parents didn't fight. Nobody in East Smithville fought—that was just another way to get taken, according to the lore. But sometimes Lee's mom had to remind Lee's dad that he'd promised to find a way to leave earlier in the afternoon, before the fog could come in. A discussion. That was all. It never lasted more than a couple of minutes.

The fog seemed to brush against the walls of the house, making soft, furry noises. The swings kept creaking. And then for a while, a dog started barking, over and over. Lee knew that everyone along the street was awake, then. A gate swung back and forth, rattling against its latch.

A light flickered against her wall through the window. A door opened and someone shouted at the dog. Another dog started barking, and Lee laughed to herself, both hands clapped over her mouth. The gate slammed shut, and then the door. The light went out.

Just as she was drifting back to sleep, she heard the sound of footsteps.

Someone was walking down the middle of the road, boot soles crunching on asphalt. The footsteps were slow and uneven. Not limping. But like someone was walking a few steps, then stopping to look around.

She got up on her knees in bed and looked over the headboard and out the window facing the street. She had to lean over and push aside the curtain to see out.

Outside her window, right in front of the house, just past the side-walk, was a man.

He was wearing a suit, a gray suit with a pattern of big, faint squares on it. He had a thin mustache and slicked-back hair. Luckily there was a street light just at the corner of their driveway, so she could see him pretty well. The cuffs of his pants were muddy, and so were his shoes, which were pointed at the tips and looked like they should be shined up so bright that you could see the moon in them, although at the moment they were clumped up with mud.

She could tell right away who he was.

His name was Bob Wodbery. She recognized his face from the microfilm; he had disappeared on April 7, 1932. He had lived on this street, near their house but not in it. The house he had lived in had been torn down for the Newcombs' new house to be built. That was why he'd stopped. He'd been trying to go home, but his house didn't look the same, and now what?

There were rules for that, too.

Lee got up and tiptoed to her parents' room. She knocked on the door.

"What? Is something wrong?" her dad asked. She could hear him patting the bed, and then her mom saying, "What is it?"

"Someone's come back," Lee said, not giving Mr. Wodbery's name on purpose. "He's standing out in the street and he needs help."

"All right," her dad said. "You go back to bed. Mabel, put some coffee on."

Her mom grunted and the bed creaked.

Lee went back to her room and watched the man walk back and forth in front of the Newcombs' house. Every time the swings creaked

The spare bedroom could be locked from the outside. It wasn't just then, though.

Lee had questions she wanted to ask. But it was a Tuesday now, and she had to get ready for school. The morning was still thick and dark with fog. Normally Lee's dad would have driven her to school, even though it was only a quarter-mile walk. Everyone got driven to school on foggy mornings, and got picked up, too, if possible. But the car was missing from the driveway.

Lee turned on the kitchen tap and let the water run. For a few seconds it was rust-colored, and then it ran cold and fast and clean. She took a drink straight out of it, bending over and slurping at the stream. The water tasted like rotten eggs. *That* was all right, then.

Or was it?

One of the stupid rules was: *rotten egg stink, fairies won't slink*. As in, when the water smelled bad, the fairies wouldn't take anyone. And she'd fallen for it. Even though she was pretty sure that the rules had nothing behind them, she still forgot sometimes.

Lee's mom had made enough toast and eggs for Lee and herself, but not for Lee's dad or Bob Wodbery. Had he left already? She couldn't ask, that was inviting trouble. Another stupid rule. She'd just have to wait and find out later at school.

She decided to leave five minutes early. She kissed her mom. "Have a good day, sweetie," her mom said, eyes fixed to the front window. The fog was too lazy to move. The wind had died down to nothing, and the leaves had sweated themselves into a mat on the ground. All the crunch would be gone.

At school she didn't talk to anyone. Soon the gossip would be flying. But there weren't any other high school students near her house on her street. The Newcombs' two kids were in elementary school, and everybody else around their house was middle-aged or old.

She went to the school library. Mrs. Akers looked up from where she was sitting on the floor in her wool skirt, a card catalog drawer in her lap. "Yes, dear?"

"Mr. Wodbery came back last night," she said. "For your information."

Mrs. Akers lifted her eyebrows. "One of the longer ones," she said. "He tried to go home, didn't he?"

"Yup. He was staring right at the Newcombs' new house like it was all Greek to him."

After lunch the questions started. Some people walked home to eat and of course their mothers would have heard by then and passed along the news.

"Someone came back last night to *your* house?"

It was worse than going to church and having a hundred old ladies ask her how school was going.

Her best friend Jenny rolled her eyes. "Why didn't you tell me?" But she was used to Lee, one minute telling her more than she ever wanted to know, the next holding back important secrets, like which boys she had a crush on.

"He was gone already in the morning," Lee said. "No big deal."

"*I* heard he was one of the long-term ones. And I bet you knew who he was. You're still obsessed with your forbidden science experiment. You know, don't you? Fess up!"

Lee confessed everything she knew, which wasn't much.

Jenny rolled her eyes again. "You're always turning things into bigger mysteries than

I n the park across from the elementary school, Bob Wodbery was sitting on a swing, shaking a cigarette out of a pack. He had a different suit on, one of the ones from the church charity box.

Lee walked up to him. "Hello. I saw you last night in the street. You stayed in our guest room."

"Hey there, kid," Mr. Wodbery said. "And thanks. I thought I was all turned around in the fog last night. Thought I got lost."

"I have some questions for you."

"I'm sure you do."

"What happened?"

He sighed. "One minute, I was driving along a highway in my car with my arm across the seat and my girl beside me. The next I was in the fog. Same as everyone else. No different."

The story that everyone who came back gave, at least, the story that everyone gave who gave a story in the first place, was that one minute they were doing whatever they'd been doing, and the next minute they were walking along an old road in the fog.

"What was it like?" she asked.

"Why do I get the feeling that you're gonna take out a notebook and start writing down my answers?"

Lee said, "I might, if you say anything worth writing down."

"Too-shay, as they say in France. I can tell you now, I don't got nuttin' worth writing down."

"You don't got or you won't got?"

"Leave me alone, kid. You're bothering me."

She snorted. "I'll tell you something interesting."

"What?"

"What happened to your girlfriend after you disappeared."

He winced. "Don't tell me. The car ran off the road with her in it, and she died some kind of horrible death because I wasn't there to stop it or run for help."

"Nope. She grabbed the steering wheel and slid over across the bench seat, then stepped on the brake, nice and slow. Then she got out of the car and walked back to town."

"Must have taken her a while. We were at least five miles out." Mr. Wodbery smoked thoughtfully for a minute. "Good for her. I worried about her a lot, I have to admit. What happened to her afterwards?"

Lee screwed up her face. "I don't know. I was mostly just interested in the people who got taken, not the people left behind. Unless she got married and changed her name, she kind of just disappears out of the records I saw."

Mr. Wodbery stared out into the afternoon. What was he doing there? Waiting for someone?

"Why all the questions?" Mr. Wodbery asked finally. "You lose someone?"

"I dunno. I just got curiosity."

"Curiosity killed the cat," said Mr. Wodbery.

She stuck her tongue out. "But satisfaction brought it back. Why are *you* here?"

"I'm waiting for someone."

So she was right. "Who?"

"None of your business."

"Someone else who got taken? You still haven't given me a real answer as to what happened to you."

"Just what I told you, kid. One minute I was driving, then the fog."

"What did you do, walk the whole time? Did you see a fairy? What?"

Mr. Wodbery's face seemed to redden. Was he blushing? "It didn't feel like 'the whole time' or anything. If you asked me the second I got back how long I was gone, I would have said it was a couple of months, maybe. That was all. And it wasn't just walking. I walked along the road until I reached the next thing. Then I stopped and did it. And when I was done, I walked some more."

"What next thing?"

"I used to work on little things when I used to live here, you know that? Mending little pieces of equipment. Not clocks or watches, but almost anything else. The fixit man."

"I...think I remember that."

"So there I was, walking along the road. It was a dirt road, with like a hump in the middle from the wheel ruts digging down into the dirt. On either side of the road there were pieces of long grass. It was sharp stuff. If you ran your hand along it, you'd end up with red welts along your skin, from getting all scraped up."

She nodded. She'd sat down on the swing beside him, but she kept the board underneath her from moving back and forth. Mr. Wodbery pivoted on the toes of his shoes, making the swing turn around underneath him.

"Every once in a while, I'd come across a bench, high enough that I could stand at it and work. There was a headlamp with a magnifying glass and everything, so I could work properly. I fixed...I don't know. While I was working on things, I knew what they were. But when I was done I forgot. It's like that. Your memories just melt away." He screwed up his face. "I think I remember asking one of them if I was doing it right, and it told me that I wasn't, that I was doing a terrible job. I remember saying, 'If I'm doing such a terrible job, what am I here for, then?' and then it hit me." He waved the hand holding his cigarette past his right cheek. "Slapped me, really. I apologized and it called me an idiot or something. It was a different word, though. I knew what it meant but the word made no sense to me."

"What word?"

"Hell, I don't know, kid." He dropped the butt of his cigarette and crushed it out with the toe of his shoe. "Sorry. Ignore my cruddy language."

"I won't tell."

He shook his head. "No, nobody tells in this town. All these rules, and of course one of 'em is not to tell."

She gave him a humorless smile. "I went over every single case that I could find in the newspaper and books and everywhere else"— she couldn't remember if microfilm had been a thing back in his day and she didn't want to derail the discussion—"and I couldn't find a single place where one of the rules actually applied."

"You looked up jobs? And they don't just take us because they can use us?" Mr. Wodbery asked.

"They take babies and old people and people who can't even talk," Lee said. "They take ten-year-olds."

"And they walk and they walk," Mr. Wodbery said, shaking his head.

"Did you meet anyone?"

"No. Or at least nobody who I can remember, other than maybe that one time. I can't be sure of much."

"Hmmm," she said. "So you're waiting for someone alive?"

"Hey," Mr. Wodbery snapped. "Don't talk about us like we're dead over there. We're not."

"Sorry."

Mr. Wodbery shook his head again. "Bobolyne."

"Is that who you're waiting for?"

"Yes?" he said. "Yeah, that must be it. I'm waiting for a Miss Bobolyne."

Lee took out a small flip pad and wrote *Miss Bobolyne (sp?)* on it. Mr. Wodbery laughed uproariously, slapping the knees of his suit.

"You do! You do have a notebook! I'm

∿

" . . . Not in the records at all," Mrs. Akers said. "Because it's not a name. It's an obscure word that means 'idiot.'"

Lee gaped at her, unsure of whether to laugh or to cry. "Seriously? It's not a last name or anything?"

"It's not a last name or anything. It's an old Tudor English word for a fool. From Shakespeare's time, but it wasn't one of the words that he created."

Lee tapped her finger alongside her chin. "I think he mixed up his memories. He's not waiting for a Miss Bobolyne. The fairies called him a word that meant 'idiot,' and he remembered the word."

Mrs. Akers said, "That's interesting. He remembers talking to the fairies?"

"He said he ask them if they liked his work, and they called him an idiot and slapped him."

"His *work*?" Mrs. Akers said. "What work?"

Lee took a breath, backed up, and related the entire incident instead of just asking Mrs. Akers if she recognized the name *Bobolyne* from the town records somewhere.

"What on earth was he doing in the park?" Mrs. Akers wondered aloud, after Lee had finished.

"He said he was waiting for someone, then told me to mind my own business, and then, just before he got up and left, he said he was waiting for a Miss Bobolyne."

It felt to Lee like she had been explaining things for hours. She hadn't; the bell for her next class hadn't even rung yet. And still it felt like she had relived this moment so often that she knew what Mrs. Akers was about to say.

There was a phrase for that. *Déjà vu.* What had Mr. Wodbery said about that? *Pardon my French?* Now she couldn't remember whether he had said it or not.

"...the records," Mrs. Akers said.

"What?"

"I said, 'Of course you know who he's waiting for, even if it's not in the records.'"

Lee shook her head. "I'm sorry. I didn't get much sleep last night."

Mrs. Akers smiled. "It's me, silly."

"You?" Lee took a step backward and almost tripped on the carpet.

Mrs. Akers steadied her. "I didn't mean to startle you. Yes, me. I was the girlfriend he left behind in the car."

"Wow!" Lee said. "Really? I had no idea."

"Yes, my maiden name was Padelford. Angela Padelford."

"That's right!" Lee said. She grinned at Mrs. Akers. "Why didn't you tell me?"

"I wanted to see if you would—"

The bell rang. Time to go.

"Figure it out?" Lee laughed. "I don't know, Mrs. Akers. Probably not. Gotta go!"

She dashed out of the library toward her next class, almost running into

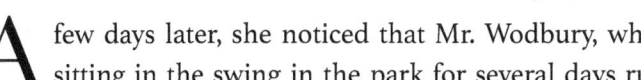

A few days later, she noticed that Mr. Wodbury, who had been sitting in the swing in the park for several days running, was nowhere to be seen. She asked Mrs. Akers about it before school started.

"I'm not sure, Lee," Mrs. Akers said.

"Have you talked to him yet?"

"No. Every time I try to work myself up to it, I keep thinking, 'What if I had come back one more time?' and 'What if I had never gotten married?' and I get so depressed that I can't do it."

"I'll tell him, if you like. And then I won't tell him where you live."

Mrs. Akers laughed. "That isn't how it works, Lee. He could just ask someone else."

Lee knew she was being childish, but she still said, "I could tell Mom to tell everyone not to tell him. You know how fast gossip and rumors fly around this town."

"I do. But thank you, no, Lee. I have to face my demons all by myself."

"You don't," Lee said stubbornly. "Not really. Or is there another rule about that? One that nobody talks about?"

Mrs. Akers laughed. "You'd think so, wouldn't you?"

That night the fog rolled in again, but it wasn't as bad, and Lee's dad didn't have to work late, so it wasn't as tense a situation as it had been before. At the dinner table they talked about Mr. Wodbery. He hadn't wanted to spend a single night in their guest room, as it turned out. He had wanted to be taken to the hospital right away.

"The hospital?" Lee said, her mouth half-full of mashed potatoes.

"Lee," her mom said. "Swallow before you interrogate."

"S'ry."

"He said he was hurt," her dad said.

"Was he?"

"Not that I could see."

"What did the doctors say?"

"They said he was in perfect health, all things considered."

All things considered meant *even though he was abducted and possibly beaten by the fairies, and who knows if he had anything to eat in all that time anyway?* Even if her dad was in a talkative mood, there were some things you just didn't say, regardless.

That night she heard someone walking outside her window again. She jerked awake from a dream about jerking awake from a dream. Or pulling her hand away from a candle flame...somehow the two things had blended together.

She turned around in her bed and leaned out to hold the curtain away from the window.

It was Mr. Wodbery again. He was walking along the street. He was still in the same suit, not the one with the squares on it, but the new one from the charity box. It was dirty and covered with mud and torn all along one sleeve. It looked like his face was bloody.

Had he been abducted again?

She tiptoed to her parents' room and tapped on the door.

"What? What is it? Is something wrong?" her dad asked.

"It's Mr. Wodbery," Lee whispered. "He's outside in the street again."

"Is he drinking?" her dad asked in a dark tone.

"I don't know. He looked hurt, not drunk."

Her dad snorted. "All right, Lee. Go back to bed. I'll take care of it."

Her mom said, "What is it?"

"The fog coughed Bob Wodbery back onto our doorstep, that's all."

"What a pain," her mom said. "I'll—"

"I'll take care of it," her dad repeated.

"You know she watches out the window," her mom said. "I wish she'd just…"

Her dad said firmly, "I know it. I'll take care of it."

In a few minutes, her dad had gone outside to talk to Mr. Wodbery. By then, Lee had cracked her window open, hoping to hear what they would say. But it was banal. "What happened to you, Mr. Wodbery?"

"I couldn't say, Mr. Warrick. Perhaps the fairies did it."

"Perhaps they did. Why don't you come in and lie down in our guest room? Unless you'd rather go to the hospital?"

"I'll lie down for a bit, if you don't mind."

And then they came into the house.

What had her mom meant, saying that she, Lee, watched out the window? She closed the sash slowly, trying to make the smooth hiss as soundless as possible.

Suddenly, she felt as if

⁓

"He won't come out," her mom said. "He's locked the door."

Lee had very clearly seen that the door was locked—from the outside. If Mr. Wodbury had locked his door, then he hadn't been the only one to do it.

But she couldn't ask about the lock on the door. She didn't know how she knew it—it wasn't one of the official rules or anything—but she knew it, with a terrifying certainty that clenched her guts. *Don't ask about the door.*

"I can ask him if he wants anything," Lee said, carefully avoiding the word *door.*

"Don't be silly. It's time for you to go to school."

It was Saturday. Lee nodded and picked up her jacket and book-bag. Her bookbag felt heavy. She'd look inside it later.

"If he comes out, ask him if he'll talk to me about what he saw this time," Lee said.

"This time?" her mom asked blankly.

"Well, he said before that the fairies hit him," Lee said. "And this is the second time he's just shown up in front of our house. I think that's what happened to him. I think he got taken and came back right away. I used to think it was a fake, that people just lied about being taken for short periods of time, but maybe not, right? And maybe this time he remembers what happened."

"You shouldn't be asking about what happened," her mom said, disapprovingly.

"I know, I know," Lee said. "But I am just burning up with curiosity!"

"Just remember, curiosity killed the cat," her mom said. Lee was tempted to sass her: *And satisfaction brought it back.*

But her mom was smiling, so Lee smiled back, gave her a wave, and just said, "See you later!"

"Be careful, you never know

W hat was in her bookbag was a book.

The cover was made of heavy, tooled red leather with gold details. The edges of the pages were edged with gold, too, and were about as thin as onionskin. The words inside were done up in the style of an illuminated manuscript from the Dark Ages.

She couldn't read a word of it. Latin? It was to laugh. The letters themselves looked unfamiliar, and she thought she would have recognized it if they had looked anything like...anything. Ancient Egyptian hieroglyphics, Chinese characters, the hooked-together words of Arabic, even Greek or Russian she would have been able to tell herself that she'd seen them before, somewhere.

She wanted to believe that it was a fairy book. That Mr. Wodbury had been able to bring something back with him from fairy, which nobody *ever* did, and had shoved it in her bookbag when nobody was looking.

She had stopped on the way to the library—the city library, not the school one—in the park. It had several different names, but essentially it was the same park, wandering all across town with a single path running along it. She had sat with her back toward the street against the trunk of a large, overarching tree. It was a seasonal tree. In the spring, summer, and fall, she liked to sit under it—but in the late fall and winter, when its branches were bare, it gave her the creeps. There was something awkward and angular about its branches that she didn't like to see. It was like seeing a ballerina with knobby toe bones sticking out.

But just now it felt friendly and safe, so she sat underneath it.

Across from her was a stream that ran most of the way through town, following alongside the various parks. In some places it was shallow and broad; in others, it was a thin, deep rill that would pull rings off your fingers and watches and bracelets off your wrist, if you stuck your hand in. In the spring the police were always watching the bad parts, scaring kids off. During floods, people were swept away and not found until they reached a big river that lay about ten miles downstream. Someone, a boy in her grade named Richard Roeglin, had tried to tell her once that anyone who went near the stream between August first and Halloween would get abducted by the fairies. She had called him an idiot. She found out later that he was so upset that he had gone out to the creek later that night to prove her wrong, and that his parents had called her parents and told them that if Lee didn't stop being a bully to their son, she better watch out.

Her dad had told her mom she better not say anything about it, so she hadn't. Lee had lived on in blissful ignorance, even after Richard had tearfully tried to extract some kind of apology from her the next day for reasons she didn't understand.

"You're...an...idiot," she had repeated. "I'm sorry you didn't hear it the first time."

If she had known that he had stood out by the creek for hours, only to get picked up and brought home by the police (and why hadn't his mom and dad gone looking for him earlier, too scared?), then maybe she would have been nicer. She could imagine standing by the creek, in the cold and the fog, and shaking with fear and damp chilliness, every sound making you jump.

But nobody told her, and so she had acted like a real ass toward him.

She leafed through the pages of the book, stopping at illustrations. The words looked liquid, as if they were changing when she wasn't looking. She had once seen a couple of boys messing around with the mercury from a broken thermometer, and the way it had oozed around as if it were alive had fascinated her. The letters seemed like that.

The illustrations showed all kinds of things. Different types of flowers, and how they looked through each season (there were sketches of seeds, plants, blossoms, wilted blossoms, and completely dead plants, often surrounded by snow). Different bugs, including a ladybug and a Monarch butterfly, but also a lot of bugs she didn't recognize. People's faces. Rows and rows of women's hats, shoes, gloves, and so on. Buildings—those she recognized, mostly. All kinds of houses, a few churches, City Hall, a new trailer court, a bunch of trailers with cars sitting in front. She was pretty sure that it was all things that could be observed around East Smithville. At least, she was sure about the water fountain, because it had been drawn right in front of the ice cream parlor, Mickey's. The letters on his awning were there, not quite in English so much as drawn-in, hand-tinted blocks of color. The s was backwards.

The contents of the book didn't feel like a story, more like an encyclopedia, as if the fairies had made a study of East Smithville. *So fascinating. So unexpected.* It was weird.

When she had looked through it as much as she could stand, she dropped it back into her bookbag and zipped it shut.

A voice said, "What was that?"

She looked up. It was him, Richard Roeglin.

"A book."

"A bible?"

She grimaced. "If this is payback for something I said in sixth grade, you can forget it."

He looked back and forth. He was wearing a leather jacket and blue jeans. He looked like the kind of guy who would end up getting a girl in trouble someday. He smelled like smoke.

He squatted down next to her. "Look, no hard feelings, okay? Everybody knows you're the class genius, and I did something stupid back then and tried to make it look like it was your fault. That ain't— that's not what this is about. I just want to know where you got that book from."

All right, color her impressed at getting an apology, even if it was almost a decade too late. She decided to risk the truth.

"It showed up in my bookbag this morning. I think Mr. Wodbery shoved it in there to try to hide it."

"What's it say?"

"I think it says something like, 'The Guide to East Smithville,' but I can't read it. It's not written in a language that I know."

"Lemme see it."

She pulled it out of her bookbag and showed it to him. She half-expected him to grab it away from her and start running, while shouting, "Ha ha, fooled you." He didn't.

Instead, he flipped through the pages, more slowly than she had.

"There's a page with the Main Street Fountain on it," she said. "You can see Mickey's behind it."

He grunted. Then, suddenly, he thrust the book toward her, hard enough that it knocked the breath out of her for a moment.

"That Wodbery, he better watch out," Richard said.

"What do you mean?"

"People who get taken by the fairies shouldn't stick around. Bad things happen to them when they do."

"That's nonsense," Lee said.

"Is it? Is that what your graphs and tables say?"

As a matter of fact, it hadn't even occurred to her to check. She knew that the abductees tended not to hang around for long, but she hadn't found out how long, or if anything "bad" happened to the people who stayed.

Not having a satisfactory response, she chose to ignore the comment.

"What do you have to do with all this anyway?" she asked instead. "Why so nosy? You don't have any family or friends who got taken. So why do you care?"

"Because they're going to take me next."

"What?"

"I'm next," Richard repeated. She shoved the book back into her bookbag and zipped it shut. He held a hand out to her, and she let him pull her up. The she brushed off her skirt and shook out the back of her sweater.

"Nobody can know that," Lee said. "That much I'm sure of."

"I've been having nightmares," he said.

"So?"

He held out his hands, not *to* her, but so she could see them. Palms first, then the backs, then the palms again. The knuckles looked scabbed and scarred, like he'd been punching things for so long that they would never heal completely over. But that wasn't what was unusual about them. It was that they were covered with long red blisters.

"Every night. I walk along a road," he said. "It's a long road, and it doesn't turn to the right or the left. It's a dirt road, and the grass has grown up all around it. I have to walk and keep walking, and I can't stop, except—well. Mostly I can't stop."

"Who's forcing you to walk?"

"Nobody. At least, nobody I can *see*," he said. "I put my hands out and touch the grass, but it stings. It tries to stick to my skin, and it kind of tears when it finally pulls away."

"Okay," she said. She hadn't forgotten what Mr. Wodbery had described about being taken, but the rumor might have gone around. Richard might be messing with her, that was all.

"I have to walk forward until I reach the next thing."

"What is that?"

"It's a car. Usually an *old* car, like a Model-T or a Model-A. Sometimes it's a racing car, like a Daimler. A lot of cars I don't recognize, though. They're always busted up somehow, and I have to fix them."

They were walking through the park together, following along the stream.

"That does sound like what Mr. Wodbery described," she admitted. "But he was actually taken. He didn't dream about it first."

"How would you know?"

"It's not in any of the descriptions, and he didn't say anything."

"Maybe they don't want you to remember that part, the part where they try you out first. Or maybe nobody wants to talk about it. Or maybe they *do* want to talk about it, but someone shuts them up."

"Shuts them up?"

"Ask Wodbery. See if he did have dreams before he was taken."

"Why are you saying all this?"

"Because you're the..." he shook his head. "I don't know. It's like I used to know, but I don't know. But I do know you should know, and that's good enough for me. I want someone to remember me, after I get taken."

"Why not just leave?" She'd seen him pull up to the school in a car before. He only lived half a mile from school; he was just doing it to be cool. "You have a car and a driver's license."

He grabbed her forearm, a little too tight. "You and me, Lee. Let's get in my car tonight and drive off together." He laughed harshly and let her go, long before it would have occurred to her to wrest her arm free. She was too shocked. "What, don't want to? Afraid that I'll disappear mid-trip, just like Wodbery? Afraid the cycle will just go back around?"

"I will if you want to," she said. "But only to go to a movie. And I have to ask my parents first. And no hands, got it? I don't want to get felt up. I just want to prove a point."

"A date?" For a second he grinned. "Sure, I'd—

That night she dreamed she was standing outside the guest room door. It was still locked. She had pulled on the Yale lock just to make sure.

"Mr. Wodbery," she was saying. "Are you in there? Are you still there?"

She scratched her fingernails against the wood. Her hand felt cramped. She stopped what she was doing to shake it out, to shake out her whole arm. It felt sore all the way up to her shoulder. Then a trickle of mud ran across her lip. She could taste it. She was soaking wet and covered in mud, as a matter of fact.

The door creaked open. The Yale lock didn't mean anything. It was a false lock. The whole door frame swung inward.

On the other side of the door

She woke up screaming, trying to scrape something off her face. Like spiderwebs. It felt like it was all over her.

Her door slammed open and her dad appeared, holding a baseball bat. "What is it? Did he touch you?"

"No, no," she sobbed, knowing that they weren't going to believe her anyway. "I just had a bad dream."

"What kind of dream?"

Almost instinctively, she lied. "About school. I was going through the hallways and it was all filled with spiderwebs. They were crawling all over me!"

Her mom, standing past dad's shoulder, laughed nervously. "You didn't get a bad grade, did you?"

Lee wiped her face with her pajama sleeve and said, "Not funny, Mom. Not funny." She heard something thump against the wall in the next room. "Oh no. I woke up Mr. Wodbery. I'm so sorry."

"I'll go check on him," her dad said, walking off. Her mom came into the room. "You're not nervous about your date, are you?"

"Sure," Lee said, laughing a little nervously. That's what her mom wanted her to be, excited and nervous—not going out with someone just to be stubborn. And because he was scared. "But I don't think I'm all *that* nervous."

"It's the weather," her mom said.

They both looked at the window. The sheer curtains blocked them from being able to see the street. Lee leaned over and pulled back the curtain.

The road was covered with fog. It had crept up on them, everyone sleeping peacefully, without warning.

"Ugh," Lee said. "Fog."

They stared at the window. It felt like the fog was underneath the window ledge, just out of sight, waiting to pop up at them like a jack-in-the-box. Lee shivered. At that moment, she would have done just about anything to make the feeling go away. That they were all about to get pounced on.

The keys jingled in her dad's hand. Then came the sound of the lock being opened. Then her dad knocked. "Mr. Wodbery? May I come in?"

A rustling noise. Then the sound of a floorboard creaking, and then a key turning in a lock. The door locked on both sides. It was a heavy door, too.

"Yes?" Mr. Wodbery's voice came. "Is everything all right, Mr. Warnick?"

"I just wanted to let you know that Lee just had a dream. It's nothing to worry about."

"What kind of dream?" he asked.

Lee put a fist to her mouth and bit down. *What kind of dream?* Why did they keep saying that, if there was nothing to Richard's theory?

"Oh, just some worries about school. Spiderwebs at school. You know how it is, in high school."

A sigh. "Good."

"Exactly. Well, goodnight. Unless you'd like to get something to eat while everyone's up?"

"I could make cocoa," Lee's mom said.

"Cocoa, please," Lee said in a small voice. The small voice worked every time, and it didn't fail her now. Everyone had to put on their robes and sit in the kitchen and drink warm cocoa. It felt like they were playing cards, everyone against everyone else, and no way of knowing who held what cards or even how many.

Finally, Mr. Wodbery cleared his throat. "Mr. Warnick, I don't know how to say this, but I think it's time that I moved on soon."

"Soon? How soon?"

"A few more days at most."

"I see," her dad said. "Well, I wish you luck."

Mr. Wodbery gave him half a smile. "Luck that I find her, or luck that I don't?"

Luck that you make it out, Lee wanted to say. *And surely someone has told him about Mrs. Akers by now, haven't they?*

Her dad laughed too loudly, then slapped Mr. Wodbery on the back. Her dad stood up, finished his mug of cocoa, and announced, "I'm off to bed. Lee, you too. You have school in the morning, don't you?"

She couldn't remember. It wasn't Saturday...was it Sunday? Or had she gone to school earlier today? It didn't matter. It was some kind of hint. Her dad wanted her out of the room while...while her mom and Mr. Wodbery talked? Something was off. She swirled the last of the cocoa around in the bottom of her mug. A big piece of skin clung to the side of the mug. Suddenly the thought of drinking the dregs of cocoa disgusted her.

She glanced at her mother, then gulped the last swallow quickly, before she could think about it. She made a face, then carried hers and her father's mugs to

～

Her notebook pages were covered with doodles, not the notes she thought she'd been taking. All during class she'd been thinking about that book that someone—Mr. Wodbery presumably—had given her, and talking to Richard about it.

Had his eyes scanned over the lines as if they made any kind of sense? Had he been *reading* it?

Was that it? In order to read the book of the fae (*The Book of the Fae*, she said to herself, testing out the feel of it; it sounded like some kind of book of Celtic legends, or an encyclopedia that didn't quite exist), one had to have gone there, either in reality or in dreams?

Could she will herself to go to the fairies, in dreams? Is that what they had all done? *Willed* themselves?

It seemed strange, the idea that Mr. Emmott's wife had *willed* herself away. Why on earth would she have done that? Or that Mr. Wodbery—in the middle of driving along with Mrs. Akers—could *will* himself out of a moving car. Wasn't he supposed to be driving? And wasn't he supposed to be happy, at just that moment?

Maybe it was happiness that pulled you away. Then again, she couldn't remember Mrs. Emmott being particularly happy, either.

Lee sat under the tree again. She'd made a habit of sitting there every day since Richard had asked her out. Soon they would go out on their date. And every day since he'd asked, he would appear, not at the same time, to talk to her. At first about his dreams, but then about other things. He would sit beside her and ask her to tell him a story. Once he even dozed off, while she was trying to tell him her version of *Of Mice and Men*.

"What did you dream?" she asked him playfully.

"Some kind of steam engine," he said sleepily. "I couldn't fix it. They were upset. I need to do some research, I guess. They're more complicated than they look. You'd think that it would be loads simpler than a combustion engine, but no."

"A car with a steam engine?" she laughed.

"Why not? In a different world, maybe that's how it would have been."

He shook himself fully awake, then stood up and, when she offered him her hand, kissed it. "My lady. I am off to the library."

"Slay me some dragons," she said. "Or fix them. Up to you."

He grinned. "I think I'll fix them. Personally, I've always sided with the dragons."

She laughed and went back to the book she was reading, a collection of short stories. None of them ended the way she thought they ought to. They were dark and violent—terrifying even. She disliked them, but she couldn't seem to stop reading, either. The introduction said that the stores were the way they were because the author was religious, and had always struggled with her weight, and also because she was a teacher, which in Lee's mind didn't explain much of anything. She knew plenty of religious, overweight teachers who didn't write like *this*.

Footsteps approached her. She looked up.

It was Mr. Wodbury.

"Well," he said, crouching down next to her. "I thought I'd come and say goodbye. I'm leaving."

She closed the book, not even putting in her thumb where she left off, and set it aside. "I'm sorry to hear that."

"Why? Because you want to ask me more questions?"

"Sure!"

"Well, it's your last chance. Lay 'em on."

"You know that Mrs. Akers is really Angela Padelford, right?"

"I do," he said seriously.

"Then she's not the one you're waiting for?"

"That's all over. No, it's someone else."

"Who, then?"

He just smiled.

She asked, "Do you know how to read the book? That is, I think you gave me a book, and I can't read it. I *think* you got it from the fairies, and you shoved it in my bookbag to hide it. And can you read it if you've only gone in dreams?"

"Who's gone in dreams?"

She shook her head. *Tit for tat, this for that, or else there come the fairies.*

"I did give you the book," he admitted. "I thought you'd be able to read it. I can't."

"You can't?" It was the worst of all possible answers.

"Not a word. Some interesting pictures, though. I thought that of anyone who might be able to read it, it would be you. I've never met someone as nosy as you. But I suppose it's too much to ask after a day or two that you could crack the code, whatever it is. Someday, maybe."

"How did you get it?"

"No idea. In fact I didn't have it when I first came back. It was under my pillow that first night, in the church basement."

"I thought you went to the hospital."

"I was going to, but I changed my mind and went to the church."

"Did someone from the church give it to you?"

"I didn't want to ask. You know how this place is."

She did.

"It was Richard Roeglin who was dreaming. He fixes cars, he says. Otherwise his dreams sound like yours."

Mr. Wodbery made a face. "Poor kid."

"Do you think he's going to get stolen?" She tried to keep her voice steady and unemotional.

"Simply no doubt about it." Mr. Wodbery straightened up. "Any other questions? I want to get a move on. I have to try to thumb a ride out of town before it gets too late. Wouldn't want the fog creeping up on me...I don't know if I could stand to go back, to tell the truth."

"I understand." She stood up, brushed down her skirts, and shook Mr. Wodbery's hand. Then, on impulse, she shoved the book back into her bookbag and threw the strap over her shoulder. "Which way are you going? I'll walk with you for a bit."

"Help me pick up a ride, is that right?" Mr. Wodbery laughed. "Young girl like you, they'll be sure to stop."

She flashed him a grin. The two of them walked together through the park, following alongside the stream.

"You two going steady?" Mr. Wodbery asked. "I think that's how you say it."

"Oh, we haven't been on a date yet," she said. "First one's on this coming Friday. We're going to a movie. He promised not to vanish while he was driving and I told him not to make any promises he couldn't keep."

Mr. Wodbery chuckled. "Well, at least you both have the same sense of humor."

"I just want to prove him wrong," Lee said.

"Many a marriage has succeeded on just that basis."

She laughed, but she knew she was blushing. "That's a bit premature. But not my parents."

"No?"

"No, they always get along."

"Alvin and Mabel," Mr. Wodbery said.

"I sometimes forget their names aren't just 'Mom' and 'Dad,'" Lee admitted.

"Don't go too fast," Mr. Wodbery said. "You don't want to end up married to somebody you don't like just because you decided to be a liberated woman."

She laughed. "Are you giving me 'the talk,' Mr. Wodbery?"

"Well, somebody has to."

"Don't worry—" She had just about said, *Mrs. Akers gave me a book* when she remembered who Mrs. Akers was, or who she had been, and decided not to confuse the issue. "—I read all about it in a book."

"I just bet you did. Well, be good. Maybe not *too* good. But good."

She winked at him. What she intended to do or not do with Richard wasn't any of his business. But she was an East Smithville girl, and East Smithville girls didn't argue.

Finally, they came to the bridge across the stream, which was the quickest way out to the highway. You just followed the path on the other side across the rest of the park, and there you were, at the crossroads. It was about five-thirty in the afternoon, still about an hour and a half from sunset. It was *that* kind of day, though.

"Thanks for the company," Mr. Wodbery said. "Here's where I leave you, I think. I should be able to pick up a ride, pretty girl or no. Good luck with the book."

"Thanks."

Mr. Wodbery looked over the bridge, squinting into the distance. She knew what he was doing: he was trying to see if there was any fog coming up from the grass in the park.

"Maybe you should wait until tomorrow?" she asked.

"No, it's time to go," he said. He didn't have any luggage with him, not even an overnight case or a satchel. But he had struck her as proud, too proud to take charity. He had probably only gotten rid of his old suit because it had been so muddy. He looked down at his feet. "It hasn't rained lately, has it?"

"No, the path should be dry."

The path, which was now two solid streaks of white gravel, had been built to follow a wagon trail that the earliest settlers had used, hundreds of years ago, and in places the ground stayed damp and, to be frank, rather bad-smelling, like a swamp.

"Then I'm off."

He seemed curiously hesitant. Lee looped her arm around his and said, "I'll walk across with you."

"Will you?" He was sweating; she could see the dark stains on his collar and the beads on his temple.

"Of course."

"It's just...it's just..."

She lifted her left foot. "With me, now. Left."

He raised his left foot. They both put them down together, lurching left.

"Right."

They lurched to the right.

"Left."

They lurched to the left, their feet hitting the boards of the bridge.

"Right."

Thump-thump.

"Left. Right. Left."

Arm in arm, they reached the halfway point. Underneath them, the low puddles of lazy autumn water caught the golden, late-afternoon light.

"Right. Left. Right."

Suddenly, Mr. Wodbury's arm was missing from hers. *Gone.* She looked around. She had turned...she had turned around somehow, and was standing at the edge of the bridge facing the park. In the distance she could see the big tree that she liked, and the swings.

Hours had passed, and the streetlights were on. Not that it did much good; the fog had rolled in.

She turned around.

The other side of the bridge was completely covered in fog. She couldn't even see the far bank, just the suggestion of a few wisps of grass on the other side.

That's where they walk, she realized. The path. It was really a dirt road, or at least it had been, before it had been filled with gravel.

The water under the bridge whispered. She looked over the edge. It was different. Even in the dark she could tell. It rushed by, almost directly underneath the bottom of the bridge. It was a flood. She pulled a dead leaf off a nearby bush and dropped it in the water. The flow snatched it away and it vanished in the fog and the dark.

The fog that surrounded her wasn't *too* bad, but more of that impenetrable fog was pushing its way across the bridge. It floated over the rushing water like it was trying to sneak up on her.

She had to get back to the tree. She'd be safe there, she knew. A new rule.

She ran for it, bookbag bumping on her back. Her parents would be worried. She had to make it back. And Richard, unless he'd been stolen already.

She slapped both hands on the tree trunk. But it wasn't enough. "Ollie ollie oxen free!"

She turned around, careful to keep her back against the tree. She let the bookbag slide off her shoulder and down to her feet. The book was heavy.

The fog rushed toward her, faster than a dog could run. She crossed her arms in front of her face and screamed.

"Ollie ollie oxen free! Ollie ollie oxen free!"

It rushed past her. It had bigger fish to

She sat up in bed. "Richard!"

The door opened; it was her dad. This time he wasn't carrying the baseball bat; Mr. Wodbery was gone. At least, she thought he was gone. He *must* be gone.

"Nightmare?" he asked.

"I hope so," she said. It was time to come clean. "I dreamed that I was walking Mr. Wodbery out to the highway, through the park to the path where the bridge crosses the stream. He was too chicken to go by himself. And midway across the bridge, he disappeared and I was surrounded by fog. And I knew that if I didn't make it to the trunk of the big tree, I was a goner. But I made it."

"Oh?"

She remembered. "And I had to yell 'ollie ollie oxen free' before it counted. That too. I remember that, too."

He nodded. Her mom's face, pale and with dark circles under the eyes, looked past his shoulder. "Everything all right?"

"Bad dream," her dad said.

"I'm worried about Richard," Lee admitted. "He was having weird dreams about getting taken. And it's a foggy night."

She didn't even have to look out the window to check.

"Why don't we all get up and have some cocoa?" her mom said.

"That sounds like a great idea," her dad said. "And I know that you're worried about Richard. Why don't we call his folks and check on them all?"

"Can we do that?"

"*You* can," her dad said with a special emphasis. "They'll understand."

"Wash your hands," her mom said, as if every girl woke up with so much mud on her hands. Lee stared at them. They were caked with it —but she hadn't gotten a single crumb or smear on her white sheets.

"Okay," she said.

In the bathroom the water ran rust-colored into the sink. She let it run for a few seconds. Then it ran clear, and she went to work on her hands with the scrub brush. Rills of mud ran down the drain, making letters. *Virginia Blackinton, Virginia Blackinton.* The water stank of rotten eggs. She bent over and drank it, straight from the faucet. It tasted terrible—but the cocoa would fix that.

"Mom, I think I know who the next person to come back will be," she yelled.

"That's nice," her mom called from the kitchen. "Hurry up, the cocoa's almost ready."

When her hands were clean she felt better. You never knew when something might happen, she realized, but you didn't have to dwell on it.

And there were only so many people you could worry about, she realized too. Because when the fairies came

ABOUT THE AUTHOR

DeAnna Knippling is always tempted to lie on her bios. Her favorite musician is Tom Waits, and her favorite author is Lewis Carroll. Her favorite monster is zombies. Her life goal is to remake her house in the image of the House on the Rock, or at least Ripley's Believe It Or Not. You should buy her books. She promises that she'll use the money wisely on bookshelves and secret doors. She lives in Colorado and is the author of the A Fairy's Tale horror series which starts with *By Dawn's Bloody Light*, and other books like *The Clockwork Alice, A Murder of Crows: Seventeen Tales of Monsters & the Macabre*, and more.

As always, this story is dedicated to Lee and Ray,
without whose love none of this would be possible.

Find out more about DeAnna at:
wonderlandpress.com

facebook.com/deanna.knippling

twitter.com/dknippling

goodreads.com/goodreadscomdeannaknippling

bookbub.com/authors/deanna-knippling

pinterest.com/dknippling

AT THE MIRK AND MIDNIGHT HOUR

DAYLE A. DERMATIS

In Michael's defense, I'll note that the snow slanting sideways down on the winding mountain road made it nearly impossible to see two feet in front of us. Plus, no one expects someone to step out in front of a car on a night like this.

But she did, and I shouted "Bloody hell!" just as Michael slammed on the brakes.

The woman collapsed in the road.

The car fishtailed, Michael overcompensated, and we spun a full three-sixty before skidding to a halt, blessedly not wrapped around a tree.

Michael closed his eyes. "Did I hit her?"

"I don't think so," I said. I jammed my woolly hat on my head and got out of the car. Michael followed.

The woman was gorgeous, unconscious, and absolutely not dressed for an upstate New York blizzard. Her skirt had rucked up, displaying an incredible pair of legs—incredible enough that I noticed, and I don't even swing that way. (Experiments while in uni don't count, especially not if you're wrecked.)

We got her into the car before she froze to death, and had a brief argument about taking her to the hospital. I was pro, Michael was con. Eventually I agreed that going all the way to Lake Placid on Route 73, a treacherous road bordered by snowbanked rocks on one side and a stomach-lurching drop to the Cascade Lakes on the other side, was asking for trouble. Mobile phones were next to useless here in the Adirondacks; more towers were in the works, but not soon enough.

The woman was breathing, didn't seem to have any obvious injuries, wasn't even hypothermic. Which begged the question where she'd come from, but that wasn't a mystery we could solve right this second.

So we took her with us to Michael's parents' cabin, a mile up the road and where we were headed anyway. We got her into the bed, and I stoked the woodstove and put water on for tea while Michael brought in the supplies.

When I went back in the bedroom, she was awake. Her eyes were such an amazing shade of aqua, I wondered if she wore contacts.

"Hallo," I said. "I'm Tamara—Tamara Carter."

"You're Scottish," she said.

"Aye," I said. "And from the sound of it, so are you."

Her delicate brow furrowed and her rosebud lips pursed. Then she shook her head. "I can't remember."

Something about her seemed vaguely familiar, but I couldn't place it.

"D'you remember what you were doing out on the road?"

"I...I was looking for something. I don't know what. It's right here —" she waved a delicate hand at her temple "—but I can't quite catch it."

Michael came in then, with a steaming mug of tea.

"This is my fiancé, Michael," I said. "Michael, this is—do you remember your name?"

She said something that sounded like Sheila, but didn't know her surname. We determined that nothing hurt and she wasn't dizzy (and there were no bumps or tender spots on her head), but we'd take turns keeping an eye on her during the night.

I was dozing in the chair by her bed when her soft crying woke me, and I moved to hug her, and the next thing I knew we were kissing. She tasted like Highland rain and smelled like wildflowers. Then Michael was with us, and it all seemed right, seemed to make sense.

Like any good femme fatale, she seduced us.

I should have known this was what being under a glamour felt like. My parents taught me better than that.

~

S tupid, weak mortals.

They'd been so easy to seduce, so easy to snare in my net. A little fairy dust in their tea, a few murmured words of magic, and they were going to make my job so much easier. Not only that, but I could bring my mother back an extra-special present.

I'd have to get rid of that Tamara woman, of course. As it was, she was proving harder to control. Some kind of protection on her, maybe? I couldn't quite tell, and I didn't have the time—or the caring—to figure it out.

No matter. She was expendable, once she'd done what I needed her to do.

∾

By the time the sky lightened—I can't say for sure if the sun rose, because heavy gray clouds pressed down, smothering the mountains—Sheila remembered something. Something very important.

"I was out there because I was looking for my baby," she said, her impossible eyes wide and brimming with tears as she clutched Michael's arm. "They stole my baby."

She still couldn't tell us who exactly had taken him or where he'd been taken from, only that they drove a green Range Rover and lived near the end of the road.

Michael had come here often when he was growing up, and his family knew most of the people on the hill. There was no phone in the cabin, so he suggested we drive farther up, stop in, and ask around.

"Maybe we could go to the end and work our way back?" Sheila suggested.

Of course we agreed, whether or not it made any sense.

The road dead-ended at an estate with a lodge-like house that was owned by downstate investors who rented it out, Michael said as we inched farther up the hill. One of the other residents had a plow, so the road was relatively clear, but the snow was still coming down hard.

The lodge's driveway wasn't plowed, but up by the house, half-covered in white, we could make out that the vehicle was a Range Rover. A green one.

Michael backed down the road, turning into a narrow side road that led to someone's hunting camp. We cut through the woods to come around the side of the lodge, where the tree line came up close to the building. We'd found jeans and boots and a jacket for Sheila, but even though they were all too big for her, she moved like a deer, graceful and seemingly unaffected by having to slog through the knee-high snow.

Something niggled at me, even as we peered in the window and saw the nursery. Something told me this wasn't right. But like Sheila's memories the night before, the "something" skittered away from my conscious brain.

"There!" she hissed. "That's my baby!"

In minutes, we had a plan. Michael would go to the front door, distract the residents, while Sheila snuck in the back and retrieved her son. He wouldn't cry, she reasoned, when he recognized her. My job was to wait down the road, alert them in case someone else came up.

I held my breath, stomping around in the snow trying to keep warm. It gets cold in Scotland, but not like this. What was taking them so long?

I heard the wail of a siren. My stomach lurched. Shite!

I took off towards the lodge, as fast as my unwieldy boots would let me.

They met me halfway. "Take the baby!" Sheila said, thrusting the bundle into my arms. I didn't question the logic. I just turned and ran.

We'd left the car unlocked, but Michael had the keys. I assumed he was right behind me.

I put the baby in the back seat. I wished we had a baby seat, but Sheila could sit back there and hold him for a short while.

I was just straightening when I felt a sharp sting between my shoulder blades, and then the world went bright and blurry and finally dark.

~

I woke up in the back of a police car, cuffed.

They read me my rights. When we got to the tiny local station, they took me into what amounted to an interrogation room.

"I don't understand why I'm here," I said, because by all that was holy, I didn't. I remembered driving up from Albany with Michael in the snowstorm, getting off the Northway and taking the smaller roads to Keene....

"You kidnapped a baby, Ms. Carter," the female cop said.

"No, that's ridiculous," I said. "I'd never do anything like that. Just ask Michael...."

"Yes, the man who rented the car. Where is this Michael?"

Sweat trickled down my back. I wasn't a U.S. citizen. Didn't that mean they could toss me in prison without charging me, never to be seen again? They had my passport.... The sweat stung, as if I had a cut on my back, and I squirmed in the hard metal chair.

I told them about Michael's parents' cabin, but they'd already been there, and nobody was there.

Still, when they let me have my phone call, it was Michael's mobile I tried. I left a message. No sense bothering my parents; there was nothing they could do.

The spot on my back still stung. I asked to use the loo; the female officer went with me. I pulled up my shirt, twisted around to look in the mirror.

"I think something's poking me," I told her. I could see something dark between my shoulder blades. She used her fingernails to pry it out, dropped it in her palm.

"Looks like a thorn," she said.

No. I knew what it was.

Elf-shot.

That's when I remembered everything.

My first thought: Oh shite, Sheila was a fairy.

My second thought: The fairy bitch had shot me, and then left me to take the fall.

My third thought: The bitch had Michael.

O nce the elf-shot was out of me and the glamour had melted away, everything was so obvious I knew my parents would thrash me when they found out how stupid I'd been. Glamour or no glamour.

The baby wasn't Sheila's, hadn't been stolen from her. She'd come to steal a baby, because that's what fairies did, when they weren't stealing your fiancé. (I wondered if she'd planned to take Michael from the start, or whether he was just collateral damage.)

Wait. When fairies stole babies, they left changelings in their place.

"Is the baby okay?" I asked.

The police woman looked at me funny, but when we exited the bathroom, all bloody hell had broken loose.

What I gathered had transpired was this: The baby found in Michael's car with me slumped over it had been taken to hospital—but when the ER nurse unfolded the blanket, it was full of nothing but twigs and leaves.

Even though I'd been allegedly found with a baby, said baby no longer seemed to exist, ergo, there was no evidence against me, argued my court-appointed lawyer, therefore they couldn't charge me with anything.

I was warned not to leave the country, and I promised not to. Technically, I wasn't lying.

I was going to leave the mortal sodding realm.

I was out of my element here in New York. In Scotland, I knew just how to find the items I needed. Here, I'd have to improvise.

Oak and ash, rowan and hawthorne. I made do with oak and apple and willow. I stuffed some protein bars into my pockets, since I knew I couldn't eat anything of the fairy realm.

My luggage, along with Michael's, had been torn apart when the police searched the cabin, but I found the locket my mother had given me, with hers and my father's hair braided together inside. I wondered whether, if I'd been wearing it, Sheila would have been able to glamour me.

Sheila. Sidhe. I really am a plonker.

I swapped my coat for another hanging on a peg by the door. It was camouflage-patterned, but there should be enough green in it. I took a fireplace poker.

I had to take the chance of going near the lodge again, but I stuck to the woods. By now it was late afternoon; what little light there was would be gone soon. It had stopped snowing, but their tracks were mostly filled in, just soft-edged, shallow depressions. I lost my way more than once.

I lost the trail completely at a brook.

I almost sat down and cried right there and then, but it was too bloody cold, and it was getting dark. The water was probably even colder; ice edged the rocks so only the middle of the brook flowed, clear and dark.

I squinted at the ice, flipped on the torch I'd brought.

Aye, some of it was broken. They'd crossed here.

I eyed the slippery stones. If I fell and broke my leg, I'd be frozen dead before anyone found me. Still, I had to go on. I supposed it was my legacy.

Gingerly, I put a foot on the first rock. Took a step to the second. I planted my foot on the third, felt it wobble. I rocked back and forth, decided that it was still reasonably stable, and took my chances. It held.

Which is probably why I was a little too confident about the next step. My foot slipped off the stone into the icy water.

I thrust the fireplace poker into the stream and caught myself before I went all the way down. Thankfully my boots were water-proof. I scrambled up onto the far bank and took a moment to catch my breath and flex my fingers, which ached with cold even though I wore gloves.

I could just make out the trail on this side, headed upstream. That made sense; civilization would be downstream. I tried not to think about the fact that the Adirondack Park was just over six million acres (a fact Michael had shared with me on the drive up) and the entrance to fairy could be anywhere.

The noise of the brook got louder as I struggled uphill, and soon I saw why: a waterfall. Not a huge one, maybe only ten or fifteen feet high. How I was going to climb up the side of that, I had no clue. I'd have to backtrack and go deeper into the woods, then cut back across.

The tracks didn't seem to go that way, but then, the light had gone from bone gray to steel gray, and I couldn't see much of any tracks anywhere.

Except...what was that?

I slogged to the edge of the falls, picked up the dark object that had caught my eye.

A left glove. Michael's glove.

Had he dropped it by accident, or had he shaken off the glamour just long enough to have the presence of mind to leave me a bread-crumb? It didn't matter.

I closed my eyes, held my breath, clutched the leaves in my pocket, and listened.

Faintly, I thought I heard the sound of bells.

I opened my eyes. They were coming from behind the falls.

Even though the water coming over the fall was probably half its normal rate due to the ice, the closer I got, the wetter I got. The spray stung my numbing cheeks. If I was wrong about this, I was starting to doubt I'd even be able to get back to the road before I got hypother-mia, or simply got too numb to walk.

I hauled myself up next to the flow of water, saw just enough space behind it, and before I could question my own sanity again, I stepped in.

There was no ground beneath my feet.

I pitched into the fairy realm.

～

The landing knocked the breath out of me. I lay there gasping, half-panicked and vaguely happy that I was so numb, because I'd probably hurt a lot more if I wasn't.

Finally, with the help of the fireplace poker, I hauled myself to my feet.

I was still in a forest, and there was still a brook and falls, but the trees were different: fewer birches and pines, more oaks and yews and rowans. The light was different, too. Instead of the dark gray of winter, here it was the midnight blue velvet of the gloaming.

In the distance, I saw a faint glow. Since there was no snow here and thus no obvious trail, that seemed as good a direction as any.

As I walked, my feet started to thaw. First a tingle, then pain with every step. I was hobbling by the time I got to the edge of the grove.

My breath stuttered and my heart ached. Fairy Court. And every one of them was more beautiful than the last.

I saw Sheila, sitting on a low throne, and she was as gorgeous as I remembered, only now I wasn't quite as enamored of her. I forced my brain away from the things we'd done. Let's just pretend I was wrecked again.

There was still something familiar about her that I couldn't quite place. Maybe I'd met her before. Maybe she'd even targeted Michael and me.

Next to her, on a higher throne of more elaborately carved wood, was the Fairy Queen. If she had a name, my parents never told me. If Sheila was one of the most beautiful there, the Fairy Queen trumped her in spades.

But I had no time to gaze upon her. On a low stool at her feet sat Michael, and he had a jewel-encrusted gold goblet in his hand, and he was raising it to drink.

Shite.

I didn't have time to think. All I knew was that I had to stop him.

Ignoring the pain, I sprinted through the middle of the gathering. They might have reached out to stop me, but I was already swinging that iron poker. I smashed the cup out of Michael's hand.

Blood-red wine sloshed out as the goblet bounced on the ground. I'd dented it, and an amethyst lay in the grass next to it.

"You didn't actually drink any, did you?" I asked him.

He gaped at me. Still glamoured. Bollocks. I draped my coat over his shoulders.

You might have thought I'd come here with a plan. You'd've been sadly mistaken. For all my trudging through the woods, I'd only gotten as far as "find the slag and save Michael. And the baby, too, if possible."

They were afraid of the cold iron I held, which gave me a small advantage. But there were far more of them that there were of me, and they could overpower me without much damage.

Sheila half-rose out of her seat, but it was the Fairy Queen who spoke first.

"You!"

I look like a mix of my parents. I've got my mother's golden hair and my father's fair face. I wasn't surprised that she recognized me.

"Aye, 'tis me," I said. "We haven't met properly, but we know each other well enough. I've come for my Michael." I waved my hand. "I would've thought you'd know better than to mess with our family again."

She whirled on Sheila, who stared at me. Finally I saw the resemblance. Sheila was the Fairy Queen's sodding daughter.

Oh, bugger all.

"Do you know who this is?" the Fairy Queen hissed.

There's always a moment where the truth is revealed. I squared my shoulders and turned to face the courtiers.

"My name is Tamara Lin Carter," I said. "I believe you knew my parents: Tam Lin and Janet Carter."

*N*o wonder the mortal woman had resisted the full strength of my glamour.

No wonder my mother was furious at me.

But then my mother smiled.

pparently the Fairy Queen hadn't been talking to Sheila when she asked if she knew who was who. She'd been talking to me.

"How fortunate that you're here," she said, her voice honey-sweet and just as barbed. "Apparently you haven't properly met your sister."

Clichéd as it might sound, I felt the blood drain from my face. Now I saw the resemblance that my mind had refused to acknowledge.

She had her mother's midnight hair, her mother's sapphire eyes. But she, like me, had her father's face. More stunning than mine, given her fairy blood, but still.

My father had been trapped in the fairy realm for seven years before he'd met my mother and, well, deflowered her. It made sense he would've slept with the Fairy Queen during that time.

I closed my eyes. The truth would kill my mother.

Then I remembered something else. "Oh, that's disgusting."

Even Sheila looked a little sick. Good.

"All I did," the Fairy Queen said to Sheila, "was send you to find me a mortal child. And this is what you bring into my lands?"

"I brought you a gift," Sheila said. "I had no idea."

"Michael's mine," I said. "Unless you want another face-off like you had with my mother..."

"Take him," the Fairy Queen said. "He has neither eaten nor drunk in his time here. I relinquish any hold on him."

"I'm taking the baby, too," I said, pointing to the crib by her throne.

"No."

I brandished the poker. "Yes. Sheila's my sister; she shares my blood. But she lied to me, making us help her steal the baby because she said it was hers. That violates your code—blood never goes against blood. My parents taught me all about the way you do things."

The Fairy Queen stared at me. "I'll come for yours," she swore.

"Bring it on," I said.

The bravado I showed didn't match how I felt. As we left the grove, I knew it wasn't over. We'd be fighting this fight for generations to come.

I just hoped the child I carried inside me would be up to it.

ABOUT THE AUTHOR

Dayle A. Dermatis is the author or coauthor of many novels (including snarky urban fantasies *Ghosted*, *Shaded*, and *Spectered*) and more than a hundred short stories in multiple genres, appearing in such venues as *Fiction River*, *Alfred Hitchcock's Mystery Magazine*, and DAW Books.

Called the mastermind behind the Uncollected Anthology project, she also guest edits anthologies for *Fiction River*, and her own short fiction has been lauded in many year's best anthologies in erotica, mystery, and horror.

She lives in a book- and cat-filled historic English-style cottage in the wild greenscapes of the Pacific Northwest. In her spare time she follows Styx around the country and travels the world, which inspires her writing.

Find out more about Dayle at:
dayledermatis.com

f facebook.com/dayledermatis

y twitter.com/dayledermatis

g goodreads.com/DayleDermatis

BB bookbub.com/authors/dayle-a-dermatis

WITH ONE SHOE

KAREN L. ABRAHAMSON

B y the time Detective Ron Conway pulled up to the Paradis house it had been forty-eight hours since Elvira Paradis had last seen her child. As Ron arrived, the gray clapboard house slouched in its postage-stamp sized yard just like the other matchy-match houses on the block; a veritable gang of houses emulating the sullen youngsters on their way to school. The house might once have been white. The trim showed a last desperate hint of green. The yard was brown from too much sun and too little June rain. No tree, no hedge, not a single damn living blade of grass. A pink sneaker lay in the middle of the lawn. Desiccated weeds filled what might once have been a garden.

Someone had cared—once—but the weight of the neighbourhood had dragged their efforts under. He recognized the place—he'd grown up in one like it—the kind of hell that stole dreams and bred nightmares. Not any place to raise a kid.

And now a fourteen-year-old was missing.

Ron climbed out of the brown sedan, letting the sun dry the damp spot between his shoulders.

"I hate these cases," his partner, Jake Spinoza, muttered as he climbed out the other side.

"Makes two of us." Ron pulled his sports jacket on.

"It's always the same. The kid gets tired of being abused. They run, and drugs and prostitution get them. It doesn't end well." Spinoza shook his head. "Maybe we should just arrest the parents. Then the kids might stand a chance."

Ron eyed the house. It didn't quite have the black-eyed look of the other places on the block. A pot of geraniums next to the front door said that hope hung on by a thread. Maybe other things were different here.

Ron was big and Viking-pale, the bulk to Spinoza's wiry Latin frame. The door opened, revealing a woman who actually looked *interested,* perhaps even worried—another first.

"Mrs. Paradis? I'm Detective Conway and this is Detective Spinoza."

"Come in. Please." Elvira Paradis motioned them inside. Small, bird-boned, and faded blonde, she had stooped shoulders and pale blue eyes that took up most of her face. She had a scent of vanilla and roses. She wore a pair of worn blue shorts that exposed thin legs, and a cotton floral blouse that that looked ironed. Another sign that someone cared.

The inside of the house showed it, too. The living room furniture was worn, but clean. A blue sofa faced the front window that had the drapes drawn. Two mismatched chairs faced the couch, draped in green throws to hide lurid yellow upholstery. Curbside finds, he'd bet. But in this house people did the best with what they had. A television sat against one wall topped with family photos of Elvira Paradis and a blonde seven-year-old child just as fine-boned as her mother, but with indigo eyes.

On the couch, Spinoza pulled out his notebook and Ron sat with his hands between his knees. "You contacted the office to report your daughter missing," Ron said.

She nodded, the most silent witness he'd ever met.

"Tell us what happened."

Her throat worked. "I got up yesterday and she wasn't here."

Definitely a woman of few words.

"When did you last see your daughter?"

Her pale blue gaze settled on his and for a moment the room changed to vivid burgundy with forest green carpets. The furniture was cream and the windows looked out onto a world of verdant hills and forest. For a moment his chest unclenched and he could breathe —almost laughed out loud for the first time in a very long time.

Then she blinked and he was back inside a faded house on Effron Avenue that parched under the Saskatchewan sun.

"At dinner night before last. Afterward she went to her room. That's it."

"Tell me about dinner."

"We had peas and mashed potatoes."

Spinoza stirred and grinned. Let the great Ron Conway drag it out of her. Spinoza was having fun.

"What did you talk about?"

"School, maybe. She was doing a project. She's a good kid, May-bell is."

"So tell us about May-Bell."

"She's smart. Gets straight A's in school."

"Do you have a recent picture of her?" Because a detailed description was clearly beyond her.

She got up and left the room. Spinoza's smile widened.

"Shut up," Ron muttered.

"Didn't say a word."

Elvira Paradis returned and handed Ron a five-by-seven school photo of the child from the T.V. photos fast-forwarded to age fourteen. Fine boned like her mother, but her small mouth was determined and those indigo eyes—there was something wild about them. He couldn't imagine her surviving in this household's silences.

He settled back on the couch. "Have you checked her room—seen if anything's missing?"

When she looked mystified, he added, "Did she take things with her as if she planned on leaving? Are there clothes missing that might indicate what she was wearing?"

"I'll show you." She led them down the hall, clearly not knowing the answer.

"Is there a Mr. Paradis we should talk to?" he asked.

She shook her head 'no.' "May-Bell and me—we're on our own."

May-Bell's stingy room held a single narrow bed under a window that gave out onto a sun-parched backyard. It held only a swing set with a single dangling swing and a yawning gap where a second swing might have been. Her room was little girl pale pink and purple, but the walls held hints of fledgling teenager: posters of animals, woodland scenes, an art poster of fairies placed at the end of the bed. Not exactly what he expected. No boy-bands or teen heart throbs.

"No unicorns," he said.

"They were extinct a long time ago."

Spinoza arched a brow at him.

"Can you see if anything's missing?" Ron asked.

She rifled through a painfully empty closet, and almost empty drawers. "It's all here, I think, except what she was wearing; blue jeans and her favourite pink t-shirt with a running horse on it."

That was something. "What kind of shoes?"

"She has a pair of pink runners. They're her favourite."

"Hold on." He led them out front to the shoe on the lawn. Pink sneaker, size five. It showed the signs of kid-wear with the heel bent in back from treating the shoe as a slip on. It lay upside down, as it had fallen. A fight, maybe? A shoe wasn't something you stepped out of and left as you walked away—at least not just one of them. This was more like the shoe had been dropped as the girl was carried away.

"Did you hear your daughter leave?" Why hadn't she noticed the shoe?

She was looking up to the sky as if the sight of the shoe pained her.

"Mrs. Paradis? Did you hear her?"

She shook her head, her hair spun like spider thread around her shoulders. "She didn't come through the living room because I was watching television." Her small hands worked each other.

He used his smart phone to photograph the shoe. "I'd like to see the backyard please."

He and Spinoza tramped after her as she flitted across the browned lawn to the side of the house and a small gate that hung open.

"Do you always leave your gate open?"

"No." She frowned.

The grass underneath May-Bell's bedroom window *did* look like some of the blades were crushed. From someone standing here? Or was it from someone jumping down from the ledge. He tested the window and it slid upward with the ease of frequent use. Had the girl flown the coop on her own? Had she left with someone?

The swing set, a factory-made metal job, sat alone in the yard, the lawn underneath faintly green compared to elsewhere. The set had been there a long time—probably put up by a family with young children before the financial crash. Along with two swings it would have had a teeter-totter at one end. Now its bright red paint had chipped and rust ate the metal. The single swing hung like an exhausted child.

"How long have you lived here, Mrs. Paradis?" He crossed to the lone swing and touched the chains.

"Almost eleven months." Her hair was silver in the sun. It would be ethereal by moonlight.

The swing itself was wooden. He hadn't seen a wooden swing since he was a kid—now playgrounds had soft rubber because wood was considered too dangerous. When he touched it, the swing groaned where the chain met the suspending crossbar and a tingle ran through him.

He settled onto the wooden seat and had the urge to lean back and start pumping. Instead he stared at the house. "May-Bell come out here a lot?"

"Some."

But this *was* the kind of place a teen would come to be alone. It was the kind of place to think. His house had had a similar swing—a lone board hanging from the strong branch of an oak tree that had long ago been cut down. He'd spent evenings there dreaming of life beyond that yard. What did May-Bell dream of? A knight on a white charger rescuing her from her life?

But the posters in her room spoke of a different kind of girl—not the boy-obsessed fourteen-going-on-twenty-four-year-olds that were everywhere today. No, this one was *interested*. May-Bell Paradis *wanted* something. If she left, it would be because she wanted something more.

Beneath the swing set long grooves had been worn into the lawn by feet dragged across the earth. The odd thing was the grooves lay under the spot a second swing should hang.

He stood. The chains that would have held another swing appeared sheared off at the crossbar.

He turned back to Elvira. "How long ago did you have the swing cut off?"

The woman's mouth settled into a sullen line. When she met his gaze he found himself in a meadow of wildflowers, the wind tossing the blossoms, the air heavy with sweetness and the hum of bees.

She blinked and he again stood in a faded backyard with a rusted swing set. *What the hell is going on?*

"There was never a second swing," Elvira said.

"Mrs. Paradis, what do you think has happened to May-Bell? Has she run away or was she taken?"

She seemed to look past him into somewhere else. Then she shook her head. "May-Bell would never leave me like this. Not of her own choice. You've got to get her back for me."

The way she'd looked away, he knew she was lying.

Alexander Junior High filled half a city block with concrete stairs and seating areas terraced up to a concrete façade. There were no trees and no grass, only concrete that reflected sunlight into Ron's face and heat through the soles of his shoes.

Inside, the air smelled of machinery overloaded by the heat of too many teen bodies. The halls were quiet, just a few wraith-like figures shifting under the fluorescents before disappearing into classrooms. The half-heard drone of teachers' voices brought another rush of *déjà vu*. He'd hated high school, had hated junior high more.

He showed his badge at the office security window and they were buzzed into a waiting area that was split by a counter. On one side were two desks and office machinery. On the other three chairs stood against the wall, a small table in front of them. The air reeked of copier ink, paper and an old woman's too-sweet perfume.

"We'd like to speak to the principal, please. It's regarding, May-Bell Paradis," he said to the clerk. Spinoza nodded.

"Have a seat. I'll tell him you're here." The clerk motioned to the waiting room chairs.

The chairs stood next to a closed wooden door. One chair held a kid with black hair that hung over his ears, and a black gaze that radiated age beyond his years. He looked up at them, and the age disappeared, leaving behind bored resignation. He wore a black t-shirt and jeans over long, outstretched legs, and had a black leather jacket across his lap. Now, who wore leather when it was a hundred degrees? Work boots with lug soles covered large feet.

Ron slouched down in the chair beside the kid and grabbed a magazine off the table. Old. Women's. He tossed it aside and sat in silence. No banter between the two admin staff. Unnatural. Unhappy.

"You waiting for the principal?" Ron asked the kid.

"The Veep. He doles out what passes for justice 'round here. You'd like him," the kid said with a lip curl.

Lots of attitude, this one. The kind that said what he thought. "You know May-Bell Paradis?"

"I might." Normal caution. "What'd she do?"

"Who does she hang with in school?"

The kid grinned. "You gotta give a little, ta get a little, man. What'd she do?"

"Disappeared. Her mother thinks she's been abducted."

The kid snorted. "That old hag don't know nothing."

Ron sat up. "So you *do* know May-Bell."

The kid shrugged, his grin gone. "She's fucking trapped like the rest of us. The world, you know?"

He leaned his head back against the wall and closed his eyes, effectively ending the conversation.

Ron settled back, too. "We want to make sure she's all right. You hear anything, I'd appreciate you letting me know." He placed a business card on the kid's knee and closed his eyes. He felt the kid stir.

"If I was May-Bell, I'd be so far from here you'd never find me. I'd never look back."

Ron rolled his head sideways to look at the kid, but the boy's eyes were still closed, and Ron's card hadn't moved. Had the kid even spoken? Spinoza didn't look up from thumbing a magazine.

The wooden door beside them pulled open, releasing a gust of sea-scented aftershave and a student moving fast toward the main office door. A big man followed him.

"You've visitors, sir. The police," said the clerk. She nodded in their direction. Spinoza closed his magazine.

The principal was a tall, thin man, verging on the cadaverous, with large hands that stuck too far out of his gray suit jacket sleeves. He turned a sunken-fleshed face towards them. "How may I be of assistance?"

Ron stood and introduced them. "We'd like to speak with you about May-Bell Paradis."

"I'm Stepford Hall, Vice-Principal. Please, come in." He motioned them into his office. Functional shelves of policy manuals, and educational theory. Above the book shelves was the expected inspirational office picture except instead of the usual words like *Strive*, or *Excellence,* this one said *Be* and showed a street scene of people going about their day.

VP Hall must have seen his glance. He smiled as he sank into his seat. "We strive to keep our student's expectations realistic—especially since the economic downturn."

It was a short interview.

Stepford Hall knew nothing about May-Bell Paradis except her attendance—excellent—and that she was a good student, but he did print off May-Bell's schedule and suggest that they talk to May-Bell's teachers, beginning with her Art instructor.

When they stepped out to the waiting area, the dark-haired kid was gone.

After receiving directions, Ron and Spinoza tramped the school halls. Posters of upcoming dances, club meetings and fashionable causes decorated the walls. The place echoed their footfalls like painful memories.

At the juncture of two halls a trophy case adorned one wall with chrome and photos of outstanding athletes. The other side of the hall displayed student art. One painting stopped Ron.

Done in watercolours, its faded blue-grays and greens hinted at tree tops and sky. In the center a swirl of color and line suggested a child in a swing so high she hung above it all. Wild blonde hair blew out from her shoulders and became part of the clouds. It was delicate and beautiful and wild. Scratched in the corner were initials he couldn't make out.

"So what'd'ya think?" he asked.

Spinoza shrugged. "Looks okay. Like someone has a thing with swings." He cocked a brow. "You maybe? You were asking a lot of questions this morning."

The wild-haired blonde could be May-Bell. If it was the Paradis swing set it was proof that both swings had been there and that one was missing—the one the girl in the painting was on. Pondering that, they found the classroom. He knocked on the door, and they stepped inside.

Bright and dark colors splattered the floor, tables and easels. Students wore paint-splattered smocks, as they dabbed brushes on canvas. The fug of turpentine and paint filled the room and a dark-haired woman paused at students'shoulders. She headed toward Ron.

She was a pretty woman, with large dark eyes, and lush lashes. She had high cheekbones with just enough natural colour and a trim figure that, though she was Ron's age, hadn't gone to fat.

"Ms. Leary?" He kept his voice low. "I'm Detective Conway and this is Detective Spinoza. We're investigating the disappearance of May-Bell Paradis. Can we step into the hall?"

"Of course." She preceded them into the deserted hallway. "How can I help you?" She looked from Spinoza to Ron.

"May-Bell's mother reported that she hasn't seen her daughter since night before last. We understand May-Bell has excelled in your class. Have you noticed anything unusual about her?"

Ms. Leary frowned. "Not really. She's the clichéd artistic genius— always distracted except for her art. She's a fantastic painter. Really talented. Someday she'll be someone to reckon with in the art world."

Spinoza's pen scritch-scritched across his notepad. "Can you think of anyone who might want to harm May-Bell—or abduct her?"

"Harm her?" Her skin paled a little. "Do you think something's happened to her?"

"We have to explore all possibilities," Ron said.

And there was that lone pink sneaker fallen on the parched lawn.

Ms. Leary crossed her arms. "I can't think of anyone. She was liked well enough. She never mentioned any issues. She seemed happy since she got a boyfriend."

That was news that Elvira Paradis seemed unaware of.

"Can you think of any reason for May-Bell to run away?"

She shook her head, frowning again.

"So who's this boyfriend?" Spinoza asked

She glanced back at her room. "I'd introduce you, but he's absent today. His name's Todd Sloan. Tall boy. Dark-haired. He likes black leather, but the kid has an artist's soul."

He thought of the kid from the office. "You don't happen to have a photo of him, do you?"

She led them down to the trophy case and studied the displays and photos. "There. That's Todd."

The dark-haired kid stared back at them, his hair slicked by sweat, muscled arms exposed by a basketball shirt. Arms like that were certainly enough to overpower a skinny wraith like May-Bell Paradis.

"Do you think I could get a copy of that photo?"

She shrugged. "The office might have one. But Todd wouldn't do anything to May-Bell. He genuinely cared for her. He's been using her as a model for his painting." She motioned to the watercolour that Ron had admired. "That's his work. He has a whole series of them."

"Really." He glanced at Spinoza and read his matching concern. Was the kid obsessed with May-Bell? "Any possibility of seeing his paintings?"

"Uh..." Ms. Leary suddenly seemed uncertain. "Todd wouldn't do anything to May-Bell. Really."

As if she reassured herself.

"Let's see those paintings, shall we?"

He eased her back to the classroom, but by the time they reached it she was visibly struggling with whether to cooperate.

"I think we may have met Todd today in the office," he said. "He expressed a bit of attitude toward authority. Is that what he's like?"

Ms. Leary looked up at him. "No. Maybe. It depends, I guess. Me, he had no problem with."

Understandable. A pretty teacher wasn't hard to take direction from.

"So those paintings?"

Ms. Leary led to them to a series of shallow drawers that filled one wall. She pulled one out.

A similar watercolour lay on top, the sky a little lighter, the trees and landscape a lot darker and a beam of light caught the figure who had left her swing behind and was leaping—or was that falling—from the swing back to earth. It looked like the landscape would swallow her up.

"A different feel to this one," he said.

Ms. Leary nodded.

He rifled through the stack of paintings. A pastel of a similar scene. An oil with the sky almost tropical blue and a dark brooding landscape with May-Bell Paradis sitting alone on a swing on a two-swing set. For all the bright colour of the sky, the landscape drained the life and color out of everything.

"These are not happy paintings. Not like the one on the wall."

He found Ms. Leary studying him.

The rest of the paintings were all dark and getting darker, except for the last one. It was done with a less skilled hand—the other paintings showed a swift progression in the artist's skill, but this one captured a wild emotion the others hadn't. It showed the same dark landscape and swing set, except that only one swing hung there. The sky was a deep blue verging toward night with the last blush of sunset still edging the horizon. Against this, miniscule from distance, a figure wildly pumped a swing through the air, suspended on nothing.

"Strange." He met Ms. Leary's gaze.

She touched the canvas almost in admiration. "This was his first work in class. He was almost embarrassed when I told him how talented he was." She smiled, but the smile faded. "You know, I didn't think anything of it at the time, but May-Bell got upset when she saw it. She and Todd got into an argument, but things blew over and they started dating."

The tiny figure in the painting seemed filled with joy and freedom, like a bird following the sunlight. He could remember childhood dreams that were similar. Escape. Salvation. So why was Todd Sloan painting May-Bell escaping?

"Can we see May-Bell's paintings, please?"

Kay slid out another drawer. "May-Bell's work is also stunningly good, but darker. There are rarely people in her work. When there are, they aren't happy."

The painting on top was an abstract swirl of dull brown with small square blotches that suggested houses covering the entire world except for a corner that held a brilliant green.

He thumbed through the others. Dark forests with the suggestion of a lost, red-hooded child. Dark alleyways with ethereal smudges that could be ghosts. The canvases got steadily darker until he reached the one on the bottom. The painting was lighter, brighter, a woodland scene of huge trees and shafts of sunlight illuminating a fantastical garden of crimson blooms and a woman in a gossamer robe tending them. Through the trees were hints of carved moss-covered stone archways.

"Why are the first paintings so different for both Todd and May-Bell?" Spinoza asked.

"The assignment, I guess. I asked them to paint something that could only be true in their wildest dreams. I always assign that first to get it out of their systems. Once they get that on the page, I can start working with them to find the beauty in the mundane."

"Interesting." Ron said. Another way to kill dreams.

"If you think of anything else, or if Todd shows up, would you give me a call please?" He handed her his card.

She looked at it, nodded. Her gaze was sad and lonely.

They left the school at three o'clock after retrieving Todd Sloan's address from the school office. The school belched out escaping youngsters. The two of them were silent as they piled into the sedan.

"So what do you think?" Spinoza asked.

"I think we need to find Todd Sloan."

Like the Paradis house, Todd Sloan's home hunkered in a parched lot of cracked earth, its walls chipped white paint over exposed grey boards. It reminded him of flesh showing through torn nylons. Old newspapers and candy wrappers piled at the base of the house as if they held up the weary structure. A sheet of milky plastic had been nailed over the broken front window.

"Imagine growing up here," Spinoza said.

"We've seen worse."

"But this area used to be nice."

Ron shrugged and climbed out of the car. The air smelled of car exhaust, dust and despair. At the house, he knocked on the door. There was movement inside, but no one answered.

"We'll get Todd's photo out to the uniformed officers. They'll pick him up," he said.

Then they left and headed for the office. Finding out what had happened to May-Bell Paradis would wait another day.

Or it wouldn't. That night, at home in his two-room apartment, Ron sucked back a beer in his t-shirt and shorts because his air conditioning had quit again. The TV in the corner droned sitcom reruns and the room smelled of his dinner of ham sandwich with sauerkraut on pumpernickel.

He leaned back on the easy chair that comprised his living room furniture, eyes closed and feet up. This was his thinking position and he needed to think, because something about the May-Bell case itched like a chigger under his skin.

Todd Sloan lived near enough to May-Bell that he could have been stalking her since the Paradises moved in just a few weeks before school. That was the only way he could have known her well enough to have painted her as his first art project.

Or else Ron was just imagining things and the kid had been

inspired to incorporate May-Bell into his painting when he'd met her in class.

But that felt wrong. And Todd Sloan had disappeared right after he knew they were looking for May-Bell. The logical deduction: Todd Sloan ran.

He recalled his few brief words with the kid. May-Bell trapped. Not abducted, but escaping. The kid had spoken with sadness and longing and—yes, bitterness. That was what Ron had heard—the bitterness.

He sat up and stabbed the TV off, then grabbed pants from the unmade bed across the room. Grabbed a shirt, his badge and gun and a jacket to hide the fact he was armed. Then he headed out.

He parked a block away from the Paradis house. At two in the morning the neighbourhood was quiet, even dogs slumbering. He started walking; the night air fresher, untainted by daytime unhappiness. A fading moon stretched his shadow on the sidewalk.

At the Paradis house he wondered whether he was a fool. The house was dark as he followed the yard around to the back. The parched grass whispered under him. The side gate stood open. Elvira Paradis had said she kept it closed.

Moonlight filled the backyard illuminating the swing set, the lone swing rocking gently at the urging of a seated Todd Sloan.

Ron stepped through the gate and Todd startled and then slumped as if he'd long given up hope.

Ron slouched across the yard. "You miss her don't you?"

Todd nodded, but wouldn't meet his gaze.

"You saw her when she first moved in. You saw her and were infatuated."

Another nod. "She was just crazy beautiful. All that wild blonde hair and eyes that were dying. She was dying just like the rest of us, moment by moment. She hated that it was happening. Before school started I watched her because I didn't have the guts to talk to her. Every night she'd climb out her window."

"And she'd come out here, to swing," Ron said softly.

"It was the strangest thing I ever saw. She'd swing higher and higher, almost desperate. I was scared she was going to swing right over the swing set's top bar, but instead light filled her and filled the swing and suddenly the chains released and she was flying—up into the sky. I watched her that first time, swooping and laughing and then she swung back down and the swing attached again. She did that every night for a week and then school started and she didn't do it anymore."

"But you painted what you'd seen."

Todd frowned. "She freaked. But we worked it out. We were together and she was happy—at least a little."

But his hands formed fists around the swing chains. "At least I thought we were. She said the reason she could make the swing fly was that she could fuel it with all the happiness she had from when she was young, from before her mother and she were banished from their—place. She said happiness was a gift, a magic, and that living here stole it from her."

Todd swung the swing back and forth, his feet scuffing through the green grass that was fading to brown.

"Night before last she flew again, didn't she?"

Todd shrugged. "The swing's gone, isn't it?" Loneliness, bitterness, the weight of the world.

"So you didn't hurt her?" How the hell was he going to report this?

The kid looked up at him. "Hurt her? She was magic, man. I'd have gone with her, but I couldn't find enough happiness anymore. I guess she knew I'd bleed it off of her, too, eventually." He sighed and his tears caught the predawn light.

Ron remembered that feeling all too well. He settled himself cross-legged on the grass beside the swing. There was nothing he could say. He'd lost the art of happiness, too.

Side by side they looked up at the empty sky. The moon was setting. Another day of heat and crime and ugliness coming their way.

But somewhere, a girl with one shoe and a swing was flying.

ABOUT THE AUTHOR

Karen L. Abrahamson is a well-traveled writer who has explored cultures and countries around the world but British Columbia, Canada is her favorite place to come back to. She is the author of literary, mystery, romantic and fantasy fiction including the highly regarded Cartographer fantasy series. She lives on the west coast of Canada with two Bengal cats that aren't quite as well traveled as she is.

When she isn't writing she can be found with a camera and backpack in fabulous locations around the world.

Find out more about Karen at:
karenlabrahamson.com

f facebook.com/karenlabrahamson

g goodreads.com/karenabrahamson

BB bookbub.com/authors/karen-l-abrahamson

ONE GOOD SNEEZE

LOUISA SWANN

Hard to believe something as small as a sneeze can change the world, but it happened to me. Could happen to you too, if'n you don't stay vigilant.

My name is Chiaroscuro Addicott Settlemire Moss though my mum calls me Chia and my da calls me a pain in the bum. That's not my full name, though. I found out the hard way it's not good to share your full name with just anyone, 'specially faerie folk. Names have power, believe it or not.

I didn't believe it. Not at first.

Didn't believe in faeries, neither. Not one mite. Which is why my world turned upside down the day I found myself in the Land of the Infamous Fae.

All because of that sneeze.

Like most stories, this adventure started off innocently enough. I'm a travel photographer and had just gotten back to the little cottage in Nevada City I currently called home after an intensive spring photo tour through Iceland. I'd decided to take a couple of friends and go backpacking in the Sierras during the summer solstice, in honor of my da who'd passed during the winter.

Da and me, we didn't get along, not really. Mum said we were too much alike, two souls trying to share the same skin, both redheaded and stubborn.

I tend to think our mutual discomfort came from being exact opposites, more like two ends of a broken stick. Yes, we were both redheads, but he took after his grandfather, a first-generation Scot with an obsession with the supernatural, while I tend to favor—in my own opinion—my mum, a third-generation Brit gone back to her "roots."

The only times Da and me didn't get on each other's nerves was when we were tramping through the woods of his beloved Sierra Nevada mountains or dancing, but the dancing times were few and far between while hiking was part of the normal course of events. Hiking beneath cornflower blue sky with the sting of pine in our noses and birdsong filling our heads, all discord fell away. Times like those we actually *felt* like family.

We talked during our hikes, really talked. Not the lecture kinda talk about how he thought I should behave or what clothes I should wear or how I needed to keep up my grades. We discussed worldly things—what was happening in the government and how he thought things were going to get better.

We talked about his family and the adventures he'd had when he was growing up. Being that Da had been an only child with parents who worked hard just to make ends meet, most of those adventures were shared with his grandfather, the man responsible for my first name—Chiaroscuro: the effect of contrasted light and shadow.

My grandfather passed away just after I was born, so I never got a chance to ask him why he chose that particular name. (Da always said I was the "effect" of light—aka Mum—when confronted by shadow—aka Da—but Mum said that was a bunch of bunk, I wasn't any "effect," I was my own self, thank you very much.)

We talked about Mum's family and which one of her six siblings had gotten into the most trouble. (Uncle Zach took the prize for Uncle Most Likely to Turn Criminal, which Da wholeheartedly endorsed despite the fact that Uncle Zach was the only other relative who shared grandfather's supernatural obsession.)

We talked about war.

We talked about grace.

And we talked about faeries.

Da was a firm believer in the Land of Fae, though I couldn't understand why. Here was a man who didn't take shite from anyone. A man who claimed he liked his whiskey hard and his women harder, though Mum always rolled her eyes at that one. Da only spent what he earned, always on necessities, nothing more. Any leftover money went in a savings account—yes, those still existed—and there was *no* allowance for frivolities, though Mum had her rainy day allowance.

Needless to say, Da was the kind of man who only believed something once he'd seen it with his own eyes—the exact opposite of his own father.

Yet Da insisted the Land of the Fae was real.

All because he had—once upon a time—met a faerie.

Those times hiking with my da were the best times despite all the faerie talk, far as I was concerned. When I was much, much younger, I used to wish as hard as I could that things between us would stay the same after we got home from one of our hikes.

Soon as we got back to our two-story tract house in Sacramento, however—a house that looked like every other house in the residential tract on the *outside* but was not like any other house in the neighborhood on the *inside*—anything resembling accord dissolved. The entire house was Da's "man cave," a place he had *allowed* Mum and I to inhabit. Even though I moved out ten years ago, Da and I still butted heads over the man cave issue along with just about everything else.

All issues that seem trivial now. Too alike or too different, didn't much matter once Da was gone.

Took him being gone, *really* gone, for me to realize how much I missed him.

Of course, I didn't understand much of anything at the time of his passing. The days had been filled with a flurry of activities, most of which passed in a blur. I *thought* my angst—the burning in my chest, the ocean of tears that refused to fall, the fury threatening to explode like a rampant volcano (how dare he up and die on us!)—was due to not really being able to say a proper goodbye.

Astonishingly enough, I found myself missing the stubborn fool. Maybe I thought going on a trek would bring me closer to his spirit. Maybe I just wanted to get away from all the shite going on in the world. Either way, spending the solstice hiking the trails in Da's memory grew from an idea into an obsession as the winter snows melted and Spring spread like a deadly disease from the foothills into the mountains, laying the groundwork for an early summer.

So, I made a plan.

I'd take a three-day trek along one of Da's favorite trails, during which time I'd tell tales of derring-do about Da. I'd do it on the solstice, the longest day of the year, a day when the faeries came out to play. At least that's when Da had met his one and only fae acquaintance.

I almost went alone, but Da's voice kept echoing in my head: "They who sow the wind shall reap the whirlwind."

Not sure why he chose that particular proverb to hit me over the head with during my formative years. Da didn't care none for bible thumpers and that particular proverb was straight from the Bible, Hosea 8:7. But he always followed up the proverb with his *own* definition, making sure his meaning was crystal clear: if'n you do something stupid, be prepared to deal with the fallout. Far as he was concerned, the only reason for something bad to happen was because the person the bad thing happened to had been stupid.

He didn't believe in Fate or coincidence or any of Murphy's Laws. Da believed in taking responsibility for one's own actions. "If a body makes intelligent, reasonable decisions, everything works out," he'd say with a nod.

Like he'd never done anything stupid in his life.

Hiking alone in the woods was stupid as stupid gets far as Da was concerned. And since this little trek was in honor of his memory, I best not play it stupid.

So, I gathered up the only two people I trusted with this special time—Murdock McKenzie, my second-oldest friend, and Doni Swift, who holds the Oldest Friend record—and filled them in on my big plan.

"Sounds...interesting," was all Murdock said.

Doni raised an eyebrow and nodded. "Whatever you need."

Murdock looks like a child's sweet teddy bear, but I'd learned long ago that teddy bear image of his was more like the real thing than a child's toy. Murdock *is* cute and huggable and his face is furry, but beneath that soft exterior lays an ocean of snark surrounding a volcanic temper. There's a heart of gold beneath the snark and temper, though. A heart both true and loyal.

Doni, on the other hand, isn't furry or nasty. Where I'm short and scrawny, Doni's tall—6 foot plus a hiccup (as she says)—rounded just enough to fill out her jeans nicely, but not to overflowing, and her green eyes always bubble with laughter. At the time of our *adventure*, her black hair was cut in a bob that never needed combing. We'd known each other since we were babes in arms and had shared practically everything while growing up—measles, mumps, chicken pox, even a boyfriend or two.

And now we were about to share a grand adventure, or so I imagined.

We threw our gear in my aging Jeep Cherokee—tent, sleeping bags, even took along cutting-edge lightweight air mattresses since none of us were feeling like spring chickens, though thirty-mumble, bumble didn't put any of us in the senior citizen category, not in my book anyways.

Murdock even splurged on a brand new Windburner radiant cook stove that promised to be the ultimate in backcountry cooking. Compact and light? Not so much. But not all that heavy, neither.

"Might as well do it up right," Murdock said when I questioned his extravagance. "This being for your dad and all."

"Long as you carry it," was all I said. I divided up the food between Doni and me—since Murdock was lugging the stove—finished loading and fastening my pack, then jumped in the driver's seat and prayed the engine would turn over.

After three false starts, the engine roared its displeasure at being disturbed while the sun was still sleeping, and we headed for the hills.

The hills were really mountains, of course. Mountains I've hiked for as long as I can remember. Our destination was two hours of driving time and a day's hike away—the Sierra Buttes, a geological formation Da called "quartz porphyry" and I called "jagged red peaks."

Da was...had been...a third grade teacher. Loved guiding young minds, he'd always said, but his true passion was geology. He obsessed over geological formations, insisting on studying the land wherever we went. You might say I picked up some of that knowledge by osmosis, but I was more interested in the pretty rocks than in whether they were igneous or metamorphic.

The trail we were about to embark on was one of Da's favorites and the old fire lookout at the top of the buttes offered one of the most spectacular views I've ever experienced. I was looking forward to seeing that view once again and sharing it with my friends.

Dawn broke as we pulled into the parking lot at Lower Sardine Lake, painting the deep cerulean sky with streaks of rose and pale peach. There was a trailhead much closer to the buttes themselves, but Da had always wanted to take the long way, so that's what we were doing.

We climbed out of the heated Jeep and were greeted by a breeze that felt like it came straight out of the Arctic. We pulled on jackets and hats, strapped on our packs, and headed up the trail without saying a word. The birds welcomed us along with the new day, twittering and chirping like a gaggle of happy children. The sharp scent of pine mingled with the ripe cat-urine stench of juniper. I wrinkled my nose at the familiar combination. Da loved juniper trees in spite of their smell. He'd always collected the berries along with the needles and bark, saying they were one of Nature's best medicines.

I refused to drink the tea he made from the needles. Couldn't get the thought of cat pee out of my head, but I found myself mimicking Da, grabbing a handful of berries or needles every time I got near enough to a tree.

The trail was more of an abandoned road between Lower and Upper Sardine, rocky and cracked by runoff, but wide enough we could walk side by side. I took the opportunity to share a few tales with my friends.

The vista opened as we crested the first ridge, the pristine waters of Lower Sardine Lake sparkling below us. I paused and studied the sky, my attention caught by the sound of an osprey's call. The shrill, yet musical whistle trilled three times, short bursts followed by a long cry.

"What is it?" Murdock asked.

I held up a hand, finally spotting the osprey—white body, brown wings—just as it drew its wings and plunged toward the waters far below in a heart-pounding stoop. "There."

We were too high to see the splash, but I could tell the osprey's hunt had been successful. He—or she—had to work hard to get clear of the water and gain a bit of altitude. The osprey's wings kept up a strong, steady beat as it headed back into the trees.

"Maybe if we ask nice, we'll get invited to dinner," Murdock said.

Doni rolled her eyes and we moved on, stopping for a quick break on the dam at Upper Sardine. After reinforcing ourselves with salami, jack cheese, and water, we shouldered our gear, and started the more strenuous part of our climb, leaving the old road behind.

The sun grew hot as the day marched on. The rocky trail insisted we pay attention—one misstep on a wobbly rock could result in a strained ankle or worse. We moved single file now, stories about my da whispered in my head instead of out loud. We stopped briefly for lunch—more salami and cheese—but I wanted to get to the top before dark, so we didn't linger.

My plan was to pitch our tents as near the lookout as we could get —which was a fair distance below the abandoned building that had to be reached via stairs...and more stairs...and more stairs—and spend two days celebrating Da and the summer solstice.

The weatherman had predicted sunny skies for the next week, but I wasn't all that surprised when sullen clouds scudded across the sun, sending the temperature plummeting. Afternoon thunderstorms were a way of life in the Sierras.

I'd figured on afternoon thunderstorms.

I'd also figured we might have to navigate across or around lingering snow fields.

I hadn't figured on it actually snowing.

In the middle of June.

Da would have detected something different about the developing storm—the shape of the clouds or the smell in the air. He would have stopped and made camp, yakking about the time he'd been trapped in a blizzard or survived a flood while we set up the tent. By the time the storm hit, we would have been sitting snug as proverbial bugs in our sleeping bag rugs.

But I wanted to camp where Da and I had usually camped. In an area of old growth trees that embraced us like sheltering arms. I insisted we move on, even after the clouds threatened to put the sun to an early bed. I was certain we would make it.

We didn't.

Have I mentioned that my life has been a series of misfortunes tied together with mishaps and misery?

I like to blame it on Da, of course.

You see, he gave me a charm on my very first birthday—a thumb-sized translucent red stone carving of something that looked more like a squished pug than anything else. Ever since then, I've felt more cursed than blessed during my thirty-some years on this planet. Anything that *could* go wrong in my life, *has* gone wrong. It was easy to blame what I called "the nasties" on that little red pug.

"You bring it upon yourself," Da said one day when he caught me bad-mouthing the pug. "They who sow the wind shall reap the whirlwind."

Yeah, that proverb again. It definitely was one of Da's favorites, though I wasn't sure how it applied in that particular situation. Anyway, I'd been wanting to get rid of that *charm* for as long as I could remember, but it hadn't seemed proper, not with it being a gift and all.

But it somehow felt appropriate to cap off my little celebration of Da's life by casting that evil charm off the old fire lookout at the top of the buttes, fare-thee-well and ta ta, that sort of thing.

Had the pug caught wind of my intentions and summoned the storm?

The wind picked up and the clouds finished devouring the sun, draining the warmth right out of the air. I shivered, and we stopped long enough to pull our jackets and hats back on.

I'd made sure we were prepared for a typical summer storm.

I hadn't been prepared for a blizzard.

Clouds obliterated the peaks from view; snow obliterated everything else. We'd been caught on one of the more open slopes, away from any sheltering trees. My heart sank as I realized I knew where we were.

There was another side to the buttes, a side few people knew about and even fewer had ever experienced. Beneath the buttes themselves, hidden deep behind bramble and rock, was a cave, the entrance to a tunnel that went who knows how deep into the mountain itself.

I'd always figured the cave was a mine—there were plenty of mines throughout the Lakes Basin, especially around Gold Lake proper—but Da thought differently.

"This place is special," he'd said over and over. The man knew his rocks. If'n he thought the cave was something other than a mine, then I tended to believe him.

That belief had flown out the door the last time we'd visited the cave.

"It's a door into Fae," he'd said in a voice so low I almost didn't hear him. "Right here. In front of me. If only I could remember how to open it."

He wasn't himself right then. Da was a big man, with broad shoulders that seemed able to bear any weight they were made to carry, the epitome of "large and in charge," of his own world at least.

But that day in the cave his eyes grew wild and desperate, his face filled with a longing I couldn't understand.

It was not one of his finer moments.

I had decided to avoid the cave during this memorial trip. There were other places, other memories I would much rather cherish.

Apparently, my wishes were not important, not on this trip, anyway. Not as far as the weather gods were concerned.

The wind howled and wailed, driving pellets of stinging ice directly into our faces.

"Come on," I shouted, trying to make myself heard over the wind. I headed for the only shelter I knew, leading the way off the trail, scrambling and sliding down rocks now slippery with snow. I shimmied around boulders, ducked beneath brambles, and finally stopped, breathing hard, hands on my knees.

For a moment I didn't look up. Didn't want to see the gap between boulders, a gap that led into darkness far deeper than any absence of light could explain—

"Would you look at that," Murdock said from just behind my left shoulder. "A cave. Cool beans."

Doni wasn't so thrilled. "I thought you wanted to stay away from this place."

"What, this isn't a new discovery?" Murdock sounded disappointed, though having to shout to be heard over the screaming wind took away from the melodrama.

I straightened and looked at my friends. The wind decided to give us a break, leaving the snow to swirl around us instead of driving it into our faces. I glanced at the gloom still hovering overhead, thought about just setting up our tents...or maybe one tent, considering there was barely enough room for the three of us to stand in the tiny hollow between boulders.

Another blast of ice crystals practically tore the breath from my mouth.

"We don't have to do this," Doni said. "There have to be other options."

There *were* other options, none of them good.

I shrugged, trying to look nonchalant. "We'd never get the tents up in this wind."

"What about bear?" Murdock shouted, his voice tight. He nodded at the opening.

The critters leave this place alone, Da's voice whispered in my mind. *They know the door is here.*

I would actually *welcome* confronting a bear in that cave, I realized. Finding that kind of evidence, evidence that Da's faeries did not exist (wouldn't the faeries keep the bears away?), would confirm that Da had been nuts, bonkers, crazy as a loon. And all would, once again, be right with the world.

In a perverted kind of way.

Clenching my jaw tight, I faced the opening that seemed to ooze darkness. Without another word, I slid my pack from my shoulders—the opening was low and narrow—and left the outside world behind.

~

W e squeezed ourselves into a tiny alcove that appeared to be created by a tumble of boulders and smaller rocks, but I knew that was just an illusion. The boulders and rocks were part of a larger cave—a cave Da had brought me to at least a half dozen times. The front of the cave had partially collapsed. We stood in what was, essentially, the entry.

The space seemed preternaturally silent after the violent screams of the storm outside. The air smelled...ancient. I could almost imagine the dust hadn't been disturbed for eons, though I knew differently. We stood for a moment, letting our eyes adjust to the tiny bit of light that had somehow managed to follow us in.

Yes, I know. It was ludicrous to think the light had actually followed us, but it seemed that way at the time.

The *entry* seemed smaller than I remembered it being. Of course, I'd been all of ten at the time—I think. Old enough to do the trek without being carried and young enough to be scared spitless when Da started blathering on about faeries and such. It just wasn't like him, you know? Not like him at all.

"Guess this will work," Murdock finally said, his voice sounding deeper and more sonorous surrounded by rock walls. Doni just looked at me, her brow furrowed, lips pulled down in a slight frown.

She knew almost everything about me, including how I felt about this cave, though she'd never been here—at least I'd never brought her. But she somehow sensed that this was the place where I thought my father had gone insane.

I listened to the still-howling wind, much fainter now we were out of it, but still going on like a raving lunatic.

"It widens out a mite further in," I finally managed to say around the lump clogging my throat. "We'll need flashlights, though."

Murdock didn't waste any time pulling a flashlight from a side pocket of his pack. Doni did the same, though her movements were slower.

I dropped my pack to the ground with a loud thud, yanked my own flashlight from the "might need it fast" pocket just above my bedroll, and flicked the flashlight on.

"Come on," I said, jerking my pack off the floor and holding it in front of me like a shield. "It gets kind of narrow for a while, but I think we can all make it."

Murdock grumbled something about being squished through a spaghetti press, but we eventually worked our way through a tunnel that got narrower before it got wide. I am not generally claustrophobic, but at the narrowest point of the tunnel, right before the tunnel opened onto what I used to call "the bubble," pressure from the rock walls became so intense—mentally—that I almost screamed.

"The bubble" was a circular cave with a dome-shaped ceiling, not quite the size of a two-car garage. The air was absolutely still and the sounds of the storm outside were so muffled I could barely hear them. There was a tinge of ammonia in the air that suggested the presence of bats, though a quick flick of my flashlight beam over the ceiling didn't stir up a cloud of flying furries.

I didn't mind bats. Bats were normal and anything normal was good, especially when it came to this cave.

Murdock set his pack on the rock-strewn floor and flashed his light around like a search beacon gone wild, the broad LED beam illuminating every nook and cranny. The walls and ceiling were just as jagged and craggy as I remembered them, though everything had that same sense of being smaller than I remembered.

Murdock finally heaved a sigh that rebounded off the walls. "No bears."

Of course there were no bears, but how had he missed seeing the tunnel?

I resisted the urge to flash my light at the back wall. I knew what was there. I didn't need to point it out.

"How about cougar?" I asked, trying to lighten the mood. "Any sign of a big cat? Or coyote?"

"Or wolf," Doni added with a grin. She let her pack slid to the ground next to Murdock's and flashed her beam across the ceiling, illuminating a dark black stain that followed the dome's slope, disappearing around a jagged ridge of broken rock. She didn't say anything, though her light lingered on that stain for several heartbeats before moving on.

"We look like kids in a haunted house," she said, abruptly pointing the flashlight at her face. She frowned, then spun the flashlight forward and pointed the beam at the back wall. "What's back there?"

Drat.

Murdock immediately flashed his light in that direction. He frowned. "Looks like a tunnel. Bears don't like tunnels, do they?"

The enclosed space made our voices sound...hollow...resonating in that odd tone voices tend to produce when speaking into a cardboard tube.

I shrugged. "I'm no bear expert, but I do know we'd be able to smell a bear if'n there was one around. Or a big cat, for that matter."

"How 'bout those wolves?" Doni asked. I could almost see her turning the notion around in her brain, looking for something juicy. "Or big dragons that like to eat itty bitty people. This looks like a good place for a—"

"Is that a *real* tunnel?" Murdock asked. He had on his "not sure I like this" look, with his mouth twisted to one side and one eyebrow raised.

I shrugged. "Looks like one."

Doni gave me a sharp look. I knew what she was wondering, but I hadn't told anyone else about Da's little episode. No matter how close a friend Murdock was, I didn't feel comfortable discussing my father's sanity or lack thereof. Not here. Not now.

But there was no reason not to talk about the tunnel. There were tunnels everywhere. Tunnels were normal, just like bats.

I just wouldn't mention Da's *theory* about the tunnel.

"Don't know how far it goes," I finally admitted. "Da checked it out when we first found the cave. He didn't find anything special."

Didn't find what I wanted to find, Da's voice whispered in my head. *It's there. Somewhere—*

"Maybe it's one of *those* tunnels," Murdock said, his voice low. "You know, like the one near Shasta. Leads to wherever the Lemurians are hiding."

Doni snorted. "The land of Mu is a myth, you idiot."

I gave her a tiny smile and turned away, flashing my light at the ground as if looking for something. I'd never told her that particular *myth* about Lemuria was what had Da all stirred up. He'd been convinced that the myth was real. Folks had just gotten things mixed up. Lemuria wasn't gone, not really. The Land of Mu, aka The Land of Fae, had existed for eons—on a different plane. The sightings of robed figures—faeries, not Lemurians—flitting in and out of caves near Mount Shasta confirmed it. You just had to find the right door.

The tunnel beckoning from the far side of the cave was one of those doors. He'd been sure of it. He'd never allowed me to explore with him, though. Said he didn't want to put me in danger.

As if he'd been immortal or something.

Murdock didn't push the subject. He'd found something else to focus his attention. A fire pit.

"You burned fires in here?"

Startled, I looked at the section of ground illuminated by his flashlight. Doni flashed her light at the ring of smoke-blackened rocks, then tilted her light back up at the ceiling.

"Ah," she muttered. "Makes sense."

She gave me a look. I shrugged.

"We didn't make fires. Da always brought his little stove, like Murdock's but smaller and lighter."

The presence of the fire ring and the marks on the ceiling was one of the things that had convinced Da he was on the right track.

"Could have been the Lemurians," Murdock said. He strolled over and stared down at the ring. I followed him, drawn as if by a magnet, though my legs felt like they were moving through a puddle of stiff molasses.

What was I afraid of? I suddenly wondered. There was nothing special about that fire ring, just as there was no such thing as faeries, no spirits of Mu, no Lemurian ghosts hanging around.

I gave myself a mental shake and stepped up beside Murdock, who was staring down at the fire ring.

The ring didn't look any different from the last time I'd seen it. A bunch of rocks set in a circle, blackened by fire. A mite smaller, perhaps, just like everything else seemed to be. There were even ashes in the center of the circle.

A chill ran down my back like a splash of ice water.

Had those ashes been there before?

It didn't matter, I decided. Someone else had probably found the cave. I tightened my jaw and flashed my light around the walls one more time. "We might as well set up camp for the night. That storm will probably be over soon, but I don't particularly relish the idea of trying to pitch tents in the snow. We'll have to go outside to tend to *business*, but this should work fine otherwise."

"Right then." Doni flashed her light around the cave, letting it settle on a space along the wall near where we'd come in. "I'll take this spot." She set her pack against the wall and pulled the lower straps free, releasing her bedroll.

"Good thing we brought air mattresses," Murdock said, finally turning his back on the fire ring. "This floor doesn't exactly lend itself to a good night's sleep."

I shrugged. He was right. The floor was strewn with rocks the size of my fist—and larger, much, much larger. But the smaller rocks could be moved and there was some sand in areas between the rocks. Not exactly the Hilton, but it would do for one night.

"I can set the stove up next to the fire ring," Murdock said. "And this little space—" He pointed at a semi clear area with his boot, "will just about fit my sleeping bag."

He moved his pack between the area he'd chosen and the fire ring, then set his fists on his hips as if waiting for me to protest.

Granted, he'd taken up most of one side. There wasn't a lot of "clear" space left, unless I wanted to park in the middle of the cave. But I didn't mind moving a few rocks.

"Fine with me." I knew how badly Murdock snored. Distance probably wouldn't help much, not with the sound chamber effect going on, but I still decided to move as far away from him as I could.

Which put me close to the tunnel entrance.

I shut down any second thoughts creeping into my mind and yanked my bedroll free.

~

The next few minutes were filled with the sound of wheezing humans as we blew up our air mattresses.

Hey, I said we'd gone all out—for a backpacking trip. Hauling along the equipment to blow up mattresses other than by mouth had not been on my "must do" list.

Once the air mattresses were filled, Murdock set up his new fancy-dancy stove and we settled in for the night.

I have to admit—the ambience was rather cozy, though a mite on the chilly side. With the camp lanterns going and a mug of Irish-crème-laced coffee in hand, that extra voice in my head—Da's voice —finally quieted and I found myself relaxing.

We turned in early, not surprising after the pre-dawn start and storm-riddled day. I dropped off quickly. So did both Doni and— surprise, surprise—Murdock.

Without a single comment about bears.

And that was where—as any avid movie goer, A or B, can tell you —everything went sideways.

I woke sometime around midnight, straining my ears to figure out just what had woken me. Couldn't hear anything other than Murdock's mind-numbing snores. If'n you've ever heard someone trying to hand-saw a wet log, you'll know exactly what I'm talking about.

I'd left one of the camp lanterns turned down low to serve as a night light, but someone had evidently decided that little bit of light was too much. The absolute darkness of the cave—the total absence of any light whatsoever—was more than a bit daunting.

I fumbled inside my sleeping bag, looking for the flashlight I always kept tucked in beside me.

And realized that—in between Murdock's snorts and snuffles—I could hear someone whimpering.

"Doni?" I said in a low voice. No use waking Murdock. We'd never hear the end of it if'n his beauty sleep was interrupted.

Doni didn't answer.

I finally found my flashlight and flicked the beam on. I sat up, shoving my sleeping bag away from my face with one hand and shining the light at Doni's spot with the other.

She appeared to be sound asleep.

Was she having a bad dream?

I climbed from my bed, trying to be quiet as a cat on the hunt and failing miserably. No matter—Murdock's snores more than made up for my lack of stealth. I tiptoed over to Doni's bag and bent to put a hand on her shoulder just as she let out another whimper.

Only she wasn't the one whimpering.

Icy fingers trailed up my spine, lifting the hair at the back of my neck. Had something come out of the tunnel, then? Murdock's bear or a big cat...

Bears and cats didn't whimper, though. Neither did dragons.

Which left Doni's wolf...

I did one of those slow-motion turns, half afraid to see what was behind me and opened my mouth, intending to shout or call for help or simply scream—

My flashlight illuminated my own rumbled sleeping bag, Murdock's stove, and three lanterns.

Nothing more.

Heart in my throat, I hurried over to the lantern perched on the knee-high rock near my bed and, half expecting nothing to happen, shoved the switch to full brightness.

The lantern flared to life, chasing the darkness back. I took a deep breath, scanned the ceiling overhead with my flashlight to verify the ceiling was also free of intruders, then moved cautiously to my sleeping bag.

The lantern was supposed to last for fourteen hours at full brightness. We had two other lanterns—and our flashlights with extra batteries.

There was no way I was going to turn that lantern off. Not tonight.

I climbed into my sleeping bag and started to snuggle in.

That's when I noticed my stone charm. Lying on its side in the sand, round puggy eyes staring at me in that accusing way only pugs can seem to manage.

I'd left that charm tucked safely in a pocket—inside my pack.

This time it wasn't only the hair on the back of my neck that rose —all the hair on my body suddenly stood at attention.

I wondered briefly if'n I was dreaming. I even pinched myself hard enough to wince.

Not dreaming then.

For some strange reason, I didn't want to wake either of my friends. They'd had a rough enough day. I was the instigator of what was rapidly becoming more nightmare than adventure. It was up to me to make sure everyone was safe.

I climbed back out of my sleeping bag. Snatched the charm from the dirt and clutched it tight in one hand. Took my flashlight tight in the other hand, brandishing it more like a club than a light.

And tiptoed toward the entrance where we'd come in.

It only took a minute to slip through the rocks to the tiny entry. No one had taken up residence while we'd been sleeping. I chanced a look outside and drew back immediately as a blast of icy wind carrying equally icy crystals stung my face.

If'n someone was sneaking around our camp, they hadn't come from this direction.

There was only one place they could be.

I don't know about you, but when I get nervous or afraid, I tend to also get angry. Anger doesn't always lead to intelligent decisions. Right then, I was not only a mite scared and more than a mite angry, I was tired—both physically and mentally. At that moment in time, I was certain the entire trek had been a mistake. I hadn't made peace with Da's memories. Those memories had done nothing but cause me trouble.

Just like Da.

I clenched my jaw, slipped back into the cave, and strode over to the tunnel, not bothering to tiptoe.

One of Murdock's snores ripped the air just as I reached the tunnel's yawning black maw and my heart jumped into my mouth.

I glared at Murdock, sleeping soundly while I was busy playing... what? Bodyguard?

I turned back to the tunnel and started to shout, "Who's there?" Before the words came out, I closed my mouth and took a moment to think.

Whatever I'd heard had been whimpering, not growling or snarling. It hadn't sounded fierce at all. It had sounded like it was hurt or...like a pup separated from its mom.

There still was no reason to wake my friends. I'd take a quick look down the tunnel and figure out what was going on.

I took a deep breath and stepped into the tunnel.

When the tunnel's ceiling dropped so low I had to crawl on hands and knees, I realized I still had the charm clutched tightly in my left hand. I'd also neglected to pull on my boots or grab a jacket.

I shivered in the chilly air, unsure how far I'd come. I hadn't heard any whimpers since I'd left the cave. It was time to turn around, wasn't it?

The stone charm had grown warm in my hand and an idea flitted through my sleep-deprived brain. I flashed the light over the rough rock walls, looking for a niche or small ledge. I'd leave the charm here instead of casting it from the abandoned fire station. The cave—this tunnel—epitomized my relationship with Da.

It was the perfect resting place...for the pug.

My nose started to itch, as if allergic to the suggestion. Remember that sneeze I told you about? The one that changed the world?

That's when it happened...

Whether it was the dust that got to my nose or the curse of the evil red pug, either way, that sneeze was so violent, my head whipped up—right into a rock just waiting to clobber my noggin.

Stars danced around the edge of my vision and everything went black.

At first, I thought I'd knocked myself out, but I could feel sand and rocks beneath my palms and knees. My head felt like I'd just been clobbered with a baseball bat, so I was definitely conscious.

I just couldn't see...anything. Except for the odd impression lingering on the back of my eyes, the type of weird afterimages that make you wonder just what you were looking at when the lights went out.

I don't know if you've ever experienced absolute dark, but the senses tend to play tricks when one of the senses goes missing. My breath echoed in my ears and I could smell my own fear. The walls had been an arm's length or so away the last time I'd been able to see them. Now, I could *feel* the walls closing in around me. I squeezed my eyes closed so tightly tiny sparks of red, yellow, and blue danced across my eyelids.

I opened my eyes and flicked the switch on my flashlight once. Twice.

Nothing happened.

Great. Dead batteries.

That meant I'd have to work my way back to the cave.

In the dark.

Added to the heavy sound of my breathing came the thud, thud, thudding of my heart. My mouth felt like a desert. The air was so thick I couldn't breathe, yet I knew there was nothing wrong with the air. Not really. The only thing that had changed was me.

I pushed myself back on my heels so I could turn around and the back of my head cracked into the ceiling—again.

Things kept getting better and better.

I felt around me, trying to remember if'n there was enough space to turn around like a dog.

There was some space, but I quickly found I wasn't nearly as agile as a dog or as flexible. There was no way I was going to be able to turn in this tight space.

But that didn't stop me from trying.

Somewhere between trying to turn around and bumping my aching head yet again, I realized I'd dropped the charm.

I started to search around in the dark, feeling like I'd lost something precious.

Then I stopped. Why was I looking? I was going to leave the dang thing behind somewhere anyway.

Besides, it was probably the Evil Pug's fault I'd gotten into this situation.

Lowering my head to avoid hitting any more rocky protrusions, I cautiously extended one leg back as far as I could while still balancing on my knees, then the other, following my legs with my hands.

It seemed to take forever until I reached the lantern light. By then I'd been able to stand and turn around, feeling my way along the wall with my left hand. Fortunately for my ankles as well as my hands and knees, the floor of the tunnel had been more sand than rock and I made the return trip in relative safety.

The camp lantern lasted until I'd staggered from the tunnel to my sleeping bag and then had flickered out.

I was going to have a talk with the salesman at our local camping outlet. He'd promised batteries with long lives; neither lantern or flashlight had delivered.

I slid into my sleeping bag with a groan, feeling a mite light-headed. Probably from all that pounding going on in my head...

The next thing I knew, it was morning.

~

At least I thought it was morning. Hard to tell the difference between night and day when you've fallen asleep in a cave.

I know one thing for certain—there is nothing in the world like waking up with an otter peering into your eyes—cute button nose, eyes that always manage to somehow look concerned, soft fur a mite on the damp side, tiny round ears, and tickly whiskers. Kind of endearing while still being a startling experience.

At least I *think* it was an otter.

I caught a whiff of something musky, then the whiskery face disappeared, leaving me feeling discombobulated. Trying to reorient myself, I studied the firelight flickering over the ceiling, dancing in and out of the nooks and crannies...

*Fire*light?

I started to sit up but froze as an eerie sensation of something crawling down my forehead set my teeth on edge. I raised my hand to swipe the offender away—

"I wouldn't do that I was ya'll. In fact, I wouldn't move at all."

The voice, dry as a desert and twice as thorny, stopped my hand mid-swipe. Out of the corner of my eye, I could see an old woman hunched next to the fire ring. The scent of wood smoke mingled with...sulfur?...tickled my nose, then was gone.

I slowly lowered my hand as the end of a blue stick rose above my right eye, waved around in the air for a moment, then settled on the bridge of my nose. I lifted my hand, instinctively wanting to brush the stick—or whatever it was—off my face.

"You might want to listen to her." The warning in Murdock's tone froze my hand in mid-air.

I let my hand dangle loosely for the length of a breath, then lowered the hand to my side. A shadow shaped like the prow of a tiny ship followed the blue stick.

What on earth?

Have you ever tried to focus on something sitting on the bridge of your nose, crossing your eyes until they hurt because you couldn't figure out what was crawling on your face?

If'n I hadn't been totally discombobulated by a) being woken up by an otter-type creature and b) being on the verge of panic at having something *odd* crawling around on my face, I more than likely would have recognized the thing using my *face* as a highway fairly quickly. But it took more than a heartbeat and what felt like an eon of eye-crossing to identify the black-and-red beast with vibrant blue legs resting on my schnozzola.

A frog.

Why did it have to be a frog?

Now I'm not a frogaphobe, not really. Frogs have their place—which happens to be anywhere else but my nose.

"Aren't those the poison ones?" Murdock asked. "The kind South American natives poison their darts with?"

I would have kicked him if'n he'd been anywhere close by. He sounded like he was chatting over coffee while images of deadly hoppers flashed through my mind, National Geographic-style. My gut tightened into a stone I hoped I wouldn't have to pass.

This couldn't be *that* kind of frog. We were more than a jillion miles—well, several thousand miles anyway—away from any poisonous frogs. Yes, we have poisonous toads, but the mountains of northern California are definitely not home to poisonous critters. We do have the odd scorpion. And rattlesnakes (occasionally). As well as sharp-tongued harridans dressed up like school teachers and road maintenance workers who derive no greater pleasure from life than making a hard-working soul late her first day on the job...

"The purtiest ones are the worst," the woman said. "That one'll kill ya in ten seconds flat."

I managed to keep from turning my head, but some sign of alarm must've shown. No surprise considering the adrenalin flooding into every crevice of my ready-to-flee body.

"Probably not a good time to sneeze," Murdock warned.

I groaned, frantically trying to think about something—anything else. Murdock had just dropped from Second Best Friend into the Dung Heap of Lost Friendship. He *knew* how insidious such suggestions were.

Not only was I going to kick him once I got out of this sticky conundrum, I was going to—

Another thought interrupted my mental tirade: Where was Doni? Why didn't my oldest, bestest friend *do* something?

"Long as ya don't touch his back, yer safe," the old woman continued. "Little bugger has an oozing problem. Secretes goo through the skin covering his spine like a kid with a runny nose. Ain't his fault. Nature made 'im that way. But the stuff is deadly—leastways to types like ya'll."

Definitely a medication moment, only I'd left my martini shaker, with all the appropriate ingredients, at home.

"You sound like you're talking from experience," I said, trying not to move my face as I spoke. A blurred movement to my left indicated the woman's nod, but she didn't offer any more advice.

I carefully took note of what little I could see of my surroundings using my peripheral vision. Woman to the left of me, cave wall to the right. And there I was, stuck in the middle.

With a frog.

On my nose.

"Where's Doni?" I managed to ask the question with a minimum of lip movement.

"Was going to ask you the same thing," Murdock said. "Until I saw you were busy."

Yes, I was definitely going to kick him and now I would probably castrate him as well—figuratively, if'n I didn't do the deed in actuality.

As soon as I figured out how to get rid of this blasted frog.

"Don't go getting yer harnesses in a knot," the old woman said. "That tall friend of yers is out watering the bushes."

I absently wondered if Doni knew what was going on in here or if'n the old woman had managed to somehow pass Doni as she tended to business.

The twin sticks parked on my nose turned, step by sticky, agonizing, step, until I was staring deep into a pair of dark, froggy eyes.

There had been no frogs in the cave when we'd gone to bed.

So where *had* this little blue-and-red gem come from?

"Uh, Chia. Did you know there's a frog on your nose?"

I choked back a snort. The Great and Glorious Doni had returned. My nose wrinkled as I caught a whiff of something... sulfurous? I tried to glare at Doni without moving, but glaring does not work well when all you can move are your eyes and the object of your glare is barely visible. What I could see of her looked rather...pale.

"You know Chia," Murdock said. "Always doing the unexpected."

I gritted my teeth.

"Doni, this is...I don't believe I caught your name?" Murdock's question hung in the air like a befuddled raindrop.

"Name's Darwin," the woman said.

"Darwin...what?" Doni asked. She sounded as calm as Murdock. Did they think I'd set all this up as some kind of sick joke?

"Just Darwin."

"Right," Murdock said.

Just Darwin, I mused. No first, last, or middle initial. Could be she thought she was famous or something. Being a photographer had allowed me to meet so many rich, famous, and otherwise abused folks during my travels and I'd never heard of anyone currently named Just Darwin.

"Don't s'pose ya have any M&Ms on ya?" Darwin had a wistful tone in her voice, like a child at Halloween.

"No, ma'am. Bad for your teeth," Doni said.

I couldn't help grinning. *That's my girl.* I must have imagined she looked pale. She didn't *sound* pale or flustered or whatever tone of voice generally accompanied paleness.

My grin faded as the cornflower-blue legs and blood-red body still parked on my face shifted slightly. How was I going to get myself out of this one?

Despite my efforts not to think about sneezing, my nose decided to develop an itch right then and there. The kind of itch that precedes a mind-numbing, head-jerking, rib-cracking sneeze.

Probably couldn't blame this one on Murdock and his big mouth.

I wrinkled my nose.

The frog shifted position.

"Hey, guys?" I mumbled. Frantic to stop the itch pre-sneeze, I pursed my lips tight together. The frog, its tiny feet cool and sticky on my skin, shifted position again.

Gathering itself for a jump, maybe, but where to?

Eyes? Lips? Hair?

Just picturing a poisonous frog scrambling through my tangled locks was enough to send shivers up and down my spine, dissipating the urge to sneeze. Clothes, skin—even lips—were things I could brush off, but hair was another matter entirely. It could take *weeks* to track down a frog that had gotten lost in the ragtag mop I called my "morning" hair.

"Guys? I think it's about to—"

A soft twang reached my ear and the little hopper disappeared from my nose. I bolted upright, winced as pain knocked against my skull at the abrupt movement, and stared in shock as the frog splatted against the wall nearest my right shoulder.

"Well, that wasn't very nice." Murdock sounded like a wounded child. He was still sitting on his sleeping bag, hair tousled, and eyes half closed, like he'd just woken up.

"How did you...*do*...that?" I wasn't sure what I'd just witnessed.

The woman grinned, flashing a set of healthy looking teeth. Her teeth looked totally out of place, teeth that belonged to an A-list actor, not a backwoods hermit lady. Her torso was covered with a ragged leather vest that barely concealed sagging breasts and ribs prominent enough to count. Her pants consisted of leather leggings belted at the waist with front and back flaps protecting the more delicate parts. A black felt hat with a wide brim covered the top of her head. A pair of long, gray braids seemed to sprout from beneath the hat, one braid dangling down across each boney shoulder.

The woman held up one hand and partially opened it, revealing a mass of what looked like rubber strings. It took a moment for me to recognize her ammunition of choice.

Rubber bands. The ultimate weapon. Why was I not surprised?

I looked around nervously to make sure nothing else was trying to sneak up on me, then watched as the scrawny woman poked a stick in the fire.

A fire.

In a cave.

I snuck a glance at the black mark on the ceiling. The mark, the ashes—somehow it all made sense, in a warped kind of way.

Was this the woman's home, then? Had we inadvertently invaded her space?

And when had she moved in?

"Ta answer yer question—about my experience, and all—it beats the snot outta me what piss frogs're doing in these parts. They don't belong in the Land of Fae. I kin tell ya that those critters been all around yer camp this morning. Done shot about eight of 'em so far."

"What do you mean, the Land of Fae?" I asked at the same time Murdock blurted out, "Eight of them?"

I rubbed my aching head and swallowed hard, attempting to coerce my heart out of my throat. Beats the stars out of me why they call the heart an internal organ. Whenever something goes wrong, the first thing my heart wants to do is jump ship. Not exactly prime captain material, this heart 'o mine. But I keep it under control.

Usually.

Da's voice was back in my head and this time he wasn't whispering. *Told you the door was here*, he gloated. I shuddered and studied the frog splat on the wall. I had to be dreaming. Any minute I'd wake up, tell my friends about my crazy dream, and we'd all have a laugh—

"You're shooting wild frogs? With rubber bands?" Doni, always the practical one, didn't seem worried about being told she was in faerie land or how many frogs the woman had bagged. She wanted to know how it was done.

The woman nodded.

"Extra heavy-duty rubber," she said, taking a moment from her fire-poking. Before I realized what she was up to, she'd slipped a band over one index finger, pulling the band taught with two leathery fingers of her other hand. She pointed her loaded finger at me, then grinned and aimed off to one side.

Twang!

I held tight, determined not to flinch as the rubber band thwapped against the wall not far from the gooey frog splat.

"We can't be in the Land of the Fae," Murdock said. "Faeries are small and beautiful and you're...different." He cleared his throat. "Interesting choice of weapons,"

"Takes care o' what needs takin' care of," the woman said, evidently ignoring his first comment. "Coffee?"

"I don't suppose you have any English breakfast tea?" Murdock asked, his deep voice full of hope. He climbed to his feet and stepped over to the fire.

"Never had any use for the stuff." The old woman sniffed as something smelled bad.

"Much better for you than *that* stuff," Murdock retorted.

My eyes widened as I stifled the urge to shake my head in disbelief. Here we were, teetering on the edge of—what? Insanity and reality? Illusion and delusion? Something else equally as tangled?—and my companions were discussing the merits of tea versus coffee.

"I'll take a cup of joe," Doni said. She walked over to the fire ring, shoved Murdock out of the way, and took a primitive-looking mug from the old woman before settling herself on a small boulder.

I squinted at Doni. The girl didn't look good. Her normally rosy face had a slightly green tinge.

"You look like you ate a week-old fish carcass," I told Doni. "You want to make like a pizza and split?"

Doni's eyes grew so wide, I was afraid they'd pop right out of her head. She sipped at her coffee, then stared into the mug and shrugged.

"I think you've got your metaphors confused," Murdock said.

"You're the one fusing metacarpals." That was stretching it, even for me. I frowned, trying to stare at my own lips. Which, of course, was not only impossible without a mirror, but stupid. So, maybe my lips and my brain had somehow become disconnected. Maybe there was something in the air affecting my lip/brain connection. Or maybe I'd gotten a dose of frog poison.

"How come we're not choking on smoke?" Murdock asked, suddenly changing the subject. He nodded at the fire, reluctantly accepted a mug from the woman, and gazed longingly into the mug as if trying to transform the coffee into tea. He took a sip and grimaced, his face settling into a disappointed mask.

"This place is special," the woman said, "being a door between worlds and all. They's old magic here. Deep down. Keeps this fire burning—" she poked at the fire again, "and takes the smoke away. Not the kind of magic I'm familiar with, but—like I said—this place is *old*. Outdates me by centuries and I'm no spring chicken if ya hadn't noticed."

I'd assumed the woman had started the fire herself. It hadn't been burning—there hadn't even been wood to burn—when we'd all crawled into our sleeping bags. I'd also wondered just how she'd managed to bring in wood and build up a decent blaze without waking any of us in the process.

And now she was saying the fire had *already* been burning?

Not possible. We would have noticed like that, wouldn't we?

Murdock sat on a rock beside the woman, looking like he wanted nothing more than to go back to sleep.

"Good morning, princess," I said.

Murdock rolled his eyes without answering.

Darwin held a mug of coffee in my direction.

"What happened to our camp mugs?" I asked, looking the mug

over with a critical eye. Judging by the primitive clay construction, the mug had more than likely been made by hand. The mugs we'd packed were tin camping mugs.

"Didn't want to intrude," Darwin said.

I could feel my eyes grow as wide as Doni's had been. Not *intrude*? Her very presence was an intrusion.

Finally, I pulled my jaw off my lap, pulled on my hiking boots and stood, giving my flannel shirt a quick tug to straighten it. I snatched the proffered mug from the old woman's hand and eyed its contents suspiciously without sitting down.

"Thank you?" I quickly soaked a corner of my shirt tail in the steaming black liquid and scrubbed at the end of my nose. If'n there was any poison left on my skin, the coffee should neutralize it.

Doni took another swallow, her cheeks once again rosy in the fire's glow.

Didn't look like the brew was going to kill us—not immediately, anyway. I took a cautious sip...and was immediately whisked back in time to the first mug of cowboy coffee Da had given me.

I'd been all of twelve at the time. Twelve must've been a magic year in Da's mind, though I never quite figured out why. On our previous treks he'd made sure to pack plenty of hot cocoa for me. This time, there wasn't a flake of cocoa in sight. This rich brew tasted just like the first cup Da had finally coaxed me into drinking. Hadn't been my last, either. I had decided way back then that cowboy coffee was good stuff.

I glared at the woman. "How did you know...?"

Know what? How to make cowboy coffee?

I shrugged. "Da used to make it like this," I said, looking apologetically at Doni, then Murdock. "When we were trekking."

Murdock nodded as if everything suddenly made sense. Doni opened her mouth, then shut it again without saying anything.

"Need some air." I turned my back on them and headed for the cave entrance. My eyes burned and a lump the size of my fist had lodged itself in my throat. I stumbled through the tight passage into the alcove and then out into the new day.

It was earlier than I'd thought, sunrise turning the sky pink and red. I closed my eyes tight then looked again, my stomach tying into a hard knot for the umpteenth time. The sky was swollen with angry red clouds, the color of blood on the bottom and topped out with cotton candy pink edges.

And that was where any semblance of "normal" ended.

There wasn't any sign of the snow that had driven us into the cave the previous night. Nor was there any sign of the brambles we'd shoved our way through. In fact, I wasn't looking at mountain vegetation at all.

I appeared to have stepped out into a blasted desert.

I gripped the mug in my hands so tightly it probably would have dented if'n it had been tin. The heat from the mug—almost enough to burn, but not quite—served as an anchor to what was left of my sanity.

Sage mingled with huge boulders that jutted from the ground like giant teeth. In the far distance I could barely make out tall mountain peaks capped in brilliant white.

Steam rose between the boulders and sage at irregular intervals. An odd sound interrupted the silence, blurping and blopping like a pot of pudding just come to a boil. The air reeked of rotten eggs and decaying vegetation overlaid with a hint of sage—not a pleasant combination.

Was this what I had smelled earlier, when Doni came back into the cave?

"Where on earth are we?" Murdock asked, coming up behind me. I didn't turn to look at him.

"I have no idea," I finally said.

"Wondered how long it would take you to figure out we weren't in Kansas anymore," Doni said as she squeezed out of the alcove. "Thought I was dreaming at first, but that ended when one of those bushes..." She pointed at a particularly nasty bunch of sage, "poked me in the bum."

"What?" I frowned at her. "You sat on a branch, you mean."

"No. The blasted thing poked me. I know better than to sit on a

173

bush. I made sure there was plenty of distance between any errant branches and my bum—"

"Bushes don't like being peed on." Murdock nodded. "I'll keep that in mind."

I shook my head and tried to get a grip on what was going on. I moved off in the opposite direction to the bush Doni had pointed at... and immediately stopped at the edge of a mud pot, of all things, in all its blurping glory. I headed another direction and ran into another mud pot. Everywhere I turned, I seemed to run into another pool of burbling mud. Or sagebrush. Or giant boulders.

I stared around in stunned disbelief. Didn't appear I was going to wake from this dream anytime soon.

Remember what I told you about dreams? Da again.

I gritted my teeth. How could I forget? When we were out on our little treks, Da was always telling me about his dreams and what they meant. Weird dreams—and odd experiences—were given to us so we can learn, according to Da.

I reached up to run a hand through my hair, a nervous habit I thought I'd broken years ago. Instead of simple bedhead hair, my fingers got tangled in something resembling polar bear fur teased into dreadlocks by all that noxious steam. Lovely.

Might as well figure out what I was supposed to *learn* from all this...balderdash, as Mum would say. I pushed my way between my two friends, cast one final, extremely irritated glance at the burbling mud pots, and headed back into the cave.

"Okay, Darwin," I said, stalking over to my bedroll—my *safe* zone —as deliberately as I could manage. I adopted a strong, no nonsense stance—feet shoulders' width apart—and faced the old woman, holding the mug in both hands as if it were a shield. A rather small, insignificant shield, I realized. Still, it was something solid to cling to.

"Where are we?" I asked. I tried to sound confident, but couldn't seem to eliminate the pleading tone from my words.

"I told ya—in the Land of the Fae," she said, leaving off the "duh" implicit in her words.

The Land of the Fae.

I sipped from the mug and pondered what I'd discovered outside. The heat from both fire and mug was soothing, the brew rich and flavorful, but too much of this *cowboy joe*, as Da liked to call it, and I'd likely find myself growing hair where hair had no right growing—

"Wait," Murdock said. He stopped as he squeezed through the entrance and stood there, half-stooped over, a horrified expression on his face. He held his mug out as if afraid it would bite. "Coffee's a drug, isn't it? Not really a food?

"Coffee's coffee," Doni said, shoving him out of the way. She took a long swallow from her mug and gave Murdock an evil smile.

"No," Murdock said, his round face as serious as I'd ever seen it. "She said we were in the Land of the Fae even though she doesn't look anything like a faerie. Everyone knows you're not supposed to eat faerie food—"

"So, tell me about the frogs," I said, interrupting Murdock's paranoid rant. I frowned. Why was I asking about frogs when what I really wanted to know was where in blazes we *really* were, how we'd gotten here, and what was the best way to get back home without the requisite pair of ruby slippers?

Darwin poured herself a cup of coffee and carefully set the pot on a rock beside the burning flames. "Them frogs showed up three cycles ago, just after a man, such as yerself, came through the gate."

This time I did roll my eyes. "One, I'm not a man. Two, we didn't pass through any 'gate.' Three, what is a cycle?"

Darwin ignored me. "These frogs, they ain't native, I kin tell ya that much. Only amphibian types around these parts are Machiavellian toads and they's about as big as my hand. Them things 'er harmless—the toads, not my hand—though they make a nasty splat when ya step on 'em."

"Excuse me?" There were toads in the Land of Fae? Not that I believed that's where we were, but it was the only thing sinking in right then.

"You look as befuddled as a hyena in a fish tank," Darwin said.

Doni and Murdock moved up behind me.

"She's giving you a run for your money," Doni said.

I wasn't sure what she meant by that cryptic statement. Yes, I like to mix my metaphors a bit, especially when I get hysterical, but there wasn't anything metaphorical about a hyena in a fish tank. Was there? Or toads for that matter—

"You take a bath in froggy pheromones or something?" Murdock asked, his voice tinged with disbelief.

Startled, I glanced at Murdock who was staring at my feet. Skin crawling, I let my gaze travel down...

Dotting the floor of the cave in a five-foot radius around my boots were a dozen or more of those black-and-red frogs—complete with cornflower blue legs.

My stomach heaved like a boat on the high seas and for a moment, I thought I would lose the contents of my stomach along with my sanity. I screeched, almost leaping out of my skin when a pug with extremely short legs darted out of nowhere and raced around my feet, chasing back the frog that was about to hop on my boot.

Mission accomplished, the pug sat on its haunches and looked up at me with a wide smile on its squished puggy face.

"Where the blazes did you come from?" I asked the little dog, stilling a convulsive shudder. Except for its size—a little bigger than a house cat—and the fact it was *alive*, the pug looked exactly like my stone charm—puggy but smooshed. It was even the same carnelian red color. I automatically reached for my pack, then stopped. I'd dropped that charm somewhere in the tunnel last night, right?

I squinted at the back wall, wondering if'n I should go look for that blasted charm, except...I squinted harder.

There was no tunnel.

Shadows flickered across the rear wall, highlighting the rough peaks and valleys of solid stone. The floor seemed to shift beneath my feet.

Had I dreamed the entire midnight escapade?

I touched the back of my head and was rewarded with a sharp pain.

Apparently, the bumping-my-head part of the dream—if'n it *had* been a dream—was real.

I cautiously let my right hand release its death grip on the mug, reached down and dug my flashlight out of my sleeping bag. Straightening, I flipped the flashlight on...

Dead as a broken twig in winter.

I flipped it back off, remembering—with some embarrassment—my panic last night. I glanced at Doni.

"I need your flashlight."

Doni looked hard at me for a long moment, then went over to her bag, set her mug on a nearby rock as casually as if it had been a coffee table, and dug out her flashlight.

I reached out to take the flashlight, then paused. I *did* tend to have an odd effect on electronics now and again.

"Turn it on." I commanded, then added, "Please," after seeing the look on her face.

Doni rolled her eyes and clicked the flashlight's switch.

Nothing happened.

She tried it again. Still nothing.

"I just put new batteries in." She shook the flashlight as if making a martini, then tried again.

The flashlight remained dead as a proverbial doornail.

Murdock went to the nearest camp lantern and switched it on and off. The lantern was as dead as the flashlight. He went to the next camp lantern and tried it—with the same result. After reassuring himself all the lanterns shared equal status, he snatched the flashlight from his bedroll and clicked it on.

His flashlight was as dead as the rest.

Curious, I pulled out my cell phone.

Dead as a zombie missing its head.

Had we stumbled into some kind of EMP tech-annihilator zone?

Murdock dug in his pocket and pulled out, of all things, a canister with real matches—the kind you have to strike on something rough. He quickly lit a match.

A tiny blaze flickered at the end of the wooden stick for almost a full minute, leaving behind a charred stick as it burned. He blew the match out when the flame reached the tip of his fingers.

At least we had that.

The pug let out a bark that sounded more like something that came from a squeaky toy than from a living animal. The personification of red evilness circled around my legs. My knees almost buckled when the little dog's feet hit the back of my calves.

"Stop that!" I turned to glare at the Evil Pug. "You want me to fall in the middle of all this?" I waved a hand at the frogs.

"Can't seem to git shed of 'em," Darwin said, her voice still conversational, "but that's what yer here for."

"Excuse me?"

"I bin cooking up all sorts a prayers and offerin's. Last night, the Big Guy in the Sky came to me directly. Tol' me to come to this cave, so I did and here ya are."

I had to restrain myself from doing a teenage eye roll. Murdock had that move down pat, a move I reserved for the most egregious of moments. This was not *quite* one of those moments. The woman was serious.

"Why me?" To be frank, I'd never been the answer to anyone's prayers before. Felt kind of good—if'n I forgot about the frogs and the stink and the fact I had no idea how we got here or how we were going to get home.

"Friend of mine did some speculating. Seems you inherited some special blood. Add that to your given name, Cinaed Chiaroscuro Addicott Settlemire Moss, and I kin see how ya were meant to be in this particular place at this point in time."

Cinaed.

A chill ran up my spine and spread like mold over my skin.

Cinaed is old school, old Scottish school, that is. Means born of fire, Da had once told me.

How had this woman known my full name? I hadn't told her. I hadn't told anyone, not even Doni. Can you imagine my friends trying to pronounce *Cinaed?*

Besides, Cinaed was a boy's name, no matter how you pronounced it. Which is why I stuck with Chia.

The petite amphibians chose that moment make a full out assault, hopping this way and that as they worked their way toward me. I tried to move out of the path of chaos, but finally froze in place, paranoid that I'd end up stomping on the little buggers. I had no idea what their poison would do to the soles of my boots. (*Probably nothing*, a little voice in my head whispered. *It's poison, not acid*, but I didn't know that for certain.)

The pug growled.

"Atta boy, Charlie," Darwin said.

Charlie leapt into action, spinning and nipping, his curly tail wagging so hard I thought he'd fall over. Lucky for him the frogs were moving faster than he was. At least for the moment.

Just when I thought things couldn't get any weirder, an otter popped out of my sleeping bag. The same otter I'd seen earlier—I think. Same whiskery nose. Same dark stripe between cute brown eyes, running up over its skull, essentially parting the fur between its equally cute ears.

The otter wiggled its nose as if trying to decipher a strange scent, then dashed into the melee, adding chirrups and whistles to Charlie's shrill bark. Otter and pug danced among the frogs, scattering the black-and-red hoppers in all directions. The otter was three times bigger than the pug, its long, lean form moving as sinuously as a dancing snake. Everything was moving so fast, I couldn't tell who was winning—frogs or furries.

That standing-on-a-heaving-boat feeling came back. Charlie wasn't *my* pug and the otter was...an otter, but all I could see was both of my new furry friends coming to sticky end, as Mum would put it.

I summoned my best Space Opera commander's voice and directed it full force at the pug. "Down!"

Charlie didn't even blink.

The otter gave a derisive snort.

Both otter and pug somehow managed to keep their noses from

contacting red-and-black skin, actually herding the little amphibian beasties...

Up my legs.

Twang! Thwap!

Another frog exploded into a mist of black, red, and blue.

"And we have a winner!" I said in my best carnival show voice. "Give the girl a prize!"

My sarcasm soared over her wrinkled visage like a vulture looking for dinner. Underneath all that leather she suddenly reminded me of a snake. Not a cute snake, like the otter. A deadly snake, all skinny and loose jointed. I half expected her to roll over on her belly and slither away.

More rubber bands flew, the loud *twang thwap!* growing like thunder in my ears.

Frogs flew in all directions, splatting against cave walls and sleeping bag alike. For a brief moment, I wondered if'n the rubber bands were spreading the poison, then promptly dismissed the notion, only to bring it back a heartbeat later when one of the frogs that had been fortunate enough to land on my sleeping bag started moving again.

Darwin calmly reloaded her rubber band "gun."

If'n she thwapped a frog directly on my sleeping bag, I would more than likely have to burn it. The bag, that is. Not the frog. Though judging by the goo plastered on the wall, it would be difficult to separate frog from bag once the double-duty rubber band had done its work.

Before Darwin loosed her Flying Rubber Band of Destruction, Charlie dashed at the little beast taking refuge in my sleeping bag's silken polyester folds, driving the frog back out on the ground.

Of course, the amphibious beast headed straight for me.

I was prepared this time. Instead of waiting for the frog to climb up my pants, I took careful aim and kicked the thing into the fire. The flames popped and hissed.

And just as suddenly as they'd appeared, there were no more frogs. Living, that is.

I wrinkled my nose, preparing for the stench of barbequed frog, but the stench never manifested.

Neither did more frogs.

A surge of relief left me feeling weak-kneed and triumphant, a feeling that faded as I studied the destruction surrounding me. Guilt washed over me in tsunami-sized waves at the sight of so much frog goo.

It wasn't the frogs' fault they were poisonous. They hadn't started out their day plotting how to take down one Chiaroscuro Addicott Settlemire Moss.

Had they?

My heart jumped into my throat as the otter pressed against my left leg while the pug pressed against my right. Without thinking, I bent and took the pug—it being the smaller of the two—into my arms. I absently scratched the pug's head and tried not to dwell on the eerie silence.

"Who was this man who supposedly came through some kind of...gate?" I finally asked.

"Speaking of gates...what happened to the tunnel?" Murdock said.

"What do you mean, what happened to the tunnel?" Doni pointed at the back wall. "It's right there, moron. Tunnels don't move."

Murdock twisted his lips and shook his head. "Not sure what you're seeing, girlfriend, but that wall looks too solid to be hiding a tunnel."

Doni snorted. She stalked over to Murdock, ignoring the frog goo coating just about everything. Grabbing Murdock's arm, she turned him toward the rear wall and pointed. "Right...there."

She glared at the wall as if to prove her point.

For all the years I've known Doni, I've never seen her stunned or at a loss for words.

Until that moment.

Doni dropped Murdock's arm like it was a burning poker. She

walked to the back wall and began running her hands over the jagged rocks, muttering to herself as she went.

"The human was more like this one," Darwin said, looking Murdock over. "Big, but not as round. Brown eyes and a black streak running through silver hair that looked fine as silk—"

"Uncle Zach?" I asked. The first part of that description—brown eyes—could fit thousands of people. But the black streak decorating Mum's youngest brother's hair was unique.

Zacharia Settlemire was the youngest of Mum's six siblings and the most likely to get into trouble. Da and I had spent many an hour theorizing just how long it would take before Uncle Zach's current Scheme-of-the-Day landed him behind bars. Uncle Zach's most recent scheme had come close—he was somewhere in South America, blasting new tunnels for mines. He'd contacted Da last fall with a tale about ancient ruins and strange artifacts mixed with a bunch of supernatural mumbo jumbo.

Da had burned the letter.

Had Uncle Zach discovered a way into faerie land?

I had no idea. I did know that if Zachariah Settlemire had decided the Land of Fae truly existed, he would have figured out some way to exploit the place. Uncle Zach exploited *everything*.

Far as I could tell, though, the only thing being exploited here had been the frogs. And they were all dead.

Weren't they?

"I'm not from around these parts, either," Darwin said, her tone laced with a note of...tension? "Came here when I was young as a ripe plum. Now I'm a dried prune. Have no desire to go back. I bin tasked with protectin' the gate. Done a fine job of it, too. 'Til them frogs come in."

She took a sip of her coffee, grimaced, and emptied the mug's contents on the ground. The black liquid settled into the sandy dirt, leaving behind a dark stain. "Don't know how ya kin drink the stuff. English breakfast tea is much better."

Murdock gaped at the woman. Darwin grinned like a mischievous child, then gestured at me. "Something 'bout ya draws them frogs. That's why ya'll were sent here. To help me get shed of the things."

She reached behind her and lifted a black cloth bag from the ground. Charlie wiggled in my arms, his puggy tail wagging expectantly. "Collect all the frogs and stick 'em in this bag. Simple as making apple pie, if ya don't count the cockroaches. Get the frogs in the bag and then ya kin go home. If ya'll really want to, that is. Lots of folks'd rather stay in the Land of the Fae."

I stared at her in bewilderment. "Didn't you just rubber band them all to death?"

"How many are there?" Murdock asked at the same time.

"How far have they spread?" Doni asked a breath later, turning from her inspection of the tunnel-less wall.

Darwin shook her head dismissively. "No idea times three. All I know is I asked for help and here ya are. The frogs come to ya easy 'nuf. All ya have to do is figger out how to get them into the bag. They only bin here three cycles—about three of yer days—and I don't think all that many got through before I got the problem figgered out. They weren't comin' through the normal way, see. They had their own special access. Plugged that hole up, pretty as ya please." She waved at the back wall. "Now I just got to empty the basket."

"What basket?" Murdock asked.

"Not a real basket," Doni said. She stared at Darwin as if the old woman had grown a second head. "The old witch is speaking figuratively, right?"

"Be careful who you call a witch," Darwin warned. "They don't take kindly to being named. And just so's we clear up the record—I'm a brownie, not a witch, though I do have some unusual...*talents*."

I scratched my head, only half listening. One of the rocks near the cave entrance had...moved. At least I thought it moved. But the thing sat still as a...rock...as soon as I looked directly at it.

Before I could look away, the rock moved again.

I shrieked and leapt toward the rear wall, tucking the pug under one arm so I could grab Doni and drag her back with me. The pug twisted in my arm as if trying to see what I was running from.

"What..." I pointed at what now looked more like a giant cock-roach shell than a rock. "It—"

The otter sneezed. Twice.

"Incoming," the shell said. Its voice was scratchy and startlingly high for such a monstrous object, though I must admit, I'd never heard a shell speak before. Giant mole claws stretched out to either side of the shell. "Incoming," it said again.

The shell started digging, huge claws throwing dirt to either side. Before I could do more than stare, the thing had disappeared into a hole that slowly filled in.

Light flashed somewhere in the entrance tunnel.

"Run," said the clawed bug from his half-buried hole. "Fast."

We did what all good rubberneckers do—we stood and stared. We were in a cave, for goodness sakes. Where were we going to run *to*?

"Frizzle nuts," the old woman muttered. I swear her joints creaked as she stood. She brushed off her hands and put her hands on her back as she stretched.

Whether the pug actually understood Darwin's words or just sensed the danger didn't really matter. He squirmed so hard I had to either put him down or drop him.

Then he ran over to the otter (who I'd silently dubbed Sir Olly).

The pair looked at each other for a long moment.

Olly leaped into the air, snatching the black bag from the old woman's hands. Before any of us could act, the otter spun and raced out of the cave, Charlie close on his heels.

"What the...?" I started after them. I didn't know what I'd just witnessed, but the pair of four-footed loonies shouldn't be running around loose if'n danger was really on its way. Besides, I was supposed to use that bag to collect the frogs. No bag, no frogs, no ruby red slippers to get us back home.

The world outside the cave looked just as bizarre as the last time I'd seen it, complete with angry red skies, burbling mudpots, sage, boulders, and sulfury stench. Olly and Charlie were waiting near the base of a large boulder thirty feet or so away. I'd taken maybe ten steps in their direction when a rock the size of a baseball slammed into my right calf—and stuck.

I stopped dead in place. I stamped my foot, stamped again, then stamped some more, trying to jolt the rock loose. No go. That rock clung to my pants like a nasty burr. I reached down, grabbed hold of the thing, and yanked it free.

"Don't..." Darwin said, but it was too late.

Pain stabbed through my calf, startling me so much I cried out. I dropped the rock and smashed it into the ground with my heel—at least I tried to smash it, but the rock rolled beneath my foot like an obstinate baseball.

"Not good," Darwin said.

"Why not?" I asked. I rubbed my calf and frowned at the smear of blood on my hand. "It's just a rock, isn't it?"

I pulled up my pant leg, stared at the blood trickling down my calf. Maybe a Mexican jumping rock capable of ripping people to shreds.

"That was a baby Flying Cockroach," Darwin said. "They leave behind a scent that attracts other Flying Cockroaches when threatened."

"Like killer bees?" Murdock asked.

Darwin hesitated a moment, then nodded.

From off in the distance rose a distinctive sound, reminiscent of... you got it...killer bees—mingled with fighting lions.

"Here they come." Darwin sighed.

Another cockroach thudded into my right thigh. This...*baby* cockroach...was bigger than the one I'd just squished—softball-size rather than baseball-size. I carefully disengaged the little being from my pants—*before* it hooked into my flesh—and studied it closely, taking care not to let any part of the thing attach to my hand.

Looked just like a normal cockroach—except for its size.

"Boys," Darwin snapped, "ya'll get over here."

Charlie raced up, Olly right behind him. The pug slammed both of his front paws against my leg. Olly sat back on his haunches and held the bag up in his paws.

"Put it in the bag," Darwin ordered. "Now!"

Without thinking I dropped the cockroach in the bag.

Olly let go of the bag like it was a hot potato. Bag and giant baby cockroach thudded to the ground.

And Olly laid on it.

Light flashed through the black fabric still visible beneath the otter as the air split in a violent roar of thunder.

"What...?"

The light faded.

Olly rolled up onto his feet and yawned as if just waking from a nap. Charlie licked the otter's nose. Olly promptly scrubbed at his nose with both paws.

Not a fan of doggy kisses.

"The baby cockroaches are bombs," Darwin said. "Nasty little things."

The angry bees/fighting lions sound had grown until it seemed louder than the recent blast. The air whistled with the sound of too many flying bodies. Were those all cockroaches?

And if the babies—enormous enough to send katsaridaphobes screaming—were bombs, what were the adults and how big were *they*?

"How did Olly...?" I started. I shook my head and tried again. "That otter should be dead."

"Remember where you are," Darwin said.

"You still don't look like a faerie," Murdock said. Then he pointed at something in the distance. "What's that?"

I looked—and immediately wished I hadn't.

What appeared to be a dark river flowed across the ground, surging around boulders and under the sage. I blinked to clear my vision and realized the river was made up of frogs.

Hundreds of them.

"Guess they want to escape the flying cockroach bomb babies, too," Doni said.

"The roaches are guardians of the border between the Fae and ya'll's world. They know those piss frogs don't belong here."

Guardians of the border.

Olly stood on his hind legs, holding the black bag in his paws. I frowned at the otter. Did my adorable new friend have a deadly side to him as well? Would he explode when petted? Or did he merely smother humans in poisonous kisses?

I finally took the bag and studied the black fabric, expecting to find it riddled with holes. The fabric looked as whole as Olly did.

Remember where you are.

"How am I going to get all those frogs into this tiny bag?" I asked. The bag wasn't very large. There was no way all those frogs were going to fit.

"That bag is bigger than it looks," Darwin said. "You just get those frogs into it. The bag will do the rest."

Olly chirped. Charlie barked and whirled in an excited circle.

"Whatever ya do, ya best hurry. Those bomb babies're almost upon us." Darwin held my gaze, expecting...expecting what?

Anything, I realized. She expected me to fix her little problem because she'd been told I would. She didn't care how I took care of the frogs as long as I took care of them.

"How many rubber bands do you have?" I asked.

Darwin shrugged. "As many as needed."

Well, that was about the most cryptic answer I'd ever heard.

But it would have to do.

"Charlie, can you and Olly make sure the frogs head this way?"

Charlie spun another circle and trotted off to one side, curly tail tight against his back. Olly chittered and loped in the other direction. They both lowered their heads, acting like cattle dogs ready to round up some cows.

I looked at Murdock and Doni. "Do you think you can distract the cockroaches?"

Doni shrugged. She studied the sage and boulders, then beckoned to Murdock. "Come on. I gotta plan—of sorts."

She took off at a jog, heading directly into the path of the oncoming cockroach horde.

I spun on my heel, racing back toward the cave's entrance, looking for a way to keep the frogs from getting around me. If'n things went terribly wrong, I could duck back into the cave...

And be overrun by poisonous frogs in a very tight, very dark space.

Rethinking my original strategy, I darted to the right and positioned myself in front of several large boulders, then opened the bag and nodded at Darwin.

The old woman already had her rubber band finger-gun locked and loaded.

"Go!" I shouted.

Charlie cut into the jumping, hopping, undulating river and drove the first group of frogs my direction.

The lead frog made a desperate leap at my leg.

Darwin fired.

The frog went airborne.

And I bagged it. Without any splatting.

Yes!

If'n you're wondering just how I was so adept at catching airborne frogs in a bag, I have to admit I'd had some experience. Every time Mum's family showed up for a get-together, it was tradition to participate in a warped rendition of Catch the Haggis, a Scottish children's game, instigated by Da and made into a total melee by Uncle Zach (yes, I know—haggis is food...except in *this* particular game).

The Settlemire/Moss version of the game involved the "hens" (the grandparents) who threw raw eggs while the "farmers" (all of the grandchildren led by Uncle Zach) caught the eggs in burlap sacks.

Without breaking the eggs.

Catching raw eggs in burlap sacks had always been an exercise in hilarity. I hadn't been the best haggis-catcher in the family, but I hadn't been the worst, either.

The skills I learned as a child were serving me in good stead now, but I could feel myself tiring. I took a deep breath and clenched my jaw tight, focusing on an incoming frog.

I couldn't afford to lose my focus. Missing even one of those poisonous frogs would mean the end of my haggis-catching career.

As well as the end of my life.

Charlie was suddenly in front of me. He gave a short bark. There appeared to be a slight gap between the first group of frogs and the group Olly was herding in, long enough to let me catch my breath and see how Doni and Murdock were doing.

The cockroaches were approaching in a flying V, looking more like a gaggle of migrating geese than flying bugs. Doni and Murdock were snatching the flying insects as fast as they could and tossing them into one of the mud pots.

The things were definitely cockroaches—except for their blowing-up phase, they were totally indestructible. Not even bubbling mudpots could slow them down.

I caught sight of swimming cockroaches, cockroaches climbing banks, cockroaches shaking mud free, but the rage seemed to be gone from the mad little bombers.

And then it was time to bag more frogs.

What seemed an eternity later, it was over.

I wiped at the sweat stinging my eyes. The frogs had stopped coming. Somehow, I'd bagged them all!

"Take that, Uncle Zach!" I mumbled under my breath. Suddenly, I found myself wishing Da was here to see this. All that Catch the Haggis practice had finally come in handy.

Olly stood on his hind legs and chittered at me, waving his little paws in the air. Charlie spun in a circle, raced over to Darwin and licked her face, then raced back and sat beside Olly, his tail wagging like a curly fry gone wild.

Doni and Murdock jogged up and dropped to the ground, close enough I could smell their sweat, but not so close I would trip over them if I moved. Both of them were covered with colorful mud.

"Praise the chipmunks!" Darwin said, flashing those teeth of hers in a huge grin. "Well done!"

I stared at her in astonishment. "What happened to your accent?"

"What accent?" she said, her eyes wide and innocent. "I don't have an accent."

Every word enunciated clearly and cleanly. I shook my head. This woman was definitely a snake, adept at shedding her skin.

"I wanna know what happened to her wrinkles," Murdock muttered in a voice so low I barely heard him.

"What wrinkles?" Darwin asked. She waited a breath and when no one answered her question said, "Your task is done. The gate is once again open."

Murdock frowned. "What gate?"

"I think she's speaking figuratively again," Doni said.

"No," Darwin said. "The gate is truly open. You can leave whenever you like."

The sky beyond Darwin was still pink and red, but it no longer appeared angry.

It couldn't still be dawn and I was pretty sure we hadn't been bagging frogs all day so it wasn't sunset. Was the sky always pink in the Land of the Fae or wherever this place turned out to be?

The color of the sky didn't matter, I decided. It was time to extricate ourselves from this crazy nightmare world.

"Don't we need ruby slippers or something?" I asked, unable to keep the sarcasm from my voice. I still didn't know where we were or how we'd gotten here.

"Don't need ruby slippers," Darwin said. She waved at the cave entrance. "Just walk through the gate." She paused, hand in the air—for dramatic effect, I supposed. "But I must warn you—as your father found out, once you pass through the gate, you'll be unable to come back...Unless, of course, your uncle does something stupid again."

"Hear that, Uncle Zach," I said, addressing my absent uncle in an attempt to match Darwin's melodramatic air. "No more stupidity." I felt silly as soon as the word were out of my mouth.

Olly came over, sat up on its haunches, and patted my leg. I reached down to stroke the otter's head, but it gave me a high five and quickly backed away.

Charlie didn't hesitate. The little pug leapt into my arms and licked my face, tail wagging so hard his entire body jiggled. I scratched Charlie's ears and gave him a big hug.

How had I ever thought the little pug was evil?

"Guess otters don't like to hug," I said to Charlie.

Olly shook like he'd just come out of the water.

"Otters like to hug just fine," Darwin said. I blinked at the woman. She looked even younger than she had a few minutes ago.

"Do I smell bad, then?" I asked, raising an eyebrow at Olly, who sat on his haunches in the entrance to the cave.

"The issue isn't with you or the otter." The voice, deep and melodious, seemed to be everywhere and nowhere, all at once. "The creature you call 'Olly' isn't an otter at all."

We all started in astonishment as a tall figure dressed in white robes came around one of the boulders. At first, I thought the new arrival was a woman from the way she moved. The features—what I could see of them beneath the hood—were delicate, the figure tall and willowy, with no defining characteristics. I gradually realized I had no idea if the creature beneath the robes was a woman or a man.

Was this what was meant when someone was said to be "androgynous"?

Charlie wiggled so hard I almost dropped him. I set the pug on the ground and he raced over to the robed figure, dancing in excited circles.

"I am pleased to see you, too, Charlemagne." The voice was too deep to be a woman's, wasn't it?

"I told you," Murdock said in a low voice. "Lemurians are real. We're in the Land of Mu!"

He scrambled to his feet and moved closer.

Doni rose to her feet, brushed off her jeans, and shook her head. "You and your Lemurs."

"Not lemurs," Murdock said. "Lemurians."

Darwin actually giggled. The vest that had once seemed oversized, now scarcely covered her ample breasts. "I think they just called you a big-eyed marsupial, Aina."

"I've heard of this Lemuria," the newcomer—Aina?—said. She

glided over to me and stopped, scant inches away, bringing with her the scent of lilacs and roses. "From your father."

Aina reached up and pulled back her hood, letting the soft white fabric fold down around her neck and back. Raven-black hair glimmered in the dawn light that seemed to never change.

"He thought he had discovered an ancient land," she continued in that deep, melodious voice. (I still wasn't certain she was a she.) "I believe he was disappointed to learn that the land he called Mu was, to put it simply, the Land of the Fae, a separate dimension, if you will, that intersects with your dimension at specific points."

She went on, but I couldn't follow her words. *The Land of the Fae is real.* Da's words kept spinning around and around in my head.

"But Da said he'd *met* a faerie," I blurted in the middle of her saying something about a celebration. "Not that he'd actually been here." I spread my hands wide.

Charlie took that as a hint and hurled his tiny body upwards, somehow managing to end up in my arms. He licked the end of my nose as if trying to comfort me.

"Your father found this cave years ago, on Midsummer's Eve. He had been hurt, you see. And had crawled into the cave like a wounded animal. I was Guardian of the Gate at that time," she nodded at Darwin, "training this one. But she had gone home for the solstice and I had no one to keep me company."

I could hear longing in her voice...at least I thought that's what I heard. Since I'd never spoken with a faerie before, there was a chance I might be misinterpreting her tone.

Pink and red glistened off the snow-capped mountain peaks in the distance and I felt a yearning in response to her tone. Maybe we could stay for just awhile. Explore this land of faeries...

Then I remembered the insanity in my father's eyes, his desperation to find his way back.

"Did Da stay long?" I asked Aina.

She blinked. "He spent some...time...among the people. But time here is not the same as time on your side of the gate. He decided to go back before too much time passed." She paused. "He missed you."

Missed me? How long had he been gone?

"Come." Aina held out her hand toward the cave entrance. "Tonight is a night for celebration, yes? You have helped your uncle—and my people—by ridding us of the invasive species that has been threatening to overrun our small lands. On the morrow, Darwin and I will take him to the place he entered so he can return the contents of that bag," she pointed at the black bag still clutched in my hands, "to their proper place. The balance will be restored, and he will be set free. Tit for tat, I believe your father once said."

My head felt like it had been squished by an anvil or run over by a cement truck, I wasn't sure which. It didn't *hurt*, my brains just felt... squished. Or exploded.

~

The fire snapped in welcome as we all squeezed into the cave. Murdock, Doni, and I sat on our sleeping bags while Darwin and Aina chose to sit on rocks nearer the fire. Charlie climbed in my lap and fell promptly to sleep, his chubby little legs jerking like he was still chasing frogs. Olly curled up nearby, glittering dark eyes shifting from one person to the other as we all started talking at once.

Darwin handed out mugs filled with coffee, though I suspected she'd made herself a mug of tea. Aina gracefully declined a mug. My gut twisted as I remembered Murdock's warning about eating, but coffee wasn't really food, was it?

No matter. We'd already partaken of the brew.

~

I don't remember the festivities winding down—all we did was talk, really, mostly about my da—but the next thing I knew someone was shaking my shoulder. I bolted upright, trying to orient myself.

We were still in the cave, but the fire appeared to have gone out. Darwin and Aina were gone.

So were Charlie and Olly.

"You wouldn't believe the crazy dream I just had." Murdock sat back on his heels, his whiskery face filled with disbelief.

"You mean the one with the frogs and exploding cockroaches?" Doni asked. She handed me a mug, reaching over Murdock's shoulder. "Sorry. You'll have to wait for the water to finish heating for your tea."

"Not a dream," Murdock muttered. "Those couldn't have been faeries—Darwin and Aina. They weren't small enough. And did you see the way Darwin *changed*?"

Yes, I had seen. But it all felt so unreal now...

Not a dream.

I stared at the mug. A clay mug.

Filled with cowboy coffee.

I sniffed the brew. Took a sip.

And sneezed.

This time I managed not to bump my head—or spill my coffee—but the abrupt movement caused something to tumble out of my sleeping bag.

"Well, I'll be," Doni said. She plucked the two thumb-sized figurines from the ground and handed them to me.

A squished carnelian pug.

And a silver-toned otter.

"Hi, Charlie," I whispered. I could swear the charm grew warm in my hand. I studied the otter in my other hand. "Uncle Zach?"

Of course, the otter didn't move. It didn't even grow warm.

Did this mean he'd completed his mission? Or that he'd somehow screwed up again?

"Tit for tat," I mumbled.

I could swear the tiny otter...winked.

ABOUT THE AUTHOR

Growing up in the wilds of the Sierra Nevada mountains, surrounded by deer and beaver, muskrat and bear, Louisa Swann found ample fodder for her equally wild imagination. As an adult, she interweaves her experiences with that imagination, creating tales of fantasy and science fiction, mystery and thrillers, steampunk and historical fiction. Her short stories have appeared in Fiction River anthologies, including Reader's Choice; Mercedes Lackey's *Elementary Magic* and Valdemar anthologies; and Esther Friesner's *Chicks and Balances*. Novels include light-hearted mysteries (*It Ain't No Bull*, *The Trouble with Bulldogs*) and her new steampunk/weird west series, *Abby Crumb and Myrtle Creek* (with Brandon Swann).

Find out more about Louisa at:
louisaswann.com

 facebook.com/swanngang

twitter.com/LouisaSwann

bookbub.com/authors/louisa-swann

DUST

LISA SILVERTHORNE

In the dark and misty rain, a man lay face down on the wet Portland sidewalk, phone clutched in his left hand. I knelt beside him, the bass thrum of dance music vibrating through my jaw and into my rib cage. But the downtown street at the edge of the Pearl District was quiet. There was no music. The man looked up at me and my heart twisted into a knot—Trent! I'd been waiting for his text to meet him here. One of Trent's feet hung on the edge of a writhing circle of lavender light that gleamed and pulsed in front of a dark alley.

The fey portal!

Again, I felt the music. Thin, crystalline threads twining out of the portal and into my eardrums, tangling along the night's sharp edges. One by one, the clear soprano notes of an ethereal melody sliced through the fog, becoming a siren song, its feathery softness outlining the passageway. Luring humans through it to a crossroads of sorts. I'd been there once before. It was a rest stop between worlds. Where Club Oberon stood, an opulent dance club, where bands of beautiful, vacuous fey hung out when they weren't here on Portland's streets—stealing human souls. They lured humans to this *exclusive* downtown club with a pinch and a promise: a pinch of fey dust and a promise of Tír na nÓg's riches if they'd only take that one last step.

Into oblivion.

My heart hammered against my chest, hands shaking as I brushed Trent's dark hair out of his eyes. He looked so weak.

"Stay with me now, Trent. Okay? Help's on the way." I stared into his familiar hazel eyes, taking his right hand in mine.

He looked up at me a moment. "Wendy?"

"I'm here, Trent. Hang on, please!"

His gaze tracked past me, toward the portal spinning in the alley. Then I saw it.

The glowing powder sparkling across his face. Mixing with the cold rain. Behind him, in front of the dark alley, the fey portal still hung open. I tapped his cheek and called his name, but he was beyond help now. Forever in their spell.

Trent—why? Why didn't you wait for me?

I shifted my black purse across my body as sirens shrieked through the busy Pearl District streets, heading toward this dark corner just past the bistros and coffeehouses. The rain-misted night smelled like fresh-brewed coffee and roasted garlic, warming the February chill. But underneath Portland's fragrant night air, I tasted a wisp of lavender and ash.

A chill trickled through my arms and into my fingers as I squeezed his hand.

"Oh, Trent," I cried, trying to hold onto him, but felt his presence slipping away, drawn toward the portal. "Why didn't you wait for me? I asked you to follow Jay, but not through there. Especially through there!"

His chest barely lifted the air from his lungs to his lips. A shallow breath rasped in his throat as he squinted at me and squeezed my hand. A small crowd had formed around us.

"Wendy...thought I could—get in and—out. It's too late. T-texted you not—to—to come here..."

Rain-slicked streets washed red and blue as an ambulance and police car roared up to the sidewalk, blocking the street. Someone had called 9-1-1. Two police officers began canvasing the crowd, collecting statements, and blocking off the sidewalk. Paramedics and two police officers rushed past the portal, but none of them even paused. They couldn't see it. Only humans that had tasted fey dust could see it.

A police officer moved all of us back as paramedics went to work, turning Trent onto his back and opening his blue-striped shirt. Breath barely shuddered through Trent's tall, lanky frame. He grew weaker, breaths growing further and further apart.

One of the paramedics, a short brunette, crouched over Trent and took a pulse, her hands in blue latex gloves. She leaned against his chest and listened for a heartbeat. Her partner checked his pupils with a light and then administered Narcan, smashing the needle into Trent's upper thigh. The other paramedic began CPR, her oval face taut and focused.

"Administering more Narcan," said her partner, readying another syringe.

None of the meds or the rhythmic thump of chest compressions could bring Trent back from his fey dust-fueled journey. I bit my lip, tears streaming down my face as the furious dance beat throbbed unwavering in my ears, the lilt of flute and harp like shattered glass.

This was all my fault.

Remnants of sparkly gold powder clung to his nose and around his mouth, the rain washing it off Trent's cheeks and onto the side-walk as his eyes fixed on a world beyond this one—one only he could see now. A place where the beating of his heart wasn't required, the breath in his lungs not needed.

With one final sigh, Trent's last breath emptied into the mist hanging low against the street, Club Oberon's distant dance beat pulsing through the portal and across my skin. His soul spilled into the night, a white mist swept up by the fey portal in a swirl of dark smoke.

Trent was gone, his soul trapped by the fey. But where was my boyfriend, Jay? Correction: former boyfriend. Trent and I had both come here to find him. Had he made it past the portal, too—into the club? Trapped by that fey bitch's spell? Time on the other side of the portal—and inside the club—stood still. But if Jay went out the Oberon's back door and into the fey world, days could pass in hours. Trent was the last person to see him tonight.

I had to go through the portal. To get back Trent's soul—and save Jay. It's what Trent would have done. My hands trembled at the thought.

My phone vibrated in my jeans pocket and I pulled it out. Trent's text! He must have sent it inside the portal, but the text couldn't go through until he was back on Portland side again. The short text sent a cold chill coiling through my belly.

Jay's w/Azriel. Hurry! U no where.

Azriel. I gritted my teeth and shoved the phone back into my pocket. The dark memory of that fey woman was a poisonous cloud hanging over my head. Cloying. Suffocating. But my rage burned hot, pushing me forward. Pushing me through it.

Even here on Portland side, I felt her miserable heavy presence linger in the cold, rainy mist. The overpowering odor of lavender and ash was a sharp sting to my senses. She was out there. In Club Oberon.

The memory of her shrill, grating laughter was visceral, the twisted melody on repeat above the distant, furious beat of the Oberon's dance music. Empty. Heartless. Coming through the portal. She was laughing at me. Laughing because she'd taken two men away from me tonight, bringing her total to three.

She was queen of the hunt, addicted to the pleasure she got from stealing other women's boyfriends and husbands. She didn't even want them, just savored the win. It fueled her jealousy of human women. I winced, the memory of her taunts and her shrill, gloating laughter like the sound of broken glass. Sharp. Grating. Cutting away the last threads of reluctance that held me back from my vengeance. I held it in my hands at last—the chance for revenge. It was a cold blue flame that turned my heart to cinder.

The crowd gathered along the sidewalk had gotten bigger, people watching the cops and paramedics, their soft voices hissing against the misty rain and swish of tires against wet pavement. I stepped through the crowd, slipping past both police officers, my charcoal grey jacket dull against the dark, the rain, and rasp of raincoats huddled around the scene. I gripped my purse tight against my body. It was just big enough to hold a few essentials. Lipstick. Wallet. Glock.

Behind me, paramedics muttered to each other about the strange sparkly dust on Trent's face, about how they'd never seen this drug before. They swabbed at the glitter-like stuff, but they'd never get it to a lab. It would disappear long before that. Then the cops would blame it on cocaine or meth or something like that and that would be the end of it. Like before. I hated that they'd list Trent's cause of death as an overdose. He didn't drink or do drugs. Ever.

The sparkly gold powder wasn't a drug. It was fey dust. And Azriel used it to lure and kill her human boy toys after she'd finished with them. She'd shut Trent up with it and soon she'd use it on Jay, too.

Stupid, cheating bastard has no idea he's prey.

Azriel wanted the one thing the fey could never have: a soul. So, she collected as many as she could steal. I wasn't even sure Jay had a soul and honestly, he wasn't worth saving. But it wouldn't stop me from hunting this fey bitch down and ending this once and for all. Even if I had to chase her ass all the way to Tír na nÓg and back.

I crouched in front of the spinning portal.

As the paramedics lifted Trent's lifeless body onto a gurney and into the ambulance, I said a prayer for him and headed toward the portal. To Club Oberon, the fey hunting grounds. To hunt fey. Azriel had stolen her last human soul.

I'd handle Trent's murder (and Jay's infidelity) my way. With absolute malice.

Taking a deep breath, I held it, trying to focus. And not do anything stupid. With a sharp exhale, I stepped through the portal into darkness as the ambulance pulled away from the curb.

Inside, I followed a dark tunnel until it widened into a twilight hillside. The air smelled cool, ashen. Brambles and white-trunked trees with gold leaves framed the hillside and indigo sky. Thick, wheaten-colored grass rolled across the hills toward a grand, white-columned two-story building—like an old southern plantation house. Made of solid marble.

I followed the smooth, grey stone path winding toward the house, the stones vibrating with that electric dance beat. The walkway was lit with gold twinkling lights and the plantation house was outlined in purple neon-like light. Large letters on the roof faded from bright blue to green and back again.

Club Oberon.

As I drew closer, the lavender and ash scent intensified. Stronger now. I felt Azriel's presence. Heavy and dark. Ahead, inside the club. Coiled and ready to strike.

With head held high, one hand on my purse, I sauntered up the graceful white staircase like I belonged here. I stepped onto the porch that trembled with deep, vibrating bass. It resonated into my jaw and throbbed through my feet. It was beginning to hurt.

Groups of lithe fey men and graceful women milled outside a tall, curved set of double doors in vivid purple. In small groups, they huddled together in tangles of velvet dusters, draped silks in soft blues and greens, and white diaphanous gowns flowing like water around perfect bodies. Soft pastels in blue, lavender, and mint and rich, deep jewel colors in wine, amethyst, and emerald. Even their silvery white faces were adorned with jewels. Brows arched with small sapphires and eyes highlighted with tiny diamonds and aquamarines. Their throats dripped with tear-shaped amethysts. And rubies, one for each human soul they'd stolen.

I gritted my teeth, wanting to rip every single ruby off their throats.

In jeans, blue blouse, and grey coat, I really stood out. I slipped past three clean-shaven men in brocaded jackets with blowsy sleeves and layered silk shirts, glancing at their elongated and pointed ears, faces long and thin with aquiline and Greek noses right out of the fashion magazines. I moved past fey women in flowing silk skirts and dresses adorned with delicate seed pearls, gemstones, and crystals. And their hair, long, heavy tresses swept into jeweled combs or flowing around their shoulders. Others wore long curls in pale pinks and blues—even lavender and mint—that cascaded over their shoulders. They all looked like models with their high cheek bones and vivid green eyes. But there was no sparkle of life in those shallow, empty eyes.

I felt self-conscious in their presence, but I kept my chin up, imagining that I wore an Alexander McQueen dress, Harry Winston jewels, and Jimmy Choos, and stepped past the throngs of fey. Into the club.

The music was loud and pulsing, a cross between electronic and ethereal, strange multi-note chords ringing into discords and harmonies and back again. Harps and synthesizers mixing with mandolins and electric guitars. The music had a way of getting inside your head, drifting through your senses, burrowing into your thoughts and then your memories until you ignored everything else around you. I had to keep my guard up. Especially in here.

Wading through the fey-filled club was like drowning in a sea of mannequins after an explosion in a dress factory. Silks and chiffon and satin floated like clouds on the ceiling and draped the walls, the colors changing every time a cool breeze fluttered through them. Shiny marble dance floors filled with plastic perfection—pearlescent, jeweled skin, lithe perfect bodies, and pale skeins of long, flowing hair. Beside them danced smaller human imitations, clinging to them like paparazzi. I'd learned to spot fey as a child, the ones on the human side, taught by my mother (it felt so long ago now). Most of them had large aquamarine or green eyes—vacant of any emotion but contempt. Some of them dressed in high fashion human designer clothes like Armani and Chanel, empty-eyed dolls delighting in their own reflections. With all the beauty and substance of a dream.

I rolled my eyes. Jay fit in perfectly here.

The bass beat throbbed through my chest, hurting my ribs as I searched for any sign of Azriel among the club-goers. Or Jay. Their perfection was nauseating and I fought my feelings of inadequacy. My shorter frame, too straight brown hair, and a few extra pounds made me plain to them (and no competition), but I felt their jealousy spark as I passed them.

To them, I was inferior in every way. From my Gap jeans to my blue Macy's blouse, white Nikes, and clearance rack purse. My immortal soul was my only bling. And they hated me for it. Especially Azriel. To her, souls and boyfriends were the latest Louis Vuitton purse that she could just snatch and model.

Dozens of human posers danced beside the fey, crowding the dance floor, filling the purple satin chairs along the oval glass and chrome bar that sparkled with colored lights. They gathered together in little packs in the white leather booths along the wall and bunched together around one large round booth, set on a dais. A complete circle of white leather around a circular glass table that changed colors. Where the fey *royalty* held court. Humans sat at their feet, wanting to be just like their soulless idols. I was never sure if these humans even knew where they were. Did they even know their idols were fey? Otherworldly? Hungry for human souls.

Maybe some of these humans didn't even know they'd stepped through a portal. Maybe all of this had been hidden from their sight? Maybe all of these people thought this was just another Portland club? Where the fey were just the beautiful people that most humans wished to be? Tears rolled down my face and I swiped them away. And their urging humans on a little trip out the back door, for just a few minutes. *What harm could it do, right?* Then, later, when you step back through to human side, thinking it'd just been a really long night, and you realize thirty years have passed when you call your Mom and no one answers because she's not there anymore...

I fought back tears and sucked in a breath, focusing on the club's layout, but it hadn't changed at all. No one appeared threatened or hunted by the fey here. Just a typical night at the club, with the fey bands warming up for the next live set in the back room.

Alcohol and fey dust flowed like rain. Only one overdose. Slow night at Club Oberon.

"Wendy?" a voice rang in my ear. "What are you doing here?"

I turned. Sandra Ling, one of Jay's co-workers. She wore a sequined red dress and black pumps, her thick black hair, high-lighted burgundy, cut into an asymmetrical bob. She looked embarrassed to see me, but she was polite enough to acknowledge me. One of Jay's better friends.

"Looking for Jay," I replied.

Her face turned pale. She looked uncomfortable, anxious, sloshing the frothy pink drink in her hand.

"You know, my *boyfriend*?" At least he was until Trent's text made it official. Maybe he'd been brainwashed or magicked by Azriel, but there were others. Sylvia in accounting. Marcie, the hair salon receptionist. His two hookups in Toledo.

Sandra's mouth bobbed open, almost in sync with the bass beat rumbling through the club.

I saw the recognition in her eyes. She realized that I knew he was here with someone else, ending our relationship without even *the talk* or a hint that something had been wrong. I'd been too trusting. Apparently, this had been going on the entire time he and I were together.

"Were you meeting him here?" Sandra asked, flipping a chunky lock of burgundy hair out of her eyes. Traces of gold powder clung to her nostrils as she ran her hand across her face, scattering the momentary glint.

"Not exactly," I said. "Trent texted me."

Fear lit her dark eyes as she glanced toward an archway on my right. It glimmered with lights that twinkled like fireflies, fading into different colors. When the lights changed to gold, I caught the outline of a closed door in the center of a white wall.

"You remember Trent, right?" I asked.

She just stared at me with vacant eyes that widened as fear crept slowly across her round face.

I pointed toward the front door. "Mine and Jay's friend. You know, the 9-1-1 on the sidewalk outside the portal?"

Her mouth fell open, but quickly closed. With a shrug, her expression was like *oh well, I'll pick up another friend at the discount store tomorrow.* Her vapid club face returned, like I'd said that Trent had only tripped and sprained something tonight, not ended the night in a body bag downtown, overwhelmed by fey dust.

I pressed my purse closer to my side, feeling the Glock's taut outline through the black microfiber. It was my only backup now.

Once more Sandra's gaze drifted across the dance floor packed with writhing dancers to that door beyond the twinkling archway. One of the private rooms. Where the fey conducted business. And snatched away souls. Where that coward Jay was hiding with Azriel— if she hadn't already devoured him.

"I'll find them myself," I said and turned away.

I made my way across the dim-lit dance floor, colored lights flashing overhead and beneath my feet. The white marble shifted colors along with the beat as I weaved through waves of writhing bodies toward the archway.

"Wendy, don't!"

Sandra's hands wrapped around my arm, pulling me back.

"Don't what?" I asked. "Don't confront my cheating boyfriend and that skank Azriel?"

She shook her head. "Jay's not worth it, okay? Stay away from Azriel. Please don't end up like Trent."

So she *did* know about Trent. The Sandra I knew was still in there somewhere.

Her eyes welled with tears. She brushed her hand across her face and just like that—the emotion was gone, the emptiness returning. Like closing a door, she was under the fey dust's spell again.

"After tonight, she won't hurt anyone else," I said and walked away, toward the archway and the narrow door.

This time, Sandra didn't try to stop me.

I passed under the arch and opened the narrow white door. I shoved past a fey man with flowing white hair drawn up into a man bun, his skin pearlescent pale. He wore grey leather pants, a silky white shirt, and a black leather duster. He ran his tongue over pale, bloodless lips as I slipped past him. Like he could almost taste my soul. A vampire would have been more honest. Fey delighted in anything and everything human, consuming and enslaving us. Collecting us like trinkets on display. Wearing our clothes and styling their hair like ours while insisting we were inferior to them. And stealing our souls.

The large private space was well-lit with high ceilings and shiny marble floors. I'd expected more white leather, bright jewel-toned silks, and colored lights, but this high-ceilinged space was the exact opposite.

The hairs on the back of my neck stood on end. Like I'd just stepped back in time.

Softly curved, oh-so-familiar furniture the color of ivory with its romantic scrollwork, delicate lines, scalloped edges, and carved flowers. Aged taupe walls with distressed molding and intricate chandeliers dripping with crystals and candlelight. Well-worn blue striped sofas and weathered floral loveseats filled the room, sheer, raw silk curtains pooled with sunlight (fey magic) on the marble floors. So achingly soft and familiar, the room smelled like blueberry scones, hot tea with lemons, and rose petals. Like I'd closed my eyes and stepped out onto the veranda as the last snow-washed moments of winter gave way to spring. Muted green grass and pale, cloudy blue sky, sun-faded tapestries, and threadbare linen tea towels.

Tears trickled down my face. Faded moments of my childhood, just before Azriel seduced my father.

Her cruelty had darkened. Deepened. Lavender and ash scent overpowered the smell of scones and lemons.

My neck muscles corded, jaw tightening as my stomach twisted into a nervous knot.

Curtains to my left fluttered open, revealing another sofa the color of crushed sage. Where Jay sat up and Azriel stretched out on the sofa, her head in his lap. His long, thin face was crusted with fey dust, grey eyes looking strung out and glassy. Once, I thought he was hot and sexy, caring and crazy about me. Now, he looked at me—no, through me—with that same fey emptiness as the others, like he'd never seen me before. Like I'd never mattered to him at all. Everything he'd ever said to me had been a lie. I saw that now as he cuddled that fey skank against his chest and stared into her large aquamarine eyes. Like they were streaming Netflix.

Azriel ran slender her fingers and long, spiky red fingernails through his close-cropped (thinning) dirty blond hair. His eyes widened when he finally saw me. He hurriedly stood up, shifting Azriel away from him, and stared at me like a burglar tripping a security alarm.

"Wendy! Wendy, listen I—"

I held up my hand. "Don't Jay. Don't even bother. You waste my time."

Azriel smirked at me from the couch, her mane of white hair across Jay's lap. She wore a short gold dress that was hiked up on one side. Stretching with feline grace, she stood up, twisting a small, white silk pouch between long reed-like fingers, daring me to act.

"Lose something, little girl?" Azriel asked, chuckling at me.

"Something of value? Not in this room. But I did earlier. Trent Davis died tonight."

Jay's mouth fell open, his thin face turning to glare at Azriel. "What? Trent's dead? Why would you kill him?"

Azriel laughed, the sound like breaking glass. "He was causing you problems, so I took care of it, love. Like I decorated this room just for Wendy."

She ran her hand down Jay's arm and I felt the white heat of hatred burn in my chest. I gritted my teeth, fingers strangling my purse strap.

"I'm sorry," she said, flipping her sparkling white hair at me. "Was he yours, too?" Her laughter crashed through the room again. Stoking my rage like a forest fire.

"Humans don't own each other," I said, a hand on my hip. I glared at Jay whose gaze shifted to his feet. "We used to have things called relationships. Which are based on trust. Love. And respect. But Jay wouldn't know much about that."

Azriel fingered a smoky glass pendant around her neck. The smoke inside the gem swirled and shifted. Like a living entity. Then I realized it wasn't a gem at all. It was the prison where she kept all the human souls she'd stolen with her fey magic.

Somehow, I had to get that necklace. To set Trent's soul—and the others—free. She could keep Jay's for all I cared. They were perfect for each other. But Trent didn't deserve this. He'd tried to help me and Jay and paid for it with his life. I'd make sure he wasn't punished for it.

"How'd you get him to snort the dust?" I asked Azriel, taking a step toward her. "Trent didn't even drink."

She crossed her sinewy arms across her chest. "I didn't force it on him," she said, her soprano voice lyrical and condescending. "Not at first anyway." Her glass-shattering laugh crackled through the room and I winced.

Jay seemed horrified by what Azriel had done, but he stayed at her side. I couldn't tell if she'd enchanted him in some way (like Trent) and honestly, I didn't care. Anyone that chose to stay with such a horrid creature was someone I didn't know anymore.

I took another step toward her.

"Such a bold and feisty little girl playing at love. Have you come to beg me to get your little boyfriend back?"

I was within reach of her now. So smug and beautiful. She had a major bitch-slap coming and so did Jay. I had to make sure she didn't call up some crazy fey magic and escape to Tír na nÓg. Like before.

Not unless I had a real good grip on her first.

"Keep him," I snapped. "I got the better end of the deal, but you're too vain to see that yet. You just wanted him because you could take him from me. And because you hate humans."

Azriel shook her head, her luminous, pale aquamarine eyes narrowing. "Then why are you here?"

I lunged at her, my fingers closing around the soul prison around her neck. I yanked hard until the chain snapped. At last, I gripped that gem in my fist—something I'd waited a lifetime for. I stumbled backward, grinning at her.

Azriel gasped, her hand at her neck, an angry welt on her alabaster skin where the chain had ripped across it. Her eyes turned dark and stormy.

"You're about to die, little girl."

I slid the Glock out of my purse and pointed the barrel at Azriel's face. "If I am, I'm taking your soulless ass with me, Azriel. Forever."

Azriel stared at the gun a moment and shook her head. "A gun?" She rolled her eyes, a guttural laugh rippling through the room. She propped a hand on her hip. "Against a fey? You insult me."

I held onto my grin, wanting to smash in her smug ass face. "I'm surprised you don't recognize this particular weapon, Azriel. It's been pointed at you before."

She frowned, a shadow against her perfect complexion. "What are you babbling about?"

"Don't remember, do you? " I asked. "Nearly forty years ago, my mother pointed this very gun at you when she caught you trying to seduce my father."

Again, that caustic laugh tore through the room and my urge to bitch-slap her rose to seismic proportions.

"I don't remember your pathetic human parents," said Azriel, stepping toward me. "And your silly human weapons can't harm me, little girl. If you had any intelligence at all, you would know that by now."

I held out the cloudy gem that looked more like charcoal than onyx.

"My mother watched helplessly as you suffocated my father with fey dust. Right in front of her. She pulled the trigger, but it went right through you as you stole his soul and took him from her. And me."

Azriel took another step toward me. I pointed the pistol at her chest. With a sneer, she moved closer.

"And yet here you are with the very same little toy, trying to shoot me with it again. And expecting a different result. The very definition of insanity."

I shook the gem at her. "My father's in here, you bitch. Along with Trent and who knows how many other human souls that didn't deserve this. None of it."

Azriel was in my face now. She was at least six feet tall, much taller than me, but I stood my ground, Glock still pointed at her chest.

"You're so envious of our immortality that you wear it like fucking jewelry!" I glared at her, studying her eyes. "But even with the weight of all these souls around your neck, you still have no substance, Azriel. You may live five hundred years, but after that, you'll be nothing more than dust beneath our immortal human feet!"

She let out a feral growl through her clenched teeth, hands clenched into fists as she lunged at me.

I'd expected her attack and side-stepped it.

She fell against the marble floor with a sharp thunk and I laughed hard at her. Pissing off the fey wasn't necessarily a good idea, but I was enjoying every moment of this payback. And how each time, her control unraveled a little bit more.

Azriel rose from the floor, crouching as I pointed the barrel of the Glock at her heart again. She hesitated a moment.

"Shooting fey just makes us angry, little girl. Surely even you must realize that. But let that toy be the tool of your own destruction."

I didn't expect her to smash her hand over my nose. Sparkling gold with dust.

The rush of fey magic exploded in my face and I held my breath, stumbling backward.

Azriel leaped on top of me, that little white silk pouch sparkling in her reedy fingers. Fingers twinkling gold with more fey dust.

I pressed the Glock against her heart and pulled the trigger.

Pop! The Glock's report startled me. I jumped as the force drove her backward a step. She pressed her hand to the wound, laughing at me with a scornful sneer.

"You insane little girl! You waste my time! Lead does nothing to the fey!"

I grinned at her. "No, but Cold Iron is devastating. Or so I hear."

Azriel raised an eyebrow, grimacing. "Cold Iron?"

She stared at me a moment. For an instant, I saw fear ripple across her perfect features and shine through her empty aquamarine eyes as she realized that, for the first time, the abyss of nothingness stared back at her. Frantic, she struggled against it.

"How did you get such a rare metal, human?"

"Had them made special," I said with a smirk. "Just for you. The fey may have Tír na nÓg, but we humans have something called the internet." I winked at her. "You can find just about anything there."

"I feel strange," said Azriel, slumping to the floor, a faraway look in her pallid eyes.

Thick gold fluid oozed from the gunshot wound and pooled on the floor.

Only then did I feel the club's unwavering dance beat vibrate against the floor again. Until now, the room had felt intense. Deathly silent. No one outside this room even heard the gunshot because of the music, but I'll bet they felt the presence of Cold Iron and acted accordingly. Jay was on his knees beside Azriel, his hand clutching hers. She pulled her hand away, glaring at him.

"Don't—you touch me," she said and spit on him.

213

Already, her body was turning to dust, shriveling, the gold fey blood turning to gritty sand on the shiny marble floor.

I slid the Glock back into my purse and turned toward the door. I paused, my hand on the knob.

"Goodbye, Azriel. And Jay...don't even think about calling me. Ever."

I slipped out of the room, expecting the throbbing bass beat and loud music, but the music and the beat had stopped. The Cold Iron bullets had magically emptied the dance floor of fey, so I ran across it to the front door. Even the human posers had fled, leaving the cavernous dance floor empty. Vacuous. Abandoned.

The scent of lavender was already dissipating, my lungs clearing as I walked toward the purple double doors leading outside. Where the path led back to the portal. Outside, the crowds of fey had dispersed, leaving the porch empty as I stepped into the silvery twilight waxing purple and blue from the still-flashing Club Oberon sign above me.

I hurried down the winding stairs and onto the smooth stony path that wound through the wheaten-gold grass as plush as carpet. Adrenaline pumped through me, my whole body quivering and my hands shaking. My legs felt like rubber as I crested the hill and saw the portal gleaming ahead. The lavender light spun like a whirlpool, the portal vibrating as I moved toward it. I glanced over my shoulder, making sure that nothing and no one would follow me through the portal.

Or follow me home.

The emptiness of Club Oberon was palpable now. Heavy. Mournful. Like the weight of Azriel's gem in my hand. They'd all fled. Through this portal or back to Tír na nÓg, either way, I didn't care anymore.

Turning back to the portal, I held my breath and stepped through. Into darkness. Rushing ahead, I ran toward the pinprick of light ahead that grew larger and larger until I stepped out into Portland's dark, chilly rain. In the late night solace of Portland's streets and bustle of the Pearl District, I could breathe again. The sidewalk where Trent had collapsed was empty, the crowd dispersed, paramedics and police gone now. My bottom lip quivered, tears slipping down my face as the loss bit through the numbness.

Azriel's gem was warm in my palm, still swirling with souls. Trent's soul. And my father's. How many other souls writhed inside this horrid little chamber? Jay's soul wasn't among them and I felt a twinge of regret.

But even he didn't deserve such a fate.

Clutching the gem in my fist, I walked down the damp street, down a few blocks until I reached my car, a red Nissan Altima. I ducked down behind it in the dark and laid the soul-filled gem on the wet pavement. The dark, rainy night was quieter now, softer somehow, distant buzz of traffic mixing with the roar still in my ears from the pulsing dance music that had gone silent now. I slid the Glock out of my purse.

I thought of the father I barely knew. Trent's last breath. And the ex-boyfriend who'd used me—and cheated on me. Angel, saint, and sinner, all three were gone. Leaving me alone again. Until now, I'd been unable to mourn those losses.

A sob rose in my throat, my eyes stinging with tears. I swallowed the sound and raised the butt of the Glock over my head. But the pain wrenched free as I slammed the gun's grip against the smoky gem.

It didn't crack. Or even chip.

Over and over, I hammered it with all my strength, but the surface didn't even scratch.

The souls were held inside the gem—protected—by some sort of fey magic.

Feeling defeated, I collapsed against the wet car, a mist settling low along the curbs and pooling beneath the yellow wash of streetlights—and gave in to my grief. I cried until my throat felt raw and my eyes burned. When I could finally move again, I sat up and pointed the gun barrel at the gem. I still had Cold Iron rounds in the clip. I had nothing to lose by using them on Azriel's little soul prison.

Pumping the Glock's trigger, I fired off two shots. The gem shattered!

I shoved the two bullet casings and my Glock back into my purse and staggered up from the wet pavement as smoke swirled out of the shattered gem. Rising in the mist. Myriad strands of smoke twisted and writhed around me, each one taking on a ghostly human shape as it rose toward the pale stars overhead.

One spirit enveloped me in warm gold light and white mist. For a moment, I felt arms around me, holding me close for only a moment. I smiled through my tears.

It was my father!

A wispy curl of white smoke reached out and touched my cheek. A warm, comforting pressure against my face. Brushing away my tears, I realized. With a feather kiss against my forehead, my father's form dissipated into the night.

His soul was free at last!

A siren screamed in the distance as I watched all the other souls take flight into the night, a flood of new tears slipping down my face.

Finally, Trent's spirit, the last one, fluttered around me and enveloped my hands, a gentle caress telling me goodbye, telling me Trent would be all right. The white mist climbed high into the night, toward the stars, as I got into my car and drove away. Moments before a police car screeched around the corner.

I knew the only thing they'd find was a trace of sparkling gold dust on the damp pavement, already disappearing as the rain suddenly stopped.

ABOUT THE AUTHOR

Lisa has published nearly 100 short stories in the fantasy, science fiction, romance, and mystery genres. Her stories have appeared in many publications from: DAW Books, Roc Books, and Prime Books as well as several volumes of Fiction River and Pulphouse Magazine. Her first short story collection, *The Sound of Angels*, and her first novel, *Isabel's Tears* are currently available in print and digital versions. Her next novel, *Rediscovery*, will be published in 2018.

Find out more about Lisa at:
lisasilverthorne.com

facebook.com/lisa.silverthorne.14

twitter.com/lisasilverthorn

bookbub.com/authors/lisa-silverthorne

TO HAVE...AND TO HOLD

DEB LOGAN

PROLOGUE

My name is Artie Woodward, and I'm the happiest girl alive. Wow! I never thought that phrase would apply to me, especially when I was a kid. I mean, I'm a seer. I see things normal people don't, things they couldn't see, even if they wanted to, which no one in their right mind would. I mean, even I don't want to see the terrors, but I don't have a choice. I was born with this strange ability to see the unseen, to know the unknowable.

I thought I was alone. Thought I'd spend my whole life alone.

Sure, my mom and dad loved me, but even they thought I was weird. They worried about me constantly and dragged me to more shrinks than I care to remember. None of them helped. After all, they all thought I was imagining things. Except I wasn't. So I learned to hide.

I became adept at hiding. I hid my knowledge from my parents. I tried desperately to hide my weirdness from the kids at school. But most importantly, I hid the fact that I could see them, that I knew they existed, from the terrors themselves. And as long as I hid, I stayed safe.

Lonely, but safe.

So how did I grow up to be the happiest girl in the world? How did my life change from hidden and lonely to fulfilled and glowing with contentment?

Jed Kendrick found me.

We recognized each other, and our loneliness ended. We were both seers, and on our first day at McKinley High we became a team, but that's another story. Suffice it to say we've fought terrors together for nearly six years and have developed an unshakable bond.

And along the way, we fell in love.

And now, I'm the happiest girl in the world because in late September I'll become Jed Kendrick's wife, and he'll become Artie Woodward's husband. The Woodward-Kendrick team will be official in the eyes of the world.

But first, we had to make a pilgrimage to Ireland. Jed's grannie insisted.

CHAPTER 1

On a beautiful summer day in mid-August, Grannie O'Toole met us at the Dublin airport. We emerged from a sea of people to find her waiting for us, an island of calm in the form of a small, lean woman with frizzy gray hair that Jed assured me had once been curly and deep red.

"Jedidiah Kendrick," she called, opening her arms and stepping toward us with lively impatience. "Come and give your grannie a hug!"

Jed obeyed without hesitation, wrapping the little woman in his long arms and lifting her right off the airport's tiled floor.

"It's so good to see you, Grannie," he said as he placed her gently back on her feet. He grinned like a loon as he released her and angled his body to include me in their conversation. "Grannie, this is Artie, the love of my life." His eyes twinkled as he reached for my hand. "Artie, this is Grannie O'Toole, the best Irish grannie a boy could ever dream of."

Grannie O'Toole reached for my other hand while still maintaining a firm grasp on my husband-to-be. As our fingers met, a circle of energy clicked into place. Suddenly, the three of us really were an island in a sea of people. The pervasive buzz of voices around us muffled, people flowed past us without seeming to notice our existence. We were a rock in the stream that they avoided without awareness.

Grannie nodded. "I wondered," she said, her voice calm and quiet. "I knew Jeremiah was a seer from the moment of his birth." She turned her faded hazel eyes on Jed. "You held the potential, but Jerry held the power. Even here in Ireland, I felt the change when he died and you accepted the mantle."

Jed startled. I felt the slight pull of his fingers on mine, saw his gaze tighten and focus as he stared at his grandmother. "You knew?" he asked. The question held a tinge of accusation, and I heard his unvoiced thought. *You knew what I was and you didn't bother to explain? Left me to discover everything for myself?*

"Aye, child. I knew."

Jed tried to withdraw, to pull away from this woman he thought he'd known, but she held him. She must've been stronger than she looked, for my big, strong man failed to break the continuity of our circle.

"Be at peace, my boy," she said in that calm, quiet voice. "It's part of the curse of our blood that we cannot acknowledge one another until our power is fully developed. I could no more help you to find your way than you'll be able to help the next seer in our line." She turned her attention to me. "But you," she said, "you're a surprise. I wondered about the young woman our Jed had fallen for, worried that she might be Fae. 'Tis why I insisted on meeting before the wedding. If you were less than human, I needed to ensure you revealed your true nature before my boy took vows that would bind him to you for eternity."

I was the one who startled now. Every instinct I owned urged me to hide, as I'd done so effectively before Jed and I found each other, but I willed myself to stillness and looked Grannie O'Toole straight in the eye. She met my gaze without flinching and I read nothing but sincerity and warmth.

"Fae?" I asked. "As in fairies? Are fairies real then?"

Her eyes widened. "Of course they are," she exclaimed. "Are you telling me you've attained the years necessary to contemplate marriage without ever encountering the Fae?"

My jaw dropped and I turned my gaze on Jed. "Is she saying that the terrors are really fairies?" I asked. "I always thought fairies were little winged creatures who danced in mushroom circles and slept on flower petals."

Grannie guffawed, there was no other word for the snort of laughter than emanated from her small body, pulling my attention back to her.

"Sorry," she said. "I can see we've a lot of catching up to do. Let's break this circle and speak of normal things until I get you home. My house is warded, strongly warded, against the Fae. We won't need physical contact there in order to have a private conversation."

And so saying, she broke our contact, as easily as if we'd both been toddlers. While she'd been able to hold me like a vise, I had no more luck clutching her fingers than I would've had capturing a moonbeam. I had the feeling Grannie O'Toole had a lot to teach me.

Thank all that is holy, I was absolutely correct.

CHAPTER 2

Grannie O'Toole's house was a charming cottage in the Dublin suburb of Shankill. With its whitewashed walls, jewel-red front door, overhanging thatch roof, and blue window boxes filled to overflowing with red chrysanthemums and white baby's breath, the cottage was everything I'd ever imagined of finding in Ireland. The only thing missing from my perfect vision was its setting. Instead of being surrounded by acres of rolling hills in brilliant shades of emerald green, the little cottage was hemmed in on two sides by neighboring homes and in front by a heavily trafficked cobblestone street.

The three of us piled out of the cab Grannie had hired at the airport and soon stood with our meager baggage — a backpack and duffle for Jed and a carry-on size rolling case for me — in the street in front of Grannie's cottage. As we approached that red door, I felt a slight resistance, as if the house pushed me back to the street. An overwhelming urge to walk past swept over me. I stopped, glanced around, and noted a puzzled expression on Jed's face. He felt it too.

Grannie smiled, placed one hand on the door, then held her other out to us. "Touch my hand," she encouraged. "Just a finger will do."

When both of us complied, she nodded and said, "Jedidiah

Kendrick and Artemis Woodward are welcome in my home. Please, come in."

The resistance vanished, as did my need to walk away.

Of course. Grannie had mentioned that her home was warded against the Fae. Evidently those wards worked against seer blood as well, and Jed and I had now been invited inside their protective shield. I shivered, but held my questions until we were safely inside those innocent looking whitewashed walls.

"I wasn't sure if you'd want to share a room," Grannie said breezily as she led us into a comfortable, lived-in front room. A well-worn sofa upholstered in a tweed fabric the green of budding leaves and heaped with throw pillows in bright jewel tones rested before an authentic fireplace complete with stone hearth and a planed log mantle. Two overstuffed chairs in matching upholstery provided additional seating. "But seeing as you're only handfast and not actually married, I've given you each your own space." She grinned. "That, and I didn't want to give up my own room!"

She led us through a cheery kitchen with white pine cabinets and pretty lace curtains, and up a narrow staircase. I hadn't expected a second floor and found myself on a compact landing between two doors leading to identical small rooms tucked under the cottage's eaves.

"These were originally children's quarters," she explained as Jed and I separated and stowed our luggage in the windowless cells. Each was furnished with a single twin bed covered with a colorful quilt, an old-fashioned washstand complete with basin and ewer, and a drawer unit cunningly built into space beneath the eaves. The sloping roof meant Jed could barely stand in his room, and only near the door. "They're tight, but you'll not be spending much time in them."

We trooped back down the stairs and Grannie completed the tour with a glimpse of her bedroom, spacious and sunny compared to the upstairs rooms, and a shared bath complete with old-fashioned claw-footed tub.

At her insistence, Jed and I settled in the front room while she bustled around the kitchen making tea. Once we were all possessed of steaming cups with a rose patterned plate of shortbread cookies resting on the pine coffee table, Grannie returned to the subject of seers and fairies.

"So," she said, settling into the depths of her overstuffed chair. "Tell me about your experience of the Fae. What did you call them? Terrors?"

I glanced at Jed, waited for him to take the lead.

"That's what Artie named them," he said with a nod in my direction. "She's seen them since birth. Like you said in the airport, I didn't see them until Jerry died. He was the seer, I was just his twin."

Grannie turned to me, her blue eyes seeming to pierce my very soul. "I know Jed's bloodline," she said, "know he inherited his ability from my line, but what about you, young woman? How do you come to see the Fae?"

Grannie's scrutiny unnerved me. Without thinking, I angled my head so that my long dark hair shadowed my face, closed my eyes, and concentrated on hiding, on being invisible. Stillness settled over the room and as I counted my heartbeats, I calmed.

Until Jed placed a hand on my arm.

"It's okay, Artie," he said, his tone soothing and soft. The kind of voice he'd use with a startled horse or a frightened child. "You're safe here. Grannie's no threat. She's family. No need to hide."

I opened my eyes and straightened, grasping Jed's hand and meeting his gaze. I nodded. "You're right," I said and turned my attention back to Grannie. "I'm sorry. You startled me and I reacted without thinking."

She stared at me a moment longer, then said with a sigh, "You've a powerful defense, Artie. Almost I lost sight of you...and me a seer. I could feel the power coalescing around you, cloaking you, and even so I nearly lost the knowledge of you."

She glanced around the room, and following her gaze I glimpsed pale runes shimmering above windows and doors and centered on walls before they winked out of sight.

"If it weren't for my wards, I think you'd have succeeded in disappearing from my mind completely." She shuddered and took a sip of tea from the rose patterned cup she still held. After a moment, she continued. "Well, I think we've established you've seer blood. From a very potent bloodline. An ancient bloodline."

"More ancient than ours?" Jed asked.

She nodded. "I've never known a seer with that kind of power, but there are legends..." Another pause while she sipped more tea. I could almost see the thoughts tumbling through her mind as she considered.

"Legends?" Jed prompted when the pause grew lengthy.

"What?" Grannie startled, her eyes widening, as though she'd forgotten our presence. "Oh. Yes. Legends. Among the Fae, there's a legend of a pair who will defend the human race, who will banish the Fae to another realm. Make it impossible for them to feed off our fears and baser instincts. A pair who will free us from them for eternity."

She studied us over the rim of her cup. "I wonder..."

I frowned. "That can't be us. I mean, if we were destined for something, wouldn't someone know? Wouldn't *we* know? And how do you know about Fae legends anyway?"

"It's my family's," she gestured at Jed with the cookie she'd just plucked from the plate, "*our* family's business to know. We've spied on the Fae for years, kept journals of all we've learned. Journals I'll be handing on to you now, my boy. Now that I've seen for myself that you've the sight and your intended is the right sort as well."

Biting into the shortbread cookie, she chewed, swallowed, and took another sip of tea. "The best thing the Fae could do, if they felt the time of the legend approaching, would be to isolate the families. If your parents, and therefore you," she pointed at me with the half-eaten treat, "were isolated from those of us who know and understand what the Fae are, you'd come into your power without benefit of training. Without understanding our ancient enemy. You'd be weak, and easily destroyed."

"As Jerry was," said Jed, a stricken look marring his features.

"Exactly," Grannie said. "Except for an accident of birth, Artie's partner would've been destroyed and she would've gone to her grave without ever reaching her potential, discovering her destiny."

"But because Jed and Jerry were twins," I said, catching the direction of Grannie's thought, "Jed's potential awakened when Jerry died." I squeezed his hand tightly. "And fate brought us together."

Jed gripped my hand with both of his and gazed into my eyes. "Not fate," he said. "Divine intervention. Don't forget Michael. Don't discount Dad's dream that sent us to Colorado."

"Michael?" Grannie's voice was so sharp I felt like she'd pounced on the name with a tiger's unsheathed claws. "Who is Michael?"

Releasing my hand, Jed leaned forward, elbows on knees, and gazed directly into Grannie's eyes. "Michael, the hunter. The archangel. The commander of God's armies. At least, that's who I've always known him as."

Grannie's eyes narrowed. "And how exactly do you know this Michael?"

"I first saw him when Jerry lay dying. When my sight awoke. Everything changed, and when I looked around, I not only saw the thing that had killed Jerry, but I saw him...the angel...Michael, standing behind my father, his eyes full of sorrow and pity. That's actually the only time I've ever seen him when I was awake. Every other time he's come to me in dreams."

"In dreams?" Grannie prompted.

"Yeah. He's used dreams to teach me. To tell me how to fight the monsters, the terrors, as Artie calls them. He's given me strategy and curses or spells to defeat them. I'm pretty sure he's the one who visited Dad in the dream that caused him to move us across the country to Artie's hometown. He knew she needed me. That we needed each other."

She nodded, crossing herself quickly. "An angel. Well, imagine that. And here I thought I'd be the one training you." Dusting the shortbread crumbs from her fingers, she stood, collected our tea cups and turned toward the kitchen. "The pair of you really are special if an archangel has chosen to involve himself." She paused, and glanced back over her shoulder. "Since you've little formal knowledge of the Fae, we'll start your education bright and early in the morning."

CHAPTER 3

The next few days were full of wonder. Who'd have guessed that I'd have to go all the way to Ireland to read fairy tales? Of course, these particular tales were true.

Grannie pulled out the family journals and we spent every evening studying the Fae. Jed and I learned about the various races of Fae, about their courts and their powers. We learned the places they were most likely to be found, the hills and rings and raths that covered the British Isles and much of Europe, places Grannie felt sure were portals to that other dimension where their true home lay.

We also learned about ley lines. Lines of power which connected those sites, running in straight lines from point to point and which the Fae traveled in processions...invisible to all but those with seer blood. If an oblivious human had the misfortune to build a structure across one of those lines, death and destruction followed when the next procession occurred.

During the days, Grannie O'Toole took us to church yards and ruins and circles of standing stones, whatever we'd studied the night before. On one such outing we visited a construction site. All three of us could clearly see the blue ley line shimmering with energy in the morning sun...and running diagonally through the steel bones of what would someday be an upscale shopping mall on the outskirts of Dublin.

Grannie sighed and shook her head. "'Tis a shame it'll never be completed. The Fae travel this path every year at Samhain. Halloween," she added, correctly interpreting my confused expression. "I tried to warn the owner, but he laughed in my face. Fairy tales are for children, and the gullible, don't you know?"

I shivered, glad I'd be safely home in Colorado long before Halloween came around. The terrors I'd learned to battle at Jed's side were bad enough, but here, in the Old Country, the number and variety of Fae were daunting.

Everywhere we went, we saw Fae. Some were kindly, child-sized brownies caring for domestic animals or lending an unseen hand with household chores; some were tricksters, dwarves and goblins amusing themselves by moving keys or hiding reading glasses; but others rivaled the terrors in their malicious intent, feeding on their victims' positive emotions so that the individuals were left with only distrust and sociopathic thoughts.

Grannie O'Toole cautioned us to act as though we were oblivious to the presence of the Fae, no matter their type.

"Don't see them," she advised. "Whatever you do, never look directly at a Fae. If you must observe them, do so only with sidelong glances or have a reason to look past them. Focus on a bit of the landscape beyond where they stand."

Jed bristled at this advice. "Artie and I don't ignore them. We fight and banish them."

"Maybe at home you can afford to fight," she said with sad resignation. "Colorado must be a wonderful place if there are so few Fae that two young people can fight and win. But not here. Not in their stronghold. There are too many, Jed. You and Artie would be overrun and destroyed — or worse, taken as their playthings — in a heartbeat."

"If we are the legendary pair," Jed argued, "how are we supposed to defend the human race and banish the Fae by pretending we're not what we are?"

Grannie poked a finger in his chest, her expression fierce. "You'll defend our people by lying low until you know enough to fight. Remember Jerry. Remember what happens when a seer tries to do that which he's not yet strong enough to accomplish!"

"That's not fair," Jed said through clenched jaws. His voice was low and controlled, but I heard the anger simmering just beneath the words. "Jerry was a child. I'm an adult."

"Jerry was untrained," she retorted, "and you've only just discovered the existence of the Fae. You didn't even know enough to know what you were battling back home in Colorado."

I stepped between them, placing a hand on Jed's arm. "Enough. You're fighting over how and when to fight."

Grannie stepped back, and Jed turned his gaze on me.

"I don't like letting them get away with things," he said, quietly, but with a sullen edge. "They're hurting people."

"I know," I said, stroking my hand down his arm until I could entwine my fingers with his, "I don't like it much either, but I think Grannie's right. We need to hide our knowledge until we've learned all we can here...and then we need to plan."

He nodded, some of the fire leaving his eyes. "You're right. Whether or not we're the pair in their legend, we won't do anyone any good if we take on more than we can handle right now."

Grannie sighed loudly, but held her peace.

"Let's take a break," I suggested. "We've only got two more days in Ireland. Let's do something fun. Grannie," I said, turning to include her in the conversation again, "there must be something we can do that has a low probability of running into the Fae. What do you suggest?"

Grannie's brow furrowed slightly, then cleared as she nodded and smiled. "That's a grand idea, Artie, but I'm thinking we should take it a step further. Why don't we take a break from each other as well as the learning? I've some errands I've been avoiding, and I'll be surprised if the pair of you wouldn't like a bit of time together without me hanging on your every word."

I opened my mouth to protest, but the twinkle in her eye combined with the happy surprise on Jed's face kept me quiet.

She laughed with delight. "As to where you should go, you might enjoy the Dublin Zoo or the National Botanical Gardens. Both are tourist attractions and full of people, and therefore Fae, but if you wander the less traveled paths, you should be safe enough from their notice."

"That sounds lovely," I agreed.

Jed stepped to Grannie and drew her into a hug. "I'm sorry for picking a fight with you," he said, kissing the top of her frizzy head. "You're right, of course, and an afternoon of sight-seeing will give me a chance to clear my head."

She leaned back and reaching up, patted his cheek. "You're a good boy, Jedidiah Kendrick, and I'm pleased and proud to be your grannie."

Stepping out of his embrace, she swiped tears from her eyes with the back of a hand before using it to make shooing motions at us. "Be gone with you now. You can catch a bus to either the zoo or the gardens at the pub where we had dinner last night. Have a grand time and I'll see you this evening."

Unfortunately, we decided not to catch a bus from the pub in Shankill.

CHAPTER 4

I'd just come downstairs from gathering my purse and a light jacket when Jed caught me in his arms.

"Alone at last," he whispered in my ear, and then his lips found mine.

My whole body responded to his kiss. My pulse skyrocketed while butterflies played tag in my belly; my toes even tingled. I was warm and happy and...home. It didn't matter that we were in Ireland, if Jed and I were together, I was home. They say that "home is where the heart is"...and Jed was, and always will be, my heart.

We broke the kiss, and I laid my cheek against his chest, listening to the steady beat of his heart. My arms encircled his waist, and his held me close, resting his chin on the top of my head.

"I've missed this," he said. "Time together, just the two of us."

I nodded, rubbing my cheek against the soft cotton of his favorite moss green shirt. "I've enjoyed meeting Grannie," I said quietly, "and I've learned so much, but I'm glad we're going home soon." I straightened, leaning back in his arms to smile up at him. "We've got a wedding to plan!"

He grinned back at me. "We certainly do." A slight crease in his brow signaled a change in subject. "Listen, do you mind if we don't go the tourist route? I'm not in the mood to be squashed on a bus and then mingle with hordes of people."

"Fine by me," I said, stepping out of his arms and catching his hand in mine. "We can see zoo animals and flowers back home."

"Good. Let's just take a walk instead. There's a really cool ruin just through the woods. Mom took Jerry and me there once. I think we were about six during that visit," he mused. "Every other time we saw Grannie, she came to us. Lots more affordable to fly one person across the Atlantic than four...or even three."

A shiver skittered down my spine, but I associated it with the mention of Jed's dead twin, not with intuition. I wish I'd heeded my subconscious mind's subtle warning.

"That sounds perfect," I said instead. "It's a gorgeous day for a walk."

Jed led me down the street, around the corner, and into a children's play park. On the other side of the manicured lawn, an old growth forest brooded. Grabbing my hand, Jed strode quickly toward the trees. As we approached, an opening in the undergrowth appeared and I saw a path of dark earth strewn with moldering leaf duff.

We stepped under the trees and the village and all its modern sights and sounds faded away. A world of shadowy greens and browns enveloped us; no sound reached our ears but a low breeze moaning through the leafy canopy.

I squeezed Jed's hand, reassured by the warmth of his fingers. He grinned down at me.

"Don't worry," he said, pulling me forward into the forest, "this is nothing. The castle is even spookier."

"Wow," I said. "Way to reassure a girl." I rolled my eyes, but laughed at myself and picked up my pace. No need to make the man feel like he was dragging me to my doom.

The day was warm and the woods were still. I felt a bit like I was walking through a dream. To dispel that illusion, and just for the comfort of hearing his voice, I asked, "So where are we going?"

"There's this really frosty ruin in a meadow just the other side of these woods. It's called Puck's Castle. Jerry and I thought it was great when we were kids."

Sunlight glimmered through the canopy, and I realized we'd reached the edge of the woods. Just beyond the trees lay a paved road with the forest lining one side and a low rock wall on the other. We crossed to a metal gate and I had my first sight of the ruin.

Puck's castle looked like a giant's face, mouth open in horror, eyes slitted against a wind only it could feel. A cap of green hair trailed across one corner of its brow.

I shivered. "Why is it called Puck's Castle?"

Jed glanced from the stacked rock ruin to me. "You know, I hadn't thought about that, but I remember now," his brow creased in a frown. "It's supposed to be haunted by a pookah, a mischievous fairy who plays the pipes and hops around on the rocks."

That was when I noticed the muted glow of the ley line.

I grabbed Jed's hand, tugging him back toward the cover of the trees. "We have to go, Jed," I said, trying desperately to mask the hysteria rising in my chest. "Now. We have to go NOW!"

The glow of the ley line was no longer muted. The iridescent blue brightened as I watched, pulsing as though to a musical beat.

Jed ignored my panicked tug. He stared across the meadow to the forest on the far side of the castle.

"Jed," I cried. "Please!"

If he heard me, or felt me yanking on his hand, he gave no sign. My love, the man I intended to marry, stood as though turned to stone and stared as a troop of fairies left the shelter of the woods and marched along the ley line straight to Puck's Castle.

Too late, I thought. *Leaving now will only draw their attention to us.* So I did what I had always done, I hid in plain sight. And prayed that my gift would shield Jed as well.

I peered through the curtain of my dark hair, watching the approaching fairies through slitted eyes. One of their number peeled off and scampered up the rock tower, lithe as a mountain goat. When he reached the top, he danced from stone to stone, lightly skipping over the ivy that trailed in a glistening stream across one corner. His dance ended abruptly on our side of the castle, and I knew I'd been unsuccessful. The pookah saw us...or at least one of us.

His surprised cry caused the troop to halt, and me to close my eyes and redouble my effort to hide.

But my attempt was in vain.

Footsteps pattered across the green carpeted meadow, and I cracked my eyes open by the merest sliver to see the pookah and two tall, silver-haired companions standing on the other side of the gate from us.

Jed shook his hand loose from mine, as if I were no more than a bothersome fly, and stepped toward the fairies.

"Begone," he said. "You're not wanted here."

"How unusual," said the pookah. "This mortal has eyes that see."

"Unusual and unacceptable," said one of his silver-haired friends. The creature crooked a finger at Jed and said, "Come, mortal. You must meet our queen."

My Jed, my partner, the love of my life, placed a booted foot on the lowest rail of the gate and began to climb over, his eyes glazed, his expression vacant.

I couldn't stand still. I couldn't let them take my Jed!

Flinging my invisibility away, I grabbed Jed's arm. "Jedidiah Kendrick, hear me! Come away, Jed. Come away with me now!"

The three fairies startled, stepping back a pace.

"What's this?" cried the pookah. "From whence did this mortal appear?"

"She holds great power," said the second.

"No matter," said the third, the one who had held silent until now. He turned gleaming orange eyes on me and spoke directly to my soul. "Come. Your will is mine. Follow where I lead."

I barely had time to duck my chin and close my eyes before his words wove their spell. A nearly irresistible urge to climb the gate and follow Jed into the meadow flooded my heart and soul. But a sliver of my will had managed to hide, and that sliver fought the fairy's compulsion. If I fell under his spell, who would rescue Jed?

The thought of losing myself wasn't nearly as terrifying as the thought of losing Jed.

That sliver of self blazed with fear for my love, and the hot emotion broke the fairy's hold on my mind. I slipped into my own spell and the creatures forgot my existence. Jed was their one and only prey.

When the troop had passed, I sank to the ground and sobbed, grieving for the life we'd never share now. I'd been powerless to protect Jed, and my heart ached with loss.

CHAPTER 5

Grannie was inconsolable. She paced the floor in front of the hearth and wailed her despair, while I held myself together, folded into one of the overstuffed chairs.

"He watched them cross the field? He stood there bold as brass and stared at a procession of fairies?" Her eyes were red with weeping and her voice scratched and cracked as though she'd inhaled a lifetime's cigarette smoke. "Did he learn nothing from me?"

She pulled her already frizzy hair, and then turned on me. "And you...how did you come home again, lassie? How are you here and not my Jedidiah?"

My own tears were gone, washed away in the flood I'd shed on the lane outside Puck's Castle. I had nothing left to give.

"I hid," I said. "I tried to shield him too, but they saw him anyway."

"You hid," she said, the words dripping scorn. "You claim to love my boy, but you did naught to save him. You hid."

"I tried," I answered, stung by the injustice of her accusation. "I cast away my protection and tried to call him back. He loves me. I love him." I sighed, futility washing over me yet again. "I thought my call would be stronger than theirs. I was wrong."

"Then how are you here?"

"I realized it wasn't working," I explained. "My sudden appearance startled them, gave me just enough time to slip back into my trance." I closed my eyes and rested my head in my hands. "Even so, I almost didn't make it. The only thing that saved me was the knowledge that Jed was lost if I gave in."

Her hand settled on my hair and stroked; the touch comforted me.

"I'm sorry, Artie," she whispered. "This is none of your doing and 'tis wrong of me to lay blame at your feet."

I rose and hugged her tightly. "I'm so sorry," I whispered. "I don't know what to do."

We separated, staring at each other through bleak eyes.

"How do we get him back?"

Grannie closed her eyes and sank onto the sofa, pulling me down beside her. "Oh, child," she said. "He's lost and there's nothing we can do about it."

I bristled, hot anger replacing despair. "I can't accept that," I said. "I won't accept that. I need him. We need each other. There has to be a way to steal him back."

She patted my arm. "I've never heard of the Fae releasing one of their toys," she said, but something in my expression made her change tack. "We'll search the old texts. Not just our family journals, but those in the clan library."

"Is yours the only seer clan?"

Grannie pursed her lips and thought. "I know a few other families. I'll ask them to search their journals as well."

I nodded, suddenly too weary to hold up my head. Research. It wasn't much, but it was hope, and I would cling to hope until I could cling to Jed again.

"Go to bed, Artie," Grannie said with a pat on my knee. "Neither of us is thinking clearly at the moment. We'll start our search in the morning."

I nodded and found my way to the second floor, where I was now the only occupant.

CHAPTER 6

Our search was long and arduous, but Grannie O'Toole was a steadfast guide. We read every word of her family journals before moving to the headquarters of her ancestral clan, the O'Connors, and petitioning to search their library.

Fortunately, the O'Connor library was located in Dublin. Unfortunately, the older texts were indecipherable to me, and eventually proved beyond Grannie's skill at translation as well.

Days dragged by, followed by plodding weeks of reading ancient script until my eyes ached. Family and friends in Colorado called asking when Jed and I were coming home. I prevaricated, misled, and outright lied. I couldn't bear to tell anyone that he'd been stolen, kidnapped by supernatural creatures. No one would believe me anyway, so I hid behind a façade of a holiday too delightful to bring to a close.

August's myriad greens turned to the golds and reds of September with no solution in sight. Despair seized me by the throat as our anticipated wedding date approached...and passed with me no nearer to rescuing Jed. I couldn't go on like this. I couldn't live without him, but I couldn't give up while he might be saved. Maybe the next document would hold the secret. I kept searching

By mid-October we had reached the limits of our ability to research, and I was desperately afraid I'd be forced to leave Ireland... to abandon the possibility of ever seeing my love again.

Just when our spirits had reached their lowest ebb, Laird Angus O'Connor sought us out. He found us in a dim library chamber where tattered scrolls and decaying journals lined shelves set against stone walls dark with age. An ancient oak table occupied the center of the room, its wood so stained and dark it seemed to absorb what little light filtered through the high, narrow windows. The most ancient scrolls dealing with the Fae resided in this room... scrolls filled with script that had defied even Grannie's ability to read.

The clan leader was an impressive man, with a broad chest, heavily muscled arms, a thick neck, and a full head of deep auburn hair. Though he was clean shaven and wearing a perfectly tailored suit, he looked like a warrior of legend.

"Maeve O'Toole," he called in a booming voice that filled the narrow chamber. "I've heard tales that you and your young assistant have fair taken up residence among the journals of our clan. Do you seek specific knowledge, or are you merely broadening your understanding of your heritage?"

Grannie scrambled to stand, so I followed suit, but when she gave the man a low bow, I merely inclined my head. He was not my laird, nor was he ever likely to become so, the way our search was going.

"Laird," said Grannie, standing as tall as her slight frame would allow. "We're looking for specific information...regarding the Fae."

"I see." He shot a piercing look at me, and I saw wariness and a shrewd intelligence in his gaze. "And who might your assistant be? If she's of our clan, I've no recollection of her."

Grannie folded her hands in front of her and lowered her gaze. "She is not of our clan...yet. Laird Angus O'Connor, may I present Artemis Woodward. Artie, this is my clan leader, Angus O'Connor."

Laird Angus held out a massive hand, and I laid mine in it.

"'Tis pleased I am to make your acquaintance, Miss Woodward," he said, lifting my hand and brushing my knuckles with his lips. As he did so, a flash of recognition seared my mind. This man was not only a seer, he was far older than his looks suggested.

He smiled, a twinkle lighting his eyes. "Ah, I see your blood recognizes mine. Good. That will expedite matters." He released my hand, sat down at the long narrow table between the racks of books and scrolls, and gestured us to chairs as well. "What do you seek, and how may I assist you?"

Grannie raised an eyebrow in my direction, but remained silent. I sighed. I preferred to leave the explaining to her, but obviously she'd decided this was my tale to tell.

"Very well," I said, and gave my full attention to the laird of the O'Connors. "I'm engaged to Mrs. O'Toole's grandson, Jedidiah Kendrick. We came to Ireland so that Grannie could meet me before we married. Once here, we discovered that Grannie is a seer, like Jed and myself. However, we found Grannie to be much more knowledgeable, so we set out to learn what we could from her before we returned home to the United States, to our home in Colorado."

I told Laird Angus everything I could, every detail of how Jed had been taken and how I'd escaped. The telling was hard. During the weeks Grannie and I had searched for answers, I'd tried not to think about that day, tried not to remember exactly how I'd failed Jed. Instead, I'd concentrated on finding a solution. But it had all been in vain.

Grannie and I avoided speaking of the future. I lived in her house and we worked side by side searching the records for clues, but I knew in my heart I couldn't stay in Ireland forever. Yet, I couldn't imagine returning to Colorado without Jed. Frankly, I couldn't imagine living without Jed. If I left the Old Country without him, what point would there be for my existence?

And so I stayed, would continue to stay, until I found Jed or Grannie sent me away.

As I finished my tale, Laird Angus took my hands in his and stroked them with his thumbs. Compassion filled his gaze as he said, "Ah, lassie, 'tis sorry I am to hear of your woes, but the chances of you regaining your love are very slim."

Tears filled my eyes, but I blinked them back. "I know," I whispered. "Actually, they're about gone since even Grannie can't decipher these final journals."

"I can see you're a steadfast lass," he said, releasing my hands, "but have you courage as well as loyalty?"

I swiped at my eyes to clear the tears and met his gaze. "I've dealt with terror since my earliest memories, and did it on my own until Jed found me. We were in our teens by then. Together he and I fought the terrors, the Fae...and won. Until we came here." I lowered my eyes and studied the delicate opal ring Jed had given me when we agreed to marry. "There are so many more Fae here, and we had so very much to learn. I guess we failed."

Laird Angus lifted my chin with his index finger until my eyes met his. "I may know a way," he said, "but you'll have to act alone, and it will require more courage than most seers possess. I'll not fault you if you choose to leave this place with the tale untold."

My heart leaped. My pulse thundered so hard I could barely hear past its whooshing against my eardrums. "Y...you...you know how get Jed back? Tell me," I demanded. "Tell me now!"

"Oh, Laird!" Grannie said, and she looked so white I worried she might faint.

The big man laughed. "Call me Angus," he said. "We've no need for formalities between us. We're seers all, with much work to be done."

The plan was simple to tell, yet seemed impossible to execute.

As Angus explained, all I had to do was pull Jed out of line as the fairy troop processed along a ley line during a full moon...and hold him until he recognized me.

"You can see them, so you can do it," Angus assured me.

"It sounds too easy," I said, frowning. "What's the catch?"

His eyes darted around the room as he looked for something to focus on that wasn't me. "The catch, as you say, is that you must hold him no matter what the fairies do. No matter what spell they throw at you." He sighed and met my gaze. "Their own laws dictate that they cannot harm you during the rescue attempt, but if you despair, if you lose hold of him for even an instant, both of you will be lost beyond recovery."

"Beyond recovery?" Grannie said, and I heard the fear and tension in her voice. "What does that even mean?"

"Exactly what it says, Maeve," Angus answered. "Only one attempt is permitted for Jed, and since Artie will be attempting to steal from the Fae, no attempts will be tolerated on her behalf. Either they both come home, or neither does."

I nodded, then made eye contact with each in turn. "That suits me fine. If I can't save Jed, I've no reason to go on."

Angus nodded, a fierce glare in his eyes. Grannie's eyes brimmed with tears, but she bit her lip and made no objection.

CHAPTER 7

Halloween, or Samhain as the Celts called it, brought the next full moon.

Grannie and Angus prepared for the attempted rescue by creating a shield bracelet for me and embedding it with every protective sigil and ward they could discover. Angus also took my engagement ring and sealed it with a spell to enhance the love it represented.

"We can't go with you," he explained, "can't help you with this task, but we can see to it you carry as much positive energy with you as is physically possible."

I spent my preparation time writing down everything I could remember of the time Jed and I had spent together. From our first meeting in social studies on our first day of high school, through every battle with every terror we'd ever vanquished, right down to the way he'd kissed me before we walked to Puck's Castle on that fateful day. Those memories strengthened me. They reminded me of all we'd accomplished, of all we'd become to one another.

Jed was my life and I was his. No matter what, I would hold him. Nothing a fairy or a terror or any other foul thing that walked our earth could do would cause me to abandon my man. Jed was the other half of my soul and I refused to continue to be separated from him.

Halloween morning dawned clear and bright and biting with cold. The time had come. Tonight the moon would be full and the fairy troop that had stolen Jed would process right through the middle of an under-construction mall on the outskirts of Dublin...the one Grannie had shown us early in our visit.

"You're sure it's the same troop?" I asked, wiping damp palms on my well-worn denim jeans. "If he's not there, we'll have to wait for the next full moon."

"I'm certain, Artie," Angus said. "I've had spies out for the last few weeks. Experienced seers who know how to watch without being caught. Jed is with this troop, and except for being completely enthralled, he is whole and well."

I nodded, busying my fingers with binding my long dark hair in a single tight braid. I'd have no need to hide behind my hair this night. "Good. That's good."

"Come, Artie," Grannie called from the kitchen. "Let me fix you a nice dinner. You'll need your strength tonight."

I shook my head, remembered she couldn't see through walls, and called back, "No thank you, Grannie. I'm too nervous to eat. Besides, I'm stronger than I look. I'll be fine."

She hurried in to the front room a few minutes later carrying a tray of steaming mugs. "I thought that might be your attitude," she said with a wan smile. "Here, at least drink this broth. It'll fortify you without weighing you down."

"Good thinking, Maeve," Angus said with an approving nod, accepting his own mug. "Drink up, Artie. It'll be time to leave before you know it."

Angus and Grannie drove me to the construction site, timing it so we arrived just as the moon rose full and bright above the horizon. Grannie hugged me and wished me well, while Angus touched my ring and bracelet. "You're well warded, lassie, and ye've a stout heart. I've no doubt ye'll prevail."

I nodded and spoke past the lump in my throat. "We'll see you soon. Both of us." I licked lips that felt more like sandpaper than flesh. "But, if anything goes wrong, you have our story. Add it to your journal, please."

"There'll be no need, at least not until you've added another fifty years' worth of tales."

A quick grin and I left them to hide myself behind a pallet of bricks that was stacked beside the shining ley line. All that remained to be done was to wait for my love, my life, my Jed.

The moon floated just above the horizon, so round and full it seemed to fill the sky. A shining white orb starred with mars and craters against a velvet black sky studded with pinpricks of light. Surely such beauty boded well for Jed's rescue.

A soft jingle of bells wafted across the silent night. They were coming.

I hunkered low in a sprinter's crouch, one eye on the ley line, ready to spring the moment I saw him. My pulse raced, my vision wavered, my ears rang with nerves.

The first fairy appeared. An ageless female in a flowing green gown holding aloft a branch of silver leaves threaded with tiny golden bells. Behind her came a tall raven-haired male garbed all in deep blue carrying a purple banner trimmed in golden threads. Next came a throng of fair folk, easily thirty or forty individuals of all species, including a few Grannie hadn't described. Another bannerman and bell-bearer brought up the rear.

He wasn't there! Jed wasn't part of the procession!

How could we have been so wrong? What could I do now?

I closed my eyes against a suffocating wave of despair. And then I heard the clip-clop of horses' hooves on the moon-drenched ground.

My eyes flew open and I beheld a snow white unicorn following the final bell-bearer. The ethereal creature had appeared as if out of thin air, and sitting sideways upon his back was the most beautiful lady I could ever have imagined. The female was dressed in gossamer fabrics, like moonbeams on an icy lake, in shimmering shades of palest blue, rose-petal pink and tender green. Her face and form were perfectly proportioned, an alabaster complexion framed emerald green eyes and her hair had the shade and shine of molten gold.

Surely this must be the fairy queen the pookah had spoken of, I couldn't imagine her as anything else.

My heart leapt and my soul stilled almost before I realized what I had seen. Jed walked beside the queen's horse, his hand resting lightly on her slipper clad foot, his eyes glazed and unaware.

My moment had arrived.

I sprinted from my hiding place, knocking Jedidiah to the ground. Encircling his left wrist with my right hand, I threw my left arm around his neck and clung to him like a burr.

Jed spoke not a word, but lay like a mannequin on the ground beneath me. Could it be this easy? Could I have won already?

Almost I loosened my grip, but the ring on my left hand and bracelet on my right flared to life and I felt their protective sigils glow.

No, I hadn't won. I'd merely surprised my enemy. The battle had yet to be engaged.

The fairy queen called out in ringing tones more beautiful than I could describe. The troop stopped. All eyes focused on me...and Jed.

Unpronounceable, unknowable words tumbled from the queen's lips...and my reality transformed.

I no longer held Jed. Instead I clung to the head of a giant snake that raised itself...and me...into the sky. I closed my eyes and chanted a mantra to the man I knew I held though the evidence of my senses told me otherwise. "You are Jedidiah Kendrick and I am Artemis Woodward. I love you and you love me. Come back to me, Jed!"

The weaving head faltered, the massive jaw closed, and a huge forked tongue darted out, tasting my scent upon the air between us.

The fairy queen spoke again, commandment in every unknown syllable.

The snake shifted and I no longer clung to smooth scales. Now my left arm wrapped the coarsely furred neck of a Bengal tiger, while my right hand fought to hold its claws from my flesh. Golden eyes stared at the pulse in my naked throat and knife-sharp teeth gleamed in its open mouth.

I closed my eyes and held on still more tightly. No matter what form the fairy queen forced upon him, I refused to release my Jed. If she made him kill me, so be it. I'd rather die than fail him again.

Fear clogged my throat, but I opened my eyes, stared straight into his, and screamed, "You are Jedidiah Kendrick and I am Artemis Woodward. I love you and you love me. Come back to me, Jed!"

The tiger's claws relaxed and something flickered behind his eyes.

The fairy queen spoke again, her words strident and somehow desperate.

Jed writhed and bucked beneath my hands, but I refused to release him. When the transformation was complete, I found myself eye to eye with the biggest bird I'd ever seen. My left arm encircled his neck, pulling a razor sharp beak too close to my face, while my right hand held tight to the pinion of his left wing.

Intelligence flashed behind his eyes as he cocked his great head and blinked a nictitating membrane. I smiled, with more courage than I felt, and repeated, for the third time, "You are Jedidiah Kendrick and I am Artemis Woodward. I love you and you love me. Come back to me, Jed!"

He lowered his feathered head, touching my forehead with his own.

"I love you, Jed Kendrick," I whispered, "and I will never let you go."

The fairy queen spoke again, but this time her voice held defeat. The great bird that had been Jed deflated and morphed and became...Jedidiah Kendrick, a mortal man with his two feet planted firmly on the ground.

Jed stared into my eyes from where we stood, my right hand in his left, my left arm flung around his neck. He raised his right hand and caught the tear sliding down my cheek on his index finger. "I see you, Artemis Woodward. I know you. You are the love of my life."

Neither of us even glanced up when the fairy queen spoke. We had eyes only for each other.

"Congratulations, mortal female," she said, her voice distant and cool. "By the terms of our law you have won back my thrall. He is free from this troop, but I warn you, do not linger on these shores for all of my other troops will be anxious to avenge this slight. I now know both of your names and I do *not* wish you well."

Jed and I held each other without speaking until the troop had disappeared and Grannie and Angus ran to embrace us.

EPILOGUE

Thanksgiving is a uniquely American holiday and Jed and I celebrated it in Colorado with our families...by pledging our lives to each other. Since our ordeal in Ireland had given us so much to be thankful for, we decided Thanksgiving was the perfect day for our wedding.

Grannie O'Toole arrived the day before, accompanied by Angus O'Connor. Jed was honored beyond words that the head of the O'Connor clan would come all the way to America just to attend our wedding.

I'd explained how Angus had been instrumental in Jed's rescue, but my love remained vague about the weeks of his captivity. Everything I told him of that time seemed to slip from his mind as soon as I said it, but I didn't mind. In fact, I envied him his forgetfulness. If I could erase the memory of my despair and grief, I'd do it gladly, except that it would also erase my knowledge of Grannie's steadfast support and how hard Angus had worked to help me bring Jed home.

The ceremony itself was a small affair. Jed and I exchanged our vows in the little neighborhood park where we'd first become a team. I wore a clean-lined white velvet dress, full length and long-sleeved in deference to the late November chill, and carried a small bouquet of gold asters and wine-red chrysanthemums. Jed looked regal in a black tux and a cummerbund, that latter in a deep gold shade that matched his aster boutonniere. Reverend Kendrick, Jed's father, officiated, and our vows were witnessed by Jed's mother, my parents, and Grannie and Angus.

Reverend Kendrick's face fairly glowed as he recited the age-old words, "Jedidiah Amos Kendrick, do you take Artemis Lucia Woodward to be your wedded wife, to love, protect, and cherish, to have and to hold from this day until the end of time?"

A slow smile spread across Jed's face, lighting his eyes and making him even more handsome than usual. He squeezed my hands. "I certainly do."

His father turned his gaze on me. "And do you, Artemis Lucia Woodward, take Jedidiah Amos Kendrick to be your wedded husband, to love, protect, and cherish, to have and to hold from this day until the end of time?"

The memory of those moments when the fairy queen had transformed my love from one deadly form to the next flitted through my mind. I had held him then, I would hold him forever.

"I do," I said without a single doubt.

Jed pulled me into his embrace and our lips met in a kiss that caused everything around us to fade into the background. I'm sure his father intoned the final words of the ceremony, but I didn't hear them. I didn't need to.

I was Jed's and he was mine...and there wasn't a terror or a fairy in sight.

What could be more perfect?

ABOUT THE AUTHOR

Deb Logan specializes in tales for the young – and the young at heart! Author of the popular Dani Erickson series, Deb loves the unknown, whether it's the lure of space or earthbound mythology. She writes about demon hunters, thunderbirds, and everyday life on a space station for children, teens, and anyone who enjoys young adult fiction. Her work has been published in multiple volumes of Fiction River, as well as in *2017 Young Explorer's Adventure Guide, Feyland Tales, Volume 1,* and other popular anthologies.

Find out more about Deb at:
deblogan.wordpress.com

facebook.com/deb.logan.750

goodreads.com/deb_logan

bookbub.com/authors/deb-logan

VENOM

BRENDA CARRE

No one knew how long the old woman had lived in the Gothic mansion with the wrap-around porch that everyone could see sitting on the hill just after you drove up the narrow asphalt road out of Matsqui. It was old—silvered by wind and rain and lack of care and it looked like the perfect place to haunt if there were such things as ghosts. Marietta didn't believe in ghosts—well at least not for five years anyway. Sure as shooting if there were ghosts, her stupid sister would have come back to haunt her, which she had not.

Marietta knew the old woman in the old house was alive. Deliveries were made. Food got eaten, but nobody had seen hide-nor-hair of her for years. It was intriguing and weird and frustratingly there were no records to research. A classmate's smelly old pipe-smoking Gramps had said that woman had been old and white-haired back before WWII started. Nonsense of course. Nobody could be that old. If the old woman had been in her sixties or seventies in the 1930's, she'd have to be over a hundred by now.

Marietta saw the house every day from the yellow bus windows on her way to Willowdale Primary. She and Laura invented stories about it. All the kids did. Marietta invented that a witch lived there who would boil and eat kids by peeling off their skins first and making shoes from the leather. Sitting beside her on the cracked vinyl seats Laura invented that maybe a good fairy lived there who was eating all the bad thoughts of kids like Marietta.

Of course Laura had to make a poke at Marietta. It was Laura's way.

Laura had ways of inventing things in that sweet reedy little voice of hers that made Marietta look bad and worse than bad. Marietta's 'big' sister was always being held up to her as the one to emulate. Laura was the one who got sent out for piano lessons no matter how expensive they were. Laura was the one who got the good grades and Laura was the one everyone praised. Laura, Laura, Laura. But until Laura's "tragic" death in the spring of 1969 Marietta never went through a day without wanting to pull out all of Laura's fabulously wavy, Breck Girl strawberry-blonde hair.

Well now Laura was gone, and those flowing princess tresses of hers were gone, thanks to hospitals with good soft pillows. Marietta wasn't sorry she'd used one of those pillows on her sister. Laura was dying anyway, that was clear. Marietta had just helped her along a bit.

After Laura died of cancer—well, that's what the report said, anyway—Marietta kept right on inventing stories about the mysterious ancient woman in the old house. The day her sister was buried she finally got to see the old house up close. Even as Father McInroy said his religious dump at the grave, under a suitably grey sky and the air smelling of the coming rain, Marietta began to plan how to get back somehow and scout around the old house, maybe peer into dusty windows and see something spidery scuttling around. From here she could actually walk between the rows of Lombardy poplars and toppled ancient gravestones and down a slope overgrown with Himalayan blackberry canes. The task would be to forge a trail somehow through those nasty rows of wicked thorns. She'd have to bring along some skookum clippers in a bag of some sort after getting the eight miles here to and from the trailer court she lived in.

She'd do it somehow. At least now she had an excuse. "Visiting my sister's grave" sounded touching and believable.

"Well, you get to see it now every day you rot here," she said under her breath to Laura as they dropped the coffin into a deep red-grey hole that smelled like squashed caterpillars and musty leaves. She was glad to drop the sticky dirt down onto the white-draped coffin. Marietta's mom wept buckets, comforted by a crowd of women with fashionable flip hair and shortie coats over their black mini-dresses—women who had until that day treated Marietta's mom like trailer dirt. Her mom was too stupid to see those women were sad about Laura and that in the future it wouldn't change a thing. Marietta saw through them all and she swore that even so much as she hated her mom, she'd get even with those women.

Those women were the ones who'd planted the idea in her mother's mind that she should get rid of all Laura's stuff. Never mind she also got rid of Marietta's stuff (her favorite books and the doll she'd made herself) as if Marietta had died too. It was all gone the day after Laura's funeral as if cleaning their end of the trailer made a difference. Now there was nothing but a bed, an empty dresser, a whole bunch of rage, and a pot of overcooked mac-and-cheese turning to cement on the dirty stovetop.

Marietta's mom even had Father McInroy come by and bless their trailer with holy water as if he was exorcising some demon. His sideways comment (while scratching his paunch) that Marietta should now "strive to be the angel Laura had been," made her want to use a pillow on him.

Marietta's teeth ached from clenching them on what she really wanted to say to that fat ass, but she went still and she planned. Some day she was going to find some door to the rage she felt and shove her mother and smelly Father McInroy through it. She couldn't use the pillow thing again but she could wait. Say anything you want about Marietta Cattermole, but Marietta had patience.

She went to the school library and the smaller one in Matsqui and tried to research poisons. Nothing presented as useful. Nothing surfaced either about the decaying woman in the decaying mansion on the hill. In the fall of 1970, Marietta went into eighth grade at Abbotsford junior high. School was far enough away that most of those kids had never heard of Laura and most of them were so intent on making their way in eighth grade that Marietta could coast beneath the radar. She still went by the old house in the rattly yellow Bluebird bus that chunked and sputtered its way up the hill.

She noted that delivery vehicles drove up a shrouded driveway that started at the bottom of the hill, but she refused absolutely to consider this as a way in. Marietta didn't know what day deliveries were made up there and she refused to risk the chance of being seen. No, this was the Fortress Impregnable and she would do it her way or not at all. Instead she took some time to make friends with Kim the bus driver. Marietta remembered enough about Laura's sickly-sweet ways and how their mom was swayed by them, that she got on Kim's good side by giving her a toy for her little girl, bought with lunch money Marietta had nicked from kids' lockers. Marietta didn't nick money often enough to get caught, but by May 1971 she had enough to buy a good pair of clippers at Beezmeyer's Hardware.

Then she wove her story of woe to Kim about how sad she was that her sister was gone and how she never got enough chance to visit Laura's poor solitary grave because her mom was working a day shift at Mission City DQ and an evening shift at the Legion Bar. True all of it, except for Marietta needing the mourn over Laura's grave.

Once a week Marietta got Kim to let her off at the side of the road headed up to the graveyard, clippers stowed under her books in her book bag. She hitched a ride home. She wasn't afraid that the story might get back to her mom. Visting Laura's grave was a waterproof lie because she *was* visiting Laura's grave. She always spent time planting blackberry cuttings over Laura's grave in hopes one day those cuttings would grow up into a massive blackberry forest that nobody could get through, and her mom's hands would bleed as she tried to clip her way through to find her precious Laura.

She always spent an hour after clipping an intricate path through the canes so she could reach the house. Marietta felt as if she was digging deeper and deeper into her own needs and reaching the heart of the mystery. Now a week before school was due to let out for the summer, Marietta broke through to the old mansion's back wilderness.

The big house had rotting gingerbread trim and tall, four-over-four windows, all warped. Some high up were broken. There was even a gray, old Desoto in the weedy circular drive. Its curved windshield and long rounded hood were dotted with decomposed leaves. It was dirty and age spotted like something from the Bride of Frankenstein. The whole place reminded Marietta of a cut that goes all slimy but never heals. Oozilly fascinating but sore.

She snuck her way through a tangle of un-mowed grass to the back door of the huge spindle-post porch so excited she could hardly breathe. Everybody knew that The Bright River in Abbotsford delivered a hot expensive meal up the round driveway twice a week. Everybody knew that a sack of groceries went into the dark covered porch with its mossy roof, and the milkman came. There had to be something worth something inside. The woman might be a ditsy old recluse but she must have money—maybe even riches stowed away in crazy places.

The mansion was even more impressive and inspiring close up. The porch's floor squeaked and snapped under her grubby high-tops and she worried briefly about weak boards, but thankfully they held. Around her was a swishing noise of the wind in a great tall fir tree lording over the back jungle. It sounded and felt a lot like somebody breathing down the collar of the windbreaker Marietta had found on top of a box at the Mission Dump.

Not a ghost though, no matter where she was standing.

Marietta dug into her plaid skirt pocket for the letter she'd written on the back of an algebra worksheet marked and passed (barely) by her math teacher, Mr. Sycamore. It reeked of eighth grade equations, but it would be just the right touch of proof that she wasn't some robber but just an innocent teen.

To finish the deal, Marietta had rubbed out her own name and put in Laura's. Say anything you want about Marietta, but say she comes prepared. She rapped hard on the door more than once and stuck her letter through the rusty slot. The door was chippy, bleached raw in places, and mustard yellow in others. The shutter closed on her finger with a rusty snap.

"Ach!" she yelped, and jammed the finger in her mouth. She'd almost said the 'F' word but that would never do if she was supposed to be Laura. Marietta looked at what the rusty mail slot had done to her finger. A drop of blood welled up and dripped on the blistered porch. Well never say things don't happen for a reason. Her letter had said, "I feel your pain." Up until now that had been a lie.

Pretty funny. Oh well. She guessed a bite was all she was going to get today, but she'd try again next week. She'd find a way. Marietta scuffed at the blood drop on the porch with the toe of her running shoe. Ground it down into the rotting boards. Nobody should guess she'd been here. That was part of the thrill of the hunt...

"Hello?" said a dry old voice behind the door, so breathy and whispery that Marietta hardly heard it over the scrape of her high-top. She heard a rasp of paper clear through the closed door as the old woman picked up her letter. It sounded like rats rustling. Now what?

All of a sudden Marietta realized a surprising worry. Should she pull her clippers out of her bookbag again just in case? Was it possible the old woman might own a gun? Kim had left her off at the graveyard but what would happen if she never got home tonight? Would her mom phone around? Phone the school?

"I'm, ummm, Laura Cattermole, ma'am. I'm so sorry to bother you, but I've come from the student paper at Abbotsford Junior High. Back in '67, our seventh grade class studied the Mission City archives and the 1946 flood. Now I'm in the high school and, well, we're—we're doing a spread on historical personages and I hoped you might consider—well, I know this might be painful for you but I want to do just one good thing before I die. You see I have to go back into hospital soon because of my leukemia—and I wanted to do something good for my school first. I thought maybe you...."

"Oh you poor wee thing!" The door creaked open and a tiny face looked out. Pleasant enough but stitched with wrinkles. The woman was shorter than Marietta by about a head. She didn't look at Marietta. She stared at the remains of Marietta's blood on her doorstep. "Oh, you've cut yourself. That cannot be good. Come! Come in my dear, quickly now. I mustn't go out. It isn't allowed. The house is a mess, but we must see to that."

The old woman's voice was as soft as a whisper, like she was afraid of waking somebody up or something.

Marietta didn't want a fuss but she realized Laura would have accepted the old woman's offer of help, so she nodded. "Oh it's nothing—I don't really need anything. It's only a small scratch." She held out her gouged digit and the old lady took it into soft little fingers. It was like being tickled by a mouse or a bird.

"My letter slot is rusty, alas. This will need Mercurochrome—come in, dear, come in. What did you say your name was—did I hear Laura?"

"Yes. Laura," Marietta lied. She looked around her with interest. It was surprisingly, precisely neat though it was crowded with antique stuff covered in dust. Two scrolly wing chairs faced each other with their tall backs flush to the wall. A table dull with heavy dust stood beside each chair, with an empty Chinese vase set dead center. It smelled like ancient baby powder and tea leaves and emptiness. Marietta sneezed.

"Bless you sweetheart." The old lady said and tapped her way ahead of Marietta, across dusty boards through the broad hall. Marietta took note of the silver horse-head on the black wood cane the old woman was using to support herself. That must be worth a lot! The old woman was dressed in a floor length puff-sleeve dress of black that looked Victorian and over this she had on a flowered apron Marietta knew was called a pinafore. Around the old woman's shoulders was a long knitted green shawl that swept the ground behind her and left a track that looked like a slug trail. Marietta stepped along behind her, with enormous interest. This place was a real treasure house!

Straight ahead the grand stairway went up to a darkened landing where it parted right and left into two stairways. Scrolly portraits glared down of ancient men and women with creepy eyes. The light in here was meager, but Marietta saw funnel spider webs in every corner high up close to the painted ceiling. Fat pink-bum cherubs flew across a turquoise sky to converge in a kissing crowd near a scrolly medallion and the dangling lamp—a lamp that held candles.

No electricity! Wow. The ceiling was foggy with dust but Marietta could still see the spiders planting their eggs up there.

Creepy but enjoyably so. This old woman was alone in here and yes, she could easily be one hundred and ten—way too old to climb up on chairs and dust the ceilings and get rid of the spiders scuttling over the cherubs' faces.

Marietta consulted her watch. Four-thirty. If she played things right she could tease a story or two out of the old recluse and get home long before the May twilight fell. On another day she could come back and maybe in time figure out what might be worth nicking in here.

"I've been longing to have a nice sit with a sympathetic soul. Please come in, dear Laura."

The old woman opened a thick door into what looked like a sitting room. The over-stuffed chairs, the curtains, the lampshade and the table cloths were all done up in layers of rose-covered chintz. There was a marble-topped fireplace on one wall and an open doorway to what looked like an ancient kitchen on the other. A third door on the library wall had shelves painted on it and on them were fake books, that looked bound in gold and silver, so the whole door fit right in with the real-leather bound books on the other shelves. This door had a painted knob on it and a painted padlock. The hasp and the padlock looked so real Marietta wished hard she could paint like that.

"Tromp l'oeil" said the old woman seeing her look. "It means 'fool the eye'."

"It's good," said Marietta.

"Isn't it? My brother painted it for me. Alas he's gone now," the old woman added with that wistful old-person sadness Marietta had seen in her friend Vera's smoky old Grampa.

"Did your brother buy you those too?" Marietta asked pointing to the china figurines that seemed to glow in the darkness. They were expensive—even Marietta could see that—some were dancing fauns from Greek myths, one was of a tall crowned prince sitting on a throne like chair not unlike the kingly chair the old lady pointed her to sit in next to the hearth. Some figurines were ruffed Bo Peeps in pink and blue and purple guiding their flocks of little white sheep. There were china fairies by the score and even a black dragon wrapped around a white fountain on the table beside Marietta.

"Let me get you something for that cut. That dragon never bites, I promise, not anymore at least."

The old woman's eyes twinkled as she tapped her way into the kitchen. She returned fast with a tiny bottle of yellow stuff clutched in her hand and another delighted gleam of a smile.

"Oh good. You're still here. Let's get that poor finger fixed up now. My name is Spenser, and yours of course, is Laura."

"Of course. Is that *Miss* Spenser, or Mrs?" said Marietta.

"My first name is Spenser. Spenser was an affectation of my mother's. She liked faeries, you see, and she wanted to name me after the poet."

"What poet?"

"What do they teach you children these days?"

Spenser pulled a pair of ancient gold-rimmed glasses out of her pinafore pocket. She placed them precisely on the bridge of her very narrow nose and peered at Marietta's offered finger. It had already quit bleeding. In fact it didn't really need the purple-yellow stuff but Marietta was happy to let Spenser fawn a little. This close-to the old woman smelled of lavender.

Spenser daubed Marietta's cut with the yellow stuff, tore off a bandage wrapper with trembling old fingers, and applied the gauze part to the meager spot: a strangely lulling experience that Marietta put down to the heat of the hearth beside her and the comfort of the kingly chair she was sitting in.

"I can see you need a bit of history, my dear. Back in the 1500's Edmund Spenser wrote what most believe was an allegory to Queen Elizabeth of England. He called it the Faerie Queene."

"Oh," said Marietta disdainfully. "An old dead guy."

"Old, certainly, but *not* dead. Well, not dead in the way most people think."

"How not dead if he lived in the 1500's?" said Marietta as Spenser settled into the other kingly chair next to the faerie king figurine. Spenser patted the little king's head like he was an old friend. "How fortunate I am to find a listening ear after such a very long time, my dear, and you with your lovely friends on the school paper to report back to on this. So few have believed me when I told them long before the second Great War that there is whole 'nother place where people go when they die. Nobody wanted to hear me tell them so though. Not at a time when so many grieved the loss of their loved ones and wanted to laurel them for their sacrifice."

"You didn't think they were heroic?" said Marietta surprised.

Spenser frowned at Marietta over the top of her gold rims. "Of course they were heroic. What they did went way beyond monuments and where they are now is not in graves. The Norse Eddas come closer to the mark when they talk about warriors going home to Odin.

"We studied mythology just this spring. I liked Ragnarok and I liked the Greek myths too, especially how Diana had her dogs chase down Actaeon," Marietta said and stole a quick glance at her watch. It read four-thirty—still. She put the watch face to her ear and noted it wasn't ticking. Some quick fiddling with the winder fixed the problem though, thank goodness. Her mom wouldn't be happy if she'd broken her watch—not that anything she ever did pleased her mom.

"Well then, if you studied the Greeks and the Norse, you will be clear there are many such places, my dear. One of those is Heaven another is Hell and every variation of both you can think of, but there are so many others all of them reached in a variety of ways. One way is death, but there are so many others beyond the veil, or the person, or the thin space or the portal if you want to think of it that way—oh, aren't you planning to take notes?" said Spenser.

"Oh yes! Of course," said Marietta annoyed she'd not thought to do this earlier. She wanted to look and act professional. Marietta took out the Ticonderoga pencil and the yellow pad of legal paper she'd brought along in her Flintstones book bag as a prop. As she did so, a cold wind blew over her, shivering up her spine in a nasty way. There had to be an old cracked pane behind those cabbage rose curtains on the wall on the way to the kitchen. Something was making them move.

This was creeping Marietta out. They were way too close to Laura's grave. "Might I ask how long you've been here, Ma'am?" she asked needing to change the direction of their discussion.

"Oh just ages, dear," said Spenser whipping off her gold glasses and poking them down in the pinafore pocket along with the bandages and the little yellow bottle.

"This house can't be 'ages' old. It's a Victorian."

"Yes it is, but there was something here before that," Spenser said with a spark of satisfaction. Something tigerish in it and—and even gloating.

Marietta shuddered and worked her way deeper into the comforting plush of the kingly chair. Maybe steer the talk around to where the good stuff was in this house, and get the old bat's agreement for her to come back and "make friends" like she'd done with Kim.

"Well how old are you then?" she asked, annoyed at having to be blunt.

"As old as my eyes and a little older than my teeth."

Spencer grinned like a pleased little kid who'd successfully passed her catechism, with a hint of "I know what you want out of me but I'm going to toy with you awhile."

"But you went through the War?" Marietta persisted.

Spenser's face drooped. "I didn't, no. My brother did though. I made a terrible mistake back then and I have paid for it ever since. I never saw him again after that."

"I'm sorry for your loss," Marietta said because Laura would have done.

"Not my loss. He lost me." Spenser's faded eyes sparked now as if this "loss," whatever it was, had turned her into a fighter. Into a person a lot like Marietta considered herself to be. There was something now in the way Spenser sat—erect like a cat tensed to pounce —that spoke of how it must have been for her long ago when she was Marietta's age.

Marietta felt kindred to Spenser now as she'd never felt for anybody else. She sensed that what she needed from the old woman lay here in the mystery of Spenser's brother, and not in Spenser's age or the age of the house or the cost of all the antiques around them. This was the heart of "I feel your pain."

"Tell me about your loss," she said and put pencil to paper.

Spenser smiled. One of those "Ah" smiles that told Marietta that she'd said the exact right thing. "Do you really, really want to know, Laura? It's a long story?"

"Yes, Ma'am, I really do want to know."

Marietta looked at her watch again. It was now a quarter to five. Still time. She tried to keep the hungry want that was rising in her breast from making it onto her face.

Spenser tucked her spiderwebby shawl closer around her against the now definite chill in the room. "There are doors all through this world of yours that lead to other worlds. They are called thin spaces, and when you die however many years from now, my darling, you will go through one."

Spenser patted the little king on the head again and now Marietta saw how shiny his small silver crown was from constant rubbing. "My brother never fought in the last war, or the Great War before it, or the Crimean One before it. But he has fought many a time in the Fey Wars and come out unscathed."

"The...*Fey* Wars?" squeaked Marietta.

Spenser pointed toward the "fool the eye" bookshelf that was pretending it was a door. "Through there lie the land of Faerie and my brother is one of the kings..."

"Nooo!" said Marietta. This was just too much. It wasn't fair for Laura to be right. This had to be a joke, a crazy old woman's joke. This Spenser had to be dottier than a magic mushroom, and farther out than Timothy Leary!

"It's true my dear. My brother exiled me here long ago for causing the terrible destruction of the woman he loved. He dragged me through that door and he set a padlock on it that I can't open. He put wards on the doors and the porch so I can't cross through. I've been trapped in this house for nearly two centuries long enough to regret my ways. I want to go home, Laura, and make amends for the unspeakable pain I caused my dear brother. Will you help me, my dear?"

Spenser's soft old voice quavered at the end.

Marietta gaped at her. "Help you?"

"Yes, by opening that door for me. I can pay you well. I will pay you well, on the life of my brother I promise you." Spenser looked diminished now and tired and so very sad. All the fight in her was gone.

"Why me?" said Marietta.

"Because it was you who marked my porch with blood and venom. Venom can be useful in so many ways. You have told me a lie —oh don't worry my dear. Don't you worry that I've caught you out. I much prefer your guile; it shows a clever mind. I don't need to know your name or why you wanted me not to know it. The important thing is, I know you."

Marietta sighed.

"OK, well, it's my sister Laura who died from leukemia and I wanted to remember her by..."

"Stop! You need not lie to me. I understand you, really I do. I know what it is to lose and before you came I never found anybody who might understand my need to get home so perfectly. Can you imagine how hard it is to go from child to old woman all alone because of something you did? No I see not. I want to go home, my dear, and in return for helping me everything here is yours."

"Mine?"

Marietta couldn't believe her ears. Here was a mansion filled with riches. This was the answer to her deepest wishes. If she helped Spenser she could go to school and lord it over everyone—but that meant believing that Laura had been right and *that* reeked. On the other hand, if there was no secret faerie realm beyond that fake door it would mean she never needed to believe in Laura ever again. Win—win.

"What's the catch?" she said.

"None, absolutely." Spenser struggled up out of her kingly chair with a gasp of pain. She picked up the little figurine and with that in one hand and her cane in the other she tapped over to Marietta and set the little king down next to the dragon. "This is him. My brother, Chalcedony. He left me this likeness to taunt me with. I give it to you now. He's handsome yes?"

He was—sharp-jawed, dark haired and proud. If Marietta could actually help Spenser through that fake door, she'd be taking Chalcedony home with her. She'd have to hide him from mom but so what?

"Ok, so what do I do?"

"Go to the door. Touch the painted lock. That's it."

And that was it. The door opened. Marietta stood on the threshold. The cottage room in front of her was like a painting with rough beams spanning the very low ceiling and a wide window with a tufted brocaded window-seat no more than a dozen good paces across the stone floor. The view out that window took Marietta's breath away: a jagged tooth of a mountain. An aqua lake with an island in it, and a castle on that island that would need a boat to get to it or somebody or something that could fly. The castle was more tooth than castle and as much of a crag as the mountain behind it. Somewhere out of sight someone—a woman—was singing a nursery rhyme.

"By-lo baby bunting, daddy's gone a-hunting, to get a little rabbit skin to wrap my little baby in..." The voice was deep for a woman's and very melodious. The love Marietta could hear in that voice gave her heart a deep twist. Oh, to be loved like that...

Ah, but this *was* Faerie. No wonder Spenser longed for this world just beyond her grasp. What if she, Marietta, were just to step into it? Who would ever care in her own world if she vanished forever into Faerie—in fact, what did she really owe Spenser? What if she just stepped through and left the old woman behind?

Just then the singing woman came into view. She wore a high-waisted sky blue dress with enough material below that waist to cover a king-size bed. The dress had slashed sleeves and a high gold collar. She looked the perfect serene and perfect-faced Madonna. Her arms were filled with a downy blanket. Marietta knew this held a baby from the gurgles of delight coming out of its folds and the chubby fist waving in the air.

The woman started and looked at Marietta.

"Ah!" she said, and her lovely face lit up. "Welcome back, Your Highness. We have waited here a year and a day for you. You look very well."

"Thank you!" said Marietta preparing to take her first step into Faerie. She didn't think of why there should be something called the

Fey Wars. She knew bad things can happen to good people and nothing comes right in the end and good things can happen to bad people and things do work out. She was just in the middle of that very first step when she felt the gentle touch of hands on her shoulders from behind. There came a flash of white light and a dizzying, stomach-turning feeling of the world going upside down and inside out. For an instant Marietta felt as if she occupied two bodies, as Spenser walked right through her and into Faerie.

It hurt Marietta as if her skin had been ripped off.

How could she be staring now at her very own back? A girl of thirteen walking fast away from her. A girl with long ditch-water colored braids, a windbreaker with Mission High written in letters across the back. She was wearing a plaid box-pleated Wallace tartan skirt, ugly panty-hose that bulged at the knee and dirty Keds high-tops. Then everything faded and Marietta found herself standing in front of the fake "fool-the-eye" shelves and she was locked out—not only from Faerie but from her own young body.

Marietta was now inhabiting Spenser's aged body, standing in Spenser's house, one quivering age-spotted hand on Spenser's supporting cane, and oh! How her joints and her back ached!

Marietta shrieked and the terrified noise echoed through the empty lonely vault of the dusty, silent Victorian. She was locked out, not just from Faerie but from her own world. Deliveries would come as they always had. Life would pass her by and she would be the mysterious woman on the hill with no new views from her upper windows but the road from Matsqui to Abbotsford, and in the back, the eternal graveyard where Laura lay.

She managed to get back and fall into the comforting kingly chair she'd sat in as a young girl. No comfort now. The fire had died in the grate and Marietta pulled the long crocheted shawl tighter around her bony shoulders. Residual memories of the woman who had once occupied this body revealed to Marietta everything that Spenser had done to get her exiled here. It had been a whole lot worse than what Marietta had done to Laura. Jealousy for her brother's love had moved Spenser to throw Chalcedony's lover into the cold vault where demons live. No chance of survival there, no matter Spenser's talk of life after life.

Hot tears of anger and despair tracked their way down Marietta's wrinkled cheeks.

Would Spenser change now she'd wormed her way back into Faerie? No.

Marietta cried for a good long time until she felt used up, which wasn't long in this old body.

After that, in the quiet after tears she started to think again.

"Venom is useful in so many ways. I know how to be patient and I know how to get even." Marietta whispered to the silent house. "I'll get there one day, no matter what I have to do to get into Faerie. I only have to wait for another angry venomous teen, but it won't take as long for me to do that as it took the old witch. I know things about my world outside that she didn't know, or only learned from the newspapers in her grocery boxes."

Marietta patted the silver crown of the small king Chalcedony. She settled back in the kingly chair and dried her tears with a corner of her pinny. There was much to do now. She'd open the blinds. She'd dust the panes. She'd stroke young Chalcedony's crown until the day she could meet him in person. There was sun behind those ugly curtains and she was going to find it.

But first, she was going to enjoy being rich. She was going to build up a decent fire in the grate beside her and take a nap.

ABOUT THE AUTHOR

Brenda Carre writes long and short fiction with a dark, mythic twist. Her short fiction has appeared in the Magazine of Fantasy and Science Fiction, Pulphouse Magazine, and Fiction River, to mention a few. Her indomitable character 'Gret' was the cover story in Pulp Literature Magazine's issue 15. She is currently working on a big book mythic/epic fantasy series she calls: 'Lara Croft meets a Wizard-of-Earthsea in the Pacific Northwest'. She also writes spicy romance under the name Tess Cornwall. Brenda is a visual artist and educator, and teaches a workshop on mapping through story.

Find out more about Brenda at:
brendacarre.com

facebook.com/carrtell

twitter.com/brenda_carre

goodreads.com/Brenda_Carre

bookbub.com/authors/brenda-carre

ALONG THESE LINES

REI ROSENQUIST

The train hissed and grumbled along the track, screaming around the sharper turns. The sound was grating, and yet oddly comforting, because the sound was the sound of motion. Movement. Change. The air was stale, though, unventilated and over-ripe with the stench of bodies who'd long since departed. Out the window, the train passed through a great black stone arch that read "World's End," and entered a long dark tunnel. Koko sat back against the stiff bench seat and let out a slow breath, trying not to choke on the stinking, dry air.

The train came out of the tunnel with a blinding flash of light. Koko leaned against the grimy window, flat nose to cool glass. Outside, the sky turned from the smoggy grey-white to a bruised green-blue, powdered with fat cumulonimbus clouds that shimmered with rainbows despite the lack of sunshine.

"Shrine Town," the locals once called this stretch of railway, since it'd once been lined with thousands of shrines for thousands of reasons. Now, this stretch of land was a graveyard to shrines and temples of old, to towers of a city gone. Blown away and burned to ash, it was. Only the ghosts and bones left to tell the tale.

Koko liked to think of this place as the "Haunted Forests" instead. More poetic that way. As if something so ugly and laid to waste could be beautiful instead of a reminder of tragedies past.

That was Koko's hope today: that broken things could be redeemed.

A dirt-caked hand lifted a tangled pile of metallic gears, rubber tubes, and shredded wires. Once a good scavenger, Koko had put the little AI doll together by hand from a self-made design, then cobbled the body together from scraps lying around the old shipping yard where Shacho and Koko lived together.

Nowadays, Koko didn't so much find and build things as wait for things to change. And their wasteland home wasn't a shipping yard anymore, because there were no shipments coming in or out. Nowhere to ship from and nowhere to ship to. After the wars ended, goods stopped coming into the burned-out city, and everything turned into trash. So, Koko built the doll out of found junk because ze liked projects like that: challenges of turning the useless into cleverness.

At least that's what Shacho used to say. Back when Shacho had been Koko's most trusted friend. Back when the two of them used to walk the shrine roads together. Koko would comment on the weeping willow branches while Shacho replaced the incense and candles. It had been a quiet and safe ritual, something that gave Koko hope even if ze couldn't explain why.

Nowadays, even saying that Shacho and Koko lived together was a stretch. They survived one another, that was it.

Today, Koko had ducked out after Shacho's relentless shouting got too intense. Only, instead of circling the yard and heading back in to grumbles and avoided eyes, Koko had decided to scoop up the broken doll off the stoop and go seek parts to repair the tangled mess. It was a distraction, more than anything useful. Fixing little things, to avoid the big things that couldn't be set right.

So far, it was working. The train had brought Koko back to the city of old, and Koko was even distracted enough to remember something kind Shacho had once said. That was good. A huge step forward. Even if that gentle version of Shacho was gone for good.

Koko pulled at a few of the wires and coiled them around the doll's twisted left arm for safe keeping. The small, heart-shaped head was built from two pieces of broken ceramic laid flat against the bent-in aluminum chest. The neck was a mangled mess of blue string and black wires. Koko gingerly laid the two tiny, six-fingered, hand-like appendages on the belly like the doll was praying for help.

"We're almost there," Koko whispered, patting the doll's limp head gingerly with a single finger. Wherever "there" was. End of the line, Koko decided on a whim. Demachiyanagi, the weeping willow neighborhood. Why not? There, Koko could see the remains of the old shrine road and try to relive some happier moment in some brighter life. Maybe ze could even find some pretty broken ceramic pieces to utilize for repairs.

Koko cradled the doll as if it had just agreed with this plan.

The doll had hit critical fail on a couple of stairs yesterday after a test-run of a new sensory upload. Koko had been sure the chip was ready, but it turned out mean-version Shacho had been right. There was something missing. It'd managed two steps with success, then hit a clump of rocks, slipped, and crashed the rest of the ten flights down to the ground.

Shacho's caustic laughter still stung in both Koko's ears, burning red hot. Part of the unbearable bad as of late. The tension, thick as smog, between Koko and Shacho, zer only companion in a world devoid of life.

"Tsugi wa Kyoto desu," the overhead speaker said in a garbled voice.

The train was wrong, though. Kyoto Station no longer existed. Even still, the train stopped as though the platform was there. Doors opened to a dirt field, and a blast of arid acidic wind blustered into the train car before the doors slid shut again with a grumbling clank.

Only two more stops and Koko would be there.

At the supposed home of the Magician.

Koko knew Shacho's fairy tale. The story of how the Magician had come out of nowhere in an archway near the old shrine road. How this magical being had given zem a spell that would stop the hydrogen bomb and end the wars. Only, none of that was real. It was a story Shacho told on good days. The story ze told on bad days, however, was too depressing to recall right now. Koko pushed the story aside and looked out the window. The bad memories slipped away like the landscape.

A sigh of relief.

Today, Koko was getting good at avoiding unpleasant things. So why not add "disbelief in magic" to the things Koko chose to forget? Maybe ze could wander around where the weeping willow trees used to grow and find the Magician, alive and in the flesh. The Magician could fix this broken doll. And then Koko would finally be able to ask zer biggest question of all. The one Shacho bluntly refused to talk about. The one that kept Koko up at night. The one that could change everything.

"Why are we still alive?" Koko said aloud to the recording of the train's clean, polite voice as it announced the next station that was also no more.

"Tobira ga shimarimasu," the train said in response.

"That's right. That's what Shacho says too," Koko replied, cradling the little broken thing and translating the speaker's words easily. "*All the doors are closing. Or rather, they're already closed.* That's why I'm going to find the Magician. I've got to try to make things better any way I can."

It was a day of pretending difficult things don't exist, Koko reminded zemself silently. A perfect day to make a change.

"Let's go," ze said aloud to nobody.

The train slid noisily down the track, rattling toward Demachiyanagi. Koko leaned a head against the window, smearing it with a greasy forehead. The ruined scenery slipped by, peppered with the bright vermillion red-orange of the past. A color that was supposed to keep the bad away. Little good it'd done as of late.

Up ahead, the river rose on the left side of the train, a dry and cracked silt relic of another time. Then the train went underground, dropping into the unknown dark. Koko clutched the handrail, suddenly realizing the track might no longer go all the way through to the station. It had been how long since they'd come out here together, Koko and Shacho? A lifetime ago. Eras back.

The train hissed to a slowing stop as the cracked and dirty platform rose up out of the looming blackness.

"Shu-ten no Demachiyanagi desu," the train announced in a glitchy gurgle, as if the recording had gotten corrupted. No shock. Everything was broken about this world. The recording had probably gotten messed up when the first of the firestorms came. The ones that turned all of Japan into an ash hole. It was amazing the train remained at all. It was as if the Magician had protected it, but forgot to ensure the full quality of the recording's voice.

It didn't really matter. Why was Koko thinking so much about it?

Another graceful distraction, this one to keep from having to look out the window. To keep from thinking about Shacho's bitter expressions or the unending arguments. To keep from crying at all the pain Koko couldn't undo no matter how hard ze tried.

"Tobira ga hirakimasu," the announcer said, and the doors chugged open on the left side.

Koko couldn't help but translate this phrase too, taking the silly prerecorded announcement as a sudden boon. Yes, a door was opening somewhere, wasn't it?

It had to be.

Koko stood, scooping up the robotic doll and tucking it as carefully as possible in a pocket. A moment after stepping onto the once-yellow platform, now mottled grey with flakes of phlegm-colored paint, the doors lurched closed. A slap of cool air whipped Koko across the cheek. It stung with that fizzy tingle that anything this far outside of the city did. Koko cringed, rubbing the slapped cheek like it was Shacho's palm instead of the wind. As Koko's taped-up sandals stepped over the metal threshold of the station onto black sand, Shacho's laughter came again, biting worse than the breeze.

"You're chasing fairy tales," Shacho always said no matter what Koko got up to.

"What else do you want me to do?" Koko always replied. "Just sit here and wait to die?"

"Why not?" Shacho would say, sitting cross-legged in a supposedly peaceful pose. "That's good enough for me."

Today, Koko had found this game worthless.

"Well, it's not good enough for me anymore," Koko had said as big as possible.

"Then, go. I won't be sorry when you don't come back. One less mouth to feed."

Koko could feel the tears biting at the corners of zer overly dry, tingling eyelids. Shacho always said things like that. "Fine, go die," and "Who cares if you don't come back?" and "We'd each be better off on our own anyway." Less friends, the two of them were survival mates. Or, up until now, they had been. They'd managed to find the same shelter when the first series of bombs went off. And they'd managed to find a food source. And water that didn't eat them up.

After all the hard stuff was solved, they'd stuck together out of habit. Because the world after the firestorms wasn't a world where you went it alone. Anybody was better than alone.

Despite Shacho's threats.

So, why had Koko gone out alone today?

If Koko was really honest? Something felt like it was pulling Koko out here. Something vague but also...big.

"Fairy tales," Shacho would snark.

Koko laughed out loud at zemself, trying to shake the feeling of weight pressing down on zer shoulders. Up the uneven stairs, zer hard, plastic soles scraped against the rickety train platform like fingernails across cardboard. Despite the bad sensation of the air and the hollow sound of Koko's own breath, everything about this station still felt familiar. Which was strange, because as Koko cleared the steps and came out at ground level, not even a single landmark remained. Not a hint of vermillion red or rich black. Not a candle holder or an incense bowl, cracked or not. Not even one weeping willow stump still standing.

Everything here was just as blasted out as Kyoto, or back home at the shipping yard.

Koko frowned. Maybe Shacho really was right, and zer words weren't abuse but...the hard, cold truth.

The two of them were just waiting to die.

Koko turned back to the station entrance and then froze, a jolt of fear sinking down into zer gut. When would the next train would come? Did the trains go both ways from Demachiyanagi? Vital questions Koko hadn't even thought to ask. No doubt Shacho would have. But Shacho wasn't such a fool as to rush out and get on a train headed to the old neighborhood.

Koko would have to sort this out mess out alone.

Ze turned back toward the rubble and, in turning, caught a glint of something in the distance. Something bright against all this muted drab. Something shiny and—dare Koko even think it?—new!

A bolt of hope jabbed into Koko's heart like a needle full of adrenaline. Ze patted the pocket where the doll's remains were tucked away.

"That's it!" Koko said and darted for the opposite side of the station.

What "it" was, Koko had no idea. But it was something different, and that was enough to chase it.

The edges of the doll in zer pocket prickled against the skin of zer leg, like it was trying to communicate something. Ze chalked it up to the weird static sensations this place gave off, huffed, and took off across the open field of garbage.

After about a hundred meters of picking across the treacherous land, an uneven buzzing sound, like the humming of a passing drone, caught Koko's attention. But all the drones were downed with the Great Sub-Orbital Blast (G.SOB), an EMP that had been installed in the international space station and programmed to discharge repeatedly as it circled the entire earth. That continual blast finally ended the world wars, stopped further weapons-making, and made the last handful of remaining governments sign treaties. Then, not long after peace was declared, the G.SOB hit humanity with its unanticipated backhand.

Namely, that humanity had no ability to survive without technology.

A couple people here and there had scraped by in the fallout. Maybe just two dwindling hangers-on existed. Maybe there were a couple more scattered like dust to wind across the sphere. Who knew? It wasn't like Koko could ask anyone. The G.SOB had taken care of all that troublesome inter-global communication. This era of postwar existence was like living in a new dark age. A blank slate, sure, but not the kind anyone ever wanted.

So, no. That glint of metal out there couldn't be a drone. It had to be something else. Something...alive, trying to communicate?

Koko's heart skipped a beat. And zer mind immediately jumped to: the Magician!

Koko coughed. Even if it was just a regular old surviving human like Shacho and zem, the thought that there might be someone else alive was exciting. Even if that someone drove a machine with sounded like a drone. Fuck, even if that living thing was a drone, somehow. It was all still better than being solo with Shacho.

Koko tip-toed across the rubble, heading in the direction it seemed the sound was coming from. Away from the city, following the course of the river, out toward where the bamboo forests used to be. Now, the unknown mangled rot of the past. Away from the broken heart of what was left of civilization, and out toward the wild sunrise.

The ground grew more uneven, addled with rocks and chunks of scorched concrete, razor sharp rebar, twisted steel. The dryness of the air didn't let up, but it changed from acidic to tacky. It clung to Koko's chapped lips like hard wax that wouldn't lick off. Still, zer tongue kept trying, tasting over and over again the bitter gack. The wind didn't help. It wasn't strong, but thin and sharp, like knives digging at Koko's exposed skin. And the buzzing air made Koko's jaw clench tighter and tighter together.

And yet, that one single tiny shard of hope—*we aren't alone*—drove zem on.

The sun dipped bit by bit behind the low blackened hills, and shadows stretched craggy fingers around corners and along paths that led to tall, spider-webbed safety glass dead ends. Koko stopped at a dip in the land where the rubble of some once-bright-and-glorious monument lay in rust, faded colors, and ashen dust. The drone-like sound seemed to grow louder here, as if this concave pit were the source. But the only thing noticeable in the pit was a huge black block of concrete. Some remnants of a skyscraper basement, perhaps. It was huge, and stuck in the ground like a root from some human-made tree long since ripped up by the trunk.

Koko stood, toes curling against the edge of the land, wondering what to do next.

The sound grew as if calling out, asking Koko to descend.

Ze leaned forward out over zer narrow hips, lost balance, and slipped on loose stones. Ze went head over knees, clattering and scrambling, tumbling and grumbling down the steep slide of land, somehow lucky to not hit more than a few round rocks. Okay, maybe it wasn't luck. Koko was adept at ducking and rolling after uncountable fights with Shacho's short-fuse temper, which in this moment suddenly felt like fate.

It wasn't fate. Koko's skills were strictly survival-based, and those skills being useful at this random moment in time was mere happenstance.

And yet, did that make the skills any less valuable?

Koko stood and dusted off from the tumble. The answer should be "no," only Koko had no proof. Life was nothing more than survival of the fittest, but couldn't one could call that drive to live a kind of fate? A combination of a conscious and subconscious choice to stay alive?

Something Shacho had lost that, maybe, Koko could find and bring back.

After all, today was about fixing broken things, wasn't it?

Without warning, the grumble that had filled the air moments ago became a sharp piercing tone. Just for a short count of three, then it went back to grumbling. But that was enough to force Koko to zer feet.

A flash of blue light drew Koko's eyes to the source. In the center of the concave dip a structure had appeared where the block of concrete had been. No. Incorrect. The concrete block had...opened up. Broke itself in half to form an archway. And in the middle of the archway, that same blue light glowed. Dimmer than the flash had been, but there all the same.

Koko tentatively approached.

Closer to the archway, the air filled with stomach-twisting smells of flayed fur, boiled blood, burnt hair. Koko knew those smells well. The telltale signs of another bombing. Of more fires starting. Of another three months hiding out. All this, a trigger that told every-thing in Koko's body—run! Hide! Burrow into the ground and don't come out!

And yet, that blue light was oddly compelling. Strong like a magnet tugging on Koko's belly button. It drew zem in as if no resistance stood between them. At the threshold of the archway, Koko came to a halt.

What would happen if ze stepped through?

"Koko," a voice filled Koko's head, without reaching either eardrum first.

Koko's ribcage tightened in panic. "What do you want?" ze tried to answer. Nothing came out but a jagged breath.

"It is I, the Magician," came that bizarre inside-voice.

The Magician? So it was true. Shacho was wrong. They were alive for a reason. Koko was going to find out why, and it was going to make everything better.

"Do you want to come to us?"

Us? That was an odd bit of rhetoric. And yet, everything in Koko said "yes." Every thought and every atom. There was simply no room for "no."

"Then close your eyes. The transition isn't easy the first time."

Koko clenched zer eyes shut. A wash of blue so bright ze could see the veins in the back of zer eyelids pulsed, filling zem with a strange calm. And then, a wash of utter peace so deep that Koko was sure this was it. This was death. And that, somehow, Shacho had been right even if the Magician was real.

Life was a meaningless waste.

You just live, and then you die based on random happenstance.

#

"Are you alright?" a gruff and unfamiliar voice asked.

Koko blinked, and found zemself laid out flat on zer back, looking up at a soft orange light glowing from a recess in a smooth, featureless grey wall.

"Where am I? Is this Death...or no, wait. If I'm here and I'm still alive then...is this...the Afterlife?"

The strange voice laughed softly. "Ha, no. There's no such thing. You're on the Ley Hachi."

"What is Ley Hachi?" Koko asked, confused, eyes still aching.

"The home of Yume. I believe you call them the Magician."

"The Magician," Koko breathed, afraid to say the name out loud.

"Yes, Yume'll be here in a few minutes. You need something to drink? The transition is never easy on a body," the stranger said.

"Transition?" Koko asked, jolting up.

Their eyes met. The stranger's were bright orange. A sandy brown face framed by a short crop of bright gold and silver hair. A sturdy but elongated stature, like a stretched out giant standing some three meters tall. The stranger's face was broad, with high cheek bones and a flat forehead. A steep chin and nose stuck out at the same angle, only the nose ended not in a steep point as Koko expected for some reason, but rather in a button-like nub. The stranger's ash grey clothes were tight-fitting and revealed a flat chest, gently rounded belly, huge muscular shoulders and impressively thick forearms.

"Yes, transition. Yume's on their way. Try to relax," the stranger said in a rush, and turned away before Koko could respond.

A door opened on the opposite side of a dome-shaped room with a deep sapphire-blue roof. The space was large for a hallway, but small for a room. In fact, the area felt more like some kind of waiting area. The air smelled sweet and aromatic, like a mixture of herbs. The temperature was warm, but not too hot. Also refreshing, but not too cold—somehow. Koko leaned back and studied the dome of a ceiling. It looked like the night sky back before everything turned to junk.

Koko started at the out-of-place thought.

Neither ze nor Shacho had lived long enough to have ever seen the night sky. The two of them had been born right before the end of the wars. "Rubble babies," the world had called them. And they'd been sick-lucky to even survive as long as they had. Scraping by but sticking together, that's how they'd done it. But never under a sky that looked like the ceiling above.

"Koko, welcome," came a voice sweeter and mellower than the first stranger. The same voice from the archway.

Koko bolted upright. The Magician, surely!

Koko stared at this legendary being who wasn't supposed to exist with shock, then awe and finally, respect. Ze drank in all of the Magician's appearance. Where the first stranger's appearance was long and strong, the Magician was slight and small. A slice of a body, nearly sheet metal-thin, advanced on dancing tip-toes toward Koko. Long carbon black hair tumbled around sharp shoulders, swept back into almost an arc. A rich, almost velvety, dark brown-black face with easy slopes of chin and nose, low flat cheeks, and a moderate brow with narrow black pinstripes for eyebrows. And where the first stranger's eyes had been bold and bright, these were a gentle violet, pale and soft. Like a pastel painting instead of a daring acrylic work.

Again, Koko started at knowledge ze shouldn't have. What was it, this tumbling of information? As if Koko were linked back into the inter-global networks that once existed. Only, Koko had never been connected to them, just heard a rumor, a whisper of reality before the wars.

"Spells," the Magician said suddenly.

"What?"

"The reason you know more than you should. It's an information spell written on the walls. You'll acclimate soon."

"Oh," Koko said in surprise.

The Magician drew in closer to Koko than the first stranger had, and ze could smell the scent of something sweet and aromatic. It popped and sparkled delightfully in zer nostrils, so much that Koko couldn't help but snort.

"I'm sorry, I hope the smell of jasmine doesn't offend you."

Koko's eyes went wide. "It's just...I've never smelled anything like it."

"I gathered it in from another world, similar to yours. However, the ecology has much diverged in recent eras, so it must be rather unfamiliar to you. I'm sorry. I wasn't thoughtful."

"No," Koko said suddenly. "I like it."

"Ah. Well, let me not waste your time. Allow me to introduce myself, though surely Radon already prefaced my entrance."

"Radon?"

"My traveling companion and crew mate. The one you've just met."

Radon. What a strange name. It rolled around in Koko's mind like it ought to mean something, even though it didn't.

"I'm Yume."

Koko couldn't move. "You—you—"

"Are real. Very much so. They/them/their pronouns, if you please. And you are Koko, I believe."

"I-I am."

"And your pronouns?"

"Umm..." Koko paused at this question. It was strange to be asked. Nobody had ever asked. But then, back home it was always only Shacho and Koko these days. No pronouns aside from "I" and "you" were needed aside from inside Koko's own head. And in zer head, everyone was the same gender-neutral post-wars popularized "ze" because, well, why wouldn't they all be?

"I can call you by the gender-nonspecific "they" if you like."

"No, umm, I mean, I guess...ze?"

"Ze/zem/zer it is," Yume bowed low in almost a curtsy. "It's a fine pleasure to meet Shacho's ward after so long."

Another unbelievable blow. *You know Shacho?* Koko shouted inside zer head because the words simply wouldn't tumble out. Instead, Koko just gaped.

Yume reached out toward a glass panel with several concentric circles etched into the surface. "Come. I have much to show you. And let's get you some sustenance. You must be famished."

The door opened inward, revealing a brightly lit room the frosted glass somehow hadn't shown. Koko stepped into a massive food hall thinking "magic, surely." The room had several long tables with high stools gathered around each. In the center of the room were what appeared to be small huts where people congregated, shifted around, and eventually left with food in hand to rearrange themselves around the tables with stools. The whole place hummed with quiet voices, clanking of dishes, steam hissing. The air was savory but sweet, spicy but salty with a fishy tang. Koko couldn't quite put zer nose on what exactly it was. Nothing specific, but at the same time—everything all at once. As if all the food from the past were represented here, only remixed and distributed in a way that was both familiar and strange.

"This is the Ex Machina Mess Hall," Yume said, waving toward a line of people.

"Ex Machina?" Koko repeated with wonder, "Is that the name of your fleet?"

"Fleet?" Yume repeated, then shook their head. "No, no. It's the name of my people."

Koko stared at the food line, the full stools, those gathered around and talking in hushed tones. All of them were as different as Koko and Yume, as Yume and Radon. All ranges of statures and body types, from short to towering, from compact to robust to lanky. A full spread of hair colors, types, styles. From what Koko would have called "natural tones" to vibrant, almost bird-like plumage piled high in impressive towers, or braided into thick ropes of rich hues. And skin tones ranging anywhere from bone white to blue-black, from pastel pink to a deep almost-green brown, from sunlight yellow to dusk red. And their clothes! Oh, such a vast array of styles, from fur blankets to tight-knit wool jumpsuits to glittery ball gowns. From elaborate and bold to muted and fleshy tones. Some wore adornments, small trinkets, stones and bones. Others wore nothing but the simplest of trousers. Even the words Koko overheard didn't all sound as if they went together well.

The only thing that seemed to bind these beings together as a "people" was the fact that each one bore a matching tattoo. A simple EM inside of a series of concentric circles that matched the etching on the frosted glass door Yume had brought Koko through.

"This is all of them?" Koko asked, marveling at array.

"Not at the moment, but all of the Ex Machina have access to this hall, similar to how we got here," Yume said.

"How *did* we get here?" Koko asked, looking back for the frosted glass door. It was gone.

"Through a portal. You'll see many frosted doors back on the ship. Each opens onto an endless number of access points. You have to watch the panels, though. Never go through a portal before you've adjusted your coordinates. But, don't worry. I'll show you how it all works when we get back."

Koko frowned and sighed, feeling overwhelmed. Nothing Yume said made any kind of logical sense. Looking down at zer hands, Koko noticed the floor here was made of hard packed red dirt. That completely sidetracked whatever conversation Yume wanted to have, because instead Koko gasped and said, "Wait! Where even is this? Earth?"

Several heads turned. Each pair of eyes, a completely different hue. Koko swallowed and tried to disappear, arms around zer middle, head tucked like the broken doll to zer caved-in chest.

Yume patted Koko's shoulder gently. "It's okay, everyone feels the same when they first come here."

"E-everyone?"

"Yes, Ex Machina is a people made up of refugees from worlds like yours."

"Worlds...like mine..." those words stung. Hearing them and echoing them back. A death sentence for the Earth, surely. Why else would Koko be a "refugee" here with the Magician?

"I'm sorry," Yume said in sad, quiet confirmation.

It was all Koko could do not to choke up. "S-so we aren't on Earth anymore," Koko said with a heavy heart.

"No," Yume answered gently.

"I'm not very hungry," Koko admitted, arms falling like over-cooked noodles to zer side.

Yume nodded graciously. "Sleep instead?"

Koko nodded silently. Without another word, Yume guided zem back toward the door they'd come through. Only, the door wasn't in the same place it had been. They had to cross the whole Mess Hall floor, passing by carts with steam rising that smelled like fresh rice and noodles frying. Koko hadn't smelled rice and noodles since... since...since too long ago to remember exactly when. Before the wars ended and before Shacho turned so nasty. The two of them used to walk the street markets at night under glowing soft yellow fairy lights, eating endless amounts of takoyaki, okonomiyaki, boxes of yakisoba, bowls of rice with fish and seaweed.

A sharp shard of homesickness burrowed into Koko's heart, then swiftly following it - a stab of guilt.

"What about Shacho?" Koko wanted to ask, only the words wouldn't come out. They turned to ash, and blew off Koko's tongue into the huge open hall full of strangers who had nothing in common but a few circles.

"Here we are," Yume said, pulling up to a massive archway marked with the same concentric circles, and lettering that Koko couldn't read. "That says Main Portal, and if you're ever lost, just look for one of these. It'll take you wherever you need to go."

Wherever you need to go.

Koko choked on those words. Because the only place Koko wanted to go didn't exist. The neighborhood of weeping willow trees, walking swept stone streets beside Shacho, staring up at the vermilion red archways while Shacho replaced candles and incense sticks. The late Autumn sun hanging red and low over green mountains full of swaying bamboo. The smell of frying noodles and cooking rice in the air.

Unavoidable tears slid silent down Koko's face. Ze tried to quickly dash them, but it was too late. Yume saw everything. They turned graciously away.

"We're almost there," Yume pulled up to a panel on the side of an archway that Koko hadn't noticed before. At the wave of a hand, the panel lit up a soft indigo.

Yume's fingers flew across the indigo light as if they were knotting string. When whatever they were doing was finished, the frosted door they stood before turned green for just a second. Yume pressed a hand against the center of the panel and pushed the door open. On the other side, there was Yume's ship again. It looked like the same room they'd left, but then maybe all of Yume's ship looked like that. Grey, metal, nondescript with weird sapphire domed ceilings. A strange place to restart a life.

This is a world where we don't go it alone. Shacho used to say with a gentle smile before the hydrogen bomb came. Koko froze. It was true. Magician or not, this all felt wrong without Shacho.

"Yume," Koko said suddenly. "Th-thank you for rescuing me, but..."

Yume looked down sideways. "But?"

"I want to go back home."

"That's a choice I think you might want to hold off on," Yume said with a wise lilt to their voice.

And then, Koko remembered. Yume wasn't just some random refugee collector. Yume was *The Magician*, and the Magician had saved their world. And, what's more—Yume knew who Shacho was. The one who'd stopped the bomb. So, maybe, it was all going to work out okay. And maybe, Koko was over-reacting and deciding things that didn't need to be decided quite yet.

It was too soon to know anything for sure.

"Sleep on your decision," Yume advised. "Please?"

Koko nodded. There was wisdom in that. Even Shacho would agree. Maybe not Shacho these days, who made flash decisions and stayed angry about everything. But the old Shacho. The one Koko missed the most. Best to take the slower logical route, set deciding anything aside for now, and pay homage to that old Shacho. The one who'd have protected Koko from anything.

"This way." Yume approached another door. This one was grey and had a silver plaque with lettering on it that, again, Koko couldn't read. "I had Radon set up a room for you. It should be just about ready."

The hallway was not nearly as grey or as ugly as Koko recalled. In fact, there were windows everywhere into small rooms full of interesting things that Koko didn't understand. Lots of strings attached to moving things.

"What is all this?" Koko asked as the two of them walked.

"The engine stations. Everything you're seeing is the internal workings of the ship. It's how we move between worlds."

"Move between worlds?"

"The frosted doors. They don't lead to other parts of the ship like the grey doors do. The panels are instructions, coordinates for which place in which world the door ought to connect you to. And when you go through, you pass along a ley line through a dimensional rift into that world."

Koko stared in through another window as the two of them passed by. Inside the wires was a kind of strange glow. The same strange glow that Koko had seen back at Demachiyanagi in the archway that had opened up.

"Was the archway a frosted door on your side?"

Yume nodded, looking at Koko with an expression that was hard to read. Wonder? Confusion? Intrigue?

Koko pushed past that odd expression through to a different one. A muddled mixture of sorrow, regret, and rage flaring up inside zer chest. Ze stopped and stamped the ground. "If that archway was a door to a better world, why didn't you come to save Shacho long before now?!"

Yume stopped in front of a grey door and opened it. "We wanted to, but the gateway on your side wouldn't work. It'd been broken a long time, and when we received the communication that things had gone wrong, we simply couldn't make it back in time. We came as soon as we could."

"I don't understand," Koko said and stamped again.

"It will make more sense once you've had some rest," Yume said and opened a grey door. "I promise."

The room beyond the door was a bedroom much like the room Koko had always dreamed of living in. It had a four-post bed made out of a dark red wood, complete with pastel purple and grey-blue velvety drapery like a sunrise on a foggy day. The bed itself was a dark midnight sky blue-black with a bedspread made of stars. Across the room, on top of a desk made of a lighter wood, sat a journal made of some kind of pale beige fiber and a tanned skin cover. Beside it rested a glass and metal pen and a small ink jar. The floor was tile, black and white in a pattern that looked much like the Ex Machina symbol, only simplified.

Yume pointed at a small ornate inlay of gold tiles in front of the door. "Your coordinates, for when you choose to go back to Kyoto."

"Where....where are we now?" Koko asked, staring at the concentric circles and the tight knot of strings in the center.

"In the in-between. But don't worry. You put these coordinates into any frosted door and off you go. I told Radon to keep the ship within radius of your ley line until you've decided for sure. We aren't going anywhere until you're certain you want to come with us or go back for good."

For good? Why: *for good?* And if the frosted doors were portals, then what was all this "range" business about? Koko couldn't make ups or downs of any of this.

Yume motioned Koko through the door. A soft candle-like glow filled the room, seemingly from nowhere at all. They sat in unison on the edge of the surprisingly firm bed. Light came from small recessed holes in the ceiling.

Once Koko stopped fidgeting, Yume explained.

"The portals work off of ley lines. They only exist in very specific places, and only connect to other very specific places."

"What's a ley line?" Koko asked.

Yume nodded and went on. "There are lines of significance which extend from one universe to the next, much like the tracks of a train extend from one place to another. There are stop-off points, stations so to speak, where universally significant things have happened. Things of great weight. Kyoto is one of them. Ex Machina has traveled there many a time throughout history. The shrines and the temples, all that spiritual weight over the generations of humanity. And even before that, the ley lines drew all kinds of magical beings to the place. It's one of the earliest in recorded time. We've done everything in our power to protect it."

"The wars..." Koko whispered.

Koko thought of Shacho and how the wars, while terrible, never went nuclear. It was all because of that magical moment when Shacho charged into what was targeted as the hypo-center of the first bomb. Shacho had run right in to one of the oldest shrines in all of

Japan and held up what history called "a wand," screaming what history called "a spell."

But Koko knew the truth of that day. The wand had been a de-atomizer, a palm-sized black box that carried a chip Shacho had invented. The chip contained certain kinds of energy (which Koko never had understood) that could neutralize a hydrogen bomb moments before it went off. And the "spell" had been Shacho speaking a necessary verbal code to the neutralizer to initiate the stop-sequence.

"The story you know is what Shacho and I agreed the story would be for Earth's history. The truth of that day is Shacho carried a ley line key I gave zem, and the spell ze spoke unlocked the ley line which lies over Big Top and follows the train line there all the way to the ocean. The spell activated the ley line's power to protect your world."

Koko's mouth hung open, getting dry, while tears welled in the corners of Koko's eyes.

"Why..." tumbled out without Koko even trying.

"Shacho was one of our best contacts, and ze volunteered zemself for the mission. We agreed to let Shacho go in, only none of us knew what the cost would be. Had I known what I know now, what the cost would be..." Yume's face paled, turning a dirty kind of mud brown. "Oh, I would have done things so differently."

"Shacho..." Koko mumbled, absentmindedly, thinking only of gentle Shacho. Of the Shacho who never came back from that magical moment. Instead, ze came back a bitter husk who, like Koko's broken doll, didn't work anymore.

Koko's doll! Koko had come here with it, seeking the Magician's advice. Only now, it felt so small and meaningless. And the Magician felt less like a friend and more like someone to distrust.

Who was to say they weren't just another person who wanted power and control over others like all the previous masters of the world? Who was to say that, given the chance, the Magician wouldn't use their ley lines to lay waste to the world like the old ruler had?

Who was to say that the Magician wasn't going to use the power of their magic to lay waste to everything once again?

Was this really a day to fix broken things—or a day to foolishly lose everything?

"I'm sorry," Yume started to say.

Koko turned away, tears dripped down like rain onto the star-colored sheets of the bed. Ze didn't want to be here a second longer. Ze wanted to go home. Broken or not.

"Perhaps it was too soon to tell you the truth about the past. Only, we don't have much time for you to decide. The ley line can only sustain us for so long before we must move along."

Koko nodded.

"I'll leave you in peace."

Yume, the great and awful Magician, rose. Their long cotton robes slid off the bed as they made for the exit. Koko couldn't bear to meet their eyes as they turned to leave.

Peace. What sort of peace was this? What sort of peace would it ever be between them? Perhaps the same kind of stalemate Shacho and Koko knew? Only this was worse. The Magician and their people were liars who used magic to lay waste to entire worlds. Thieves who sucked up the best of people, and left them in the waste like broken dolls. Why had Koko ever thought coming here would solve anything?

"I want to go home," Koko said out loud as Yume opened the door.

Yume paused. "I'll prepare the key."

Koko nodded without a sound at Yume's back.

Yume turned for a brief moment, trying to catch Koko's eyes. Koko looked down, feeling for the edges of the broken doll in zer pocket. It was still there, tucked away safe as it ought to be. Koko held the broken doll's tiny hand, thinking of Shacho. Yume sighed heavily, gathered themself, and left the room without another word. The grey door slowly closed behind their back and Koko was left alone.

That night was full of tossing, turning, tears clutching the broken doll and twisting the sheets.

The doll, like Shacho, would never go back to normal.

How could Yume have let that happen? How could Yume, the great Magician who owned a ship that traveled across universes on fairy magic, allow someone to pay such a high price? Allowing Shacho to take magic nobody understood into a battle no one knew the outcome to was as good as signing Shacho's death sentence, wasn't it? And what's more, here was Yume living fat and happy while Shacho suffered alone in a world that hadn't even been worth trying to save.

Because despite what Shacho did, nobody else survived anyway. Only Koko and a broken Shacho who didn't even know ze'd saved anything at all. The question that had driven Koko here—"why are we still alive"—was only more poignant now, not less. And in the face of real magic, it stood even less of a chance of coming out to a happy answer.

Poor choices, that was all Koko had. Mistakes foolishly made by those with the power to give out keys and spells, but not the power to do anything when things went wrong.

The grey door cracked open. Koko was about to tell Yume to leave, only to meet the bright, bold eyes of Radon.

"Come in," Koko said instead. Maybe Radon had some other explanation. It was worth a shot.

"You're upset," Radon said directly, coming in and shutting the door with a clack.

Koko nodded, trying not to cry.

"Understandable," Radon said. She walked over to stand in front of the bed, hands in deep denim pockets.

"How could Yume..." Koko began softly.

Radon's face screwed up in a flash. "Sorry? What was that?"

"Yume let Shacho..." Koko couldn't get the words out.

Radon's expression tweaked up more, not less. Those bright eyes flared with a cold fire Koko hadn't seen before. "Hey, what the hell do you think Yume has to do with it?"

Koko jolted back against the back of the four-post bed. "Excuse me?"

"Shacho made zer choices, as do we all," Radon said bluntly. "Yume only ever tries to help us. How dare you!"

Koko backed away further, knees to chest.

The door opened further. In it stood Yume. "Radon, what are you doing?"

"Trying to talk sense into our new crew mate. If you expect me to work with someone who has no respect for you—"

"I'm not expecting anything but kindness from you right now," Yume said, coming into the room.

Radon huffed, drawing hands out of pockets and flinging a finger at Koko's head like a weapon. "But Yume, this brat—"

Yume put a hand up in Radon's face. "Radon, please step out of the room. Koko has decided to return home. There's nothing to argue here."

Radon balked at that, mouth hanging open. "What the fuck? To that ruined world? Why in hell?"

"It is zer choice to make," Yume said, putting a hand firmly on Radon's shoulder. "Leave us?"

"Tch," Radon hissed, stomped across the room, and slammed the grey door shut. "Fine. You want trash. Go back, you ungrateful—"

"Radon," Yume cut in again.

"I'm gone," Radon snapped and slammed the grey door shut with an impressive bang.

Silence and the echo of the door filled the room. Neither Koko nor Yume moved. After an uncomfortable amount of time, Koko finally cleared zer throat, if only to ease some of the tension. It felt like Shacho had just charged out of the room, and clearing zer throat was habitually what Koko always did to try and move on. Still, the tightness in zer chest didn't ease. Not even a little bit.

Yume sighed and frowned, motioned at the door.

"I'm sorry about Radon. She still has a lot of pain she carries around inside. Her world burned to the ground, and there was nothing the Ex Machina could do to help. The wrong people got control of some powerful old ley lines and unleased the power as an act of greed. Foolishness, it was. Utter foolishness."

"What happened?" Koko asked, curious.

"The result was much like what would have happened to your world had those nuclear bombs started going off, only...worse. The whole universe imploded. And there was nothing any of us could do to save any amount of life there. She...well, she's working through losing a lot. No coordinates to take her home. She is one of the what we call true refugees."

"True refugees?"

"Those whose worlds have been annihilated by magic. The ones we can't save."

"What about natural annihilation?" Koko asked, wondering about a world like theirs...zers and Shacho's. Was it not lost? Was there hope?

"Natural death is never true annihilation. An end within the pattern always becomes a return over time. Energy is never created nor destroyed. Until you are dealing with inter-dimensional magic like the ley lines. Then, there is true destruction that can never be undone. That's why we Ex Machina exist. To prevent that kind of ending."

Koko saw in a memory the words over the archway that used to lead to Kyoto Station. "World's End." A hint that should the ley line following along the train tracks there be activated for the wrong purpose...

"You mean, my world! It could be saved?" Koko blurted out.

"It already was saved by Shacho," Yume said quietly, then shook their head, seeming to remember themself, and looked ashamed. "I'm sorry. I'm sorry for your loss. For all of this. For Radon and how she came at you. For bringing you here. For taking you from the things you love. None of this is your struggle. Forgive me."

Yume stood, as if preparing to leave again.

Koko blanched, feeling a sudden urge to stop them. To reach out. To do something. "Wait, but—"

Yume paused and looked down. "But?"

But what? Koko didn't know. Only that letting Yume walk out of here felt wrong. Like being here without Shacho felt wrong. Like not going to Demachiyanagi with the broken doll felt wrong. Like sitting beside Shacho day in, day out, felt wrong. Koko didn't know what to do instead, but doing nothing couldn't be the answer either. And letting Yume leave and going home would be doing nothing.

Yume's head cocked, waiting patiently.

Koko opened zer mouth and let whatever words came tumble out. "R-radon. Ze—I mean she—said *crew mate*? Does that mean I could stay if I wanted? And...and, I don't know? Help save worlds?"

Yume nodded. "Yes, if you had chosen to stay. This would have been your home, too. And yes, saving worlds is what the Ex Machina do. Only, I completely understand why you want to return home. To Shacho. Ze was a great friend and a great companion. Full of bravery and hope. Ze should not be alone."

Yes, that was right. And if Koko didn't go back, Shacho would be alone. Broken or not, Shacho didn't deserve to be the only human left in a wasted world. How was that hope? How, then, had Ex Machina saved anything? Koko recalled suddenly the ash and the broken buildings, the ruination of their entire country. The burning of the fields, black smoke towering for days. Smoldering for months. And yet...hadn't the smoke cleared? The ash settled? And what came from ash but new growth? Wasn't Yume right? Any death only fed more life?

Surely, the Earth would bounce back from the firestorms, from the wars, from the mar that humanity had left with its endless fighting.

Ugly as it was, it wasn't the ending of the story.

"Why?" Koko suddenly burst out with.

Yume gave Koko a confused frown. "Why what?"

"Why are we alive? Any of us? What's the point?"

Yume's face fell into a kind of gentle grimace. And while the expression was sad, Koko could almost call it a subtle smile. "Ah, the age old question, hm? Crops up in every universe at one point or another. But, the tricky thing of it is: only you can answer for yourself."

Koko huffed. Avoidance tactic. Too obvious. "Sure, but why do you think?"

"Me?"

"Yes!"

"I don't ask," Yume said, bowed, and turned away again.

"Why not?" Koko did ask.

"Because the question 'why' is never as important as: what do I do now that I am alive?"

Koko's eyes went wide. It was the perfect phrasing of the most obvious truth. So obvious Koko had been missing it zer entire life. Like the chunk of concrete, this new truth opened up and became a portal to a whole different perspective. Only, Koko didn't know what to do with it. It felt too big to swallow just yet.

"I'll leave you to prepare for your departure. If you reconsider, you only need call. I'll be on hand in either case."

Yume left Koko alone again.

Koko stood from the bed, and in doing so the broken doll fell out of zer pocket. Tangled wires and all. Koko reached down and gingerly picked the doll back up, laid it in zer open palm. The little head rested almost peacefully against the chest, despite how blank the doll's expression was. Koko tilted the head back up, spread the arms out wide, and tried to remember what the doll had once looked like in the moment before the fall.

Perched on the edge of the top stair, head turning this way and that to comprehend as much of reality as possible. Arms out wide for added balance. Prepared for anything, that's what the look had been. Ready, even, to fall and come apart.

What about Shacho? What had zer expression been the moment right before the bomb came? Right before the key opened the ley line? Right before the power blasted clean zer mind?

Prepared for anything?

Was it really not Yume's fault that gentle Shacho was gone and in zer place was an angry, bitter, cruel replacement? Was Shacho just like Radon? Suffering and bearing up too much?

Could Koko do anything to change that by joining the Ex

Machina and using their knowledge to help Shacho, to help the Earth, rather than just running away?

Koko paced across the room, pushed open the grey door, and decided to go for a walk to have a look around. The hallways were mostly empty, and Koko wandered freely through corridor after corridor. How big was this ship? Bigger than it ought to have been, or so it seemed to Koko after several long minutes passed of hallway after hallway. Then, Koko found the hallways of frosted doors. One in particular stood out. This door had a symbol on it that looked like a bunch of complicated lines. Somehow all those confusing lines equaled words, Koko was sure without knowing why.

"It says: the dream of the magicians," said a voice from behind.

Koko jumped and whipped around.

There, smiling, was Yume. They pulled up to Koko's side and tapped a finger against the indigo screen beside the door to activate the frosted portal. Koko stared, wide-eyed, between the door and Yume. Had Yume said *magicians*? Plural?

Was this door where Yume got their title from? And, if so, was this a doorway to more magicians? No, but Yume was *The* Magician. One and only. Right? Not to mention, what did all of this have to do with the mission and getting Koko ready for it?

The door opened, swinging inward like all the other doors on the ship. Inside, there were no screens and technology, but long dusty wooden shelves full of what appeared to be nothing more than ancient books, themselves covered in layers of dust. Ancient tomes they were, leather and wood, bound with thick straps and heavy buckles sealing each one closed.

Yume stepped into the room practically on tiptoes. Koko remained outside, marveling, confused, and unsure. Yume rose a hand over their shoulder and waved.

"I have to look for something very important in here. You can come in, just be careful not to disturb the fairies."

"Fairies?" Koko gasped, too loud.

In response there was a rustle like a grumbling wind. Koko looked down and saw the ground wasn't tile like the bedroom or brushed steel like the hallway. Instead, it was like the Mess Hall had been, made of dirt. Only here there were all kinds of little grooves dug into the dirt. Circles formed in various places. At these, Yume pointed.

"Those are fairy circles, where the fairies congregate and discuss matters beyond mere mortal comprehension. Watch your step."

Koko was too curious to not go inside, and see for zemself what this room was all about. So, ze tip-toed into the room—an impressive library. Shelf after shelf was lined with books. The air inside buzzed with the high singing hum of tiny wings. The shelves weren't dusty after all, but covered with fairies. The tomes were covered in even more fairies that gave them, from a distance, an odd, dirty look. Closer up, Koko could make out the tiny body of each one. A hand unconsciously went into Koko's pocket, touching the pieces of the small doll.

"What's that?" One of the bigger fairies fluttered in front of Koko's face, pointing at zer nose.

"My friend," Yume said, "Koko."

The fairy cocked a tiny, flaming orange head. "Why does your friend Koko carry a doll made of fairy parts?"

Koko jolted back, nearly tripping on a fairy circle and crashing into one of the bookshelves. But Yume was quicker than Koko's blunder, and grabbed Koko by the waist and steadied zer back on the ground.

"Careful," was all Yume said, and returned to a selected tome with a silver and gold cover full of leaves and flowers.

Another fairy fluttered up from the circle Koko had almost trod in. This fairy looked angry, if anger was the expression on that miniature blue and gold face. It was kind of hard to tell because the face was so small.

"Why do you have our things? Those don't belong to you!" the blue fairy asked rudely.

Koko flinched away, resisting the urge to swap at the fairy like a roach. "I-I'm sorry? I don't—"

"In your pocket," the orange fairy said, hands on impressively curvy hips.

"Show it to us!" the blue fairy demanded in a birdlike chirp.

A hand like a hypodermic needle extended toward Koko's pocket. Afraid of what these fairies might do, Koko swiftly extracted the doll and all its broken parts. The wires unraveled like loose spools of thread and the head fell, sad and slack, against Koko's hand.

"Oh! I just knew it!" the orange fairy exclaimed.

"I thought we'd never see you again!" the blue fairy cried, clapping.

All the fairies, a wild splash of all imaginable colors, joined hands and began speaking. The sound of their voices was like sticks of bamboo trees rubbing together in a gentle wind. It reminded Koko, in a sudden rush of nostalgia, of the last breaths of life in Kyoto's once lush green ecology. The last forest that Shacho had taken Koko to, right outside one of the oldest mountain shrines. There had been a path people had been walking for generations upon generations. Koko and Shacho had stood hand in hand before the firestorm reached that far north. After the blaze went out and the bamboo ashes settled, a big thunderstorm whipped through and knocked down the last, clinging remains of the trees. Nothing grew back after that. Nothing to date, anyway. Only now, Koko had this eerie sense that—if they could just stop Shacho from ruining everything— maybe the forests would grow back and fill the Earth again with green lushness.

The fairies broke hands and clapped twice.

That same buzzy feeling that had called Koko to the archway back home filled Koko's palm, and the doll sat up of its own accord. The head still lolled this way and that. A hand came up and felt the ruination of the neck. And then, as if alive, the wires rose into the air and wrapped around the base of the neck to support the head. More wires filled in holes in the shoulders and knees, elbows and ankles. The doll stood, tottering at first, and then steady in the center of Koko's sweaty palm. The little face came to life, both worn-off eyes blinking open and looking this way and that. Koko gasped. Somehow, the fairies were activating the doll's busted AI unit? Or, was this pure magic?

"I'm sorry. I did all I could, but we failed," the doll said in a ceramic, hollow voice that sounded sadder than a doll should. Koko had never programmed the doll to speak. In fact, the doll didn't have a speaker unit at all. No audio input or output. Those pieces simply hadn't been available. So this life in the doll wasn't AI. It wasn't human technology at all. It was magic.

"We know," the orange fairy said, looking sadly up at Yume. Suddenly, the fairies looked less cute and playful. They looked older, more serious. The orange fairy's face was a mask of shadows, dark and complicated. A hand rubbed at a shoulder, and then reached out and touched the doll's face gingerly. "The key told us everything. I'm so sorry."

The doll bowed, a cracked hand pressed against the fairy's touch. "We did our best."

"But now," the blue fairy said, alighting on Koko's palm. "We have another chance. See, the Magician is back!"

Koko jerked up at the words: *The Magician.*

So, it wasn't just Shacho. And it wasn't just some weird lines on a door. Yume really was the Magician, at least according to a room full of ancient books and fairies. That seemed pretty legit. But why? What set Yume apart from the rest of the Ex Machina?

"Yume!" the smaller fairy called and darted away.

Koko decided to take a chance and try talking to the fairy who stayed behind.

"How do you know my doll?"

"We made it to help protect Shacho. Only, we failed..." the blue fairy said quietly, voice filled with regret.

Another fairy darted over, this one bright green, like leaves in spring. It glared at the smaller blue fairy. "We didn't fail! We didn't know what that ley line would choose to do to a non-Magician."

"The ley lines have a will of their own?" Koko asked the green fairy.

"Yes, indeed," Yume answered instead. "They aren't like the Ex

Machina coordinates. They are a symbiotic living effect of another living entity we call The Fae. The Fae are much, much bigger than you or me or even the whole of Ex Machina put together with all of our fleets. They live out their lives in the freeform space of the Zeroth Dimension, where the source of all magic originates from. Their interactions in the Zeroth Dimension give birth to the ley lines, complicated and tight-knit living weaves that spread out like sheets across the entirety of existence. You could think of the Fae like spiders, and the ley lines we find are the webs they've spun in order to catch life."

"They eat us?" Koko gasped, horrified.

Yume laughed. "No, that's where the metaphor of spiders falls short. They don't eat us. The ley lines catch and gather life in order to help protect the Fae."

"From what?"

"From annihilation. Each ley line contains many connecting points to several Fae, and as such, it contains a portion of each of their life forces. The older the ley lines, the deeper those connections run. As in all truly symbiotic evolutions, the one can no longer exist without the other. Should all the energy in the ley lines be broken or spent, all the Fae would die too."

Much like technology and humanity, Koko thought then, but said nothing. Because now was a time to comprehend, not take up space. So, Koko nodded at Yume and asked. "So, where do you fit in?"

"Yume was the first," the green fairy said, flying up and alighting on the top of Yume's head.

"The first?" Koko asked, then wondered at how old Yume really was. Billions of years? As old as the stars in the sky of Earth? Older, still? Older than these ancient books in this room, to be sure.

Yume lowered the book they'd been looking at. It was full of marking that Koko couldn't read.

"You can read that?"

"It is my first language, yes."

"What does it say?"

"This is my story."

Koko's eyes went wide. So, this room and these books were older. And the fairies themselves? Were they ancient too?

"We wrote it down so that no Magician would never forget," the spunky blue fairy said, answering Koko's question without meaning to.

"Oh," Koko gasped in reverence, feeling completely out of zer depth in this room. Ze looked back at Radon, who leaned against the metal wall across the hall. She now seemed the wiser of the two of them. Koko tried not to faint, not to fall onto a fairy circle of some of the oldest beings in all of reality.

"Something wrong?" Yume asked, reaching out to Koko.

Koko could feel the top of zer head getting too light. Tunnel vision started to close in and the world threatened to disappear in a dark wave. "I-I think I should go."

"I'm just about done here," Yume said, closing the tome and bowing to the fairies. "Thank you, friends, for the assistance."

Koko didn't say a word as they carefully navigated the way through the fairy tunnels and circles, roads and pathways. Outside, Koko wanted to collapse, but Radon was waiting with a frown. Yume turned back toward the hallway of frosted doors.

"What did you find?" Radon asked, pulling off the wall and standing tall at Yume's side.

"Exactly what we will need."

Radon's eyes rolled. "That being?"

Yume smiled as if it was a secret. "A formula to permanently seal a ley line that's in danger."

"In danger?" Koko asked curiously. "But, nothing's in danger."

"More importantly," Radon cut in. "How could we permanently seal one?"

Yume grinned at Radon, ignoring Koko's confusion. "Think of it like a faulty wiring job. If one can't rewire the building, they may to choose to permanently turn off the problematic breaker and lock that breaker for good, rather than risk burning down the entire block."

Yume wasn't talking about *their* ley line, about the one Shacho had used and been ruined for...were they? The idea of Kyoto's power being locked away forever was...well, it was terrible. How long had Kyoto been a part of the human narrative? Part of ceremony? Part of the magic of what being a human looked like? So many places people for nameless generations came to and laid down their hearts for a moment of peace. And now, it would be switched off like a faulty breaker. Locked away for good.

"Can it be undone?" Koko asked.

"If we do it right?" Yume paused and gave Koko a sad shake of their head. "No."

Right then, as if on cue, an alarm blared, the hallway filled with a shrill screaming that bounced off the walls and came back doubly loud. Red and blue lights filled the hall, flashing and making it impossible to move. Koko hit the ground, afraid, and curled up and reached inside zer pocket for the tiny broken doll. Its little body crumpled up against Koko's clenched fist. The wires and twisted bits jabbed at zer tender palm like teeth sinking in, saying "let me go!" Only Koko squeezed harder than ever. The alarm got louder and louder, shaking the ground . The whole hallway felt as if it were caving in.

"Get up!" Radon shouted.

Koko's head snapped up automatically, eyes wide in terror, face drenched in sweat. "Wha—?"

"The alarms. We have a sit.u.ation! Move it!" Radon screamed over the wail of the sirens.

"Move it? Where?"

"Out of the way!" Radon said, slapping Koko out of the way and darting into the room Koko had just left. Only, as soon as Radon's clanking boots landed on the clacky tile floor, she turned and charged right back for Koko. Two huge, strong hands grabbed Koko by both shoulders and wrenched zer body around roughly. Their two foreheads nearly crashed together.

Only then did Koko see the look on Radon's face. Wide-eyed, blanched, drenched in sweat. No, not sweat. Tears? Both bright eyes were dulled, the whites blood-shot and wet.

"Koko. Where. Did . Yume. Go?" came out not in a shout, but a desperate and trembling breath.

"I—I don't know."

Radon let go, spinning Koko away down toward the hall away from the grey door, the coordinates, and the bedroom. All of which had nothing to do with the alarm going off. But then, what was it for?

"What's going on?"

"The ley lines. They're in danger."

"Where?" Koko gasped.

"All of them. But specifically, Kyoto."

It couldn't be. Not Koko's Kyoto.

Surely some other universe's version. Like the world where Yume got the jasmine flowers. Somewhere similar but different. A parallel Kyoto. Some other world without Shacho, broken and abandoned in it.

"Yes," Radon confirmed in a bark. "Your Kyoto."

"I never meant for you to go, Koko!" screamed a voice from a device on Radon's wrist.

The voice was unmistakably Shacho's.

"Why did you take Koko!" Shacho screamed, more violent than ever. "I'll end you all!"

Koko froze in the middle of the hall and stared at Radon like zey'd been tazed. A shaky hand pointed at the device on Radon's wrist that, for all intents and purposes, looked like nothing more than a basic wrist watch.

"What's that?"

"A Watch. It keeps guard over all the keys."

"Why can I hear Shacho through your Watch?"

"Because the key we gave zem to stop the bomb has been turned back on."

"Shacho's key still works?" Koko balked.

"Yes. The portal may have broken, but the key to activate the ley line still works fine. That's how Shacho called us back ."

"Shacho called you back?" Koko asked, confused but also scared.

"No time to explain," Radon bit. "Right now, Shacho is going to destroy everything if we don't *do* something. Ze are going to pull up the ley line and activate it without a proper directive. And when ze do, it'll rip a hole through reality and, since Kyoto's ley line is so old, it could burn all up all the other ley lines we know of."

"But why would Shacho—?"

Radon's expression turned dark, masked, and hard to read. "Ze're angry. We stole you away."

Suddenly, Koko was back in the bedroom with Radon screaming in zer face. Back in the rubble with Shacho screaming about some broken piece of junk.

Shacho and Radon's faces were exactly the same.

Not anger, but pain stuffed down. Hurt pushed aside for too long. The effects of suffering with no end in sight. How many times had Koko talked Shacho down from rages just like this? There was a better solution than rushing around the ship trying to find Yume. If Koko could just talk some sense into Shacho.

"Can I talk to Shacho through your Watch?"

Radon frowned. "No, that aspect of the key broke when the bomb was stopped."

"Why didn't you come back to fix it?"

Radon turned away. "Right now, we need to find Yume."

Koko didn't follow. "I won't help you."

Radon whipped back around. "What?"

Koko puffed up, stood zer ground. "I don't trust the Magician."

There. It was out.

Radon huffed. "Fine. Have it your way. Let your world end while we stand here arguing. You want to know why we didn't come back?"

Koko nodded stiffly.

"Shacho told us not to."

"What? Why? Why would Shacho say something like that?" Koko asked, but already knew the answer.

Bitterness.

Radon softened, only a touch. "Our magic is what changed Shacho. Ruined zem. Understandably, ze didn't want anything to do with us afterward."

315

"But Shacho called you back to help me, didn't ze?" Koko asked.

Radon shrugged. "Don't try to understand the contradictions of decisions made in rage. Those kinds of choices don't make sense. They don't *need* to make sense. They just are."

Radon's shoulders, strong before, slumped now. As if she were talking less about Shacho now, and more about something else. Something personal.

World's End, Koko thought of the archway again. It had more than one meaning. The ley line's power, yes. But also, the heart's power to destroy itself from the inside out.

Koko understood now.

Yume and Radon had done all they could. Shacho had, too. Sometimes, things play out badly no matter how hard everyone tries. All of them had been asked to bear up under the burden of trying to stop a really bad ending from being the last story humanity ever got to write.

It only made sense the effects of such a burden would be awful for everyone involved.

"I trust you. And Yume," Koko said.

Radon eyed Koko suspiciously. "Even if it means destroying the ley line in your world?"

Koko looked down at Radon's watch, thinking of Shacho, of the ley lines and their power, of the keys and remote communication devices. Of Radon and other refugees from other worlds. How important this ship's work really was.

"Yes. Even then."

Radon relaxed visibly and rolled her eyes. As close to a smile as Koko was going to get.

"Come on. We need to run. Now."

They ran, side by side, until they came to an entire hallway of frosted glass doors. Koko marveled at the sheer number of them. All access points to other universes, other worlds the Ex Machina had helped, saved—or...as in Radon's case, had failed to save. How many doors were success stories? How many failures? How many of these worlds teemed with life, and how many looked like the one Koko had left behind? How many estranged friends, lovers, families had been abandoned? How many refugees were like Radon and had nowhere to ever return to?

"Why so many?" Koko whispered as the two of them rushed down the hall. It felt as if the doors might go on forever.

"This ship was designed for a host of agents. Each was assigned their own door. Only..."

"What happened?"

"Bad times," was all Radon said, her voice choking up on the words. "There!"

Radon's hand pointed at the end of the hallway where a clear glass door stood open. Inside, Yume stood in a tight jumpsuit made of what looked like white rubber in a room full of curved glass panels, one layered upon another like bleachers. On each glass panel was a different face, with the same expression and the same tight white jumpsuit. One of the faces, a heavy-lidded face the color of black sand with freckles like white and yellow stars across a low, flat nose, spoke in a low, clear tone.

"Ley Hachi is in position to remotely deactivate the line, correct?"

"Yes.," Yume answered.

"And you found the deactivation spell we asked you to find?"

Yume's head fell. "Yes, but, my fellow magicians—" Yume stammered, voice strained, addressing the dark face, "We can't possibly—"

"You know as well as we do. We must do what must be done," the dark face cut in.

So that was why Yume had gone to the fairy room. To find this spell to counteract what everyone but Koko had already known Shacho was capable of doing. Pulling up the ley line and destroying everything. Only Koko had been too busy being fascinated over fairy-tales and too captivated by the power of this place to put two and two together. And now, it was too late. The great and awful Magician Yume was going to work with this council of beings to take Shacho away from zem and to shut down all of Kyoto's power, forever.

"No," Koko said accidentally.

Yume turned, briefly, and Koko looked right into their face. Eyes pressed closed, finger pinching the bridge of their nose, lips in a tight downward curve. The face of someone very unhappy. Full of regret.

"You know as well as we do what must happen," another face said to Yume, ignoring Koko's presence entirely. This one had a translucent-skinned face with gills and a brilliant blue fin along the top of a crown-shaped head instead of hair. Eyes wide like two indigo globes positioned at a slant along the head focused on Yume.

"But deactivating the ley line without due process will ruin that world," Yume tried to argue "We'll lose all the work we put into saving it."

"We hear you, but Yume," the first black sand and stars face spoke again, gentler now. "If you don't deactivate the ley line now, we could lose everything."

"We can't let that happen," Koko said loudly, stepping around Yume into the line of sight of everybody.

Now, all the faces on all the glass plates refocused on Koko.

"Who is this?" the fish-like head said in a shrill, watery voice.

"This is Koko, of the world whose fate we discuss," Yume said, sounding more sad, not less.

"A recent refugee, good!" said another face. This one looked so much like Shacho that Koko had to look away. "Then all is not lost!"

"No, Koko here wishes to return home."

"But..." the fish voice gasped.

"There will be nothing to return to," Radon said, advancing from the doorway to join at Koko's side. Her eyes were red again, imploring. "We can't let *that* happen. Can we?"

"There has to be another way," Yume said. "Give us time to think?"

"We have no time," Black Sand and Stars barked, lips a straight line.

A hard edge no one was going to cross. Their impressive voice shook the room through the vibrations of the glass panel. Koko could feel the hairs on the back of zer arm trembling.

"I'll go to Shacho!" Koko blurted out before the words could run away. "I'll stop zem."

"Who?" the Shacho-like face asked in a calm voice.

"The key holder who is pulling up the ley line as we speak," Yume said.

Radon held up her wrist. "I have zem on Watch right now."

"And you are sure you can get to zem in time and prevent the ley line from being activated?"

"We will do all in our power to stop zem, yes," Yume said, taking Koko's sudden suggestion as everyone was. Like it was real. And possible.

Koko's gut twisted up with fear. Would this even work? What if Shacho was just like Shacho always was these days? Unmovable and cruel? What if Koko failed? Was the whole universe going to implode?

"And if the human fails?" the Shacho look-alike asked.

"I will remain on board. And should the mission fail, I will deactivate the ley line myself. Through the kill switch."

"Then, I see no reason to not proceed," Shacho look-alike said quietly and bowed.

And suddenly, Koko wondered if this Shacho look-alike was Shacho in another universe. And if so, did they both feel any connection to one another? Did multiple yous in multiple worlds work like that?

The Shacho look-like rose out of the bow and locked eyes with Koko. Though the irises were a completely unfamiliar shade of green-blue, Koko felt the feeling ze used to feel back when Shacho was gentle and would hold Koko after nightmares. A warm, drenching comfort. Koko looked away, face hot in embarrassment.

"It's decided," Black Sand and Stars said.

All of the cascading faces nodded in a rippling unison. Like waves, spreading out from a single drop.

That drop was Koko, and Koko's suggestion had become Koko's mission.

Yume turned from the curvatures of blank glass and put both hands on Koko's shoulders. "Let's get you ready. I need to give you a key that I'll hold Watch over. You will—"

"You're not coming?" Koko interrupted.

"No. I have to remain here, on board, as I promised."

Promised? Promised who? But then, Koko caught Yume sharing a look with Radon, and Koko just knew. The promise must be to Radon. The promise not to die. Koko could understand being unwilling to lose the only person you have. The thought tightened Koko's chest.

Koko could almost hear the echo of Shacho's words through Radon's Watch. *I never meant for you to go.* And suddenly, Koko understood.

"I'll go. Even if this doesn't work, I'm going to Shacho," Koko said, even though nobody asked.

"This will work," Yume said, nodding. " I'm sure of it. You have nothing to worry about. If Shacho is going to listen to anyone, it will be you."

If Koko could win, they all stood a chance. Winning this round with mean-Shacho was the most important thing, ever.

Talk about training. All those fights, learning how to word-spar with Shacho's twisted mind. Learning how to take hits from zer cruelty and not fall. Even if Shacho didn't believe in fate, Koko was beginning to.

Koko turned from Yume and faced Radon. "I'm ready."

"I'm going with you," Radon said without a blink.

Yume looked between the two of them, concern growing like vines in a hothouse, spreading quick and twisting against itself. "Koko?" was all Yume said.

Koko nodded, reaching for Radon's hand. "Fine. Let's hurry. If I know Shacho, we don't have much time."

Right before they arrived, Koko stumbled and nearly fell.

"Careful." A small voice on Koko's shoulder mimicked Yume's voice from the fairy room.

The doll! It was still with zem. Koko felt bolstered by this. A doll built by some of the oldest beings in all of reality! The presence of the magical doll, alone, was a comfort. A reminder that even when Koko couldn't keep up with all these amazing people, still ze weren't without protection. Ze weren't abandoned and forgotten, left to death and a death world. And even when it looked like ze were being left behind, ze weren't alone.

Koko pushed harder, forcing zer legs to pump as hard as ze could to catch up. Because Shacho needed to remember that truth too.

Ze were not abandoned and forgotten. Ze were not alone.

\#

"I'm activating the portal. Stand by," Radon said in a crisp voice.

"Standing by," Yume's voice came through clear on Radon's watch.

Radon looked down at Koko, dressed now in a tight white suit that matched Yume's and the rest of Ex Machina's. They were woven with special fairy-made threads that connected back to the energy of the Fae, and had special protective powers from attacks and special communication powers with other suits. Only, unlike the ley lines, they were not interconnected with the Fae and their life force. So, if the suit was destroyed, it was a loss for the bearer of the suit, but no greater harm was done.

Koko slipped on the white rounded helmet and tapped the left side. "Radon?"

Radon tapped the side of her own helm. "Here."

"Do you think we'll succeed?"

Radon chuckled, tapping the indigo screen. The frosted door flashed green. "That's up to the universe. We can only do our best."

"Remember, you two. Fail or succeed, Shacho is an individual and will make whatever choice ze sees most fit. If that's to activate the ley line, don't try to physically stop zem," Yume's age-wizened voice joined Radon's inside of Koko's helmet. Only, Yume wasn't here at the frosted door standing with them side by side. No, Yume was back in the control room of the ship where there was no risk of being ruined, because Radon wouldn't let Yume risk themselves this time.

"I love you too much to lose you now," Koko had heard breathed from Radon's lips right before they left.

"I love you, too, Radon," were the last words Yume had said before the clear glass door clicked closed.

Now, in front of the frosted door, ready to jump—Koko wished they hadn't been able to convince Yume not to come. Because Koko was terrified. Zer trembling hand reached into a pouch in the white suit. There, the doll in its own white suit was folded up, hands gripping the fabric like a flexible railing. Koko patted the doll's head.

"We're going to be fine," Koko forced out aloud, not sure if it was true or not.

"What do we do if Shacho fights us?" Radon asked.

"Come back to the portal," Yume answered matter-of-factly, "I'll take care of the deactivation from here."

"But, that means..." Koko's helmet fogged up with hot breath, eyes clouded with tears.

Radon's hand reached for Koko's. "We'll do our best."

"Ready to go?" Yume asked.

"Ready."

Radon pushed open the frosted door. There, framed by the neat lines of Ley Hachi, were the crumbled angles and busted up shapes of Koko's Earth. Stepping through the portal felt like stepping from hope into death. Koko tried to shake the feeling of becoming a ghost, but it wouldn't shake. This mission, it was madness, wasn't it?

"There," Radon said, her hand pointing out straight ahead of her.

There, beyond a series of wires and beams that hung in the shape of a weeping willow tree, Shacho stood, one hand held high into the air. Something metallic glinted in the high noonday sun. In zer other hand, a bot made of parts similar to Koko's doll, only the pieces didn't make a humanoid shape at all. The unit looked more insect and more alien. Koko wondered what kind of dark waves could be going through Shacho's brain.

"Koko!" Shacho shouted.

"Shacho!" And without thinking, Koko darted to zem, arms outstretched.

"No!" Radon called out, but it was too late.

Koko rushed right into the trap. The glinting metal sliced through the air, a sharpened shiv. It sliced across Koko's cheek and bicep, on the way to zer chest. Zer heart. But, the shiv hit resistance. A hiss and shriek came from the pouch where the magical doll crouched, waiting and ready to help. The little body squirmed, stabbed through. Shacho stumbled back, eyes wide and wild.

"You. You left me here. Left me for those liars. They ruined me and here you are, looking just like one of them. How could you? How dare you!"

Koko didn't move for fear that Shacho would realize the shiv hadn't hit zer chest. Instead, Koko stared blankly at Shacho. At the one who had held up a fairy key, raised a ley line, and saved life on Earth. Shacho who had just tried to kill the only other Earth-born person left alive.

What could possibly be blowing across the blackened, ashen landscape of Shacho's burnt-out mind? What feelings passed like storm clouds across the twisted up landscape of zer ruined heart?

"Get back!" Radon shouted, rushing to Koko's side.

"You." Shacho spit dirty yellow mucus to the ground. It landed on zer own shredded up boot.

"Give us the key, Shacho."

Shacho took a step back, eying Radon's Watch. "Why would I give you anything? You're a liar. And a traitor."

Liar, Koko understood. But traitor? What did Shacho mean? More illogical babble or something true and scrambled.

"I didn't betray you, Shacho. I told you the truth," Radon said.

"You told me I would be fine!"

"No. I told you we hoped you would be fine," Radon replied.

"You made me believe I could save us!"

"And you did!"

"Look around you," Shacho hissed, frothing from the narrow space in zer tight lips. "Is this what you call saved?"

So, that was what Shacho meant. Shacho had thought stopping the bomb would instantly end all the wars. That it would make all the countries and factions and rebellions and governments lay down their arms, come to agreements, and carry on in gentleness and love. Only that's not what had happened. Instead the nukes were written off as faulty, and all the fighting factions turned to older, trustier methods of death. Agent orange and firestorms. Scattershot bombs and machine guns. Archery and biological warfare. It had ruined wide swaths of land, and had eliminated humanity's chance.

So, just like Koko's departure—Shacho was right. Stopping the hydrogen bomb hadn't saved the world. And, Koko had left Shacho alone to go and find the Magician. Only in both cases, the reality of the truth didn't mean what Shacho thought it meant. Koko saw that now.

"Shacho," Koko called as gently as possible.

Shacho turned, eyes still full of the white flames of rage. "You should be dead! Don't you speak to me now."

Koko took a big risk and pulled the shiv out, revealing that it hadn't pierced all the way through.

Shacho, instead of flying into a rage, gaped, eyebrows creased. "How?"

"The same way our world isn't dead, thanks to you."

Shacho's face was emotionless. "What the fuck are you talking about?"

"Magic," Koko said and reached into the pouch, pulling out the doll that had fallen apart again. Only this time, the face was unrecognizable. Koko wondered if the fairies could fix it anyway. *Yes, they can,* a deep comfort seemed to say. Koko held the broken pieces out to Shacho, who staggered forward and examined them.

"My doll," Shacho mumbled, seeming to remember something. "The fairies..."

"They said it protected you," Koko said, offering the doll up.

Shacho pushed it away, looking betrayed. "Looks like it's yours now."

"Only for holding," Koko said, not giving in. "I think it would protect you, again and again."

"Tch. Why would you help me? I tried to kill you just now," Shacho said, looking down. The look was the same as Radon after she'd snapped at Koko that first time in the bedroom. A confused regret. Something buried deep under layers of rubble.

"They don't call us rubble babies for nothing, you know," Koko said. "What do we know but suffering? I get it. We all mess up. It's okay."

Shacho said nothing but turned away, back toward the riverbank. Back toward the thinnest ground near the ley line—Koko's heart said without explanation. A hand reached into Shacho's pocket, and from it withdrew the small thin metallic plate with the Ex Machina concentric circles on it. The key.

Koko reached out toward Shacho. "Wait. Please."

"I tried to kill you," Shacho insisted without turning.

"But you didn't really mean to," Radon cut in. "And you didn't manage, anyway."

At the sound of Radon's voice, Shacho whipped back around. "Does that even matter?"

"I think it does," Koko and Radon accidentally said in unison.

Radon shared a look with Koko, and for the first time Koko felt like the two of them were really on the same team. It was so much like when Shacho would give after a fight. They'd sit and reminisce about the past, talk about what they'd do now. Those moments, brief gaps in time with the old Shacho, made all the bad worth it. Because, like the ruined Earth, Koko's heart still had hope that it could get better. Life could start again.

Radon strode across the rubble as if it wasn't there, stood square and towering before Shacho, and held out her massive trunk of an arm. In the open palm rested another thin metallic plate with more elaborate markings on it. The locking key. The one that they'd all agreed they'd try to convince Shacho to use. This key would forever close access to the ley line here in Kyoto, protecting it for good. It would mean no more weight, no more power here. No more shrines, rebuilt. No more pilgrims on their way for a spiritual journey. No more magical energy. But, it would mean saving the rest of the Earth's ability to carry on.

"You know what this is," Radon said matter-of-fact.

"I do," Shacho answered back in a matching tone.

Bite for bite, bitterness for bitterness, brokenness for brokenness —Koko couldn't help but see that for all of their differences, they were also the same. Like all of the refugees of Ex Machina. It was more than a simple tattoo that bound them together. It was more than magic and ley lines and fairy tales. It was this: that underneath all of their pain and suffering, there was still life. They were fighters who did not give up, even when hope seemed impossible.

"Will you do it?" Radon asked.

"I..." Shacho hesitated.

"Please," Koko added softly, trying to tap into Shacho's hope.

"Why?" Shacho bit back instead, sinking back down into zer anger, hiding from the tough decision.

"Because you opening this ley line will end it all," Radon said without pause.

"And if I don't?" Shacho snapped.

"Then, the Magician will remotely deactivate the ley line, and that will be it."

"Yume? Here? Where?" Shacho barked.

"Not here," Radon said, tapping her Watch. "Here."

"Coward! How dare you not face me! I knew you wouldn't come! Because you're a coward! And a liar! And a murderer! Do you see me? I'm the result. I'm what you did! And you can't face it, can you!?"

Zer eyes went a new kind of wild. Desperate, like a starved dog smelling a scrap of meat. The look was dangerous and scary. Koko shriveled back up against zemself, arms across chest, protecting the heart Shacho had already tried to stab. Suddenly, Koko was glad for Radon's foresight to keep the ancient Magician away from this mess.

Shacho's voice cracked, ragged and raw. Ze doubled over in a violent cough, bolted back up as soon as it was done, and screamed into the air more. Again, zer voice broke and ze tumbled to the rubble, spitting blood.

"Are you done?" Radon said coolly, holding ground, key still laying in her open hand.

Shacho's coughing became sobs. Koko's fear evaporated, just like always did at this point. And suddenly, without second guessing if it was safe or not, Koko rushed over. The two of them had been here so many times over the past years. Shacho losing zer shit and then breaking down. It took so much to knock out the walls of zer heart, and Koko understood why now. Because those walls had to be incredibly strong just for Shacho to find a way to get through the day.

"Oh, Shacho," Koko said, arms out.

"Koko, no, don't," Radon said again, only quieter and less certain this time.

Shacho's hands reached out. Another glint of metal flashed, too late to stop or change direction. Koko gasped and braced for the stab. It'd go through the heart this time. No magical doll to stop the blow.

It only seemed fair, in a cruel kind of way. The world had taken everything from Shacho, so why shouldn't Shacho turn and take everything from Koko, right when the world could be saved?

For Shacho, it was just too much to get through. The wells of sorrow burrowed too deep for too long in zer broken heart. Like the doll, only magic was simply not enough. The risk to open up, to big an ask, and against that ask, Shacho's defenses were solid and well built. The walls between hatred and love, too strong to tear down.

The two of them crashed together. Chest to chest. Bone hard against bone. Only, there was no punch of metal, was there? No cutting slice through Koko's white vest. And instead of a fist pressed close against the skin, both Shacho's hands lay flat against Koko's sides.

Koko pulled away, gasping, uncertain whether or not this was the end. Zer hand searched. No blood? But then, what had the glint been?

Shacho held out a thin metal sheet and tapped it in a series of places. The key flashed gold for a second, then blue, then back to normal. Shacho braced, but nothing happened.

Radon rushed over. "Why didn't that work?"

"I don't know." Shacho looked crumpled up, like blasted metal.

"Because the ley line is refusing to respond to it," Yume said through Radon's Watch. "It won't close back down."

"Why?" Radon asked into the Watch.

"It's trying to help, is my guess, only it doesn't understand how powerful it is."

Koko thought of Radon and Shacho at the same time. They could both be like that. Sometimes, people try to help, only they don't know that what they're about to do is the worst thing. They don't see how they're just repeating a cycle.

The ley lines weren't so different from people, after all.

"We need to deactivate it before the power breaks through," Yume spoke. "I'm sorry, but we have no other choice."

"Shacho. Give me the key," Radon said, hand out.

Shacho offered the key in a shaking fist. "Take it. I'm useless."

"That's not true," Koko said, but now wasn't the time to argue. Now was the time to act. That buzzy feeling from before filled the air and Koko reached out without questioning why.

"Give me the old key," Koko said.

Radon took the key from Shacho and handed it to Koko. "What are you going to do?"

Koko looked at the key. "I don't know."

"Take both keys and put them together over the ley line," Yume explained.

Koko followed the instructions, pressing the two keys together. A vibration shook Koko's hands violently as the two keys sealed together. Koko laid the new, thicker piece of metal old-key down on top of the train track they stood beside. Right ahead of them, the tracks went underground and came out at the station platform. After this ley line closed, would the train work anymore? Had it been magic all this time?

As soon as the combined key lay on the metal, the track began to glow. The light was the same indigo of the screens beside each frosted door back in the ship, Ley Hachi. Koko took a step back and found both Radon and Shacho at zer side.

"Ready?" Yume asked, as if they knew exactly what was going on with these keys.

"We're ready," Koko said automatically.

Ready for what?

"Take shelter, will you?" Yume asked.

"We're fine, Yume. Just do it," Radon said back, deadpan.

They'd discussed this part back on Ley Hachi before embarking. If anything went wrong, taking shelter would be useless. If locking the ley line dispersed any kinds of spells, they'd all get hit with them regardless of what Earth material stood in their way. Because ley line magic penetrated everything, down to the core vibrations that made up reality. If they were going to be shaken loose, it'd be the same facing it openly or cowering behind a wall. Both Radon and Koko had chosen. They'd rather stand their ground, together. The rigid lines on Shacho's face didn't make zem look like ze'd want to duck and cover, either. The three of them joined hands and waited for the magical end to begin.

"Initiating the deactivation," Yume said.

A brilliant wave of pure white light washed over all of them. Then, after the initial blast, colors spread across the sky like a beautiful sunset. Pastel pink, orange, purple, red, and green-blue. Next came the waves of warm air, almost like the gentle push of the ocean rising as tide comes into shore. Over and over, the soft warm ripples washed over Koko's whole body, filling everything from zer skin down to the marrow of bones with a deep peace.

Koko marveled at all of this, wondering how something so tragic as locking a ley line forever could be so good.

As the light and the warmth slowly faded, the three of them released their hands and turned to look around. Everything about the world felt...the same. No more magical, but no less. No more saved, and no more dead than before.

"Is that it?" Shacho asked, surprisingly calm.

"That's it," said Yume's voice in Koko's helmet.

"It's done," Koko echoed with a strange certainty. As if Koko's heart understood things Koko's mind didn't yet. Was that what it felt like inside Shacho? Only, backwards? The mind knowing things the heart couldn't yet touch? Like not wanting to kill Koko, and trying to do it anyway? Yes, maybe it was something like that.

"What now?" Radon asked, looking from Shacho to Koko. The implied question: are you coming back with me or do I go alone?

"We'll send you back," Shacho said, looking at Radon.

"But, will the portal still work?" Radon asked.

"No," Yume said. "But I already thought of that. Koko, pick the melded keys up, please."

Koko did as instructed, picking up the metal sheet from the track that once the oldest magical power line on Earth. Touching the metal, it felt no different than before on the surface. No different than before Koko had come down the track line and met the Magician. Only, it was different. It was nothing more than metal, now.

"Set the keys on the old archway. Can you find it alone, or shall I upload a map?"

"A map, please," Koko said, marveling at how the helmet was still working. How the keys would still work. As if the ley line hadn't been the only thing magical about the universe. As if somehow magic were woven into everything. Every atom, every particle, every vibration, and every thought.

"You guessed it," Yume's voice whispered into Koko's ear.

Koko wondered if Radon heard that or not. Or if it had come from the helmet at all. No way to know for sure, but Koko had a hunch that it wasn't through a speaker or a device installed in the helmet. Just like the doll's voice.

The doll! Again, Koko had forgotten it. Ze whipped around looking for it, and saw Shacho cradling the broken doll in two palms. The doll, however, looked like an AI device again. And Shacho looked like ze were trying to repair the busted chest with a metal plug. The doll didn't seem to protest or agree.

Koko turned into the map that came up on a heads-up display inside the helmet. The archway was just across the tracks, down a narrow passage, and around a large concrete block.

"This way!" Koko called out to Radon and Shacho.

"Where are we going?" Radon asked, pulling up alongside.

Koko noticed Shacho hung behind with the doll, which was fine. Radon and Shacho didn't need to get along for this to work. They could be distant crew mates, right? At any rate, Yume would know what to do.

"We're going to the portal."

"But, it won't work," Radon argued.

Koko started. "Didn't you hear Yume?"

Radon laughed sharply at that. "No, Koko. Yume can't contact us anymore. The ley line is gone, remember? And with it, all the powers we had. All that technology all ran off the same energy, and it's gone now. What are you on about?"

Koko ignored this logic. For as true as it sounded, it couldn't be true at all, because Koko had a map from Yume who was still back on Lei Hachi.

"Just come with me," Koko said, and decided not to explain any more than that.

Radon shrugged. "Sure, why not. We have all the time in the world for broken plans, now."

Koko found the portal easily. Walked right up it and pressed a hand against the Ex Machina seal as instructed. The parts started moving. The metal started glowing. And in a matter of seconds, the portal was open.

"Come on," Koko waved a gaping Radon and Shacho through.

"How did you do that?" Shacho marveled on the other side as they stood in the same room Koko had come through the first time.

Koko shrugged. "I have no idea."

The door, which Koko recognized as a frosted glass door with a protective shade over it, opened and there was Yume.

"How come that worked?" Koko asked.

Yume grinned knowingly. "Because you have a unique connection to magic."

"I do?" Koko started.

"Obviously," Radon snarked. "The keys, the deactivation, the portal. How did any of that work, anyway?"

Shacho just made a grumble that sounded like a feral bark.

Yume ignored them all. "Koko accesses the ley lines directly, as I do."

Everyone gaped. Koko felt punched in the stomach with shock. "What?"

"Yes, I had wrongly thought when I first came to your world that it was Shacho I had been pulled toward. Only, when the magic didn't save them from the effects of the ley line activation in the past, I had serious doubts. A Magician should not have been ruined in that moment. Only, I figured I had been wrong altogether about a Magician existing on your world. Shacho's imprint of power was strong enough to trick me, that was all. Maybe, I kept thinking, it wasn't Shacho who bore the power inside zer cells after all. Only after you opened the portal did I know the full truth."

"I opened the portal?" Koko asked, startled. "But Shacho called you back, not me."

"But you activated the key without even holding one when you approached the archway."

"I did?"

"You did." Yume pointed at Koko's heart. "Inside your heart, you carry a magical charge that is energized with each beat. Normally, a Magician manifests earlier than you did, but with the trauma of your world and Shacho's unique protections gained from their familial history, the late manifestation makes sense."

"Wait. Did you say a m-magician?" Koko stuttered in shock.

That couldn't be right. Yume was mistaken. Or rather, it had been a slip of the tongue. Because it just couldn't be true. There was only one Magician, and that was Yume. As proved by the fairies and that room and, and, and well everything. Koko wasn't like that. Koko was just a single human born on a dying Earth at the right time to do some good. Rubble baby, remember? A unique connection to magic, sure, but no magician.

"You remember when you were born?" Yume asked, pulling up alongside Koko as if out of nowhere.

"Of course, doesn't everyone?" Koko said.

Shacho, who was locked in some argument with Radon at the moment, stopped and choked. "What the hell did you just say, Koko?"

"That I remember the day I was born. You do too, right?"

"No. And you don't. You're making that up."

Fairy tales, Shacho might as well have said. Koko clammed up, looking down, ashamed.

In the corner of zer eye, though, Koko could see Yume shaking their head at Shacho. "I don't think you are making anything up. Describe what you saw to me."

Koko spoke without looking up.

"Well, there were massive mountain-like shapes, only they were more shadows than shapes. Places the light didn't penetrate. The light came from a web full of interconnected threads, And, in places where the most threads knotted up, there were droplets of water, only not water, energy. Life. And the droplets of life vibrated and pulsed all the time. Then, one of the dark shapes moved aside, a long thin shadow cast across one of the threads, and like a finger it penetrated into one of the droplets. And that's when I came to life."

"That's no birth," Shacho scoffed.

"No," Radon breathed, eyes wide. "That's—"

"The birth of a Magician. One who comes from the realm of pure magic, the land of the Fae, the Zeroth Dimension into a natural world at a time when a Fae has gathered enough energy in reserve to produce an extension of itself," Yume explained.

"You're saying," Koko had to suck in a long, slow breath. "You're saying that I'm an extension of a Fae?"

Yume snapped their fingers. "Correct."

"I'm like you," Koko marveled.

Yume smiled. "Correct again."

"How many of us are there?" Koko asked.

"Oh, a handful. And each is a fleet leader among the Ex Machina," Yume said with a tilt of an eyebrow that said: won't you be one too?

"You think I could...lead a fleet? I don't even know what that means!"

"But you could learn," Shacho said.

Koko turned to Shacho.

"Shacho..."

"I'd go with you."

"You...you would?" Koko asked. "But why?"

"Because it's what I was born to do. I never meant for you to go,

Koko," Shacho said, repeating those awful words from before, the words that had that almost ended all universes. Only now, Shacho was calm and the words came out gentler than ever. "I made a lot of mistakes, and I was wrong about a lot of things. And…I want to make it up to you. All of it. I want to go back to the way things used to be. When I protected you, instead of all this fighting. I know I'm not who I used to be but…neither are you…and…maybe…"

"None of us are who we used to be," Radon said. "That's what growth is, kid."

"But, what changed your mind?" Koko asked carefully, wary of another fight.

"I finally saw how busted up I was," Shacho said and pointed at Koko's chest.

Koko looked down. The little broken doll had somehow come back to life, climbed back into Koko's pocket without Koko realizing, and nestled in to sleep. The hole in the white jumpsuit where Shacho had tried to stab them both through was still there, only now the doll's arm dangled out, like a baby's arm hanging from a crib.

"When you deactivated the ley line, I started remembering things. Before my parents died in the wars, they always said I had to do my duty. My family had always lived in the neighborhood of weeping trees. And for generations, we cared for all the shrines around Demachiyanagi. When the wars started, I knew I couldn't leave. No matter what. I was protecting something very precious, only I didn't really know what."

"What was it?" Koko managed to force out, knowing the answer.

"You," Shacho said. "I thought I understood when Yume came to me the first time. It all made sense in a way. The ley lines. The power. I was their protector. Only, I didn't see any of it for what it really was. My heart kept trying to tell me I was wrong. My family, we hadn't promised to protect Demachiyanagi. Demachiyanagi had been built to protect *you*, our greatest connection to the ley line of Kyoto and the Fae. That's what I'd been doing here all along. Only, after the ley line went off, I forgot so much. And instead of coming to you for help like I should have, I tried to secretly call Yume. And when Yume didn't answer, I decided it was time to push you away from me. Only that decision turned me mean and angry with myself. Angry, by association, with you."

"But, Koko. I was wrong. And I'm for how I treated you. I'm sorry I didn't explain any of this. I'm sorry for what I became."

Shacho stopped talking then and looked away from Koko, zer eyes turning red and dropping to zer feet.

Koko, uncertain what to do with this sad, vulnerable Shacho, looked to Yume. Living with Radon, surely they knew what it was like to be hurt for no reason. If anyone would know what to do, it would be Yume.

The soft, almost sad look on Yume's face said, "maybe today really is for redeeming broken things" without words. Koko dug down deep and found at the bottom of zer heart a cascade of breaks. All the things Shacho had said and didn't mean. All the wild rage-filled words. All the decisions that made no sense.

Don't try to make sense out of decisions made in rage. They don't make sense, Radon had said. *They just are.*

Maybe it wasn't a grudge Koko was holding as much as an inability to comprehend what it looked like inside Shacho's head. But finally, Shacho was opening up. If Koko chose to hold on to Shacho just like the broken doll, maybe the fairy magic of acceptance could create a portal to more of the truth. More vulnerability. More of the gentle Shacho who wasn't gone, just lost.

"I forgive you," Koko said.

"Thank you," Shacho said, looking up again. Zer cheeks were wet with streams of tears.

Their eyes met, and Koko remembered their first meeting.

It'd been spring. The sakura were in full bloom. The air was sweet and the bells of the nearby shrine were ringing. A wind kicked up and rain drove them both down to the shelter of the bridge's underpass. They made eye contact and started talking instantly. Over time, they became friends by fighting for the end of the wars. And after? They'd stuck together because it'd felt right.

And what did "right" mean in this case, but that buzzy pull of magic?

"Earth isn't our home anymore," Shacho said. "Let's stay here, learn what we need to learn, and go save more people like us."

Koko's heart skipped a beat at *people like us.*

The broken. The homeless. The lost. The ones who don't know their own power because they feel too stuck in the muck of their own suffering. Sure, there was a lot of brokenness to try and overcome. But, there was also forgiveness and trying again. Just like Yume and Radon did. Just like how inside of Koko zey were both human and Magician, both a small person who didn't always know what to do and the powerful extension of a Fae—one of the greatest beings in all the known universes.

Koko recalled what Yume had asked when the two of them had been alone in Koko's room. The question Koko had yet to answer even inside zemself.

What do I do now that I am alive?

Saving worlds from complete annihilation, rescuing people from broken places, and growing and helping others sounded far better than trying to figure out why things were alive at all. Happenstance, Shacho would say. And ze would be right. But, that didn't make life any less worth doing something amazing with.

Koko's heart buzzed with that feeling of heading in the right direction.

"Yes," Koko said finally, reaching out a hand for Shacho. "Let's do it."

Across the room Yume shared a look with Radon that looked exactly like how Koko felt about Shacho. And suddenly, Koko wondered how long Yume and Radon had been together. Radon didn't look much older than Koko, but then, did a body even age in the limbo space that the Ex Machina inhabited?

More things to learn. Always, more things to learn. But, first things first.

"So, when do we set out to save our first world together?" Koko asked.

"We're already en route, but first, let's properly introduce you both to the Ex Machina. I haven't explained exactly who you two are. I think they would be honored to know," Yume said, motioning for them to head to the command room.

"So long as we don't have to retell the story of the past," Shacho said, darkening.

Radon laughed and draped an arm over Shacho's back. "Not yet."

"Leave that for the fairies," Yume added and smiled.

A new glint alit in their eyes. A glint that seemed to hold the light that Koko remembered from that very first day of life. The light of the Fae. Koko wondered if that same light glinted in zer own eyes at first, but then turned to leave the portal room and caught zer own expression.

Sure enough, there that light was. The light of a million ley lines and the heart of some brilliant Fae very, very far away.

ABOUT THE AUTHOR

Rei Rosenquist is a queer agender (they/them) speculative fiction and romance writer who depicts a wide variety of identities struggling to find a place in a wide variety of worlds. They are also a barista, baker, musician, and lifelong semi-nomad.

Rei has traveled to many countries, engaged many peoples, picked up new habits, and learned new languages. Across lands, they find constant inspiration in the stories we tell each other, the food we share with one another, the music we make together, and the world we can build when we allow ourselves to dream.

Find out more about Rei at:
reirosenquist.com

facebook.com/reirosenquist

twitter.com/rylrosenquist

instagram.com/rylrosenquist

goodreads.com/reirosenquist

AT THE CROSSROADS

LINDA JORDAN

Maureen crouched down on the gray, limestone berm and stared at the dozen flower stalks lined with delicate, white orchid blossoms. The green centers of the flowers stared back. The plants were what—eight inches tall?

What was their name? She couldn't remember.

Stupid, stupid, stupid. She'd spent nearly the entire flight from Seattle to Ireland glued to her guidebook, memorizing plant names and attributes.

She leaned over and smelled the teeny blooms. Sweet, almost a vanilla scent. Still, no name came to her.

Rubbing her face, she stood up, and the wind coming off the sea hit her full force. Gulls flew high above, soaring on an updraft caused by the tall cliff face. She was alone out here today. Just the way she liked it.

The Burren had too many tourists. Even though, technically, she was a tourist too. Only staying for a year.

She picked up her water bottle and sipped the cool water. It didn't taste anything like home, although she couldn't describe the difference. Water in Seattle, admittedly put through a filter to remove all the crap, still tasted like home. The water from the cottage she rented tasted like something else. Strange water with peculiar minerals mixed in.

Maureen rubbed her eyes, knowing she shouldn't. They hurt, and were probably bloodshot. She felt tired almost to the point of delirium.

She hadn't been able to sleep all the way through a single night since arriving. She'd often wake in the middle of the night. There were strange noises. Loud sounds, almost like a party going on. Dogs barking, music playing. Except there wasn't a party. The surrounding cottages weren't even rented out. The tourist season was waning and the not-so-warm summer temperatures were growing cooler as the season moved towards fall.

And it wasn't jet lag. She'd been here two weeks now.

The sun retreated as the days grew shorter. She was used to that, having lived in Seattle, and promptly bought some vitamin D and began taking it. Seasonal Affective Disorder was *not* going to get her this year. Sleeping through the night would help a lot, though.

She finally gave in and looked up the name of the plant in her field guide. *Spiranthes spiralis*, autumn lady's tresses. The small orchids grew from tubers, each flower attached to a different rosette of leaves and a different plant.

She slid her pack off and set it on the ground. Pulled her iPad out and added the orchid to her list of alkaline plants growing in the limestone areas of the Burren. Acidic plants grew in the limestone as well, near pockets of peat. Her lists grew longer every day. She still needed to come up with a good title for her thesis.

And she needed to get more groceries, and do half a million other things, but this was a gorgeous day. Despite her lack of sleep, she'd loved spending it outside, walking the Burren.

The sun was moving lower on the horizon and if she didn't turn back now, she'd be riding the bike home in the dark. Again. The last time she'd done that had ended in a collision with a boundary marker, torn pants and a badly scraped knee. She wouldn't do that again.

She packed her water bottle, book and iPad into the pack, then slung it over one shoulder. It took half an hour to walk back to the path she'd left her bike at. She unlocked it. Put the helmet and pack on. Then peddled off down the bike path.

Should she stop for some fish and chips for dinner? No. She'd done that too much lately. Her exercise wasn't offsetting the calories. And her budget wouldn't allow much more of that. She still had soup from yesterday in the fridge. Leftovers again. She'd get groceries tomorrow.

Maureen pedaled up the long hill to the Cottages of the Wood. A group of seven, one bedroom cottages set on lawn in front of a woodland. They were all new construction, the rental agency had told her. So, new plumbing and electrical. Which meant untested, she'd found out when the electricity fluttered badly during most of the hard storm, earlier in the week. What would happen when winter came?

She'd gone out and bought a very large battery powered lantern the next day. She was experienced with power outages. Too bad the cottage didn't have a wood stove or fireplace.

Maureen got off the bike and walked it up the path to her front door. The short stone wall near her front door was knocked down. She hadn't noticed it when she left this morning. Had that been the noise she heard last night? She should call the rental agent and tell them, so the owner wouldn't think she destroyed the wall. After dinner. She'd call after dinner.

She parked the blue mountain bike just inside the front door, which was the living room and kitchen of the cottage. Then wriggled out of her pack and set it on one of the wooden kitchen chairs. Took the bicycle helmet and strapped it to the bike. And took off her khaki-green raincoat, hanging it over the chair holding her backpack. At least it hadn't rained today.

She sat in the overstuffed, blue chair and slipped off her running shoes. Then pulled her iPad and phone out of the backpack and plugged them into the surge protector on the kitchen table. More desk than eating area. Although she ate there too.

She pulled the plastic container of soup out of the fridge and opened the lid. Kale and white bean soup. It wasn't exciting, but it would do.

Pouring some into a bowl, she set the bowl in the microwave, turning it on. And returned the rest of the soup to the fridge. Another day without cooking. Avoiding cooking was a good goal. She pulled some bread out of the fridge and toasted a slice. Then sat down at the table to eat and look over her list.

The soup still needed more salt, but she kept forgetting to add it. The bread with fresh butter tasted wonderful. It was whole grain with sunflower seeds in it. Rolled oats were sprinkled over the top, creating a nice texture.

The bread tasted like her grandmother used to make. At the thought of family, a wave of grief washed over her. She had used up so much of her life taking care of her family. First Grandma, then Dad, then Mom. She'd quit school, just short of her thesis. Then quit her job. Then given up her entire life, as she nursed each one of them. While death relentlessly took each one of them from her.

Enough. She'd done everything she could for them. Now it was time for *her* to live. Except that she didn't have any dreams left. Except this one. To come to the Burren and explore it. To find its secrets. Maybe write that bloody thesis and get her master's degree. Maybe just write a paper for herself. She didn't know.

She had no idea where to go from here. Mid-thirties, out of ideas about what to do with her life, and suddenly alone. Filled with both sadness and relief.

Maureen sighed and got up to wash the dishes. She left them in the drying rack and sat down again, looking at papers of the project she'd outlined some ten years earlier. The words seemed to come from someone else. A stranger.

What she probably needed to do tomorrow was walk through the woodland behind the cottages and categorize the plants there. Then begin making the list of plants living in acid seeps. Including what stage they were in now, in August. Next August it might be a different list. Plants didn't do the same things year after year. Their lives were dependent on their age, the weather and shade vs. sun. Including whether they'd been dug up, or stepped on by people, or by the cows who grazed the Burren. Things like that.

After dinner Maureen called the rental agent and got a message machine. She left a message about the wall, asking them to confirm they got her message.

Then decided to make an early night of it. She couldn't have stayed awake much longer anyway. She could catch up on sleep. Her phone read 8:10 p.m. She locked the doors and got ready for bed.

At midnight the noise began, waking her out of a deep sleep. It started as a low thrum and then escalated into shrieking and yelling. She sat upright in her bed. Then got the lantern and looked out the back door, but saw nothing. She could still hear the noise though.

Dogs barked. No, that wasn't it. They were hounds. Baying, not barking. And there was that music again. It sounded like several different horns. Not metallic horn like trumpets. These horns were deep and bellowing. Like old-fashioned ones made from cow horns.

No way was she going out there.

She closed and locked the back door and went round to the front. Still couldn't see anything. The noise sounded louder in back.

Was it coming from the woodland? Maybe. She should look for signs of local kids having a party back there. Tomorrow, when it was light out.

She went back to bed and turned the lantern off, but the noise continued. Maureen lay back on the pillow, growing angrier by the second.

She heard foxes making that weird screaming noise like her first night in the cottage. Maureen had described it to the woman at the grocery store. The older clerk told her it was a fox.

Then thundering, like a stampede. The cottage shook from the vibrations of the sound. Or was it a quake? Did Ireland have earthquakes? Or volcanoes? Iceland did. Ireland wasn't that far away. Was there a ring of fire on the Atlantic like there was on the Pacific? Geology wasn't her strong point. She knew just enough about it to understand how soil was created.

The noise continued, getting louder and louder. It sounded like someone was banging on her back door. Then the side of the cottage.

Was the land haunted? Even though the buildings were new? Maybe it had been a rundown castle where horrible things happened. And they tore it down to build the cottages. And the ghosts were pissed off.

Damn, this was so annoying.

She got up and went to the back door, flinging it open.

"What the hell do you want?" she yelled out into the pounding rain.

A cold, wet wind blew through the cottage. Swirling around. Papers flew off the table, caught up in a whirlpool.

Dark bluish figures rushed in through the darkness. Why hadn't she turned the lights on?

There were horses and dogs. Big dogs, barking and snarling. People in cloaks and long, flowing clothes rode the horses, racing through the main room of the little cottage as if the furniture didn't exist.

Maureen stood there for a second or two, frozen with horror. Unable to really process what was happening. She felt stunned and had to make an effort to close her mouth.

They looked like ghosts, but Maureen could feel the cold, wet fur of a dog who rubbed against her pajama pants.

With a great deal of effort she made herself move. Maureen ran for the front door and flung it open.

"Get out!"

The throng stampeded out the front door, although more were still coming in the back. It looked like an endless parade.

Maureen backed towards the bedroom, trying to get out of the way.

Drums pounded and horns blew. She could smell mud, horse sweat and the sea. And always the salty sea on the wind, overpowering everything.

She was nearly to the bedroom, almost escaped to invisibility, when one of the riders bent over and grabbed her. Picking her up by the waist with two strong hands. He dragged her up aboard the steaming, black horse.

"Let me go, you bastard!" Her screams were lost in the din of the horns, but she pounded on him with closed fists, tried to hit his face. Missed.

He pushed her head down as he ducked when the horse went out through the front door. It was fairly light outside. The half-moon high in the clear sky out over the ocean. Above the land, rain clouds hovered, opening up to release their burden. In seconds she was drenched.

They galloped off down the pathway, through the dark, wet night. Joining the others ahead of them. As they moved onto the road, the horses' hooves clacked on the concrete. Maureen squirmed, trying to wriggle loose. He held her with both arms and she realized the horse wore no saddle or tack at all. The man, or whatever he was, controlled the horse with his mind. Or maybe didn't control it at all. After all, these people and animals were not of this world.

His arms felt like stone when she pounded on them. Maureen only caught glimpses of his face, beneath the dark hood. She could smell the wet wool of the cloak. His eyes gleamed pale blue in the light from the moon. He had no beard, but his features looked firm, strong and perfect in an inhuman way. There was the faint touch of a smile, which scared the hell out of her.

The horses and dogs continued to race, running throughout the entire village. Maureen fought him every step of the way. Finally, he must have grown tired of her struggle. He raised his hand in front of her face, the palm facing her. The next thing Maureen felt was her mind and body sinking into unconsciousness.

Maureen woke later, instantly alert, but confused. Slowly sitting up. She was in a large room, filled with the prone bodies of women, men and hounds lying on mats covering the floor. It was light outside the ornate stained glass windows. Sunlight streamed through the windows, causing them to glow.

The people wore no clothes, but many had blankets draped over themselves. Others lay completely naked. Boots and clothes lay scattered, as if quickly discarded.

Maureen still wore her pajamas, which were now dry. The room felt warm. The man who'd brought her here lay asleep in a pile of blankets next to her. He had long, dark hair and even now, no beard or hint of one. Then she saw the ears poking out from his wavy hair. They were pointed. Like Legolas in those movies, what were they called? Lord of the something. Was he an elf?

That made no sense at all. She must be dreaming.

That was it. She'd finally gotten into a deep enough sleep, and after so many nights of no sleep, this was a dream. A very strange one.

Maureen stood as quietly as possible. She wove her way through the sleepers. One dog, a shaggy tan hound, raised its head briefly. It looked at her and went back to sleep.

The building had one room. It was shaped like an octagon, but with more sides. What was that called? She didn't bother to count the sides. Each panel had a window or door in it. The golden brown wood which held the windows and the two doors was elaborately carved into shapes of flowers and trees.

She opened the door. It made no noise. Maureen slipped out into the sunlight, wishing she had shoes, but this was a dream. So the stones beneath her feet couldn't hurt her.

The sun shone through tall trees, deciduous and evergreen. Oaks and yews glowed with its golden light. And the oaks were leafed out in spring green leaves. New and fresh to the world. There was a large grassy meadow in front of her, bordered by a hedgerow, the wild roses in full bloom. It was obviously spring here in her dream, in contrast to fall in the real world.

At the far end of the meadow grazed horses. Blacks, browns, grays, buckskins and whites. They were stunningly beautiful. Some tall and slender like hunters. Others stocky like draft horses.

A calico cat walked up to her and rubbed around her shins.

"Well, hello," Maureen said.

The cat meowed and walked off to go about her business.

Maureen had no idea where this dream was set. She'd never been any place like this. Not that she remembered, anyway.

Walking across the stone path, she moved quickly, because the rocks were poking her bare feet and they hurt. How was that possible? To feel pain in a dream?

Once in the meadow, she could walk normally. The grass felt soft beneath her feet. There were boulders arranged in a circle. Like one of the stone circles she'd visited when she first came to the U.K. Or maybe more like one of the old stone forts in the Burren. There were tall, upright stones in the center circle. An outside circle had gray stones that looked the perfect size to sit upon. So she did.

What was this dream? It felt real, but it couldn't be. She could only have dreamt the invasion of her cottage. There was no other answer that made any sense.

But her dreams usually had things happening in them. Nothing was happening here. It was quiet and serene.

A raven flew over and sat on one of the upright grayish stones, preening its feathers and staring at her.

"Hello," said Maureen.

"Hello," said the raven, in a cracked, but understandable voice.

"You can talk? Now I know this is a dream."

The raven cackled at that.

Then it said, "This is no dream."

"It must be."

"No dream. This is real."

"Where is this?"

"Faerie," said the raven.

"Faerie? Faerie doesn't exist."

"It's more real than you are. What are you?"

"Human."

"I've heard about you. You're bad people. Destroying the world."

"Yes, I guess we are," said Maureen. "Some of us are. Others are trying to save it."

"Which are you?"

"I'm trying to respect nature. But I guess I've done my share of destruction, too."

"Hmmph," said the raven. "Both good and bad."

The door of the building opened and a man emerged, completely naked. Maureen looked away. So, she was supposed to believe this was Faerie. Not possible. No way did these people look like faeries. Not a one of them had wings, that she could see.

The raven squawked and flew away.

The man came over and sat on a stone next to hers. Making no attempt to cover his nudity. His skin was an ivory color, his eyes an eerie pale blue.

He had carried himself like a dancer. Not a wasted movement, yet behind that lay great strength and power. There was a strange light around his skin. He actually glowed.

"You are awake early," he said, in a voice with an accent she couldn't place.

"Where am I? Why did you bring me here?"

"You are in Faerie. I brought you here for many reasons."

"Like what?"

"First, you were in danger of being trampled."

"So, you rescued me?"

It hadn't felt like a rescue.

"Yes."

"And in order to do that, you had to knock me out?"

"You were fighting too hard. I was afraid you would slip off the horse and injure yourself."

"Did it occur to you that I might not want to be rescued?"

"It did not. Who would not want to come to Faerie? Also, your home, or whatever you call it, sits in the middle of one of our roads. It should never have been built there. We have the right of way."

"It's not my house. I'm just renting it and I didn't build it. I'm sure the owner doesn't even believe you or Faerie exists."

"Then that human is ignorant as well as foolish."

"Possibly."

Maureen noticed the surrounding meadow was filled with flowers being pollinated by buzzing bees and flies. Butterflies of all colors, from tiny ones the size of a fingernail to larger ones the size of her palm, drifted from flower to flower.

"I don't understand any of this," she said. Her head throbbed.

"That is because you are human. It will take some time to adjust to being in Faerie."

"I'm not staying. I want to go back. Now."

"You are not ready to go back."

"How the hell would you know?"

"You have not learned what you came here for," he said.

"I did not come here by choice. And what does that mean—being here to learn?" she asked, snapping.

"You opened the door," he said, grinning at her with perfect teeth, which only made him all the creepier. "I do not know what knowledge you need. I do know you have lost your soul."

"What?"

"It is visible to anyone looking at you. Your soul is missing. Sometimes, it is that way with humans who have given away so much of themselves that they lose who they truly are."

"You've known a lot of humans, have you?"

She was getting angrier by the moment. Despite the beautiful sunny day in this perfect setting.

"I have known many. I am much older than you."

"Just what were you doing riding through the village?"

"We must ride the old ways at various times. It keeps our world, and yours, alive. It heals the earth we all live on."

"You are crazy," she said.

"I am not. Just because something is beyond your understanding does not mean it is a lie. Or crazy. You humans have a limited understanding of the worlds."

"Worlds?" This was not happening. She must still be dreaming.

"Worlds. There are many. The human world and Faerie are just two of them, even though humans persist in believing theirs is the only one. Humans are shortsighted."

He waved his hand and a golden flask appeared in his hand. He drank from it and offered it to her.

"What is it?" she asked.

"Water."

"I can't eat or drink anything from here, can I? Or I'll have to stay. That's what all the old tales say."

"Ah, so you do acknowledge our existence? The old tales are twisted, by the corrupt times in which they were created. Nothing is holding you here, except yourself."

She glared at him, but took the flask. Maybe the water would help her headache. She was dehydrated.

She sniffed at the flask, then sipped the cool liquid within. It tasted cleaner and clearer than any water she'd ever had. Filled with minerals, full and complex. Between sips, she examined the flask. The image of a beautiful, rearing horse was carved into the side. Inside a frame of vines. She turned to the other side to see a carving of a woman, wearing a long dress. She had a stag's head and horns. With more prongs than any creature could possibly hold upright. Each point of the antlers was tipped with a glowing light. The intricacy of the carvings was incredible. They looked hand done, not by machine. It must have taken a great deal of work to make this.

"Who made this?" she asked.

"I did. A very long time ago."

"How old are you?"

"I am old enough to remember a time before humans came to this island."

"That's not possible."

When had humans come to Ireland? A very long time ago, that much she knew. 7,000 B.C.? 8,000? Maybe.

"You use that phrase a great deal. All humans do. You see such limited possibilities. Immortality is common among my people. Death, rare."

"Then what do the cycles of the seasons mean to you, if not death? You said you had to ride the old ways during different times."

"We understand little deaths, endings, but we do not experience death as you do. As a complete end. Nor do we understand your Christian mythology. We live in what you would call heaven," he said, spreading his arms and taking in the meadow.

"So none of you will ever die?"

"Sometimes, one of us is called to death, by an injury, or just from having lived so very long. It does not happen often." He rubbed his eyes.

"Why are you not back with the others? Still sleeping?"

"I thought you might need some assistance. Some help understanding where you were. Humans who come to Faerie often experience confusion. It used to be more so, even though they believed in us. However, they believed wrongly about us. They thought us cruel and called us tricksters. We only had their growth in mind, but often they could not see that far. They were angry, and not ready to change and grow. I fear you are angry too."

Maureen handed him the flask. She was angry. Furious. She'd

354

been trying to start a new life, find her way in the world. And here she was, whisked off to Faerie. And she didn't want to be here.

But what had he said about losing her soul? Giving away too much? That was exactly what she'd done. Given away so much of herself, to her family. She had kept nothing back. Hadn't taken care of herself. And now she no longer knew who she was or why she was still alive. Let alone where she should go.

She couldn't just pick up the pieces of her old life. Because the woman she'd been at twenty-five was dead. The one who'd worked at a nursery while going to grad school, nearly ready to finish. Gone. She was someone new now and had no idea who that was. Didn't know if it was even possible to revive the old life.

He made the flask disappear into thin air. Not that he could have hidden it anywhere. His nakedness felt threatening. In her world naked men generally meant only one thing.

"You seem uneasy," he said.

"Why don't you wear clothes? You were wearing them last night."

"Because we were moving through parts of Faerie that intersect with yours. We wear clothes and weapons there. Danger has often greeted us in your world. Here, there is no need for clothes, unless it is for ornamentation or a celebration."

"And that's normal for here?"

"Yes. You look rather strange wearing clothes."

"I probably look strange here anyway."

"Well, there is no mistaking you are human. You have no glow like we do. And even though your ears are hidden, they are human ears."

"Why do you glow?" she asked. Her stomach began a low rumble. The water she drank hadn't been enough to satisfy her hunger.

"Because of our magic. Those with the most magic glow more. Our elders are something amazing to behold."

"How old are your elders?"

"Nearly as old as the ground we walk on."

"Where did they come from?"

"That is something we do not discuss with outsiders."

"And I'm an outsider?" she asked.

He merely gazed at her. She knew the answer anyway.

"Come, you are hungry. Let us find some food."

He rose and Maureen decided to follow, otherwise who knew when she'd be able to eat? She didn't trust him. But she hadn't trusted anyone in a very long time.

Except death. She trusted death. It always came.

They walked back towards the building and around it. Behind it stood a beautiful food garden. Laid out in an elaborate pattern, like Celtic knotwork. Each bed planted with something different. With everything ripe at the same time.

She saw strawberries. He picked one for her and handed it her. Then took one for himself and ate it. The berry was the best she'd ever had, sweet, fruity and intense. They tasted raspberries, blackberries and blueberries. Apples, pears and peaches. Trees hung heavy with fruit and nuts. He cracked open a walnut and handed her the meat inside. Then a hazelnut.

They grazed their way through the garden, ending with ripe figs.

"Why is everything ripe at the same time?"

He shrugged, "This is Faerie. Everything is always ripe. We want for nothing."

There were two other faeries in the garden, one pruning some grapevines with a knife, another harvesting carrots and putting them in a large, woven basket. They too were naked. One man and one woman, both with very long hair, perhaps down to their knees. Each one had their brown hair tied back and braided, probably to make their work easier.

Some beds were filled with herbs, others with vegetables. It was the most bountiful garden she'd ever seen. Bees pollinated blossoms. A flock of different types of small songbirds fluttered through the garden. They looked like yellow, red and brown flashes in the foliage. Picking insects off leaves or berries off vines. Singing in beautiful voices.

Maureen also heard music coming from beyond the other side of the garden. She could pick out a flute and a fiddle. And another instrument, she didn't recognize. It was a melodic tune, slow and sinuous. Almost hypnotic. Good music to wake to.

They continued on down a path and there stood a much larger building. Many faeries sat outside on a porch, listening to a trio of musicians.

The building looked strange to her. It had three steps surrounding all sides, as far as she could see. It was many-sided and roundish, like the sleeping building. It had only one floor, but the footprint was large, about the size of a football field.

The upright corners were made of massive oak trees. The spaces between the trunks filled with vines climbing to a great height. Wisteria, rambling roses and clematis all woven together and in full bloom. The scent was amazing. Ravens nested high up in the trees and she could hear their conversations, but not understand them.

Out at least two of the sides extended large gold tubes. Smoke came out from both of them, creating clouds which drifted off.

Then a strong breeze blew towards her from the building. On it came the scent of roasted meat and the yeasty smell of baking bread. Her stomach began to growl again. The fruit and nuts had not been enough.

The faerie led her up the steps and in through one of the arched openings. The inside was quite light. On one side was a kitchen, with several subdued fires burning. Two were in large stone fireplaces where it looked like bread was being baked. One was in an open pit, over which roasted the meat. It looked like a deer or goat. Above the fires were the other ends of the large, golden tubes she'd seen on the outside.

Most of the room was taken up by carved wood tables and benches. Many faeries of all shapes and sizes sat, eating off wooden plates. They drank out of crystalline goblets that formed prisms and created rainbows throughout the room.

All skin colors were present, even blue, green and purple. Some of the faeries had wings, others scales. Some were so ethereal she couldn't stop looking at them. Others looked like things from her worst nightmare.

More than a few of them stared openly at her. Well, they'd be staring whether or not she was walking around in her pajamas. It made her feel uncomfortable though.

She didn't belong here. She was an outsider.

He led her over to a stack of plates and handed her one. It felt so light in her hand. Then they walked past platters of food and dished up. She took some roasted meat. Deer, he said. And some cooked mushrooms and onions. There was a salad of leafy greens and straw-berries. And some soft cheese, like mozzarella, but with more flavor.

He led her to a table. They sat down and a tall thin male faery with blond hair, poured wine for them and left.

She wrinkled up her nose at the wine. It smelled sweet and tasted fruity. But wine for breakfast. It only made her head reel even more.

"I do not know your name," he said.

"Maureen. What's yours?" she asked

"Donal," he said.

Maureen said nothing. She chewed on the deer meat, which was moist and intensely flavored. The bread tasted even better. But even the glorious food wasn't going to change anything. The rich meat roiled around in her belly, just like her anger.

This entire thing was complete bullshit.

She'd spent years upon years taking care of her family. Watching them all die. Yes, she'd lost her life. But no, she hadn't lost her soul. That just wasn't possible. It wasn't like she'd gone out on a killing spree or done other terrible things.

Maureen felt like she was going to implode.

"Is it safe for me to go walk around alone in Faerie? I need to be alone."

"Yes," said Donal. "But there is no alone in Faerie."

"What do you mean?"

"The earth is alive. Everything is alive. The trees, the stones, the plants. There are lichens, bacteria, mosses. Insects live everywhere. Even the water is alive. Can you not hear it?"

"No. I can't. Humans don't have that ability."

He looked at her with horror.

"What?" she asked.

"Little wonder you destroy your world, if you cannot hear its voices. I am sorry for you."

"I don't need your damn pity," she said.

Maureen got up and left the building. Walked away from the sweet music, the food, the dancing.

Rage filled her. She walked across the grassy meadow filled with grazing and sleeping horses. She didn't belong in this beautiful world. She belonged at home. But there was no longer any home. She'd sold the house and put her meager possessions in a storage locker.

She'd wanted to travel the world, not be tied down anymore.

Well, she was traveling. In a place no one would believe in. Neither did she.

In front of her lay a tangled forest. But there was a path going in and she took it. Her bare feet felt the crunch of yew needles. She walked carefully, taking care not to injure her bare feet. It was darker here. A few feet in, the underbrush thinned. The sun didn't penetrate much here. It was a mix of yew, ash and hazelnut. Here and there an occasional oak tree spread its arms. Beneath all the foliage lay thick moss covering rocks.

Tears of rage streamed down her face. She wiped them off and kept walking. They kept coming, seemingly endless.

Maureen walked for what felt like hours, listening to the birdlife and the wind among the trees. She didn't recognize insects. Or even the squirrels who chattered at her. They were reddish with white bellies. Tufts of hair stood straight up on the tips of their ears.

This world felt completely alien to her. Although the wildlife might live in Ireland. She'd studied only the plants of Ireland, not anything else. It was certainly different than the Pacific Northwest. She used to hike as a kid and knew the forests and animals there.

Were there creatures she should be wary of here? Maureen had no idea.

She kept walking. Thinking if she could put some distance

between the faeries, maybe she could find her way back to the Burren. And her cottage. If it was still standing.

Or maybe she'd just wake up, because this had to be just a really bad dream.

It began to get darker and Maureen grew tired. She came upon a huge patch of holly trees. She'd had to walk around them, leaving the path. Thorny leaves dropped by the trees formed a space she just couldn't walk over with bare feet. Even decayed they were sharp and would cut her skin. She felt tired and thirsty. She heard the sound of water. By the time she found the stream it was dusk.

She cupped her hand and sipped some of the water. It tasted refreshing and felt really cold as it ran down her throat, into her empty belly. She kept drinking until filled up.

Full darkness came suddenly. Maureen felt her way back towards a large oak tree she'd passed on the way to the stream and sat down on the tree's roots. She felt exhausted. It wasn't exactly comfortable, more lumpy. She fell asleep anyway.

She woke once in the middle of the night.

Two eyes glowed nearby in the darkness. Low to the ground and staring at her. She could almost see an outline as the moon above filtered through the trees. The creature looked like a fox. Maureen wondered at the strangeness of the night. Tree branches and downed trees formed eerie shapes in the silvery light. Peculiar screeches pierced the near darkness. The fox stared at her for a few moments and then vanished as if never there. Maureen went back to sleep.

The next time she woke it was morning. Birds argued noisily in the nearby trees. When Maureen could finally unglue her eyes, she realized they were ravens. Sitting up, she felt the ache of all the knots in her muscles. She hadn't moved the entire night long. And it had been cold.

She gradually unknotted herself and walked over to the stream, drinking as much as she could, then washing her face in the cold water. She tried to comb her shoulder-length hair with her fingers. All the tangles came out, but it probably looked terrible. She needed something to tie it up with. But there were only twigs around. They certainly wouldn't work.

Maureen felt tired. Where the hell was she going anyway? Her stomach growled in response. Water wasn't going to be enough.

Maybe she should go back to the buildings. That would be admitting defeat. She didn't want to be here. Wherever here was. She wanted to go back to the Burren. Try to pick up the pieces of her old life. But that wasn't going to work, was it?

But if not that, then what?

An empty future loomed over her like a monster.

Without a plan that was at least partly familiar, the future lay completely open. She could do anything. The vastness frightened her more than anything.

"Empty. It's empty," screeched a raven, perched on a nearby branch.

"Yes, it's empty," she said.

"Fill it up. Find a way," the raven said, cocking its head at her.

Maureen sat down on the mossy ground, smelling the rich moist soil.

"How do I fill it up? I don't know how."

Maureen watched in awe as the raven took flight and then swirled in a cloud of black, transforming into a woman. She had pale bluish-white skin and black hair down to her knees, the front part braided into two thick plaits with golden ribbons woven throughout them. She wore a long, black velvety dress, unadorned except by a wide, brass colored belt that hung over her hips. She came barefoot across the moss and stood nearby.

The woman held her hand out to Maureen.

"Come," the woman said.

Maureen stood and took the woman's hand. There was no way she could not take it. There was a bidding beneath the woman's word and she couldn't refuse.

"Who are you?" she asked, as the woman led her through the forest.

"I am Morrigan."

The name sounded familiar, but Maureen couldn't place it.

"Why are you here?" Maureen asked the woman.

"You need help."

"I don't know where I belong," Maureen said.

"Not in this world that is certain. You belong in your own world."

"And what am I to do there?"

"What do you love?"

"My family. But they're all gone. Dead."

"What else?"

"Plants."

"Anything else?"

Maureen thought and said, "No. Not really."

"Then plants it is. How can you devote your life to plants?"

"By studying them."

"And how do you study them?"

"Grow them, I guess. And watch them. Find out where they do well. What they need."

"Than what?"

"Write about them? Teach others. You have not been truly alive in your own world for a very long time. Recapture your joy and passion, share it with others."

"How does that sound as a life to you?"

Maureen touched the soft waxy needles of a yew tree as they passed it. That sounded like a good life to her. A simple, clean life. Not a life filled with pain. She'd had enough pain to last forever.

"Good," said Morrigan.

They walked in silence for a time. Then they walked past an oak tree, the largest and oldest Maureen had ever seen. Its branches must reach sixty or seventy feet up. Some of the lower branches rested on the ground, drooping with age. Morrigan led her up to the tree and put Maureen's hands on the trunk.

"Listen to this tree. She will take you home."

"Thank you," said Maureen.

"You are welcome. Remember why you are alive."

Maureen was about to ask why when Morrigan vanished completely.

She turned her attention to the tree. The grayish bark felt rough and furrowed with age beneath her fingers. Closing her eyes, Maureen could almost sense the tree's energy running just beneath the bark. Nutrients moving from the roots up through the trunk and branches, out to the new leaves. Other energy, sunlight, moved back down from the leaves to the roots.

The tree held so much life. She could feel her hands absorbing that energy.

A deep voice said, "Heal, heal other plants. Teach your kind how to revive and make whole their world and themselves. Plants will restore them as well. Humans can help the earth renew instead of destroying it. You are part of this circle. Make it move."

Maureen heard and felt the voice deep within herself. A knot had formed in her chest as the tree's voice repeated itself. She felt the tangle loosen and began to cry. To finally grieve deeply for her loved ones, and her lost life.

After a long time, the pain and tears were gone. She felt refreshed and renewed.

Maureen patted the tree and said, "Thank you."

The tree stood silent. Waiting for her to do her work.

Maureen walked over to the stream and sipped water again. She rolled her pajama bottoms up and waded through the muddy stream and across. Cold water chilled her feet.

On the other side a dirt path climbed upwards. She followed it and the trail changed from dirt to mossy stones formed into stairs. By the time she made it to the top, Maureen's breath came in gasps.

Hazelnut and ash trees grew near the top, covered with yellowing leaves. As if it were fall here. Very unlike the spring she'd left down below.

She followed the path, now smelling the salty breeze. Looking back down, the oak was gone from sight, the valley below covered with hazelnuts, ash and willows, most of them moving towards fall.

She kept moving up the path, which changed back to dirt running through a grassy meadow.

Around a swath of shrubbery, her cottage came into view. The back door stood closed. She turned the knob and it opened. Inside, everything was as it should be. As if she'd never left. The front door was also closed. Her papers were neatly stacked on the table.

Maureen checked her phone. It was only two days later. She could have dreamt all this.

Except for her cold muddy feet, dirty pajamas and hunger.

And the dream in her heart.

ABOUT THE AUTHOR

Linda Jordan writes fascinating characters, visionary worlds and imaginative fiction. She believes in the powers of healing and transformation.

She's fascinated by nature's peculiarities, mythology and spirituality, what makes humans (and aliens) tick, political systems and the creation of music and art. She loves including all this and more in her stories.

In another lifetime, Linda coordinated the Clarion West Writers Workshop as well as the Reading Series for two years. She also spent four years as Chair of the Board of Directors during Clarion West's formative period. She's worked many other jobs, more than she cares to count. Eventually, she fled the city to live out among the tall cedars.

She lives in the rainy wilds of Washington state with her husband, daughter, four cats, a cluster of koi and an infinite number of slugs and snails.

Find out more about Linda at:
lindajordan.net

facebook.com/LindaJordanWriter

twitter.com/LindaAJordan

bookbub.com/authors/linda-jordan

WATERBORNE

ANTHEA SHARP

C onnacht, Eire, 9th century

B rea Cairgead bent over her father's second-best fishing net, her fingers crusted with salt as she mended the coarse weave. A warm wind blew in from the sea, ruffling her long, dark hair and the thatched roofs of the cottages, and making her neighbor's bright flowers sway.

The sky overhead was a pale summer blue, the weather fair for a good catch. Heat reflected from the whitewashed wall behind Brea, and before her lay the harbor and an endless view of the broad back of the sea.

Brea glanced at the waters, searching for a sign of her father's boat, but there was nothing to see but the white tips of the waves. He would not return home until deep into the twilight hours.

"The long days cannot be wasted," he'd told her once, when she had complained of his absence. "Come winter there will be time enough to sit by the fire and tell tales—but if I do not work now, what will we have to eat when the darkness descends?"

And so Brea had learned to bite her tongue and accept loneliness as her constant companion. The other children had always treated her warily, and as they grew into young men and women, paired off. No one came courting for Brea.

Finally, two summers ago, she had discovered why.

Brea shook her head, trying to dispel her melancholy mood. Sometimes she thought she should visit the sacred spring, located some distance from the village, and fasten a fluttering thread of a wish upon the hawthorn tree growing there—but she had no wishes to leave for the Fair Folk. All her hopes were kept imprisoned deep in her heart. Speaking them aloud, even tying a wish upon the tree's branches, would only increase her sorrow sevenfold.

I wish for a true love of my own. I wish I had sisters and brothers. And the biggest, most painful of them all: *I wish I could remember my mother.*

Her father would not speak of Brea's mother. If Brea pressed him too closely, he would storm out of the small cottage and down the road to Biddy's Pub, and not return until he was reeling drunk, the fumes of *uisce beatha* filling the room until Brea barely could draw breath.

So, she had stopped asking.

But two years ago, on a summer afternoon much like this one, something had possessed her to go over to her father's bed and pull the mattress up. It was heavy, stuffed with straw and a thin top layer of goose feathers. She'd grunted as she heaved it up, bracing it against her shoulder.

And found, lying against the thin slats of the bed frame, something altogether mysterious.

It shimmered, opalescent, roughly the size of her hand. Brea snatched it up and let the mattress fall back onto the frame, then went to the window to examine her find.

She might have thought it was a fish scale, but no fish she had ever seen would have a scale so large. It was flat and thin and roughly triangular. She held it up to her nose and sniffed, but it carried no odor. A quick taste yielded a faint salt flavor, but that might have been the sweat from her own hands.

Brea turned the scale back and forth in the light, so caught up in its rainbow shimmer that she did not see her father arrive. One moment she was admiring the scale's glimmer, the next it was yanked from her hand. She looked up in surprise to see a storm gathering in her father's eyes.

"Da," she said, hoping for an answer before the squall broke. "What is it?"

"Something best left alone," he said.

He stalked to the bed, paused a moment, then thrust the scale beneath his mattress once more. Brea caught the tender flash in his eyes, like the flicker of the winter lights that streamed across the sky, if one looked for them.

"Does it have to do with my mother?" she asked.

His expression shuttered then.

"I'll be at Biddy's," he said, turning on his heel.

That time, he had not come home for two days. Brea did not broach the topic of the scale with him again, and when she next went looking for it, the mysterious object was nowhere to be found.

She was a clever girl, though, and slowly a sketch of the past unfolded itself. Her mother had come from the sea—some sort of ocean being who had become, for a time, a wife. Surely she was not a selkie, for then Brea would have discovered a sealskin. Or transformed herself into a sleekly furred sea creature.

The more she thought on it, the more convinced she grew that her mother had not been a normal human woman, but a mystery born of water and starlight.

It would explain so much.

From a young age, Brea had been nearly as comfortable in the water as she was on land. At first, she had thought the other children disliked her because of her uncanny swimming ability—but it was more than that. It was the fey blood that ran in her veins. No wonder the other villagers treated her with distance.

I'm still just myself! she wanted to cry out. *Just a girl.* Other than her talent in the water, there was nothing remarkable about her.

Indeed, since the discovery of the scale, and the notion that her mother had not been human, Brea had tried to reach something within herself. Something powerful and elusive and mysterious. If the neighbors looked askance at her, and no young men came to call, then she wanted to at least be able to do *something* otherworldly.

She'd taken to swimming alone in the cove a mile to the north. It was secluded and peaceful, with only the cries of the gulls to interrupt her efforts. But no matter what she did—held her breath underwater until she was dizzy or swam so far out into the waves that the shore was merely a blur—she never transformed into something more. Never found a wellspring of magic within her soul.

Her tears of frustration mingled with the seawater, and she beat at the waves with her fists. But still she did not change.

So that summer passed, and the next, and Brea found herself, at nearly seventeen turnings of the sun, with no clear future ahead.

Most of the girls of the village were courting or married. Some had moved away to other towns, and the handful left single seemed content to care for aged parents or tend the crofts.

But that afternoon, mending the nets, Brea's soul stirred with a fierce longing for *more.*

A pity she had no bardic talent that would take her away to the halls of Tara. No wise ways with herbs and tonics or deft hand at healing.

Perhaps she might go to one of the large towns in the east, where no one knew her name or face. But even there, she would have no prospects. Who would hire a girl from a fishing village for more than a lowly serving wench—or worse?

Fingers re-plaiting the coarse rope, Brea stared sightlessly over the sea. The echo of the surf on the black rocks below was the beat of her heart, the sough of her sighs.

At length, when the shadows cooled and the sun began its long slide toward twilight, she set the nets aside and went in to make supper. Brown bread and fish stew with a few bartered vegetables. It was not much, but 'twas warm and would keep their bellies filled.

Dusk sifted over the village, the sea turning silver with the last light of day. Brea lit the beeswax candle on their plank tabletop, and the one in the window that stood sentinel for her father's return.

Worry did not start nibbling at her until most of the village quieted. Often her father returned late from hauling in his day's catch. He had no sons to help him, and as much as Brea begged, he sternly refused to take her out in his curricle.

Now, she wondered if he feared losing her to the deeps. Not by drowning, but perhaps from the heritage of her mother's blood rising up to claim her.

She went to the threshold and stood, looking down the darkened and winding streets, hoping for a sight of her father's lantern. She waited a long time, until the lash of the rising wind and the spatter of stinging rain from the west drove her back inside. Black clouds scudded across the pewter sky, stealing the last light and extinguishing the stars.

Fear settled like a fist in her stomach.

The storm was blowing in off the ocean—where her father in his small boat was ever at the mercy of the winds.

For three days the tempest raged, tearing thatch from the roofs and carrying away anything left unattended. On the second day, the wind snatched their bucket straight off the hook outside the door. Brea had no hope of catching it. She watched helplessly from the window as the much-mended bucket rolled and clattered away down the street to smash against the sea wall.

She kept the hearth stoked with peat, and carefully portioned out the rest of the stew and bread, though it was tasteless in her mouth.

Da will return. She clutched the thought like a blanket, even as dark knowledge spread through her. He was likely never coming back.

On the morning of the fourth day, the dawn broke clear and golden. Brea grabbed her woolen shawl and hurried down to the dock.

She was not the first there. The gathered fishermen stood about the wreckage of a small boat, and Brea's steps slowed.

Please, no.

It was the remains of her father's curricle, flung ashore in the heart of the storm.

"Terrible sorry, lass," one of the men said, and the rest nodded, sympathy sitting uncomfortably on their worn faces.

"Likely won't be a body," another said.

The rest murmured in agreement.

Brea caught her breath on a sob and ran back to the cottage, tears blurring her vision so that she nearly lost her footing on the cobbles. She slammed the door behind her with a heavy thud, then sank to the floor, sobbing, as her heart broke thrice over.

The neighbors brought food and awkward comfort, but as the days passed their eyes hardened. After a week, old Biddy herself came to pay a visit.

"He's not coming back," she said. "'Tis a hard truth, but it must be faced."

Brea nodded. She could not yet speak the words aloud, but she knew in her heart that her father was gone. Taken by the sea.

Late at night, when sleep taunted her from the corners but would not settle upon her, Brea imagined her father and mother finally reunited. They sat together on thrones of coral, their hair lifted above their heads by the caress of the waters surrounding them, sunshine slanting down through the green sea in shafts of light to illuminate their pearly crowns.

It was a pretty thought, but in the light of day it burst like soap bubbles too-long exposed to the harsh air.

"What will you do now?" Biddy asked.

It was the question Brea had been pondering for days, and she was no closer to an answer. Her aunt in Corcaigh was half the length of the country away. Brea had never met the woman, as her aunt had left the fishing village as soon as she could and never looked back.

Biddy took Brea's silence for the lack of plan that it was.

"Well, now," the older woman said, her seamed face losing some of its sympathy. "Have you had any young man come courting?"

Of course not, and everyone in the village knew it.

"No," Brea said. She wove her fingers tightly together.

"Anyone who might take you in?"

"Can I not simply stay here on my own?" Brea asked, panic beginning to rise in her chest.

"No, lass. There's others have need of a fine, stout cottage to raise their families in. Why, the Reedys have seven people all beneath one roof. Their son and his new wife have a baby on the way."

"I could stay on and help them..."

Brea trailed off at the look in Biddy's eyes. The strange lass had been tolerated while her father was alive, but now there was no place for her in the village. A strained silence filled the room, chilly despite the peat burning upon the hearth.

"Very well," Brea said at last, dropping her gaze. "I'll gather my things and leave tomorrow."

What else could she do? Better to depart on her own, dignity intact, than have the villagers come and pitch her out of the cottage.

"There's a good girl." Biddy patted her knee. "I've a bit of coin set by I can give you for traveling money, and the roads should be safe enough."

Brea hoped so. Earlier in the year, reports had come of brigands prowling the countryside, but they seemed to have departed for richer pickings.

Where will I go? The question quivered on Brea's tongue, but she would get no answers from Biddy. Already the woman was taking her leave.

"I'll bring you the coin tomorrow morning," Biddy said, pausing at the threshold. "Nothing like an early start."

Brea nodded mutely. The sound of the door closing behind Biddy echoed hollowly through the room. Through Brea's heart.

There was nothing for it except to pack up her meager belongings. In the morning, she took the good blanket from her father's bed and fashioned a bundle to hold her spare clothing, the kitchen knife and a wooden bowl, a linen kerchief, and the small carving of a fish her father had made one summer from a pearly shell.

She made one last effort to find the scale, and at last discovered it tucked behind the chimney. It was dark and opaque, all the light gone from it. She did not know if her father's death had made it so, or if it had become singed black from the heat of the fire. Regardless, she tucked it into the folds of her second-best skirt. It was all she had left of her parents.

Just after first light, Biddy rapped on the door. She nodded when she saw the bundle on the floor.

"Affix it to the end of a stout stick and carry it over your shoulder," she advised. "'Twill be easier to manage than carting it about in your arms."

"I will," Brea said, accepting the small purse the other woman held out. "Thank you for the coins."

"Hide them, and use them sparingly. Safe travels to you, Brea Cairgead."

It was a clear dismissal. Under Biddy's watchful eye, Brea tucked the purse away beneath her petticoat, then lifted the woolen blanket containing all her earthly possessions. Head high, despite the weight of stone in her heart, she stepped over the threshold and did not look back.

Down the street, she could see the Reedy daughter and her husband pulling a cart filled with household items. The air in the cottage would not even have time to cool before the new occupants took up residence.

"Farewell," Brea said.

To Biddy, to the huddle of cottages, to the rocky shore where she had last seen her father. There was no one and nothing else to say goodbye to. Taking a deep breath, Brea set her feet on the path leading southeast from Ardglass. The crying of gulls overhead gave voice to the tears she could not shed. The sigh of the surf was her own sorrow at leaving the only home she had ever known.

The path curved, and Brea knew that if she cared to turn and look, the village would no longer be visible. She did not turn, only set one foot on the earth, then the other. The bundle grew heavy in her arms, the wool prickling her palms.

Another league ahead lay a hazel wood. Perhaps she might find a stick there to attach her bundle to. And just before the wood was the sacred spring. She would tear a strip off her kerchief and tie it to the wishing tree there, hoping the Fair Folk would bestow luck upon her. Certainly, if anyone had need of it, 'twas herself.

The morning sun grew in strength, though the high clouds meant rain later. She hoped she would find shelter by the afternoon, or she would add being damp and cold to her overall misery.

But first the sacred spring, and the wood.

The path turned again, this time to follow the bright stream that led to the spring. The water made a merry sound, sunlight glinting off the surface, and Brea could not help but be a little cheered. She allowed herself to rest beside a tumbled granite boulder, and drank from her cupped hands. It was too much trouble to fetch the bowl from her bundle.

The stop revived her, and her bundle felt a bit lighter when she picked it up in her arms again. She was thankful for the burbling companionship of the stream as she strode up the heather-banked path.

At length the heart of the spring came in sight, just when Brea's shoulders were beginning to ache. She hurried the last few paces and set the blanket down on the ferny moss surrounding the spring. The wind rustled the leaves of the wood beyond, mimicking the sound of the sea.

Beside the cool, clear pool a bent hawthorn tree grew. Bright bits of cloth fluttered from its branches—wishes for luck and healing and to honor the Fair Folk who dwelt in the land.

Brea pulled her linen kerchief from the bundle and tore off a small strip. Luck she needed, surely, and a wish for safe travels as she went, friendless and alone, into the wide world. She knelt at the edge of the spring, dampness seeping through her skirts. Dipping her cupped hand into the water, she murmured a blessing upon the spirits of the place.

The water moistened her lips, but she was not fool enough to guzzle from the pool. She had a skin of water from Ardglass's stream to quench the thirst of the road. A soft wind shivered the surface of the water, and for a moment she thought she saw a face looking at her, a reflection of a fey woman with tangled greenish hair and stars for eyes.

Then a raven called harshly overhead, and the moment was broken.

Brea stood and made a curtsy to the waters. Her skirt was muddy at the knees.

"I hope I've not offended you," she said. "My apologies if I have. I'm but a wandering girl, and mean no harm."

The raven called again, a softer sound this time, as if reassuring Brea all was well. Heartened, she strode to the wishing tree and tied her strip of cloth to an empty branch. The cloths fluttered, some faded nearly white, others still bright with woad and berry juice.

A third time the raven called, taking startled flight into the air, and Brea heard the heavy tread of footsteps.

A moment later, three men crested the hill, their clothing

rough, their beards unkempt. She shrank back, but there was nowhere to hide. She snatched up her bundle and backed toward the woods.

"A lass!" the black-haired one cried, looking at her as a wolf regards a lamb. "Aye, and it's a fair day for us indeed."

Greatly misliking his tone and the leers of his companions, she turned and ran for the trees.

But she was too slow, and awkwardly burdened. In four paces the men caught her, the first one grabbing her arm while the second snatched the bundle from her.

"A prize carrying a prize," the black-haired man said. "What's in the blanket, love?"

"Nothing of use to you," Brea said, her mind whirling as a dark fog of fear crept over her.

"We'll be the judge of that." The brigand holding the bundle pulled it open, letting the contents spill upon the ground.

The third man snatched up her bowl and knife, and toed her extra garments aside.

"Not much here," he said. "She's a right poor one."

"Shake out her clothing," the black-haired man said. "What's on the ground first, then what she's wearing."

He gave her a nasty smile.

Brea tried to pull away, but her captor's grasp was hard upon her. There was little chance she would escape the men until they were done with her. She swallowed hard, fearing what the next minutes would bring.

When the brigand took up her extra skirt, the blackened scale slipped free. It slid into the sacred pool with scarcely a ripple.

"What was that?" the second man asked, leaning over to peer into the water.

"Well?" Her captor shook her. "Answer."

"A scale I found on the beach," she said, her voice trembling. "I thought I might use it for a mirror, but it turned black."

"Not black now," the second man said. "Bright silver, it is."

"Well, fish it out," the black-haired leader demanded.

He marched Brea up to the pool's edge, where they could both see the scale, shining against the soft mud at the bottom.

The second man rolled up his dingy sleeves and sprawled on the moss. It was a desecration for him to reach his grimy hands into the clear waters, and Brea winced as he splashed about.

"I can't quite reach it," he said.

"Carrig, take his legs," the leader said, gesturing to the third man.

With much grunting and groaning, the second man was levered out over the surface of the pool.

"Still can't," he said.

"Then best hold your breath," the black-haired man said. "For I've a mind to fling you into this bedamned spring."

Brea bit back her cry of protest at the thought of a brigand's grimy body befouling those sacred waters. With the men's attention on the elusive scale, her captor's grip had loosened. If the moment presented itself, she would wrench herself free.

But then what? They had already proven they could catch her.

If she could gain the wood, perhaps she could lose them amidst the trees, or climb high enough that they could not pursue her.

Too many perilous chances to lose her life—yet she must act, and soon. She had no taste for becoming a brigand's doxy. Better to fall from a high branch and break her neck than the fate the men intended for her.

"I'll have to go under," the second man said. "Hold fast to me legs, Carrig."

He took a deep breath, then plunged his head and shoulders into the pool. In the clear water, Brea could see his hands flailing about, stirring up the soft silt at the bottom. The silver scale seemed to elude his grasp.

"Argh!" He surfaced with a shout and splash, red-faced.

"Try again," the black haired leader said.

"But—"

"'Tis your fault the bauble fell into the spring. Now fetch it out."

Hair plastered to his knobby head, the second man glared at his leader, but did not seem inclined to argue further. He blew two breaths out of his nostrils, then sucked in a mouthful of air and submerged his head and chest once more.

The bottom of the spring was murky now, but Brea glimpsed flashes of bright silver. And something else, lurking in the watery shadows beneath the bank. Something with green hair like kelp and glowing eyes, and a sharp-toothed mouth open in a terrifying grin.

One moment the second man was lying on the mosses, his upper body submerged. The next, he had been yanked into the pool with a mighty splash. He flailed in the silty spring water while something fey and sinuous wound about the man. A smack, a gulp, and the water stilled.

Brea had the sick knowledge that he would not rise again.

Carrig scrambled to his feet, looking into the spring with wide, fearful eyes. The leader's face grew pale, but neither of them made any move to go to their comrade's aid.

Not that they could have helped him. The power of mortal men was of little use when the spirits of a place took their revenge.

"I held him tight, I swear it," Carrig said. "Something pulled him under. You saw it."

"Aye," the black-haired man said. "Let's away from this foul place."

Brea gathered all her courage and briefly closed her eyes in a prayer of supplication. Her heart cried out to the spring and its guardians for succor, for mercy. This was her moment. Now, before the leader tightened his grip and they towed her away.

"Look!" she cried, pointing into the waters.

There was nothing to be seen—the drowned man had disappeared entirely, along with the water creature who had taken him. But it was distraction enough. The bandit holding her leaned forward, his grip slackening as he peered into the water.

Brea wrenched out of his grasp, took two steps, and leaped into the pool.

She let herself sink, expelling her precious air in a long stream of bubbles, a string of pearls reaching back toward the pale surface of the water. Dappled light sifted through the waters, though shadows gathered at the pool's edge. Her lungs went slack, then began to burn. She forced herself not to rise. Not to take a desperate, futile breath. The men waited up there for her, but she would never return.

Something cool brushed her fingers, and she turned herself about in the water, her long, dark hair swirling past her face.

It was the silver scale, coming as readily to her hand as it had eluded the brigand's. She smiled, tasting the clear, cool water against her teeth, and brought the scale to her heart.

Mother, I call upon your blood running salty in my veins. I call upon the ancient spirits of this watery haven. I call upon the hawthorn tree bound with wishes and the pale stars hidden behind the sunlit sky.

Take this human body and give it fins. Let me breathe water instead of air. Carry me away from the coarse hands of mortal men.

Her chest was full of coals, but she would not ascend back to the daylit world. Brea clenched her cold fingers, fighting to remain still. Submerged. Warm salt escaped her eyes and floated away, diluted to nothing. At last she could bear it no more, and drew in a great lungful of water.

As if waiting for that surrender, her body began to change. Her arms pulled in to her sides, her legs fused together. Her eyes shifted, her mouth pursed, the blood in her veins cooled even as her heartbeat surged. Liquid fire scalded every cell of her body as she transformed.

The surface of the spring shivered. A fey breeze stirred the wishing cloths tied to the hawthorn tree.

A heartbeat passed. A year, a day.

The girl-that-was flicked her tail and followed the shining current down and away. A thread of magic called her into the wild waters. Called her into the star-speckled, unchanging twilight far from any mortal shore. Called her home.

ABOUT THE AUTHOR

Growing up on fairy tales and computer games, Anthea Sharp has melded the two in her award-winning, bestselling Feyland series, which has sold over 150k copies worldwide. In addition to the fae fantasy/cyberpunk mashup of Feyland, she also writes Victorian Spacepunk, and fantasy romance. Her books have won awards and topped bestseller lists, and garnered over a million reads at Wattpad. Her short fiction has appeared in Fiction River, DAW anthologies, *The Future Chronicles*, and *Beyond The Stars: At Galaxy's Edge*, as well as many other publications.

Anthea lives in sunny Southern California, where she writes, hangs out in virtual worlds, plays Celtic fiddle, and spends time with her small-but-good family.

Find out more about Anthea at:
antheasharp.com

f   facebook.com/AntheaSharp

🐦   twitter.com/antheasharp

BB   bookbub.com/authors/anthea-sharp

AND THEN THERE ARE CATS

JAMIE FERGUSON

Abby squeezed through a small gap in the thick bushes that bordered the little city park, wincing as the branches scraped against her bare arms and legs. She found herself standing on newly mown grass next to a pair of crabapple trees, their leaves rustling in the warm July breeze. A clump of low bushes stood next to a wide bed filled with daisies, asters, snapdragons, and lavender. An elderly couple strolled down a wide dirt path about thirty yards away, a woman sat under an oak tree reading a book, and a group of little kids played on the monkey bars in the playground near the bushes that lined the far edge of the park.

But her orange tabby cat was nowhere in sight.

She pulled a twig out of her hair, straightened her light cotton blouse, and squinted around the park. Where had Neill gone? She'd taken off his collar earlier to scratch his neck, so if he got lost, no one would know to call her. And she'd never forgive herself if he got hit by a car.

Neill had snuck out of the little house she shared with her two roommates when she'd opened the screen door to the back patio. She still wasn't sure how he'd managed to get by her, but he had. She'd thought he'd be easy to catch, but hadn't realized just how fast he could climb the six-foot-tall wooden fence. He'd dashed across the street, which fortunately had been free of cars at the time, and had run down to the park at the end of the next block, Abby frantically running after him.

She tucked a lock of hair behind her ears and scanned the park, and then her breath caught as she spotted a tiny splotch of orange out of the corner of her eye. The tip of Neill's tail peeked out from under a bush. She tiptoed toward her cat, or at least did as reasonable an approximation as one could do while wearing flip-flops.

Neill's escapade had not only interrupted her work on the essay she needed to turn in tomorrow for her mythology class, but if she didn't catch him soon she'd miss the landing of the Apollo 11 lunar module. Sure, that wouldn't be as exciting as the blast off had been, or seeing people walk on the moon for the first time ever, but still. It was 1969, and the future was bright. In another ten years or so they'd have flying cars, robots would do all the housework, and everyone would have televisions hooked up to their telephones. Determined to be a part of all of this, she'd majored in mathematics, and would one day be building robots or spacecraft or something.

If only she had a robot right now that would catch Neill for her.

"Come on, little guy," Abby said. She stepped toward her big, orange, naughty tabby, keeping her tone light and cheery even though her insides felt as though they'd been tied into knots. "Let's go home, and I'll give you a whole can of tuna."

Neill poked his head out from between the leaves, blinked his amber eyes at her, and meowed, the picture of feline innocence.

"I'll play your shoestring game for a whole hour," she said. Just one more step... She crouched down and reached for him.

Neill leapt out from under the bush and darted past her in a rush of orange and white fur. Abby reached for him, but it was like trying to catch a gust of wind.

She chased after Neill as he scampered through the flower beds, ran across the sand of the playground, and then followed him through a gap in a clump of bushes. The summer sun beat down on her, her blouse and shorts were drenched in sweat, and she wished she had worn something more conducive to running than flip-flops. She squeezed through the bushes and found herself on a faint, shaded trail that wound through the grass in between a row of bushes. Neill trotted down the center of the trail, his fuzzy orange-and-white tail held high, as if he were daring her to follow.

Abby ran after him, but no matter how fast she moved she couldn't seem to catch up to her cat. The air had grown cooler and was filled with the tantalizing scent of some sort of flower—maybe lilies? Or lilacs? Her pace had slowed, as had Neill's. She knew she should sprint and grab him, but her chest ached, and her breath came in great gasps.

After a while she felt sure that they'd gone several times the length of the park - although of course that made no sense at all. But, then, neither did this trail. She didn't remember ever seeing anything like it in the little city park.

The path seemed almost golden in color now, and looked more like a band of light than a strip of tamped-down grass. She couldn't see the bushes on the side of the path very clearly—if there were even bushes there anymore. Off to one side she caught a glimpse through the branches of things that couldn't possibly be in the middle of the city: what looked like a lake, a rock outcropping, a wide expanse of sand. Every time she turned to look straight at any of them, everything became fuzzy, as if she were looking through a cloud.

She shook her head. She had to be imagining all of that. Of *course* they were still in the park. She was just over-tired. Or overheated. Or both. Neill was only a few feet in front of her. If she could just catch up to him they could go home and get off this strange trail—and watch the Apollo landing, if she hadn't missed it already.

Neill stopped in his tracks and looked back at her. The tip of his tail twitched, and then he leapt off the path into a clump of bright pink flowers.

Abby jumped off the path after him, and then stopped and raised a hand to shield her eyes against the sunshine, which seemed startlingly bright after the shade of the trail they'd been on. She looked around, blinking, as she caught her breath.

She stood in a small meadow in the middle of what appeared to be a forest. Several large boulders were scattered around in the grass; their stone was black and gray, and occasionally streaked with white. Tall oak and hawthorn and ash trees bordered the edge of the meadow; saplings and flowering bushes grew underneath them. A grove of aspens made up the swath of forest to her left, their leaves making soft, whispering sounds as they were rustled by the gentle summer breeze. White, feathery tufts of cottonwood seeds floated by, bobbing up and down as they were carried by tiny currents of air.

Abby turned and looked back the way they'd come. The path they'd followed ran from a small opening in between the trees, and looked like a ribbon of golden light as it wound through the meadow. The grass she stood in was about six inches high, and was dotted with clusters of purple, pink, and white flowers.

Except the grass in the city park had just been mowed. And the park was in the middle of town - not anywhere near a forest.

Prickles ran down her spine.

Where were they?

The sound of Neill's meow made her jump. She whipped around to see him sitting about ten feet away from her. He yawned, the tip of his pink tongue curling up, and then batted at a daisy with one paw.

Abby glared at her cat. Wherever they were, it was all his fault. If she could just catch him, they'd retrace their steps and get back home. She took a deep breath and began to walk toward Neil. The long grass tickled her ankles, and the sweet scents of lilacs, lavender, and what smelled like cotton candy filled the air.

Neill shot her a glance and then bounded across the meadow, a flash of orange fur.

She gritted her teeth and sprinted after him, her eyes focused on his bright coat. He dashed into the trees, Abby hot on his heels. Neill leaped up on a wide granite boulder that sat in the dappled shade of a giant ash tree at the edge of the meadow. She had almost reached the boulder when a woman suddenly appeared, hanging upside-down from one of the lower branches of the ash.

Abby skidded to a stop and stared, open-mouthed.

Streaks of white ran through the woman's coal-black hair. It had been plaited into many long braids, with small twigs and leaves wound through them. Her clothing looked like a bunch of brown, green, and tan strips of linen and gauze tied together. It covered some of her warm brown skin, but her arms, legs, and midriff remained bare. Her pale green eyes locked with Abby's. It felt as though she could see inside Abby, as if she were inspecting Abby's very soul.

Abby shivered in spite of the warmth of the day. Great. One of those intense hippies who didn't understand how annoying constant eye contact was. She probably lived in this tree. Abby pulled her eyes away from the strange woman and back to her cat.

Neill stared at the woman's braids, which dangled just above the surface of the boulder. After a moment he sprawled out on the rock and began to clean his back toes as if he were sitting on the sofa at home.

Abby had no idea why the woman was in the tree, much less hanging upside-down, but she was ready to be done with this unexpected adventure. She glared at Neill. He'd had his fun. Enough was enough.

"Pardon me, I just need to grab my cat," Abby said. She took half a step toward Neill, trying to figure out which direction he might run next. She was hot and sweaty, her legs and feet ached from chasing after her cat, and she had a stitch in her side. Neill, on the other hand, looked as fresh and relaxed as if he'd just woken up from a long nap. Wasn't he tired after all this running around?

"Why do you want to grab him?" the woman asked. Her voice was rich and melodic, like the voice of a trained actress or singer.

The woman dropped from the tree to the boulder, flipping in midair as gracefully as a gymnast, and landed on her bare feet next to Neill. He ignored her and began to wash his face. She sat down, pushed her mass of braids back from her face, and hugged her knees to her chest. Intricate designs—tattoos? Henna?—were drawn on her legs in dark brown, and she wore an anklet made of daises woven together. She had a soft, earthy scent, like pine and cedar.

"I've been chasing after him for half the morning," Abby said. "He snuck out the screen door. I don't know what got into him. I've got to get him back home and get back to work on my paper."

Abby began to run a hand through the tangled mess of her hair, but stopped when her fingers got stuck. She extracted them from a snarl, wincing as she pulled out a small clump of hair in the process. She took a deep breath, and then reached out and picked up Neill. Amazingly, for once he held still. She squeezed him tight against her chest and pressed her cheek against his head, feeling his soft fur against her skin. Her eyes filled with tears as she realized how terrified she'd been that she might lose him forever. He rubbed the side of his face against her chin, his whiskers tickling her neck, and purred.

She glanced at the other woman, who was staring at Abby as if fascinated. Abby felt as though she were standing on a stage under a spotlight. She took a deep breath.

"Uh, have a nice day," Abby said.

She turned toward the meadow, more than ready to go home, and squinted as she tried to spot the path she and Neill had followed. She could see the clump of flowers right where she and Neill had jumped off the path, about twenty yards away...but where the path had been, there was only grass.

The back of her neck prickled. The path was still there. It had to be. She just couldn't see it from this far away, that was all.

She tried not to think about the fact neither the meadow, nor the forest she stood on the edge of right now, existed in town.

Abby walked across the meadow to where the path should be, careful to keep her grip tight on Neill. He purred madly away, and seemed happy to be carted around.

She reached the bunch of pink flowers she remembered. There were faint indentations in the grass from where she'd stood in her flip-flops, but the path was gone.

Abby swallowed and walked a few more steps until she knew she stood exactly where the path had been...but it simply wasn't there.

She turned to walk in the direction she *knew* she and Neill had come from, and then stopped as she realized a lilac bush stood directly in her way—right where the path should have led.

She pressed her lips together, shifted the bulk of Neill's non-trivial weight to her other arm, and turned around. The woman who'd climbed down from the ash tree stood a few feet away, staring at Abby with those beautiful, pale green eyes that seemed startlingly light against her dark skin.

"Isn't this the way I came?" Abby asked. Not that the other woman had necessarily been watching when Abby and Neill showed up, but she *had* been in a tree at the edge of the meadow, so maybe she'd seen something.

The woman blinked, and then gave a nod.

"Was this bush here then?"

The woman nodded again.

Abby took a deep breath. The sweet scent of the lilacs was soothing. But even that seemed odd, for it was July, and all the other lilacs in town had stopped blooming a month or so ago. Plus this scent seemed more...purple. That made no sense, of course.

But, then, neither did the fact that the path she'd followed to the meadow had completely disappeared.

"Would you mind telling me what I'm missing?" Abby asked.

The woman waved a long, graceful hand at the lilac bush.

"The Straight Track curves there," she said, as if that were a logical explanation.

What did that even mean? Maybe she meant path instead of track? How could something straight curve?

"I don't understand," Abby said. She shook her head. She was hot and tired and thirsty. Her arms had been scraped up by all the bushes she'd squeezed through while chasing Neill, she was drenched in sweat, had probably started to get sunburned, her feet ached, and on top of all *that* she was well on her way to getting blisters in the place between her toes where the rubber thong of her flip-flops rubbed. Maybe if she got out of the sun she'd think more clearly, because nothing seemed to make any sense at the moment.

She walked back to the shade of the ash tree, slipped her feet out of her flip-flops, and sat down on the wide, warm boulder, Neill still held in her arms. The other woman followed.

"He won't run away," the woman said. She sat down on the far side of the rock.

Neill began to squirm. Abby tried to maintain her grip, but he was too wriggly. He landed on the boulder, yawned, and then stretched out on his right side.

Abby glared at him. At least he didn't look like he was going anywhere. Yet. She wrapped her arms around herself and bit her lip

"I don't know where I am," she said, her voice wavering. "I followed him down that trail that ran through the city park, but this place doesn't look anything like the park. Could you please tell me how to get back?"

"Your friend brought you to this place for a reason," the woman said. She held her hand out to Neill. He gave it a polite sniff, and then rubbed the side of his head against her knuckles.

"What do you mean?" Abby asked. "Are you saying that Neill brought me here on purpose? That's crazy. He's just a cat. A very bad cat."

She glared at Neill. He twitched his tail, and then licked the back of one of his white-tipped front paws.

"There are cats, and then there are *cats*," the woman said. She smiled and scratched Neill behind his ears. "My name is Giàrana."

"I'm Abby. What do you mean by *cats*?"

"Abby, your...*cat*...is not like other cats. He is a faery cat, one of the *cait sídhe*."

"I have no idea what you're talking about" Abby said. A *caught shee*? Wasn't that what the woman had said? A faery cat? The hippie woman didn't look like she was on drugs, but she certainly sounded like it.

A trickle of sweat ran down the side of Abby forehead. She tried to wipe it away with the back of one hand, but instead managed to smear sweat across the side of her face. In contrast, Giàrana looked as though she'd never sweated in her life. Abby squinted across the meadow, but the path she *knew* she'd taken continued to fail to materialize. And she had almost certainly missed the Apollo landing. They'd probably show it again on the evening news, but it wasn't like she could just go watch the whole thing over in its entirety whenever she wanted to.

"I will help you return to your world," Giàrana said. "But you will need to take something back with you."

"What do you-," Abby began, and then she froze as she realized what the woman had just said.

Your *world*.

Had she really followed Neill to *another world*?

There weren't other worlds. Maybe other planets, but you'd have to take a spaceship to get to them—not walk through a park.

But paths didn't just disappear.

And paths generally didn't look as though they were made from golden light.

And Giàrana had said Neill was a faery cat.

Abby swallowed and squinted at the sunlit meadow. It looked calm. Peaceful. And nothing at all like the city park she'd run through after following Neill—who was just a cat.

Wasn't he?

"Where..." Abby's voice wavered. Her stomach felt as though it was full of butterflies. She straightened her shoulders and cleared her throat. "Where am I?"

"This is the Land of Faerie," Giàrana said.

"I don't believe you," Abby said. She clenched her fists together and shook her head. "That's just a made-up place. It's not real. I must have taken a turn I didn't realize."

Although she knew she hadn't. She'd chased after Neill many times the length of the little city park. Even if she'd accidentally left the park and ended up on a path that ran in between the neighborhood houses that bordered the park—and not noticed any of the houses, in an area that was packed full of homes—she'd run for so long she should have hit one of the cross streets.

Except she hadn't.

"It appears to be real," Giàrana said. The corners of her mouth twitched, as if she were trying not to smile.

"Does that make you a... A faery?" Abby asked. This was crazy. She bit her lip. Was she really talking to a faery?

"I am a dryad," Giàrana said. "I do not know how much of our world you understand. The ash we are sitting under is my tree. My home. My friend."

Abby glanced up at the branches above her. Did Giàrana mean she lived in a tree house? Was she really *friends* with this tree?

"Is this like in Greek mythology?" she asked.

Giàrana shook her head. "I do not know what that means."

Abby took a deep breath. "I am taking a class on this type of thing now. The book we're reading says that there are nymphs, young women, who are associated with individual trees. If their tree dies, they die as well."

She shot a glance at the other woman. Giàrana was beautiful, but there were laugh lines at the corners of her eyes, and the streaks of white through her many thick, black braids made it clear she was not a young woman.

"I speak to the trees," Giàrana said. "But I am not a hamadryad. I am a dryad. I speak to all trees, not to just one. This ash is... My closest tree friend, in a sense. But if someday it dies I would be very sad, but I would remain."

Abby took a deep breath and tried to remember if they'd covered the difference between dryads and hamadryads in class. Maybe that was in an upcoming chapter of the textbook. But it was all mythology. Giàrana was just a regular person. A hippie who hung out in trees in a forest next to a meadow, neither of which existed in the city Abby lived in.

"Magic isn't real," Abby said, her voice cracking on the last word.

Giàrana raised an eyebrow and then turned her face upward, looking at the green leaves of the ash that stood above them. The light breeze that had been blowing earlier had stopped. She held out her right hand, her fingers stretched out, and her palm facing up.

A small branch that hung off of the lowest bough reached down toward her hand, as if it were being gently pushed by the wind.

But there was no wind.

And none of the other branches were moving.

The branch stretched toward Giàrana as if it was reaching toward her, and then stopped right above her hand. Its leaves turned, rustling against each other, as they moved to point toward her palm. Those closest to her touched her skin, rubbing against her palm in what looked almost like a greeting, or a caress. And then the branch began to move back up, the leaves fluttering toward Giàrana for a moment as though waving goodbye, and then slowly turning back to the sky. Finally the branch reached its previous position, and it and its leaves grew still.

That had to have been a trick. Giàrana had pulled the branch with a thread so thin it was almost invisible.

But even if that were possible, the air remained still, and there was no logical explanation for the movement of the leaves. As a graduate student studying mathematics, Abby studied facts. Numbers. Formulas. She wrote logical proofs.

What she'd just seen didn't fit any form of logic she knew.

And trails didn't just disappear.

Abby shivered and drew a shuttering breath as she realized magic really was real.

"You said you can help me—and Neill—get home?" she asked, her voice small. She pushed a tangled lock of hair behind one sweaty ear.

"Yes. But in return, you must do one thing for me. Will you agree?" Giàrana paused and looked at Abby.

Abby bit her lip as she faintly remembered something her Irish grandmother had told her about faery bargains. Granny had never spoken of dryads—what little Abby knew about them, she'd learned in her college course. But Granny *had* talked about faeries. She'd told Abby stories about how mortals often thought they were agreeing to something innocuous, but in reality, didn't understand what they'd committed to. Did that apply to dryads?

"Maybe," she said. "But I don't know what I'm agreeing to do."

"My tree," Giàrana began, and then she stopped and looked up at the branches of the ash above them. She paused for so long Abby wasn't sure if she was going to continue, and then turned back and met Abby's gaze. Her pale green eyes looked serious and sad. "I will give you seeds from my friend, this ash tree. You will take them back to your world and plant them."

That was it? That seemed easy enough.

"Okay," Abby said. "But I've never planted a tree before. Where should I plant them? How deep should I put the seeds? I don't know anything about this kind of thing."

What if she screwed up somehow? What if she planted the seeds in the wrong place and they didn't grow? Would a horde of dryads leave their world and hunt her down?

Giàrana reached out a hand and rested her fingertips on Abby's forearm. Her touch was cool and soothing, like pressing up against the bark of a birch, or an aspen.

"The seeds will tell you what to do," she said.

How could seeds talk?

Abby swallowed. This made no sense.

The dryad pushed herself to her feet and stood on top of the boulder. She reached up, grabbed the lowest branch of the ash, and hoisted herself up. She stepped along the thick branch toward the trunk, her steps smooth and lithe. When she reached the trunk she pressed her face and palms against it, and then her body began to slide *into* the wood, as if she were merging with the tree.

And then she was gone.

Abby bit her lip and glanced down at Neill, who lay sprawled out on the boulder next to her. He lifted up his head and met her eyes, and then blinked slowly. Once. Twice. Three times.

She'd raised Neill since he was a tiny, fuzzy, six-week-old orange and white kitten. Could he really be a faery cat, as Giàrana had said? Had he really led Abby to this place so that she could take ash seeds back to their world?

Abby started as Giàrana swung down from a nearby branch, a stem with a cluster of small, dried, brown pods in one hand. How had she gotten up there? She'd just gone—merged? How could you even describe what she'd done? Into the trunk of the tree. She placed one hand on the branch of the tree and swung down in a graceful arc, landing on the soft grass that carpeted the forest floor. She walked over to the boulder where Abby sat, and held the pods out. Neill's ears pricked forward. He sat up and sniffed the seeds, and then gave a big yawn and lay back down.

Abby took the stem and stared at the pods. They were flat, with a tiny bump on one side that must be where the actual seed resided. She felt a tickle in the back of her head, like hearing a whisper, as though the seeds were speaking to her, but the sound of the words was so faint she couldn't make them out.

She glanced at Neill. His amber eyes watched her. It felt almost like he was reassuring her, although of course that made no sense—but, then, neither did any of this. Was he really a cat? Or a *cat*? And what did that mean anyway?

"Why do they need to be planted in my world?" Abby asked.

"Because the trees told me this must be done," Giàrana said. She inclined her head. "Thank you for helping them."

She reached up to the lowest bough of the ash and pulled herself up, and then clambered up to the next branch. She was almost hidden by the leaves and branches when Abby realized the woman was leaving.

"Wait!" Abby said, her heart thumping. "How do I get back home?"

Giàrana's face appeared in a space between the leaves, far above Abby's head. Her long braids hung down, framing her face.

"Go back to the meadow," Giàrana said. "Your...*cat*...will allow you to see the Straight Track now."

She vanished into the canopy of the tree.

Abby looked at the seeds she held in one hand, and then slid off the boulder. Neill yawned again. She picked him up, careful to position him so the little sprig of seeds remained free, and began to head across the meadow. Even from this far away she could see the path she'd followed winding its way through the flowers and grasses, like a thin ribbon of golden light. Neill seemed perfectly content to be carried like a purring sack of potatoes, but even if he hadn't, she was no longer afraid he'd run away and be lost forever. She wasn't entirely sure what he was, but it had become clear he was not a normal cat.

She'd missed seeing the Apollo 11 landing, but she and Neill would soon be home. The return of the spacecraft no longer seemed as important as it had earlier. Abby suspected that by taking the seeds back to her world she'd agreed to more than she realized, just like in the old tales her grandmother had told. But she could still hear the whisper of the ash seeds in her mind, and knew her path had changed forever. Next semester she'd start studying botany.

And without knowing why, she knew that once the ash seeds began to grow into trees, they'd speak to her again.

ABOUT THE AUTHOR

Jamie focuses on getting into the minds and hearts of her characters, whether she's writing about a saloon girl in the American West, a man who discovers the barista he's in love with is a naiad, or a ghost who haunts the house she was killed in—even though that house no longer exists. Jamie lives in Colorado, and spends her free time in a futile quest to wear out her two border collies since she hasn't given in and gotten them their own herd of sheep.

Find out more about Jamie at:
jamieferguson.com

facebook.com/jamie.ferguson.author

twitter.com/jamie_ferguson

instagram.com/jamie.ferguson.author

goodreads.com/jamieferguson

pinterest.com/jamieauthor

bookbub.com/authors/jamie-ferguson

NIGHT SHEPHERD

SHARON KAE REAMER

Friday night, late, at the University of Cologne. The place was dead quiet. Had been for hours.

Something lost, something found, something made and something bound.

The chant ran through my head. I didn't know whose voice was speaking or where it had come from. I shook my head. Too many hours on the bench this week.

The gene sequencer, occupying a square-sized chunk of granite-topped counter, hummed to the end of its program. It made a series of sleek beeps and then went on standby. Sitting next to it, I put the finish to my handwritten notes.

Old-fashioned? Yes. Necessary? Yes. Secure? Somewhat, as long as no one found my combination college-ruled and gridded spiral block. And even then. They'd have to decode my shorthand. The diagrams might be easier to decipher. Graphic displays are second only to math as a universal language.

I hopped up from my office chair and turned to the standalone deep sink to wash my hands. I took a step backwards when I realized a creature sat on the sink, dangling her legs. She was smallish, not much bigger than my brother Theo's cat Snowy, skin creamy with a pale greenish glow, hair dark with darkish red streaks—or were they purple? They seemed to pulse and change. Disproportionately large feet swung out and back together at the end of those legs. Not large-ish, but large. They were finely boned delicate feet, just much too long for the cat-sized woman-thing on the sink. She stared up at me with her moon-face, not smiling, not frowning, just curious and... wanting. What did she want?

"Hi, uh...where did you come from?"

"You don't know?" she said, in Breton, the ancient language I knew; a Celtic language variant that had borrowings, mostly from French.

I spoke a form of it, passed down from my parents and their parents before them and on back, with a curious family dialect that was a regional mixture from both upper and lower Brittany where my family had roots. The von der Lahns were a curious mixture of

Breton-French and German. We'd mostly dropped the really archaic language bits, though. It got too many strange looks from the modern-day Bretons when we tried to speak it.

But the archaic stuff did get a good workout when speaking to Otherworld inhabitants like the one sitting on the lab sink in front of me.

I tilted my head just a fraction and smiled. Answered her in the same tongue. "You didn't come through the Opening. I'd have heard about it."

"Other ways than that," she said. "Wardens don't know everything."

She was referring to us. The von der Lahns had been responsible for rending the veil separating the real world—the waking world—from the Otherworld, which we called Ande-dubnos, and now we were stuck with the chore of gatekeeping it. This had all happened when my three siblings—my two wombmates and Brevalaer who came later—and I were still in diapers. That didn't mean we had no responsibility. We did. And plenty of it.

And we were old enough now to take our turns as defenders of said Opening, which was to be found in the back of a bar-pub-bistro (or *Kneipe* in German) called *Skogkatt*. Located on our property and just a few kilometers (as the crow flies) from Burg Lahn, our cozy castle near the Rhine, *Skogkatt* belonged to my father and his twin brother and my mother. It didn't get a lot of human traffic because the locals were afraid of it.

I didn't blame them.

At least there was decent food and drink (and sometimes music) to be had while all the defending was going on. We were charged with making sure that the things, non-human and, at best, part-human, that wanted to come through were the kinds of things that we *wanted* to come through.

"Okay. You came in from a different place. I am interested in that. Intensely. But what do you want?"

Now her look of longing changed to something fierce. Anger and sadness all mixed together. The expression disappeared after an instant. But it scared me. This creature would not have made it through the Opening. Not even close. She wasn't one of the Folk, who we called the *Tud*, which meant the same thing in Breton. Or was she?

She looked similar in size and appearance to one of her fellow creatures, the only one of that kind I'd ever encountered, who made her home in our neck of Ande-dubnos, our private piece of Other-world real estate that we called the Schattenreich.

We called her Korri. When she'd settled there, no one knew. Ages ago, centuries in waking world time. But Korri had proved useful to the family over the years, so she had been allowed to stay.

So this was another one like Korri. Were they related? I seemed to recall that they were all female, or at least most of them were. Did they all look the same?

"You're a Korrigan," I said, feeling stupid. Of course she was. I was about to ask her name, but that would have been even more stupid. She would probably have told me and then I would have owed her a favor, a *geis*.

She wiggled her toes. "Sticks and stones."

She had several sticks...and leaves...stuck onto the mossy green linen dress, darker in color than her skin, that she wore over a fine, very fine, white wool tunic. No stones that I could see. Standard Korrigan uniform, perhaps.

"Uh...okay. Can we switch to English? Or German?"

The Korrigan nodded once hard. "Okey dokes.

I laughed, despite still being troubled.

"Juliette, Jules, my brave little wolf, omega—"

"Hey! Stop raiding my memories. That is *so* not okey dokes with me"

She grimaced in a facsimile to a smile. "Just wanting a look at your other faces."

I drew a hand over my eyes and took a deep breath. "We're not in a good place to talk. Here. Other humans could see us. It wouldn't be good. They don't know about your kind...or any kind that dwells in—"

"I know that. But no one else here. Can disappear if I have to."

"Really?"

She nodded again in that little-girl defiant way. "You are a Maker."

"A…maker?" The way she said it sounded like a title. Like Baroness or Doctor. I was the first (only by a few minutes) but not yet since my father was still alive and well and would hopefully remain so for many years, and also not yet the second, although I was working on it. Unless I got caught with a Korrigan in one of the Uni Cologne genetics labs. That would probably be considered decent grounds for expulsion.

No telling what they would do with the Korrigan. I had a horrible vision of the tiny creature in front of me pickled in a jar of formalin.

She glanced around the room. The lab was sparkly clean, the black granite counters scrubbed. The glassware was washed, sterilized and drying. A residual odor of butanol had oozed out from under the hood, and the weird burnt curry smell that was also slightly sweet, emanated from my lab coat, my hair, my skin. The smells even tasted sickening. Need a sure-fire diet? Work the bench in a biology lab for a month. Appetite suppression guaranteed. Oh—and your water bill will go way up because you'll stand in the shower for about ten times longer than necessary to get rid of the smells.

To stall for time, I moved next to her. She smelled pleasantly of moss and tree bark and loam. I wondered if she smelled that way in Ande-dubnos. I washed my hands with too warm water and dried them off. I tried to be casual as I plopped into my chair and swiveled to face her again.

"I'm going to call you Korri Ann. Because we call your…fellow, um…" I stopped and waved my hands, "kindred…we call her Korri."

"If you ask, I will tell you my name," she said with a toothy grin.

I laughed. "Do I look that stupid?" I had almost asked, but hadn't quite been that stupid. I'd have to watch out for other mistakes. Other than her being here. Which was a huge mistake. "Are you going to tell me why you are endangering me here in the waking world?"

She held out her hand, palm up. A wisp of gauzy material floated there that looked like a mix of spider silk and Spanish moss. The dirty gray made it look like spun smoke, as delicate as cotton candy. I expected it to melt at any second. The structure unfolded into something that looked like a wing. I gasped at its beauty, a pattern of whorls within whorls that reminded me of a nested triskelion. A shredded area along the inside of the wing, where it would have attached to its owner, was the only flaw that I could see. A single tear escaped Korri Ann's eye.

I stood to get a closer look. The flimsy nature of the wing made me want to hold my breath, but the wing seemed impervious to air, not bending as Korri Ann turned it to and fro for me to examine. A partial memory triggered, but I couldn't call it forth.

"Is it yours?" I asked. I couldn't remember if the Korrigans were winged creatures. I thought not.

She shook her head as more tears escaped. Her sorrow touched me deeply. I suddenly understood what it had taken for her to come here, to risk detection. Other than the occasional sighting in the *Bretagne*, on the west coast of France, the Korrigans were the stuff of legend and comic books—there and only there—and mostly reduced to stories and tales for children. And merchandise for tourists to the increasingly popular area of France caught up in the neo-Celtic revival.

"Okay, Korri Ann. You need to be specific now. I know it's hard for your kind. You don't really live in any kind of linear timeline. Am I right?"

She bit her lip. Then nodded.

"But if you want me to help, you need to stay in the here and now for a few minutes to get this sorted. First—"

"He's gone," she said. "The Last One."

I pinched the bridge of my nose. Doubt that we could get this sorted in a few minutes rose up, making my head buzz like it was full of a swarm of gnats. And so I was well on my way to being truly caught, even without a *geis*. But I needed to find out what was wrong, before making a commitment to the Korrigan to help her.

I went to the door and peered out through the hall windows. They showed a silent empty courtyard, the tall grasses and landscaped bushes invisible in the darkness. A light burned in a couple of offices in another wing of the building, but that was all. Business as usual, just after midnight. Except for the hired guards, the vigilant knights of the parking lot gates downstairs, I had the place to myself.

Good. But it still wasn't safe. We needed to go someplace else to finish this discussion. I'd have to smuggle the Korrigan out of the building. She'd fit in my backpack, of that I was sure. Whether she'd let herself be subjected to being stuffed in a small dark place and transported by bicycle was another question.

"Are you afraid of being in a small enclosed place?"

Korri Ann's face lit up briefly. "We love small places...where we can hide and watch."

"Wow. Okay. We need to go somewhere...else. I can give you something to drink, some sweet tea..."

She seemed oblivious to the offer of drink. "But we need to hurry. You can Make him again?"

"Does he have a name, this 'Last One'?"

"*Bugul noz.*"

"That's his name?"

"It's what he *is. Noz* for night, *Bugul*...I don't know the word in English. Maybe someone who keeps others together and keeps them safe."

"Like a Guardian."

"Like with sheep."

I pinched the bridge of my nose. *Bugul noz.* The night shepherd. I'd come across the reference before, somewhere in Brittany when we'd all been on vacation. One of my brothers' many comic books. The *Bugul noz* had been depicted as an immensely ugly creature, but not evil, and not harmful. I snorted. *Ande-dubnos creatures* and *not harmful* were two phrases that didn't go well together. But how could a creature with such delicate wings be ugly?

Korri Ann tilted her head at me.

"Sorry, just thinking to myself. Is that his wing?"

"No—but same as his material. You need material to Make, right?"

I shook my head to clear it and pushed out a sigh. "We need to go. Can you make yourself smaller, like pixie small?"

Korri Ann snorted in return. "Pixie? I can do anything those hated pixies could do. But one should not speak ill of those who are gone forever." She bowed her head sadly.

I went to the locker and exchanged my lab coat for my fall wool mantle; black and elegant, it had been a gift from Fenris, a thank you for my gift to him of Ickles, the bunny. After stowing the laptop and notebook, I showed Korri Ann the inside of the backpack so she could judge the size. She looked at it with great suspicion.

"Hurry!" For some reason, I was afraid of discovery.

She disappeared the *Bugul noz* wing and then shrunk herself into a bite-sized Korrigan. I gave her a gentle shove with my hand and she hopped into the backpack. No sooner had I closed it, when the door opened and one of the security guards poked his head in the door.

"Are you okay...Frau von der Lahn?"

I breathed out shakily. "I'm fine, thanks. Just on my way home."

"I'll go down with you. Some reports of a stranger in the building —a beggarwoman or some such in weird clothes. And it's not even Karneval yet."

I smiled at his joke and wondered where Korri Ann had gone to first before she'd found me.

After I unlocked my bicycle and rode it out of the parking lot in the direction of my apartment—a miniscule breathing space just off the Cologne Altstadt—the brooding started. Korri Ann stayed put. I hoped she was snug and not too disturbed by my laptop with its metallic parts. I thought I heard her singing weakly.

A shepherd for Korrigans? And he had wings? Was the *Bugul noz* some kind of dragon, maybe? I'd not come across too many dragons in Ande-dubnos. The one I'd recently met had no wings. Not technically a dragon, he was a Naga lord; he'd been pretty buff, too. Then there was Melusine, who we called the Smoke Dragon, although I didn't know exactly why. She guarded the Dreams and hung out mostly in the Between Lands.

411

Whatever the *Bugul noz* was, he wasn't any more. And Korri Ann wanted me to make him again.

My mouth fell open and the bike's front tire wobbled as I lost control of the handlebars. I steadied them before my bike spilled me onto the sidewalk, and pulled to a stop underneath the *Bahnhof Süd* train overpass. Clothed in darkness and, I hoped, alone, I took deep breaths and wished I hadn't. Sour and unpleasant, the smell of old piss and stale *Pommes* accosted me along with the cold January air. But I swallowed and breathed some more.

I realized what Korri Ann really wanted.

She wanted me to regrow a creature out of myth and legend. A being as old as the land in which it had lived, where the current human inhabitants only had a distorted-through-thousands-of-years memory of what a Path Guardian had been.

Before Christianity had taken the place by storm. A quiet storm mostly, the Breton people were deeply religious. It had been no work at all to convert them. They'd kept their creatures, their mostly invisible spirits, and their Ankous, but it had all gotten jumbled up. Both in Ande-dubnos and the waking world.

Sometimes I felt sorry for all the beings, deities and whatnot that still existed in Ande-dubnos, pitied their existence and how they yearned for the Dreams of humanity to make them more than what they'd become. Waning memories, at best. Degradation to demons, at worst. But my pity was limited to *sometimes*. Mostly I was just happy when they left me alone. Did that mean I hated Ande-dubnos? I'd had bad experiences there lately, and the shock of it all still hadn't ebbed enough for me to be able to judge my true feelings about my relationship to the Otherworld and its inhabitants.

One thing my recent adventures, the terror receded but not gone, had reinforced. Not to go it alone. I needed help with this. Serious help. Who should I call? My siblings? Possibly. But my tiny little apartment was too small for all of us to sit comfortably enough for brainstorming. That meant going to Burg Lahn and risk having my parents find out about Korri Ann. They'd send the little girly-thing back where she came from without a moment's hesitation. And they'd be totally right to.

That left Fenris. He lived a few blocks over from me in a luxurious restored *Jugendstil* apartment. He had a name out of old tales, but Fenris wasn't old. He was two years younger than me, reckoned in waking world time. I was still not sure about our relationship, Fenris being my cousin and half human, and that meant trouble. Neither of the parental units had tried to have a Serious Talk with me about Fenris, which I chose to assume meant they weren't worried about the cousin part. The half human part was perhaps a bit more troubling.

Maybe they were waiting to see how things developed between us. Or not develop.

I was, too.

I decided to ping-text him first, and with gloved fingers clumsily stabbed the message into my wrist flimsy.

Are you awake?

Maybe he had company of the female variety. It was Friday night and late.

While I waited for him to answer, a passing train rumbled through overhead and a couple of dubious characters—of the drunken and arrogant male variety—stumbled down the train station stairs. I moved my bike out of the underpass tunnel and into the light. That didn't seem to be a problem for them, as the pair made like an inebriated arrow, wobbly but straight for me. Korri Ann had stopped singing.

My flimsy pinged back at me. I didn't have time for Fenris's reply and readied myself, dropping my bike and backing towards the rough cement of the overpass wall, keeping my eye on the two drunken idiots. I couldn't tell if they were Germans or foreigners in the darkness. It was hard to tell if they were bulky under their puffy jackets. I certainly wasn't man enough to deal with two of them. And right now, nationality didn't matter.

They laughed as they lurched towards me. I dropped into a loose stance, ready to use my one sure-fire karate kick. I did have my best lace-ups on. Random Guy One on my left and Random Guy Two directly in front of me. Who would be first? Just a couple more steps—

Random Guy One screamed and pulled at his hair.

Random Guy Two laughed at his pal and leered at me. His leer got wiped. He screamed and put his hands to his eyes. Blood ran out of his nose.

The other one swayed and shouted in German, calling me a *Hexe* and some other names as well.

But I hadn't done a thing. I still stood there, every muscle tense. My neck ached from the strain.

The two of them continued to curse and moan. Now they were not only drunk but angry. Sweat dripped down my forehead even though my skin felt icy.

I decided to make a break for my bike. I got hold of the handle bars when Random Guy One grabbed my arm.

Random Guy Two shouted. My attacker and I both looked.

A ghostly apparition of a beggarwoman with stringy white hair and glowing red eyes had appeared between me and the bad guys. Her skin was wrinkled, and she sang a very creepy-sounding song in Breton, a Grimm-style gnome if ever there was one. The song sounded like she was counting off the days of the week using a Stockhausen non-melody.

I bit the man's arm and grabbed my bicycle. He and his companion backed off. They shouted *Hexe!* again, and a cloud of fog enveloped them.

They ran, fell, staggered up and ran some more.

I didn't wait around to see if they would change their minds. I sprang onto my bike, riding forward and quickly hung an illegal left at the stoplight. I raced down the narrow street, pedaling as fast as I could go and hoping no one got in my way.

I braked hard at the next stoplight and grabbed my backpack. Loosening the drawstring and peering inside, I breathed out heavily. Korri Ann had drawn herself into a tiny ball. She glowed with the same sort of fog that had enveloped the Random Guys.

A late night dog-walker heading to the nearby park went past me. The piebald Jack Russell terrier lifted its head as if it sensed Korri Ann—which it very well might have—and tried to trot back to us, but its owner jerked on the leash and they went on.

"Are you all right?" I asked.

Korri Ann lifted her head and smiled weakly. I took that as a yes.

"I'm closing up again. We need to go a little further."

I slung the pack on my back again. Awkward as it was to bike that way with my wool coat, I wanted to keep Korri Ann close to me while riding rather than strap the back to my bike rack. My phone chirped angrily from the bottom of the pack. Korri Ann squawked.

I dug around after shunting the Korrigan carefully to the side, and found the archaic digital phone. I kept it because. Reason. I called her Mama. She insisted we all carry one because she hated texting. Still. Papa had adapted without looking back. He'd loved texting, apparently, from day one. Most people, especially people over a certain age, still had phones, but you never saw anyone use them in public. They were considered so *outré* these days, like smoking but not *quite* as bad.

"Hello?"

"Juliette."

Fenris's gruff worried voice startled me into a gasp. I'd forgotten that I'd texted him.

"Fenris, hey...um, did I wake you?"

"No."

"Oh. Sorry to bother you—"

"What makes you think you're *bothering* me?"

Embarrassment and anger flared. "Well, because it's Friday, the time when people are usually entertaining, sometimes with someone they, you know, are attracted to, and because it's late and—"

"Entertaining?" He laughed. "Is something wrong?"

I pushed down my irritation and told him about the Korrigan, just a rough version about her showing up in the lab, and that I needed help.

"Should I pick you up?" he asked, his gruffness gone.

"I'm on my bike. I can be there in about ten minutes or so."

"Your bike? Did you know winter is officially declared as having started over a month ago?"

"Yeah. I kinda knew that. I'm toasty warm with that lovely coat you gave me."

"Would you like tea or coffee?"

"Stronger stuff."

"Gaelic coffee?"

"Perfect."

Fenris opened the door to his flat as I was coding the bike lock.

"You can bring it in. No one would steal it then."

"If they try to steal it, they'll get a shock, and the alarm on the lock is loud enough to wake the dead and the scare the shit out of the undead."

He snorted. "Your bicycle looks like it survived the last Ice Age. I doubt anyone would even bother to steal that one."

"Not true. In Cologne, they'll steal any bike. Anytime."

My brand new, most expensive bike got stolen over a year ago. The new, less expensive one just a few months after that. Then I bought a cheap city bike from a former student and got my cousin Jeremiah to hack an off-the-shelf lock to make a few enhancements, one of which was the alarm and the mild electric shock. He'd done it no charge since he'd also lost a couple of bicycles to Cologne bike thieves.

I walked up the front steps and Fenris gestured me inside. He was dressed casually, jeans (black) and a cashmere (his weakness) pullover, with a black Tee underneath. So *not* in his pajamas. I laid down the pack on the gleaming black and white tiled foyer floor and began shedding; fleece headband, gloves, my coat. But before I got past the gloves, I was drawn into a tight warm embrace. Warm kisses followed. He had that familiar, wild woods scent of rich earth and fallen leaves. He tasted as good as his arms felt around me. My fingers tingled underneath the fleece gloves I still wore.

"Hey. Fenris," I said when breath returned.

"Juliette." He touched my nose with his forefinger and tugged on the headband. "See?"

"See what?"

"As of now, I am *entertaining*. Someone, you know—

"Thanks. I, uh..." Looking for a way to best describe my mixed feelings without going maudlin, I failed utterly and dripped awkward onto the tiles.

He helped me take off my coat, and hung it on an antique dark wooden coatrack along with my scarf. The coatrack was kind of ugly and so unlike Fenris's refined modern taste that I figured it was probably an heirloom. I'd never asked him about it.

I stuck the gloves and headband in the coat pockets while he waited. I picked up the backpack and pointed to it. "One Korrigan. Many problems."

His look of disgust would have been comical if it didn't have a frightening, wolflike edge to it.

"What?" I asked.

"Why did you bring a Korrigan here?"

"Um. Because? She needs my—our—help?"

He snorted again and turned away, going through a side door that led into his sitting room. It was lit in candlelight from real wall sconces and a few thick square (black, of course) candles on the table by the picture windows facing out to the garden. Nothing to see there in the darkness, but I remembered the recent enchanted moonlit evening when we'd sat here and looked out over a pristine snowfall-laden vista. A small vista since it was a city garden, but it had been magical and intimate.

I followed him in and sat across from him on the facing couch, both couches stylish and comfortable and separated by a shiny black (I'm not using the word lacquer, here, as that sounds cheesy—and nothing about Fenris was cheesy) massive coffee table. It held a tray with two mugs of steaming (and, I assumed) cream and whiskey-laden coffee.

He leaned back, an arm across the back of the couch, his look questioning.

I held up a finger and opened the pack. Korri Ann looked up, her eyes bright with anticipation and fear. I held out my hand, palm up. She shook her head, her arms crossed. What? Was she going to do an old-timey *I Dream of Jeannie* exit? No way. I'd already told her to back off from raiding my memories, and it would have pissed me off particularly if she knew I'd streamed the ancient series hundreds of times. I don't know why. Nothing really to be embarrassed about. Except for that one time in sixth grade I had Mama buy me a harem-type Karneval outfit that I'd doctored to look exactly like Jeannie's.

No, Korri Ann didn't. She made her way out of the pack using one of the drawstrings as a climbing aid. She looked around quickly, spied Fenris, and then hopped onto the couch. Once there, she returned to being cat-sized, like an image in a pool of water that shimmered and then changed.

She sat next to me and glared at Fenris, her legs dangling over the edge of the couch.

I picked up my black (yes, lacquered) mug and lifted it in a quick toast to Fenris. He didn't move to do the same.

"Would you like something to drink?" he asked Korri Ann, a broad hint of sarcasm in his voice.

He spoke to her in Breton. I'd not been aware he could speak the language, but, yeah, it made sense. He was family, through and through. Except for the non-human part of him.

"*Eigi einhamr*," she said, and nicked her head in a bare show of respect.

"Have you come to steal babies?" Fenris growled.

I took a sip of the still hot coffee and felt the tingle of the alcohol going down, the warm and sweet aroma in stark contrast to the sticky sour atmosphere in the room. The suddenly silent room. I wished for snow and intimacy. And that Korri Ann would go away. Now.

"We don't steal babies," she said and her face heated in anger. "Only take those offered. Why do your kind abandon babies?"

Fenris sat straighter, his eyes wary. He'd been challenged. And I could see doubt in his eyes. "If you speak truth, then..."

She nodded. "We do not deceive in that way, as you must know.

Only in self-defense, may we speak untruth. But there are no more babies to be abandoned in these times. Not in the Lands Beyond."

He nodded in acknowledgement of the fertility problems with those of his Folk in the Lands Beyond, the *Jötnar*, or so-called Frost Giants. They were neither frosty nor particular giant-sized, so I had no idea where the name had come from. Maybe the Germanic tribes and Norse tribes had meant something else, or it was a translation problem. Or Jacob Grimm and his colleagues just got it wrong.

The Korrigans had often been accused of stealing human babies, but Korri—*our* Schattenreich Korrigan—had told me once that human babies did not interest them enough to *steal* them. And had sniffed loudly at the thought. I believed her, especially since baby-stealing was not a deed attributed only to beings like the Korrigans. Trolls, demons, gnomes, fairies, etc. had all been accused in times past.

My father concurred with some folklorists who claimed that the stolen babies (substituted with changelings) meme was a coordinated —and mostly successful—anti-propaganda campaign by medieval clergy to encourage the peasantry to have their children baptized. It could also have been an older propaganda campaign, as in pre-Christian older, to explain away defective babies (and justify abandoning them).

But I doubted that the Korrigans had anything to do with baby-stealing in the waking world. Adult males—they were fair prey— were another story. I gave Fenris a brief but thrilling account of Korri Ann's help against my attackers.

Fenris glared at me, but the effect was ruined by the worry in his eyes. We'd had this discussion before. I insisted on working late. He insisted that he'd come pick me up in his chauffeured (black) Audi sedan. Since neither chauffeur nor sedan lived in the flat with him, I assumed they were housed elsewhere, but not too far away. We'd not been able to come to a satisfying *compromise* on the subject yet. But it wasn't for lack of trying. The arguments usually ended up being defused by kisses. No complaining about that. Nope.

"And now you owe her for her help?" he asked.

I shrugged. "Not directly. But I'd already decided to help her. Only problem is, I'm not sure I can."

"Make *Bugul noz*," Korri Ann said and the tears welled up again. "Gone. Gone forever."

I prompted her to show Fenris the wing.

He lifted an eyebrow after he saw it. "Can't say I ever saw...is it a him?"

She nodded.

"Only those comic book creatures," he said. "Supposed to be ugly."

Korri Ann stiffened and shook her little fists. "Not ugly. Beautiful. Stupid peasants."

I coughed out a laugh. That she would call the present-day Bretons peasants was kind of funny.

"He's dead, the *Bugul noz*?" I asked.

"Not dead, gone. Like us. We just turn to this," she said and held forth the wing, "when we go."

While we admired it, the wing just disintegrated, like a sculpture made of snowflakes being blown away in a fierce winter wind. Nothing remained. Korri Ann grasped after it, but there was nothing left to hold onto. Even though Korri Ann said the wing didn't belong to the *Bugul noz*, it still seemed kind of sad. But where had she gotten it from?

The memory I'd had a glimpse of earlier sprung forth in fullness. Our Korrigan in the Schattenreich had a mound-hut dwelling, covered with moss. Out front was a deep small pool, of cenote deepness. I'd always wondered who got sacrificed there in times past. But I didn't *really* want to know. Inside the hut, well, yes, it had a hobbit-like quality, especially if hobbits were much more sinister creatures than Tolkien had visualized them. And if they could shapeshift. Then they would be Korrigans.

But the important part of the memory was out back of Korri's house. There existed a place I only glimpsed through an oval window and had been admonished to never ever never under any circumstances try to go to. The dying, nearly dead orchard of trees resembled live oak with immense amounts of what I'd always assumed was Spanish moss or stringy spiderwebs hanging from their branches. Very beautifully patterned diaphanous material, like the wing Korri Ann had held in her small hand.

Fenris again raised one of his lush but elegant eyebrows and we exchanged a look.

"You turn into creatures made of that stuff?" I asked and rubbed the bridge of my nose again. It was late, and I sensed I was going to need a lot more Gaelic coffee to get through this.

"That is only a part of us. The rest is invisible. Until we get hungry. Then we're not invisible."

"Hungry," I said and knew instantly where this was going. "For human blood?"

She gave me the Korrigan version of a shrug, very subtle. But the frown on her face told me volumes.

"You turn into non-dead kind of vampire things? Like invisible dragons...or what?"

Her look didn't change. And she didn't look away. "Dragon-like. We...they...don't get hungry very often. Not unless something wanders by. Used to be things could get in from here." She gestured around us, meaning the waking world. "The *Bugul noz* was the one who kept humans safe from wandering in, so they wouldn't get eaten. He made the paths and also scared the mortals away. But since the veil closed, that didn't happen very much anymore." She sat straighter and closed her hands into tight fists. "Now, though, with the veil open..."

"He had too much work to do," I said.

"Too many paths to make. And it used him up."

I sat back and took another sip, letting the coffee, cream, and smoky whiskey flavors blend before swallowing. The fire in my belly made me feel as if things were going to be okay. I knew it was an illusion. As long as the veil stayed open, these kinds of things would keep happening. And ultimately, the fate of the *Bugul noz* was then, without a doubt, our fault.

I sighed.

I wondered how extensive Korri Ann's knowledge of my far-flung family was, some of whom, like Fenris, were not entirely human. Like my other cousin Jörmundgandr, whose name was a mouthful, even for a native-born German. And she was a handful. She's not properly a dragon. I'd guess you could name her serpent. Or wyrm. And an *eigi einhamr*, a Germanic skinwalker, like Fenris; they were both from the *Jötnar* side of the family. Jörmundgandr's spirit form, which was a dominant part of her personality, was of the Grendel variety. Only not ugly. Orrie, as her siblings called her (much easier to say), was beautiful. And sinister. And she had no wings.

"Dragon-like. You mean the *Bugul noz* is now a big—"

"Is also a Guardian."

"Guardian. Okay. You said that already. Then—"

"You Make things. Can you Make him again?"

"But...the wing is gone. How..." I rubbed my forehead to force my brain to focus. "I don't understand how this can work."

She lowered her head, another tear escaping. The Korri who lived in the Schattenreich was also emotional from time to time. Sad, somehow.

"Is he a Korrigan?" Fenris asked.

Korri Ann opened her mouth to answer, but hesitated. "It's possible. We don't know, just that he's always been there. As we are. But there is only one of him."

"But what does he *guard*?" I asked.

"He used to guard the sacred place. And the paths."

"Paths...as in the path you took to get through the veil?"

She nodded and two tears slid down her cheeks. "Korrigan paths. Special. For me...us. Paths for the ones left. He makes with his words."

While I thought, I hummed a tune that sounded a little like the gene sequencer in action.

"Wait," Fenris said and held up a hand. "Where is this *sacred* place?"

"Everywhere and nowhere, like all the places in Ande-dubnos," she said.

I leaned forward, my arms across my thighs. One of the big square candles on the table began to sputter. Then another one.

"This is all academic. And I do mean that." I looked up, directing Fenris a critical once-over. "One. How are we supposed to get the *Bugul noz* out of the sacred place in order to remake him?"

Korri Ann sighed and her whole body shook. I waited, but she continued to stare at the candles as if hypnotized.

"Two. If we get him out, I'm still not sure how you think we can restore him."

"Make him," she insisted. "You have done it. I heard of the things you make."

"Have heard of what—"

Right then, a fluffy black bunny hopped in front of Fenris's feet. We all stared at it. Its cashmere fur looked as soft as Fenris's sweater. More crushably soft than the plushiest plush toy.

It lifted its little bunny nose to sniff at us, both ears tilted forward. Fenris leaned over and scooped up the bunny with one hand and put it on his lap.

"How is Ickles?" I asked.

He smiled. Korri Ann pointed to Ickles the bunny. "It is made. You made him."

It was true. Fenris's bunny was one of my more successful designs.

I executed my designs on my own specialized hybrid computer (also assembled by Cousin Jeremiah) and in my favorite color, dark blue, and with a retro keyboard (where the keys clacked), but the programs I ran did not conform to the 2025 Geneva Convention Genetics and Reproduction Protocols. Not by a long shot.

However. The Geneva Protocols only covered reproduction of waking world life. The real world. The kind of genetic designs I worked on in my spare time, my professional hobby, were not the kinds of things you would find in the real world. Their essence was designed to work in the Otherworld. Ande-dubnos. Through our ancient bloodline, we had access to the Otherworld. And we could do things there that most people would call magic.

We called it *Schattenwerk*. Shadowcraft. All of us of the blood had our specialties. Designing unusual, (magical) shadowcraft creatures was mine. It required manifesting my craft into the waking world, because I hadn't yet been able to construct a fully operating genetic laboratory in Ande-dubnos. Not yet. I had started though. I had started to set up a lab in our Otherworld castle, the equivalent to Burg Lahn, called *Lahn dunum*. I just hadn't had enough time lately to mess with it.

So I interpreted my designs as not *exactly* contravening the Geneva Protocols. What they *exactly* did was sometimes unpredictable. But interesting.

Much more interesting than my doctorate work.

"Korri Ann," I said and cleared my throat.

"Korri Ann?" Fenris said and made a canine-like snort.

I ignored him. "Ickles the bunny is a waking world construct. His...material comes mostly from the same stuff that makes up all life on our planet."

"It is all connected. We are reflections of you," she said, and opened her arms. "We are a part of your Dreams, your memories, your past. Maybe, your future...but that is not known."

I jumped up and walked to the window. It was a problem that now, I knew, would never let me go until I figured it out. Were the Ande-dubnos creatures alive? The Korrigan had just answered the question. They lived. Through us. They were our reflections, as a fun house mirror that shaped and distorted, in this case by time and place and the growth of rationality and modern religions antagonistic to their existence.

The question remained: would it be possible, was it even imaginable, to *remake* Ande-dubnos creatures? Here would have been an ideal opportunity to test out my secret *Lahn dunum* evil scientist laboratory and its capabilities. An opportunity and a danger. Aside from the danger of being eaten by Korrigan zombie vampires. What kind of new monsters could I make? A funny tickling in my belly made me think that my parents would definitely not be amused by the idea. Or the actuality.

I turned around. Korri Ann now sat on the couch next to Fenris.

She stroked Ickles' head.

"Let's go get the *Bugul noz*. Petting bunnies will have to wait until later."

"But how do we get there?" Fenris asked.

"I know how. And it's not far at all. We just have to take a stroll through the Schattenreich."

∾

I'd crossed with Fenris before to the Schattenreich. It had involved a passionate kiss and a betrayal. This time my family would not be waiting to ambush Fenris after we crossed. I counted that as a positive development in our relationship.

Fenris couldn't yet cross to the Schattenreich on his own. We hadn't given him permission. He had access to a small closed off portion of the Schattenreich that had been formed by his human father, my uncle Kilhian. Deceased.

This time the kiss was just as passionate, but tempered with the experience of learned trust between us.

As with most things having to do with the veil, the less you tried to think about it directly, the easier it became. The kiss deepened and made it hard for me to concentrate on crossing.

The crossing happened effortlessly.

The illusion of dropping, not falling, not exactly, while my body slipped sideways, caused us to break off the kiss. Did crossing the veil feel the same way to him? We opened our eyes at the same time. Fenris smiled. Caught. A wimpy gasp escaped me. Korri Ann had traveled with us by hanging her arms around my neck and making fake gagging noises during our kiss.

"We're here."

"Should we transform?"

"Not yet. I may have to do *Schattenwerk* and that requires an opposable thumb. And have to hope that it works," I said, mumbling the last part.

We also brought Ickles. It made me sad to do so, but I had to insist over Fenris's objections. I wanted to snicker at his attachment to the bunny. But I didn't. One didn't snicker at lovers. We weren't quite there yet. Maybe wouldn't ever be. So, carefully not snickering.

The meadow clearing with the mostly silent River of Life to my left and the Schattenreich forest to my right was also still in the grip of winter. The grasses felt stiff and dry. The meadow flowers dead until spring. The branches of the deciduous trees—oak, maple, birch, willow—hung leafless and forlorn. A few clothed black pines, reminiscent of a warmer northern European climate, huddled in between.

I gave Fenris's hand a quick squeeze and let go. We headed through the forest. I kept a brisk pace for about half an hour. Korri Ann rode me piggyback while Fenris mumbled, a step or three behind.

I did hear him say clearly at one point, "We'd go faster if we were in wolf form."

I had some sympathy for his annoyance. Fenris was *eigi einhamr*; he had more than one skin. He was a rarity: a Germanic skinwalker inhabiting a twenty-first century male body, the essence of his non-humanity. The pressure to change into his monstrous beautiful wolf form when he was here in Ande-dubnos, even when just in our small neighborhood of it, must have been immense.

When we reached the mound-hut of our Schattenreich Korrigan (just plain Korri), the first thing I noticed was the devastation. Trees had been uprooted and thrown into the cenote in front of Korri's hut, warped sticks dunked in a dark dip of murky water. The vivid green moss that decorated the hut now looked brown and dead. The kludged-together collection of boards that constituted the door lay in pieces in front of the hut. Within was dark and deserted, although I remember it always looking dark and deserted the times I'd been here before.

We halted a few meters away from the hut. I tried to dislodge Korri Ann's arms from my neck, but she wouldn't budge and began to whimper.

"Does it always look like this?" Fenris asked.

I shook my head, a lump in my throat forming when I thought of something bad happening to Korri. "No." My voice came out as a squeak.

Fenris didn't need any more encouragement. He transformed in an instant, the handsome man replaced by a mega wolf. His black fur, shot through with bits of gray and brown and iridescent silver, bristled. His tail stood straight out behind him, a warning for anyone who could read it. With eyes intently focused, coffee-with-cream colored irises almost hidden by the enlarged pupils, he surveyed the ruins.

I entered the hut, the long dark hallway that appeared to slope down, my hands brushing along the smoothly worn, pebble-textured walls.

After a few twists and turns, the hallway opened out into a narrow room lined on one side with crude shelves that looked like shaved pieces of bark with a thin layer of wood still attached. Odd collections of stones, dried leaves and other scavenged debris lined the shelves. On one edge were three chipped teacups in their saucers and a teapot, the spout partially cracked.

Fenris padded up behind me. I set Korri Ann on the tree-trunk table. She let go of my neck reluctantly. The room had a Korrigan-sized wooden door that led to Korri's kitchen, which she never allowed guests to enter. The visual focus of the room was the oval picture window, minus the glass, that dominated the wall just off to the side of the kitchen entrance.

Fenris took a few steps towards the window. There never had been any glass in the window that I could remember, but it looked as if something had come through in a hurry; the window frame and sill were cracked and battered.

I went to stand next to him, my arm across his canine shoulders. Standing, his torso came up to my waist. That's how big he was.

"That's it out there," I said.

He turned his head to spare me a look, but then returned his attention to what was outside the window. The murky twilit grove of sickly trees, their branches being strangled by clumps of a kind of fairy moss, but this moss had never been seen in the waking world. It all formed an eerie landscape unrelieved by birdsong, the scent of rich loam. It lacked strong color, somewhat resembling a sepia landscape with dark shadows lurking everywhere. Not an inviting place to go for an afternoon stroll. I never had, and neither had any of my sibs. We'd been warned against doing any such thing. Many times. Not known for our obedience, in this case we had all complied even if we didn't know what was out there. Even Korri had never suggested we *go take a look*. My father would have incinerated her with one of his *Schattenwerk* fireballs on the spot.

"What is that stuff?" Fenris growled, the wolf in his voice vibrating through my arm, still draped over him.

"That stuff is what I'm guessing Korri Ann was talking about—the remains of the Korrigans. Their wings."

We both turned to look at the Korrigan. She stared out the window, her eyes bright with a manic gleam, as if she was hypnotized by the spectral tableau. The mossy substance on the trees did not—or did not any longer—bear any resemblance to the delicate wing that Korri Ann had showed me. What remained were now just the tattered remains of wings. Whatever had caused their destruction, the wing-like substance had become something less beautiful, like insect wings, crushed and discarded.

"What happened?" I asked.

"Drained," Korri Ann mumbled, still in her trance.

"By what?"

"*Bugul noz*. Hungry. Angry."

"What keeps them in there?" Fenris asked.

"You mean *kept*," I said. "I'm guessing it was *our* Korrigan, the one who lives—or lived—here in the hut. But what happened to her? And what is the reason for this destruction?"

"He's gone," Korri Ann said in a distressed whisper. Her whole body shook.

"Who's gone? You mean the *Bugul noz*?"

"Some of your people will die," Korri Ann said. "We were afraid of that. That's why I asked you to Make him again. So this wouldn't happen. Should have hurried."

"But what happened to our Korri?" I asked to no one in particular.

"She tried to help him," Korri Ann's timid voice disappeared, replaced by a voice that sounded like something I was familiar with when dealing with Ande-dubnos entities. It sounded like *troidell*...the Breton word for a contrivance or, more bluntly, a trick. "We decided to bring him to you...so you could Make him there in the place where you do the Craft." She took a deep breath and spurted out, "And then he...he must have gotten out." Her lips clamped shut.

"What? Korri...I mean, you and our Schattenreich Korri, planned to bring the *Bugul noz*—or what was left of him—to me in my lab in Cologne...and you are just *now* telling me this?"

"I didn't know she had failed...until we got here." She stuck her nose up in the air.

My skin felt inflamed with anger and I smelled tar and burnt matches. My nostrils flared. I clenched my fists, wanting to hit something. Anything. Korri Ann would do for a start. I could slap her from here to next week. Fenris growled loud and long. Oh, how I sometimes hated Ande-dubnos and all its natural—or unnatural—inhabitants.

"So what is he now doing and where?" I asked.

"He's doing what he always does," she said.

"He's...making paths?" I asked.

She nodded.

"Paths to...in here?" I pointed at the dreadful tree grove.

She nodded again.

The trees outside the window made a nasty creaking sound, like bones clattering.

"You can change back now, Fen," I said. "We have to look elsewhere. And fast."

It seemed the formerly harmless-to-humans Night Shepherd had become a not-so-harmless Night Shepherd in service to Korrigan vampires. Except the ones that had gotten in his way seemed to be have been *drained*. But I guessed there were more that had fled from his wrath and now waited for his return. And the humans who would follow him to their doom.

The question was where to find him.

And Make him again.

Or kill whatever he had become so that it *couldn't* come back.

PART II. SOMETHING FOUND

W e watched the *Tanzbrunnen* from a short distance away. The 'dancing fountain' was an impressive circular water feature built nearly a hundred years earlier just a stone's throw from the Rhine river. In the middle of the fountain was a raised round open stage roofed with a wavy stretched white sailcloth. I'd been here once for one of my uncle's concerts. His rock-folk-veering-into-folk-metal music, his loyal fans, and the fine atmosphere had made it a magical summer's eve.

We crouched behind some permanent freestanding constructions shaped like convex umbrellas (also with sailcloths) that served as both sunshades and rainshades for visitors. The waters of the fountain were drained for the winter, the place deserted. The *Rheinpark* was deader than dead, the gardens waiting for spring and a horde of gardeners to make them come alive again.

We parked Fenris's sleek Audi sedan—minus chauffeur—in the official parking lot with no one here to question our invasion. One phone call from Fenris got us access to the now deserted lot. I wondered exactly what kind of influence he had here in the city. My mother had told me recently that his father, her evil twin, had had plenty of mojo in Cologne to spend from all his financial connections. He'd been richer than our family and not afraid to throw his influence around to get what he wanted.

Korri Ann thought that a fountain was the most likely place for the *Bugul noz* to make an entryway for his paths. The Korrigans needed to be near water. They weren't water sprites or fairies (don't ever call any of the Folk fairies), but water was an essential part of their existence. She didn't say why. I was tired and hyped up with worry, but I had to know. Korri Ann thought that our Korri *might* have led the *Bugul noz* to water, hoping we'd be able to find her.

Why or how she knew that...I had only nodded.

And wonder what else she hadn't told me.

Water was a tricky proposition in Cologne with its many fountains, not to mention the Rhine itself. Some 'water features' were classified as wells and some were even old examples of animal troughs. Some dated back to Roman times. We'd already checked the *Heinzelmännchen* fountain in the city center across from the rowdy *Früh Kneipe*, the *Petrus* fountain, and the *Dom* fountain (with its curious mosaic that looks like swastikas, but isn't because it was built around fifty years before the Nazis started fouling the air by taking breaths).

The fountains were all pretty close together, around the Cologne cathedral and the Roncalliplatz, and therefore quick-and-easy to check. No giant evil ugly monster dude with spider silk wings was anywhere around.

Fenris was the one who suggested the *Tanzbrunnen*. It was in the middle of a huge public area that included a beach club direct on the Rhine, the beautiful *Rheinpark* gardens, two theaters in addition to the *Tanzbrunnen* stage for shows, and an outdoor bar/restaurant that was a nice place to sit and have a drink on a summer's evening. I could easily imagine coming back with Fenris for just such an occasion.

Someday.

If we survived this without getting eaten. I wasn't feeling too optimistic.

Especially if the *Bugul noz* was now in Cologne. And if our Korri, with the escaped *Bugul noz* in pursuit, had been forced to choose a place near water to make a path to lead large numbers of humans to be slaughtered by fairy vampires, this was the place to do it.

Fenris half-dozed next to me while leaning against the pillar. Korri Ann fidgeted inside my backpack, her head sticking out and one hand resting on my shoulder. Ickles the cashmere bunny stuck his nose out next to her. His whiskers twitched against my neck.

The alcohol from the Gaelic coffee had worn off, but the caffeine had kicked in, and I felt antsy and uncomfortable in my skin. The air smelled cold and fresh and menacing. I couldn't smell myself under the coat, but I imagined it wasn't pleasant. Not much I could do about that now. Maybe my body (mal)odor would be strong enough to vanquish the *Bugul noz* or knock him out. Not feeling too optimistic about that either.

I snorted, my exhalation making a little cold cloud. Fenris opened an eye, his eyebrow raised.

I shook my head.

In front of us, something shimmery moved. The fountain, which normally took over a day to fill, was full. Spontaneously. It sprang into fountaining, with all the jets on in all their glory and lighted. These weren't the installed lights, which were magical enough, but some sort of otherworldly lights—true fairy lights that appeared to float on top of the water—white and pure and ghostly with a haze of curling, spreading fog and the inviting soft music of bells. I didn't recognize the melody, but it made me start forward.

I was quickly lost in the fog. I could no longer see the fountain or its surrounds. I walked on.

Fenris called my name faintly from somewhere over to my right. I turned in that direction, but the sound ceased.

He called from my left. I turned that way.

Nothing.

The entrancing bells and a sweet fresh scent, like a flower shop heady with carnation and lavender and the sweet delicate powdery fragrance of violets came from ahead of me. I followed my nose.

The fog cleared. I walked on through an alleyway, the backdrop a green-tinged horizon lined with trees with exquisitely textured white bark, only a few of which still grasped their colorful leaves, drained of the green, photosynthesis on hold until spring, the ground strewn with shed leaves in bright fall colors.

I looked down.

I wore white satin slippers and a Regency era sleeveless white ball gown, the skirt trimmed in lace and satin, the bodice in satin and bedecked with tiny pearls. My dark chestnut hair hung long and wavy down my back. My skin seemed paler than usual and had a weird translucent glow that only increased the farther in I went.

Ahead of me was *something* tall and large. He would dwarf even Fenris, with broad heavy shoulders, long legs and arms, and dark hair with streaks of green in loose plaits trailing down his back. He wore a velvet coat and old-fashioned yellow breeches that were stretched across massive thighs, but looked soft and supple and made from animal skin. Two delicate wings extended from his shoulders. Butterfly wings made for a giant, gray and translucent and beautiful, they consisted of a soft and intricate pattern of whorls.

Those wings were the only thing that differed. But the rest was my Beauty and the Beast Dream made real.

I was no Beauty. The other von der Lahn women, my mother and sister, were better candidates for that role. And this Beast walking away from me was not the one I dreamed about. My Beast was a man who hid his wolfskin from the waking world. *My* gray wolf was my spirit animal that I could transform into in Ande-dubnos, but it was a part of me, just as his wolf skin was a part of him. It neither detracted nor added to my basic humanity, but I liked to think it made *me* more *me*, was part of my inner natural self. Was that any different from a Germanic skinwalker?

Very.

Fenris wore his wolfskin without shame and had no wish to be rid of it, to be fully human. Fenris's wolf was big and dangerous to those who opposed him. I had tamed him once, through guile, but it was to save him from being hurt even worse.

In the process, a spark had ignited between us. The spark was there before, when I first laid eyes on him, not knowing who or what he was. He had known who I was, and it was perhaps his recognition and a measure of surprise that had started the whole thing between us.

Do you believe in love at first sight? Me, neither. But I do believe that something happens sometimes, like a finger snap, when two people meet. And that's what happened. Between Fenris and me.

I didn't believe there was a real chance for us to be together. For it to work. My waking world self just didn't believe it. But the Dream, of us, the one that woke me, alone in my bed at night, feverish warm and yearning; that was different. In that dream I was dressed like this, and he was dressed like that. Transported into an era that a slew of romance novels were made of, we danced in his snow-laden garden and the world was ours alone.

We ran together then in that Dream, through the night, through the trees, transformed, two wolves in the grip of the now the speed the movement. Aware of the night and the silence that caressed us.

Transform, came the command. It was a powerful urge, to become my wolf, to run, to catch up with the Beast in front of me, the one who had found and stolen my Dream.

Juliette, came the call from somewhere else, from the voice of my Dream. From Fenris.

Mind awake at Fenris's call, I shook off the Dream and with it the lethargy that had gripped me in the fog that led me here.

I resisted.

Because I knew that if I gave in and went to the thing in front of me, I would die.

No distinct smells, just deadness, and that's how I knew I was in Ande-dubnos. But where? And what was in front of me?

He stopped and turned to face me. *Come to me. This is* your *path.* Before I looked away, I had a glimpse of dark round eyes and a lined face, skin pitted with holes and bumps, and cruel fleshy lips open to reveal many, many uneven teeth. A thick neck and bulging chest.

He was visible. And that meant he was hungry.

He was not ugly. He was worse.

I turned and ran, exchanging the ball gown with the flick of a hand for a simple cotton T-shirt and stretchy leggings, feet bare. Gaining speed. I pushed at hard cold ground that burned the soles of my feet, crunching leaves, trying to chew up distance and just get away.

A tearing, ripping-of-flesh noise from behind caused me to stumble and shudder and want to scream. A snarling growl, as of a large, very large wolf made me spin around fast. Fenris-as-wolf was grappling with the Regency-clad monster man.

The creature recited something in a short snatch of a deep sing-songy voice, and grabbed onto Fenris, throwing its arms around him.

Fenris appeared dazed for a few moments; his eyes had a druggy look to them. But he shook his head and pushed off the *Bugul noz*— the nattily clad horror could only be him or what was left of him— with his slender but powerful hind legs while snapping at him, massive wolf jaws threatening serious damage.

There was no doubt that Fenris could carry through with ripping the *Bugul noz's* throat out.

They stared at each other for a few seconds. Stalemate.

I took a few steps forward, and reached around to my backpack to grab Ickles. I would have to destroy the bunny to get to the geneti-cally engineered organic polymer inside him. Ickles was one of my best tricks, a piece of Ande-dubnos shadowcraft and *that* had been my real present to Fenris. The polymer could be used to capture the *Bugul noz*. I silently begged Fenris's forgiveness.

But my backpack was not there. I had lost it and the creatures inside it somewhere in the fog.

The *Bugul noz* disappeared. Fenris leapt after him—into nowhere —they were both just disappeared. There followed a loud click-BAM. As of a door. Slamming.

The path was closed.

My knees tensed and my body was ready to bolt again. But there was no one there, no alleyway of trees, no green glow, just rough paving stones and the dead of night.

The thousands of gallons of water that had so recently filled the

Tanzbrunnen now shimmered, the liquid as ghostly as the fog that had swept me away just a few minutes...hours...ago. Its many jets were quiescent. The fairy lights extinguished. Dawn couldn't be far away. We'd left Fenris's place sometime after midnight, close to 2:00 in the a.m. It was now close to 4:00.

I ran up to where they had stood and fought, Fenris and the *Bugul noz*, and there it was on the ground. The beautiful wing that had been attached to the creature. I stifled a cry. I had no idea where to find them in that ghostly awful sacred place where dead Korrigans went to spend eternity.

And where the fuckall was Korri Ann? Note to my smarter self: never trust a Korrigan ever again.

I picked up the *Bugul noz* wing and felt childlike arms around my neck.

"Korri Ann?"

She hugged me tighter.

"Where is the wolf-man?" she asked.

"He's..." I choked.

I pulled on one arm to bring her around to my side and then grabbed her upper body, holding her in front of me, her mossy dress clasped in one fist, the *Bugul noz* wing in the other. She felt so light, almost as light as the filmy wing, as if she wasn't really made of solid substance at all.

"Where is Ickles?" I asked.

She gulped and pointed to my backpack that lay in a little crumpled pile near the fountain. "He's not damaged, just a little blood. We had to fight off a few of the...others—"

"What others?"

"From my kind, the others that have passed on." She put her arm across her eyes and stifled a sob. Then she ran over and got the pack, tucked Ickles under her arm and dance-hopped back to me. Ickles looked terrified—frozen in shock, its big bunny eyes glazed over. It had expected to die. It still might. At my hand.

I shook the Korrigan in front of me, not meaning to, but my energy was fast giving out. The adrenaline the fight had produced started to wane. It made me feel sick to my stomach and even more antsy than before. "And Korri?"

She glared at me with a childlike grimace of horror.

"She's gone," I said, a wave of sadness making me dizzy.

"Too late. Not fast enough," Korri Ann said.

In my world, the waking world, Korri Ann, had she been human, would have no doubt been labeled a snowflake. Even for her kind, she gave off that specialness vibe in a way that I'd never noticed in Korri from the Schattenreich. I wondered, again, if it was real.

"Korri Ann," I said, and let her go, taking Ickles the bunny away from her, tucking our only chance of detaining the *Bugul noz* under my arm.

She whimpered and turned her wide-eyed worried glance on me.

"Let's stop all this. I want to you tell me what is really wrong. Right now. Or I won't help you anymore. *Our* Korrigan has *died* because of this."

"Really wrong?" Her accent was detectably British, something I hadn't noticed before.

"Do you want me to *Make* the *Bugul noz*? Is that what we are doing here?"

She opened her mouth. Closed it.

I pointed a finger at her. "Don't lie to me. I'm not threatening you. But I need to know. *Now*."

She sighed, and then it was as if she deflated, the air went out of her and she shrunk even more. "I am not true Korrigan."

"Not...what are you?"

She sank to the ground and put her head in her hands. "Like wolf-man. I was *Jötnar*. Long time now. They put me out. Sent me away. Too small, too ugly to be *Jötnar*. They were...are proud Folk. But stupid, too."

"You are one of Fenris's...I mean of his mother's tribe?"

She shook her head. "No...I mean, maybe. So long ago. I was just a baby. They left me so the Korrigan would take me."

Too tired to stand any longer, I sunk to the ground next to her. My head swam and my arms tingled with the cold, but I hardly felt anything except a stunned sort of exhaustion that made my feet feel like they were encased in lead boots.

"And so you grew up to be a Korrigan."

"Had no choice."

"My father, a very smart man, says, '*Choice is. Always.*'"

She shrugged. "Was okay to be Korrigan."

"But?"

"*Bugul noz*...he does have a name. Long name. Beautiful. He is beautiful. I..." She hugged herself tight.

"You fell in love with him?" A snort escaped me. I couldn't picture the Regency monster dude and the little Korrigan in front of me as a pair.

"Both ways. Love. It was both ways. He was not monster then."

"Mutual. He loved you back."

She sniffled.

"And? What happened?"

"It's not allowed. And I am not Korrigan. He...we thought we could make another one. Of him."

I slapped a hand to my head. "A baby? Is that what this is all about? I don't believe it."

"They kicked me out. Banned. Just like the *Jötnar* sent me away. Broke his heart, it did. He never had a...friend before."

I petted the bunny, maybe a little too vigorously. It stiffened even more. "Let me guess, then. So he kept making his paths for you to get back to..." I paused to make a spirally motion around her, "being able to meet with him. They killed him for it?"

She shifted and put her hands under her tiny thin thighs. I wished I had thighs like that. Sort of.

"Nonono...no not like that. It was as I said. He kept making too many paths. They kept erasing them, to keep me out. It exhausted him. And his heart broke. And he just passed on." Now she broke out in sobs.

I'd never seen any of them so emotional. But she wasn't one of them. She was related to Fenris!

"So this isn't our fault at all. It's not about the veil being torn open.

About those who guard the ways. *That* was a lie." I'd finally caught her.

"I didn't say it. You *thought* it."

"I...you implied it."

Somehow my legs propelled me upward, despite the achy feeling. Fenris was still in danger and it was all so not worth it after all. "I'm going to get Fenris. You...you will take me to the path, where they are." I eased the *Bugul-noz* wing into my backpack. Carefully.

"Will you still Make him?" she asked, jutting her chin out in defiance.

"Is this a hostage situation?" I asked.

"Hostage?" She looked away.

"Is Fenris a prisoner?"

"Not a very good one, I don't think."

I grabbed her and held more tightly onto Ickles, who tried to squirm out of my grip. I marched over to the fountain, preparing to cross. "Take me," I said, intending to walk right in. "Now."

The Korrigan squealed. And then she took me and Ickles through. The door opened, the fountain gone, we were back in the alleyway of trees. I was not in the Regency dress, but had returned to my battledress of T-shirt and leggings. Since I was last here, what seemed like about ten seconds ago, the trees had lost all their leaves, and were just bare skeletons. The dead leaves were either gray or brown. In the middle of winter-dead, then. Gray iron sky. What *was* the time differential?

Not knowing where to look, I loosened my grip on the Korrigan. She slipped out of my grasp, made herself very small, and started running.

"Not so easy, Miss I'm-not-a-Korrigan."

I waved a hand and threw one of my location spells at her. It would help me track. It used scent and markings, both better than DNA in Ande-dubnos where genetic markers were but a memory, history, of a time long past.

Tracking the Korrigan led me to Fenris. He lay on his side, blood starting to cake on his flank. I rushed to him. He wasn't entirely awake, but lifted his head and nuzzled me with his nose, bruised and also bloodied. I cradled his wolf's head in my arms. He relaxed and breathed out heavily, his eyes closing.

Now that I had Fenris, the problem was to get him back home; wolf or man I didn't care. But in either form, he was too big for me to transport. I didn't know whether the place we were in was a regular part of Ande-dubnos or someplace else, like the Between Lands or even further out. But transporting directly from Ande-dubnos to the waking world was not one of my talents. I could do it easily from the Schattenreich. But here, I'd need an intermediary, or a path.

Just then the *Bugul noz* lumbered into my range of vision. He stood a distance away from me and his body, as such, heaved with the effort of breathing. I'd wonder about that later. He stumbled closer, one step at a time.

I took Ickles by the scruff of his neck, kissed him on the head and wrung his neck, killing him instantly. I died a little inside at that, but I'd mourn him later. His pelt peeled away at his death, and I reached into the mass of his still-warm organs—the stink of a tiny life rudely ended wrinkled my nose—to remove the organic polymer bind.

I waited. The *Bugul noz* came closer. Just a couple more steps. I saw the tiny Korrigan scooting in front of him, waving her arms. He looked down at her, but lurched forward again. She jumped out of his way.

One more step.

He took it. I flung the bind at him and murmured my own chant.

The polymer expanded to accommodate his girth and height. He was wrapped in my *Schattenwerk* construction, Ickles' sacrifice. He was trussed, as my mother would say in her remnant Texas accent, and not going anywhere.

Korri Ann started screaming at me in her tiny tinny voice.

"Help me get Fenris back to the waking world or your *Bugul noz* will stay that way forever," I said, gasping with the strain of holding Fenris. I didn't know if what I told her was true—how long Ickles' polymer would hold—but she didn't need to know that.

Fenris breathed shallowly, his chest rising and falling too rapidly.

I was afraid.

I put my hand over his rib cage, bunching the soft beautiful mélange of brown, rust and black fur, the ends tinged with silver. He calmed under my touch. I felt for wounds and found two around his ribcage, deep but with surprisingly little blood. Maybe that was a good thing. I just didn't know.

If I had Jeannie's power, I could just blink us back to Fenris's place. But I didn't.

I stared at Korri Ann. She had that power, or something very much like it.

"Get us back," I said through gritted teeth. "Before it's too late. If Fenris dies—"

My voice caught.

She put fists on hips, at least where hips should be—there wasn't much curvature to her—and sniffed. "Now you say is time to hurry."

"Do it!"

Korri Ann stared into the near distance. A path opened up in front of us, obscuring the trees and everything else faded as if part of an unreal backdrop. She gestured at Fenris and he became tiny, a furry lap wolf. I held him tight in my arms and followed that path as if my life depended on it.

In a way, it did.

PART III. SOMETHING MADE

Time to head to the lab and transform.

Not to my spirit wolf. It was time to embrace my evil mad scientist.

We'd left phones, flimsies, and laptops at Fenris's place since we'd expected to cross the veil. Even if they'd traveled with us, they wouldn't have been any use. I hugged my laptop to my chest. My backpack was on my lap on the drive from Fenris's place to the Uni.

I paid the taxi driver and was hurrying along the sidewalk before he even pulled away from the drive.

Time to Make the *Bugul noz*. And it needed to go down fast.

Once inside the lab, I pushed up the lid. My laptop went live. I pounded keys and sent programs to run.

I checked the QuickWomb™ to make sure there was nothing else brooding in there.

It would soon have something new. I pushed buttons and called on my shadowcraft so that the creature I was about to make registered as something mundane, like mice clones, rather than what was actually gestating in there. In the meantime, the gene sequencer beeped that it had finished analyzing Fenris's blood sample, much quicker than I thought. I extracted a few drops of my own blood after pricking my finger—I already had my DNA on file in my computer.

That there wasn't any genetic material from the *Bugul noz* to work with—any waking world material—was just something I would have to live with. Improvisation in science was a highly underrated activity. I added the essence—as close as I could extract it—from the torn gossamer wing from the *Bugul noz* to the genetic cauldron I was making.

I used one of the denuded bunny stem cells we had on reserve to deposit the material in. They had proved the easiest and most reliable animals to use for my shadowcraft experiments. Maybe because of their affinity for being pulled out of magical hats over the past few centuries...well, humanity's superstition and Ande-dubnos reality were definitely connected. So not so far-fetched. Whether the new improved *Bugul noz* would be downsized on account of that was something I would just have to wait to find out.

Appropriately enough, the QuickWomb resembled a toddler-sized toy oven, but made out of metal instead of wood. I wasn't sure myself what was going to come out of it, certainly not mice, and, with a significant probability, something much, much larger than a regular-sized housecat, the limit to the QuickWomb's capabilities.

But this wasn't an ordinary organic print job. The lab swam with shadowcraft, potential and actual, swirling bright clouds of blue and deep gold reminiscent of a van Goghian starry night. These were eddies of power, invading reality. Visible to me, perhaps an uncomfortable feeling to others. I breathed in the sweetness of fresh mown grass and bay laurel, not unpleasant.

A good sign.

The manifestation of my shadowcraft in the waking world was unique to me. It caused a tightening in my belly, a nausea that quickly passed, but was the sign that I had called forth my craft. It was limited to the act of biological creation, as my sister Jax's shadowcraft was attached to her music and my brother Theo's to his science —the structure of the cosmos. We'd never discussed with each other the particulars—the how and the why and the what-the-fuck. Some things were best kept secret, even to former wombmates.

Usually, when I did my printing, whatever came out *could* come in handy sometime. It or a variation thereof. I'd had to destroy the results more times than I was comfortable with, but there was no other way to handle a biogenetic experiment gone bad. I'd never attempted to print anything remotely close to being sentient. Until now.

These kinds of experiments were my life's work. The life I'd chosen. I needed the front of my doctorate study in biogenetics to give me the freedom to do the things I wanted to do.

My parents had no idea. They'd object. Strenuously. My three siblings (and my cousin Jeremiah) did know, to a certain extent. They kept my secrets, and I'd keep theirs.

Unless something went terribly wrong.

Which could happen. Like right now.

Good things had happened. Like Ickles the bunny that I'd printed for Fenris. His black fur, soft as a quiet autumn night, his dark blue eyes like my father's. Midnight blue. I'd made Fenris promise not to rend Ickles on one of his wolf hunts. He could buy a pet shop variety rabbit if he wanted to do that. I'd explained to him about the rabbit's gut, a special polymer that could be used to bind a monster.

And it had worked. That I'd had to destroy the little bunny made me sad. But it had been in dire need. I'd once bound Fenris that way.

When I first brought the bunny to him, Fenris thanked me with a gentle kiss and went about constructing a rabbit pen in the small town garden of his immaculate posh flat. When I next saw Fenris, the rabbit was riding around on his shoulder. And he'd house-trained Ickles, he'd informed me.

I told him that one didn't name rare Ande-dubnos protective devices.

He had shrugged and given me one of his posh smiles, a Grantian Smile, somewhere on the scale between Cary Grant and Hugh Grant, and there's not a bad point anywhere on that axis. Yeah, I know. I'm a sucker for old romance movies (and television series). The older the better.

The QuickWomb hummed. Feeling the shadowcraft hum through *me*, like a strong electric current, like acupuncture gone mad, I turned my back on the machine slow and easy. It was pure superstition, the feeling that the machine could implode from too much power. At least I assumed it was superstition.

The clock indicated a slower gestation period than I was comfortable with. I'd have to come back tomorrow afternoon. Doable. Sundays, the lab was even deader than Friday nights. I took deep slow breaths and gathered my things.

Time enough to check if Fenris still lived.

I called a taxi, blinking in the harsh Saturday afternoon sunlight. Fatigue descended.

I'd laid him on his large, very comfortable-looking bed with a beach-sized towel underneath to catch blood or other leaking fluids. He'd reverted to mega-wolf-sized wolf when we gained the inside of his flat. He lay there still. Immobile, his jaws partly open, a thread of drool visible on the towel. Korri Ann was nowhere to be seen. I didn't much care. She'd have her prize soon enough. I hoped she'd be happy with it because it was all she was going to get from me.

Fenris seemed to be sleeping more easily. Maybe the *Bugul noz* phantom had sent him some good Dreams. Did he dream about me?

The skin around the wounds didn't look swollen. His breathing had deepened even though it was still a little bit ragged.

I wet a washcloth (black cotton terrycloth) in the bathroom sink (smart, black marble countertop, amazing roomy shower stall). After wiping Fenris's fur clean and dribbling on drops of hydrogen peroxide for good measure, I sat in the room's only chair, a roomy and comfortable lounger, determined to stay awake.

When I woke, sunlight was streaming through the blackout

shades that weren't entirely drawn, a few rays landing on my face. I turned to look at the patient, and I imagined that Fenris breathed easier. A glance at the bedside clock, another ugly antique, white with gilded gold edges and Roman numerals, told me that I'd slept straight through the late afternoon and evening and it was early Sunday morning. I sighed in relief that there were still a few hours left before the QuickWomb was done.

The gaudy antique clock amidst the upscale, very masculine bedroom, clean and minimal; that was the conundrum of Fenris. Like the furnishings in his apartment, he was a combination of old, ancient old sometimes, but modern in his thinking and his basic humanity. That he hadn't changed back to his man-form when we'd returned to the waking world was a revelation.

None of us, of the blood, had ever to my knowledge manifested our spirit animals in the waking world. But I was a bare twenty-four years old. What did I know of such things? Fenris's skin was a part of him no matter which realm he occupied, so maybe that explained it, though I'd never seen him in his wolf form in the waking world before.

My bicycle was still out front. A quick inspection of the bike lock showed at least one person had tried to tamper with it. I hoped their fingers were still smarting from the shock. I rode it home in the crisp clear air, feeling a chill in my bones that wasn't entirely due to the cold late January air.

Once at my tiny apartment, I picked up dirty pajamas off the floor, shook the duvet into a less crumpled form, and emptied the trash. The forced busywork did nothing to dissipate the uneasiness I'd felt since finding Fenris injured, despite his now being out of life-threatening danger.

I took a shower and changed into my most comfortable flannel-lined jeans. A slouchy loose-knit gray pullover that I'd stolen from my sister Jax went on over a tissue-thin, long-sleeved tee. The clothes were relatively clean, as they had only sat on the floor for a couple of days. I slipped on soft sheepskin boots and wool socks—not cashmere—and then decided to walk back to the Uni for the fresh air and to think, stuffing my laptop and handwritten notes into a cross-shoulder messenger bag. I'd have to walk fast to get there before the gestation was completed. I wasn't sure what to do with the *Bugul noz*, but letting him loose was not a viable option. My nervousness and general feeling of something ominous about to descend on me guaranteed my steps would be quick.

Something lost, something found, something made and something bound.

The words echoed again in my head, and again, it wasn't my inner voice. Someone else was speaking. I still didn't know where the words had come from, but knew I had heard them or read them somewhere before. I tried to remember if they were part of one of my Great Aunt Bertha's trove of fairy tales, but the exact memory eluded me. Was it her voice? It could have been, but I wasn't sure.

The ice skating rink on the south end of the Heumarkt sparkled in the sun. The cobblestones were still slick with morning dew, and the frigid air hurt going into my lungs. I turned right near the trams and headed towards Neumarkt, taking the long way along mostly deserted Sunday morning streets.

The shops were all closed. Only a few bakeries were open, and the doughy smell of freshly baked bread and the enticing fragrance of pastries made my stomach gurgle and then roil. Food would have to wait until this was over.

Something lost was the *Bugul noz*, surely. And we had found him again. Korri Ann had found him, her secret love. Whether he would be the same *Bugul noz* that I returned to her was doubtful. But he, or something very similar to him, was being made. It had a little bit of Fenris and a little bit of me as well. But something bound? I didn't have a clue about that one.

When I got to the lab, the feeling of disaster deepened. I opened the door to find broken glassware strewn about. The stainless steel latches on the QuickWomb had been popped open, not broken but bent. It was empty, although the clock showed another half an hour incubation time.

The new and improved version of the *Bugul noz* had been liberated. Korri Ann. The iron on the QuickWomb latches must have burned her when she'd pried them open. I wonder if she sobbed while doing it. She had decided he was ready and didn't want to wait any more. I jogged up and down the corridors, peering into labs and offices, hoping to find them, a renegade Korrigan and her Night Shepherd. But they were well and truly gone. I held out no hope that the experiment was a success.

Something made. But what?

I'd have to go in search of them.

With heavy sighs and a heavy heart, I spent the next hour and a half cleaning up the lab. I called on my shadowcraft again to repair the QuickWomb; that was my choice, one I might regret. It was a stopgap measure until I could do something more permanent and elegant, but it might just be the push I needed to step up the pace on completing my Otherworld laboratory.

After things looked normal again, it was time to go and look in on Fenris.

PART IV. SOMETHING BOUND

The deep breaths came and went in little puffs of cloud. I'd messed up and *Made* something that I shouldn't have. And now it was on the loose.

Messed up. Big Time. And not only the laboratory. I'd taken the time to clean up the mess, because...covering my tracks was also important. Part of me hoped, intensely, that I could still fix the rest. Help was needed. I had only one option.

It was time to call my father. Something I should have done before things went south (something my mother was fond of saying, although for some reason, her exclamations usually included the back end of a horse). I gestured excitedly while talking to my father on my ancient digital phone instead of just pinging him. This was too complicated for texting. My father listened. And listened some more. He agreed to meet me at my apartment.

I stood before Fenris's door a few minutes later, breathing hard. The key turned in the lock, but the door opened on its own.

Expecting to gaze into Fenris's intense amber eyes, I was surprised to see a complete stranger staring out at me.

"Uh," I said.

"Frau von der Lahn?" he asked me.

I gulped and nodded. He wasn't a complete stranger, I realized, but I'd never seen him when he wasn't behind the wheel of an Audi sedan.

"I was looking for Fenris, for Herr ar C'hoed," I stammered.

"He's not presently here," Fenris's chauffeur said. "He left this for you."

I took the creamy gray envelope from the man. He smiled kindly at me, but not too kindly.

"Thank you," I managed to say, but it felt like someone else speaking. "Did he say..." I shook my head.

"I believe you will find the information you are looking for in his communiqué," he said.

I nodded again, feeling stupid and awkward. I didn't even know the man's name. "I'm sorry, I don't know—"

"Felix Oskar. Just call me Oskar," he said and smiled. The kindness was not feigned, even though he presented a formal front. Maybe the formality was a part of him. That didn't surprise me in the least. He wasn't human, but could pass for one. He was at least half *Tud*. I wondered which lonely corner of Ande-dubnos Fenris had found him in.

"*Auf wiedersehen*," I said and turned to go. He coughed. I turned back.

"If you require my assistance, at any time for any reason, I am at your disposal." He bowed and handed me a business card with a digital imprint that buzzed in my hand.

"I appreciate it," I said.

He closed the door.

I stumbled down Fenris's front steps. And ran.

I slowed a block or so later when I felt a presence, as if someone was following me.

I stopped and turned quickly. The man stopped, too.

"Papa! What are you doing here?"

"Taking a Sunday stroll with my daughter in downtown Cologne," my father said. "Where are we going?" His gentle smile warmed me as he moved to my side. He had on a gray wool overcoat, finely brushed lambswool, and the silly misshaped navy scarf my mother had knitted for him. It had become even more ragged over the years. His dark chestnut hair, nearly the same shade as mine but streaked with silver, hung a little longer than usual, reaching the collar of his coat.

"To my apartment. I thought we were meeting there."

"And how is Fenris?"

"He's not feeling well, and I wanted to look in on him."

My father nodded as if he understood more than I was saying. I had left Fenris out of my explanations to him on the phone. But he had somehow figured out the missing link.

We walked together through Cologne side streets, now busy with pedestrians out for a late lunch or coffee and cake with friends and family. The pubs had also started filling up.

"Want to tell me what else is bothering you?" my father asked.

"You mean besides escaped *Bugul noz* creatures and wayward Korrigans?"

"Besides that, yes. Did something happen between you and Fenris?"

How did he know these things? "I thought only Mama had that kind of intuition," I said.

"Do you want to know the first word you spoke to me?"

I nodded.

"Mama," he said.

I laughed. "I never was very smart as a kid."

"Your mother thought it was brilliant. She'd just...just come back from the Lands Beyond, and I'd been caring for the three of you since your first weeks of life...as a 'single' parent."

"Aha. Then not so stupid?"

"I didn't think so. It was a genuinely blissful moment for me."

I let the silence build as we neared my apartment. He had let me lead.

"How do you know where Fenris lives?"

"Juliette. I am your father."

"That's your answer?"

He laughed. "You mother was here once. She told me, not gently I might add, that I'd find you here."

His confession made me smile. "Papa, did you ever do anything stupid, I mean really unbearably stupid?" I asked.

"You mean, things like trading my youth for power? Or incurring a *geis* from Cathubodua that left me in a coma and nearly cost me everything, including your mother?"

His eyes held a hint of sadness, of regret and chances lost.

"Oh yeah. Those kinds of things."

"Which flavor of stupid do you think you've done? I mean, only if you want to tell me."

I shook my head while I thought, then stuck my hands deep in my pockets. My scarf and gloves were still hanging on Fenris's coat rack, where I'd forgotten them earlier this morning in my haste to leave. The air had not warmed much, but the sun felt good on my face.

"Well, that one time I lost my Siamese cat, Purrface. I've never gotten over that."

My father looked over at me. "That was regrettable, but I wouldn't say it was your fault, except perhaps the *name*. He just decided he wanted to live in the wild rather than curled up in your bed. Purrface, if I recall, wasn't a particularly bright cat."

"No, but he was mine, and I lost him...through neglect. I took him for granted. It was awful. I thought he was dead, locked in one of the cellar rooms or eaten by one of the creatures the Burg uses to protect itself. He *was* a stupid cat, but I loved him."

My father didn't comment, just waited for me to continue.

"That made me afraid to form any attachments with people. That they would leave me, like Purrface."

"Really?" he asked, his tone skeptical.

"Well, yeah, except for Jax, Theo and Brev...and you and Mama and Heiner. And Opa. And Tante Bertha. Oh, and Gesine. And Jeremiah and Lissy. And Uncle Gus and Aunt Susanna. And Frau Morelos. And..."

My father's crooked smile told me I was being stupid again.

"Okay, I mean the idea of a, you know, love story kind of attachment."

"I didn't want that either at your age. No hurry in your case, really, as far as I am concerned," he said, the hint of irony in his voice exaggerated to make me laugh.

I did laugh. I was a Daddy's girl, more than Jax who worshipped our Uncle Heiner. My father and I had always been close. My parents had avoided having 'favorites' among their four children, but there was a cerebral connection, me with my father. We had a similar way of approaching problems, and that engendered deep affection between us that the others just didn't have.

I sighed and waved my hands around. "I've messed everything up. There's a dangerous creature on the loose that I've created. Fenris is injured. And Korri is dead. And I repaired some lab equipment with *Schattenwerk*..."

"Hmm. I am assuming you will be able to rectify the lab equipment problem?"

I nodded. "It will be okay."

"It is a shame about Korri. She served a useful purpose for a very long time. As for Fenris, well, did he leave you a message?"

"How—"

"He contacted me as well."

"He...what?" I nearly screamed at him.

"Before we talk about Fenris, there's something else."

"The mess I made. And people, they're in danger," I said, trying to keep my voice from turning into a sob.

Hagen von der Lahn, my father, the baron of Burg Lahn, successful philanthropist, and one of the Guardians of the Opening to the veil between the waking world and Ande-dubnos, offered me his arm. He had broken an army of female hearts in his youth, and was still an exceedingly handsome man.

I always felt happy in his presence, secure that I belonged to him, even when he wasn't happy with me. I was puzzled that he didn't display any displeasure at any of the things I'd confessed to him. But I was even more disturbed that Fenris had contacted him.

"I want to show you something," he said and pulled my arm through his.

"Where are we going?" I asked.

"There's a *nemeton* nearby, the location of a former Roman temple that was built on top of an even more ancient spot used by Celts. It's easy to cross there."

"Cross? In broad daylight? Is it far?"

"Not far at all. Just around the corner." My father smiled. "But of course. We only need a few shadows, and the sun's going behind a big raincloud."

I was a little breathless when we arrived at Korri's hut. Fatigue and stress chipped away what was left of my strength. The front door was now repaired, although no more sophisticated than it had been —a few boards nailed together—and as dilapidated as the old one. The door was closed. The deep pond in front of Korri's house had been cleared of its tree trunks. The water was a clear deep blue-green again, free from debris. The air of desolation was gone.

"Did you call the emergency clean-up squad?" I asked.

He laughed. "Something like that occurred, but it wasn't me." He pulled open the door and gestured inside with a sweep of his arm. "After you."

We made our way into the room that served as a dining/consultation room, the one that afforded a view into the space that contained the dead Korrigans. That was where I had saved Fenris and detained what remained of the *Bugul noz.*

The formerly dented and damaged window frame had also been repaired, and the oval picture window looked out, as usual, onto a perpetual winter landscape of skeletal trees and wings made of spider-silk, the only visible parts of the no-longer extant creatures. I took a few paces towards it and then stopped and turned to face my father.

"What happened?" I asked. "The place was trashed the last time we were here."

"We?" he asked.

"Fenris, one of the Korrigans—I call her Korri Ann—and me. We came in search of the *Bugul noz* or whatever remained of him."

The door to the kitchen squeaked open a crack. I backed up toward my father.

The door opened and Korri Ann stepped through.

She looked almost angelic, not like a mischievous little Korrigan at all. Her face had changed, revealing something I could only classify as happiness.

Anger shot through me, and at the same time pity welled up. I tried to fight the latter. She scooted into the room, her mossy linen dress covered in even more bits of bark and stuck-on leaves than the last time I'd seen her. Her hair, turned a sparkling pure white, flowed in gentle waves around her shoulders. She had on pink ballet slippers. Not wanting to think about where she'd stolen them from, I opened my mouth to speak.

But before any words came out, another creature emerged from the kitchen. He wasn't as big as the monster *Bugul noz* I'd captured earlier, but he did bear a resemblance. He also wore a look of happiness. And Korri Ann was right—he wasn't ugly.

Of course, he did carry some of Fenris and some of me, so he couldn't be all monster.

And it showed. Not a pretty face unless maybe you were a Korrigan. He had the same crazy greenish-dark plaits that stuck out all over his head. And he still had fleshy lips, but they weren't scary gross. Bulky on top, smaller-proportioned on the bottom, he had a kind of a hulk thing going on.

No wings. So I had succeeded. The Night Shepherd had been remade.

I sighed.

We left them a few minutes later, and my father explained some things on our way back to the Schattenreich clearing where we would make our crossing back to Cologne.

"I've offered them sanctuary as long as they fulfill the job that Korri did—keeping the things outside that window from getting into the Schattenreich. They seemed very happy about it all."

"Yeah, I think they're very happy to be together. If the other Korrigans find out, it could cause trouble."

"Not on our turf. The Korrigans can't stage a massive presence in the Schattenreich. It's just not possible."

I nodded. It's what we'd always been told. "But since the veil is open..."

"We've warded the borders solidly over the years and put in protections. There are creatures who are permitted to cross from Ande-dubnos to the waking world, but they don't make detours through the Schattenreich."

I hoped he was right for Korri Ann's sake.

As my father and I sat in the grassy clearing, my eyes misted over thinking about my crossing with Fenris earlier...had it only been yesterday...and our kiss. He wouldn't need that kind of contact with me once we officially gave him the right to cross into the Schattenreich without a chaperone. But that hadn't yet happened. I took out the envelope from Fenris that I'd brought with me. My father sat patiently, waiting. I opened it and read it silently. It was as if Fenris was standing in back of me, the words landing gently on my ear, his voice soft in a way I wasn't used to. His intimate voice that I'd never really heard but so wanted to.

Dearest Juliette,

My apologies for leaving without saying farewell, but you have left me no choice.

Our blood has mingled and, although I expect you didn't know what you were doing, you have put me in an awkward, even difficult situation. Exchanging blood among our people in the Lands Beyond has significance. I'm sorry to say, I have to handle the situation immediately.

Or there could be serious repercussions.

There might be anyway.

So that is why I have to leave.

I don't know when I'll return. At the latest, when the repercussions have settled. At the earliest, well, don't expect me before the trees begin to bud out in Cologne.

In the meantime, you need better protection. Therefore, I entreat you to stay at my flat until I return, where Oskar will be able to look out for you.

Try not to mess the place up too much.

I have already spoken with your father.

Oh, and thank you for saving my life.

Until we meet again,

Yours,

Fenris

I frowned heavily at my father.

"He has informed me that he will be officially courting you when he returns," my father said.

"He what?"

My father shrugged. "It seems the two of you are now bound in some way?"

I nodded. "Our blood. I used it to remake the *Bugul noz*."

"Ah. And mingled blood in the art of creation constitutes some sort of bond, then, among the *Jötnar*."

I shrugged. "He wants me to stay at his place until he comes back. Seems to think I'll need protection."

"Very mysterious. But I'd like you to take him up on it. You can keep your apartment, of course."

"Naturally, especially since you own the whole building."

He smiled. "You found that out, did you?"

"The von der Lahns have never been squeamish about owning real estate," I said in a snobby upper-class German accent.

"With good reason."

I sighed and then remembered. "Something bound!"

"What?"

"Something lost, something found, something made, and something bound. It's a phrase that popped into my head before all this happened." I ticked off on my fingers. "Something lost *and* something

found *and* something made was the *Bugul noz*. But something bound
—that, apparently is me and Fenris."

"I see. A prophecy." He held out a hand to me. I took it and
clasped it tightly. "The von der Lahn women have been known to
make them from time to time."

"Papa...I don't know what to do about Fenris. I mean, he's—"

It was my father's turn to tick off items. "He's your cousin. He's not
entirely human. And he's dangerous."

"All that." I didn't want to tell my father that I rather liked the
dangerous part. But then again, the way he was eyeing me, I didn't
have to.

"It will work out. Trust your instincts. And prophecies...well, it
seems it has all come true then."

"I'm so sorry for everything, Papa."

He stood, pulling me with him. "You're all grown up. It's time you
made some unbearable stupid mistakes. In this case, I think you did
rather well."

I wasn't sure what he meant by that, but let it go for now. "If I'd
called you to begin with, none of this would have happened."

"Maybe it would have gone down differently, but *something* would
have happened."

I closed my eyes in preparation to crossing back. I only
hoped we wouldn't scare the daylights out of any wayward
pedestrians.

"Juliette...you didn't say whether you were upset at the possibility
of being courted by Fenris."

"No, I didn't. Because I have no idea what that means or how I feel
about it."

The voice of the man I most looked up to in this world and any
others became soft and light, unlike Fenris's. "You have time now to
think about it. That's a very good thing."

I needed to make my own path, like the *Bugul noz* made paths to
keep humans and Korrigans safe. I had time to do that and to find my
way. Unlike Purrface, Fenris had promised to return. I would work on
strengthening the path that led to his return, among others of my

own making. Thinking about him being gone made my heart ache, but in a good way. A fond way.

I planned on enjoying every minute of it.

I wondered if I would have that Dream of us again when I slept in his apartment. Or maybe now some other ones, definitely not of the fairy tale variety.

ABOUT THE AUTHOR

Now a full-time writer living near Cologne, Sharon Kae Reamer's speculative fiction is inspired by her participation in various archeoseismology projects during her twenty-something years as a senior scientist at the University of Cologne. Locations that include the Praetorium and medieval Jewish settlement in Cologne, ancient Tiryns in Greece, and Greek ruins in Selinunte, Sicily, provide perfect backdrops for creating fantasy stories rich with history and mythology, such as her *Immortal Guardian* and *Schattenreich Mystery* novelette series and her five-book *Schattenreich* novel series.

Her love for mixing and mashing science fiction and fantasy continues unabated. *Night Shepherd*, in the *Schattenreich* universe is a spinoff (one of many) of her soon-to-be-published first novel in *The Sundered Veil* series, a further conception of science fantasy.

Sharon still pursues archeoseismology projects. She also cooks daily (German-English), gardens (chaotically, at best), knits (badly), does needlepoint (rather well) and reads (everything) all the damn time.

And, of course, she has cats.

Find out more about Sharon at:
sharonreamer.com

 twitter.com/sharonkae

bookbub.com/authors/sharon-kae-reamer

ABOUT A PROCESSION OF FAERIES

D oorway into Faerie is the second volume in the anthology series
A Procession of Faeries. If you enjoyed this collection, check
out the others—and follow the series on Facebook!

www.ingramcontent.com/pod-product-compliance
Lightning Source LLC
Chambersburg PA
CBHW071632260626
47170CB00001B/70